MW00778688

COLLECTOR'S EDITION

W

wild & free

F

USA TODAY BESTSELLING AUTHOR

K WEBSTER

The Wild & The Free Collector's Edition

The Wild
Copyright © 2017 K. Webster

The Free
Copyright © 2019 K Webster

Cover Design: All By Design
Photo: Adobe Stock
Editor: ellie at Love N. Books
Formatting: Champagne Book Design

To my husband…I believe in happy endings because of you.

the wild

*"She had a wild, wandering soul
but when she loved, she loved with chaos and
that made all the difference."*
—Ariana Dancu

Warning:

The Wild is an extremely taboo story. Most will find that the themes in this book will make you incredibly uncomfortable or maybe even offend you. This book is only for the brave, the open-minded, and the ones who crave love in even the most dismal of situations. Extreme sexual themes and violence in certain scenes, which could trigger emotional distress, are found in this story. If you are sensitive to heavy taboo themes, then this story is not for you.

Seriously, you've been warned.
Don't say I didn't try.
You're probably going to cringe many, many, many times.
Even if you're on the fence, it's probably not a good idea to proceed.

However, if you're intrigued and fearless and *kind of sort of* trust me, then carry on. This book *is* for you.

prologue

REED

Past

LOSING A CHILD IS INCONCEIVABLE.

Anyone with a child always has that worry playing continuously in the back of their mind. Each time they're at the water park. Every time they buckle their kiddo into a car seat. All those times they send their little ones off to spend the night with a friend.

Every second.

Every day.

Without fail.

That fear lingers in the shadows of your mind like a monster just waiting to come out and devour everything you hold precious.

Most of us don't have to deal with such atrocities.

The rest of us get to know firsthand what it's like to watch them lower your heart into the earth. Too soon. Too fucking soon. We get to watch our spouse collapse in on themselves and choose darkness over the rest of the family members who are still here. All of us who do lose a child get to know how it feels to have every memory ripped from your chest and scattered into the wind. There will be no new memories—all you have left are the ones that quickly slip from your grip.

"Daddy?"

Her voice, so much like her twin brother, both soothes and crushes me. My wife and I lost our son. But Devon lost her brother. The other half of her soul. A human she shared the womb with. Those two worked as two halves of a whole. Always anticipating the other's emotions and aiding them when they needed it. Siblings who, even at ten years old, didn't fight in our home.

They laughed.

They sang.

They played.

They loved.

"Daddy?"

I pinch the bridge of my nose and long for more of the whiskey but it's gone. Downed the entire fifth tonight. Nothing can numb the pain that sears through me though. Fucking nothing.

"Yeah, Pip?"

When she was a toddler, she used to seem to squeak compared to her loud, wild brother. I'd called him Rowdy because he was rambunctious as hell and her Pip for pipsqueak.

Another throbbing ache in my chest.

"I miss Drew." Her tone is sad. Nothing but a whisper.

the wild

I lean back in my office chair and regard my daughter. The only child I have left. For ten, she's tall and lanky. Her wide blue eyes are innocent and full of soul. Lately they flicker with worry. Both of her parents have fallen off the deep end.

"I do too, baby." I pat my lap and she runs over to me like she would when she was small. When I pull her into an embrace, I inhale her hair. Same shampoo Drew used. An obnoxious, ugly sob rips from my throat. "I-I'm s-so sorry," I choke out, my hot tears falling relentlessly down my cheeks.

She sniffles and I hold her tighter. The counselor says we need to be strong for our remaining child. Sabrina can't get her goddamned ass out of bed. It's up to me to pick our family up and glue it back together.

Sometimes I wonder if we're too broken.

Unfixable.

Lost.

"Did Mommy love Drew more? Is that why she's so sad and won't talk to me?" Devon's voice cracks with emotion. She's heartbroken for so many reasons. Losing her brother and mother essentially at the same exact moment has to be hard on her. It's devastating to me and I'm a grown-ass man.

"Of course she loves you just as much," I say fiercely. I stroke her satin blonde hair. "We just need to give her time. She's sad. We're all sad. Each of us will grieve in our own ways."

"Promise you'll always talk to me, Daddy," she begs tearfully. "Even when you're so sad or angry. Don't leave me alone."

More tears roll out of my eyes and soak her hair. I cry so hard that I can't formulate words. All I can do is nod. Kiss her head and nod. She holds out her pinky and I hook mine with hers.

A pinky promise is what she calls this.

I vow to talk to her and love her even during the darkest of times. Although, I'm not really sure how life can get any darker than this.

You could lose your other child, the dark, menacing monster in my head growls.

I squeeze her tighter.

Nod.

Kiss.

Nod again.

"I promise." My words are a faint whisper but she hears. She always hears.

"I love you, Daddy."

Nod.

Kiss.

Nod again.

"I love you too, Pip."

I'll be goddamned if I let anything happen to this kid too.

That's a promise I make to the ugly monster inside of me and force him back into the shadows where he belongs.

chapter one

REED

Present

SABRINA STARES OUT THE WINDOW, HER FEATURES hard behind her oversized sunglasses and too much makeup. I squeeze her hand but she doesn't squeeze back. Six years after Drew's death and my wife has yet to snap out of it. Depression is her middle name. Losing Drew was the final straw after years and years of tragedies that plagued our family. There was no coming back after that. She was lost. For me, losing Drew, was the most crushing of all the heartaches in my life. It was real. Tangible. Horrifying. And yet I couldn't abandon our other child. She was still alive and very desperate for love.

Devon and I had to keep on living while Sabrina got to live in the past. With him. Obsessed over the memories they shared. Suspended in a time that doesn't exist anymore.

This move is my last-ditch effort to bring her back to us. A Hail Mary.

My last hope for a miracle.

"According to data compiled by the Wildlife Land and Water Coalition, people are forty-five times more likely to be killed by a dog than by a bear, one hundred and twenty times more likely to be killed by bees than a bear, and an incredible two hundred and fifty times more likely to be killed by lightning than a bear," Devon chirps from behind me, her long skinny leg stretched out to nudge me in the arm to get my attention.

Our eyes meet in the mirror and I laugh. This girl and her useless facts. "Too bad we stocked up on bear spray then, huh?" I tease.

Her eyes are hidden behind her sunglasses that are similar to her mother's but her smile is wide and carefree. At sixteen, she's brilliant and full of life. "How many bears you think we'll see, Dad? One a month? Two a month? One a week?"

Sabrina tenses from her seat. She was cool with every part of this move. The bears have her scared shitless though. I vowed I wouldn't let her get killed by a bear.

"A buddy of mine who did a sabbatical in the Alaskan wilderness said he saw several a day. They're plentiful in these parts." I grin at her in the mirror. "But that's why God made guns."

"Dad!" Devon complains. "Don't shoot any bears."

I shrug. "Not a promise I can make, Pip. If it comes between a bear living to catch another fish tomorrow or my baby girl remaining unharmed, you better believe I'm going to kill that bear."

At this, Sabrina snorts. "Okay, Davey Crockett."

the wild

Devon giggles from the back and passes her mother a brochure she picked up at the last gas station before we began the hard leg of our journey. "Look at the map, Mom. Bear Country is what they call it. Five bucks says Dad tries to carpet the house with bearskin rugs."

Sabrina takes the brochure and stares at it. Her lips are pressed into a firm line. I'm sure she's coming to terms with reality right about now. In another six hours or so, we'll be right in the middle of our property. I liquidated every dime of my multimillion dollar global real estate company and purchased thousands of acres deep in the Alaskan wilderness.

After a humiliating episode between my wife and a woman at one of California's most elite country clubs we were a member of, I knew we had to do something drastic. Sabrina had taken to slapping a woman because she didn't like how the woman was talking to her son. It was the meltdown of the century. Screaming. Crying. Cursing. Sabrina had to be escorted off the property and we were banned from the club for life. To make matters worse, with social media being a bitch, her psychotic rage was filmed by dozens of others at the club. It spread through the internet like a goddamned forest fire, burning our family's hard-earned reputation in its wake.

I moved fast.

Instead of watching developers and buyers walk away from Jamison Enterprises, I began liquidating and selling. It took nearly a year, and that long to plan, but we're finally ready to move on with our lives.

Just the three of us.

Off the grid.

3

Like those crazy bush people, as Devon likes to tease.

When I mentioned it to my wife and daughter, I'd expected resistance. I should have known Devon would be on board first. We spoke with her teachers at her all-girls private school and they let her double up her studies so she could graduate from high school early. My daughter, brilliant as the sun's rays, crushed her sophomore year which ultimately also became her senior year.

Sabrina was a little harder to convince. She couldn't see my vision. Despite the blueprints I'd drawn up of a cozy log cabin and ideas for collecting water and planting crops, she was confused. Her life was our million-dollar home in San Francisco. Her life was nothing but pictures and things that belonged to our son.

But I did convince her.

Told her she could bring those memories with her.

That Drew would have loved the wilderness. Our son was adventure on top of adventure. A true wild one.

She said yes and here we are.

Hours along a dirt road lined with thick trees toward the place we'll make a home. The trailer we're pulling is full of tools we'll need. We'll stay in the RV I purchased until I get the cabin built. Together, as a family, we'll build new memories. We'll make a life where we can be happy and free of the stresses of the outside world.

Me being an orphan, I have no family that would care. And we promised Sabrina's snobby parents that we'd come down to California once a year to visit. Other than that, we're free.

"University of Alaska has a high suicide rate among their students," Devon blurts out. More useless information. "Looks like college is out of the question."

I shake my head. "Two years and then you're going. You promised. That was one of the caveats," I remind her.

Our Siberian huskie, Buddy, barks as if in protest. Six months after we lost Drew, I brought her home that dog. It didn't replace her brother but it gave her a playmate.

She pops her gum and laughs. "Can't blame a girl for trying, Dad. What can college teach me that I don't already know?"

"Manners," I grunt.

This gets a chuckle from Sabrina. "Maybe how to get a boyfriend."

"No. Boys. Ever," I say in a dramatic tone that earns me a huff from behind me.

"Whatever, Dad."

"Just being real, Pip."

She snorts. "Don't try to be hip. You're not hip."

"She's right," Sabrina says, a smile lighting up her pretty face. "You're not hip. You're old."

"Well, while you've been getting massages," I say and point at Sabrina. "And while you were taking Snapchat selfies," I say and jerk my head toward Devon. "I was taking the survivalist classes. I chopped all that damn wood for practice too. I may not be hip but I'm basically a god. God of the Great Unknown."

Both my girls laugh and my heart nearly leaps out of my chest.

This is exactly what we needed.

"Where's your mom?" I ask as I step into the RV. Buddy trots in behind me and walks right up to Devon to give her a wet kiss.

After wiping her cheek, Devon looks up from a book and frowns. "Headache."

I roll my eyes. Anytime Sabrina is depressed, she plays it off as a headache. She knows I won't argue it and she can sleep in peace. "It'll be dark soon. Want to explore, Pip?"

She tosses her book down and grins. "Let me grab my hiking boots."

Once she dresses and pulls on a hoodie, I grab my rifle and together we set out on an exploration. We're another three or four hours from our destination I mapped out but I didn't want to chance driving the RV and pulling the trailer in the dark. The farther we get inside the dense forest, the harder it will be to travel. According to the previous owner of the land, Atticus Knox, I know that at the end of the road is a small clearing that overlooks a gorge where a fresh water river runs through it. I'd fallen in love with the pictures he emailed me and paid the hefty sum. He assured me that the area was unpopulated. No people for hundreds of miles. Secluded as fuck. Exactly what I was hoping for. Since we were traveling out of state, I negotiated for him to leave some equipment I'd purchased from him. When we get there, I can essentially start working on our dream home right away.

Devon squats to inspect a plant and I notice a bush with many berries. Her dog sniffs around and his ears perk up when he hears a sound beyond the trees.

"Look," I tell her with a grin as I step through some brush to reach the bush. "Berries."

"Dad! No!"

Buddy barks as if to yell at me too.

I jerk my hand back and frown. "What?"

"Baneberries. Those are poisonous. We don't need you going into cardiac arrest." She stands and makes a motion with her hands. "Step away from the white berries if you want to live."

I laugh but wisely step away. Apparently more than useless information rattles around in that brain of hers. "Okay, so which ones can we eat, Pip?"

She trudges along a few hundred feet and stops before a bush with red berries. "These aren't ripe yet, but they're safe. Promise me you won't eat anything without asking me first?"

I hold my hands up in defense. "Promise."

She sticks out her pinky and her lips quirk into a sweet smile I remember from her when she was a kid. I hook my pinky with hers.

"Pinky promise," we both say.

Her eyes are filled with love and happiness. I knew this move would be life changing. We'll eventually pull Sabrina out of the dark hell she lives in. With time, everything will be perfect.

She releases my hand and continues walking along the edge of the thick forest that overhangs into the road. I've already had to stop more times than I can count to either move limbs or hack through them with the chainsaw. Atticus promised the last few hours of the journey were the hardest. He hasn't been to the property since before winter when I purchased the land from him. Winters here are harsh and unforgiving. The trees are casualties.

Buddy growls and the hairs on my neck stand on end. Heavy crunching resounds about a hundred feet into the thicket on our right.

"Dad…"

"Stay calm."

Despite all our researching and classes, we're still city folks. It's all fun and games until someone sees a bear for the first time.

We wait for what feels like ages. Buddy gets bored and shits. Nothing terrifying emerges from the woods. The sun is setting fast and I fear our little exploration is over for the day.

"Come on, Dev. Let's get inside and see about dinner."

She trots back over to me, sidestepping Buddy's bomb, and I hug her to my side. After Drew died and I picked myself up off the floor, I vowed to give the love I had for two children to the one we had left. I took her to the movies and shopping. Every day I took her to school and picked her up. Any opportunity when I wasn't traveling or working, I spent with my daughter.

Sabrina sure as hell wasn't doing the job.

"How about Frito chili pie?" Devon asks. "It's Mom's favorite."

I squeeze her. "You cooking?"

She looks up at me and grins. "I'm the only one who knows the recipe."

At this, I snort laughing. "Step one, open a can of chili. Step two, heat said chili. Step three, pour over Fritos. Step four, sprinkle the cheese and onions on top. Did I miss anything?"

"You're such a sarcastic shit, Dad."

She flings the RV door open and rolls her eyes at me before clomping up the steps.

"Don't say shit, Pip."

I close the RV door and lock it out of habit even though nobody will get us out here. By the time I kick off my boots and pull off my jacket, Devon is hard at work on her specialty. The way she effortlessly moves about the small space softly singing one of her favorite pop tunes reminds me of the way Sabrina used to be.

So. Full. Of. Life.

"I'm going to go check on your mom," I tell her as I pass her in the kitchen. I drop a kiss on the top of her head before scooting past her. Once inside the back bedroom, I close the partition door. It's dark inside. Sabrina sleeps naked. An invitation. Sometimes when she's in a dark mood, the only way to bring her back is through sex. The RV is small and the walls are practically non-existent but Devon will be distracted cooking dinner.

I peel off my clothes and crawl into the small bed beside my wife. She's awake but doesn't speak. I've been through this song and dance enough times to know all the motions. Each time I pray she'll snap out of it long enough to love me the way she used to. But every time I'm disappointed. Doesn't stop me from trying.

My mouth finds her throat and I kiss her soft flesh. Her breasts are still firm despite her now being well into her late thirties. I fondle them even though she won't respond. When I start kissing down her throat on a mission to her pussy, she shakes her head in the dark and says one simple word.

No.

I groan in frustration and begin our usual routine. Parting her thighs, I settle on top of her. My dick is having trouble staying hard so I stroke it quickly before pushing into her heat. A sharp gasp is the only evidence I'm fucking a woman and not a corpse.

My mouth tries for hers but she turns her head to the side. It's as though she punishes herself from all forms of pleasure and happiness. If Drew couldn't have it, then why should she. It kills me that she thinks this way.

I desperately try to be quiet, but our bodies slap together. The grunts coming from me are feral and borderline angry. Sometimes I want to grab her by the throat and shake some goddamned sense into her.

Sabrina never comes.

Never.

She lets me use her as an outlet so *I* can come. So she can tie us together—no matter how loose it is—in the only way she knows how. It's always been enough. Just barely.

"I love you," I whisper, my breath hissing from me.

She doesn't respond.

My eyes clench shut and I come hard. I've barely finished spurting out my release before I'm yanking out of her. I snag my shirt and wipe my dick off before tossing it into the corner. Neither of us speak. I just came and I should be relaxed but I'm pissed off. This trip was supposed to help. If anything, she seems worse on the first night on our land.

"Dinner will be ready soon. Devon cooked your favorite," I spit out as I yank my jeans on.

"I'm not hungry."

It takes everything in me not to go off on her.

"Night," I bite out.

She doesn't respond.

When I yank open the divider, Devon wears a guilty look as she stares down at her bowl of Frito chili pie. She's set out two more bowls and even made her mother a glass of lemonade. Bitterness threatens to tear me in half but I swallow it down.

"Smells good, Pip," I say, my tone gruff.

Her watery eyes lift to meet mine. It fucking breaks my heart. No sixteen-year-old girl should have to deal with this shit. She glances at my bare chest and then looks down at her food.

"I'm sorry you had to hear that." The sex. The rejection. The slow death of my marriage.

"It's fine, Dad."

I settle in across from her and eat dinner alone with my daughter. Just like every other goddamned day.

And I eat Sabrina's untouched bowl just to make Devon smile again.

chapter two

DEVON

I TRY MY CELL PHONE, BUT I HAVE NO SIGNAL. I LOST the signal days ago. We're really doing this. Living off the grid. I'm going to find me a hillbilly toothless wild man deep in the woods and have all his babies.

When I chuckle, Dad's eyes meet mine in the mirror. His kind brown eyes always bring me comfort.

"What's so funny back there?"

"Just imagining finding a hillbilly boyfriend. We're going to have lots of babies," I explain.

"No. Boys. Ever."

Buddy barks again. Stupid dog seems to agree with Dad on that one every time.

"Guess I'll have to wait until college to get my freak on," I say with a sigh and feign boredom. Truth is, I wouldn't know what to do with a boy if I had one. Having gone to an all-girl school my entire life, the only interaction with guys were the ones from the neighborhood. I've not been kissed, and I certainly haven't done anything more.

Dad growls and Mom laughs. She's more herself today. A few smiles here and there. She even sang with me through a couple of oldies on the CD I'd burned back home. I'd never seen Dad look so happy. One of these days I'm going to help Mom to remember that we're her family. That we need her. She'll laugh and smile and love us like we love her.

And Dad can be happy again.

Truly happy.

Reed Jamison puts on a strong face, but I've seen him at his lowest. Bawling his eyes out like a child. It crushed my heart. When Drew died, I cried. But when my father cried, I think I lost a part of my soul that day.

Mom has always been sad. Detached. Lost. Drew and I always felt as if we were a burden to her. And when he died, she went completely off the deep end with no hope of ever coming back. Dad seems hopeful and for him, I hope too.

I promised myself that I'd always be his sidekick. His best friend. His little girl. I would do well in school, behave always, and never argue about chores. Dad did so much for our family. It was the least I could offer for him.

"Don't eat the white berries," I remind everyone in the car for the millionth time. Buddy agrees and barks.

Dad winks in the mirror. "We'll save them for your hillbilly boyfriend."

I'm happily reading one of my romance novels when the RV starts to slow.

"Oh, shit. This one's big," he complains as he rolls to a stop in front of a massive fallen tree.

"I'm glad we're stopping," Mom says in the detached voice I know so well. "I have a headache coming on."

Heat creeps up my throat as I remembered last night. They had sex. It didn't sound very fun. Dad seemed angry. Mom didn't make a peep. All I could hear was their heavy breathing, the slapping of flesh, and his grunts. The entire RV shook and rattled. I was so embarrassed. Sure, I've seen sex in movies and read about it in my books, but that was the first time I've ever heard it. Experienced it in live action.

When I lift my eyes, Dad's are on mine. Once again apologetic. I want to tell him it's not his fault she's the way she is but he won't believe me. He's exactly like me. Confident we can somehow fix her one day.

"Come on, Pip. I need an extra pair of hands, and your mother has a headache," he seethes, his jaw clenching as he turns to regard her.

She's unfazed and simply shrugs.

With a strangled curse word, he slings the door open and steps out. The door slams behind him scaring the crap out of me.

"Go help your father before he has a coronary," she says in a bored tone.

"It's hot," I whine as I swipe sweat from my brow.

Dad is hot too because he's long since yanked off his shirt. He's pissed and has been taking it out on the tree for the past three hours. I've escaped only long enough to fetch us water.

"Go inside with your mother," he barks out before kicking the tree.

I flinch at his outburst. "Dad…"

He jerks his fiery gaze my way. My dad is usually all smiles and full of love. His anger toward my mom though has cast a permanent scowl on his face today. I want to make it go away.

Running over to him, I throw my arms around his waist. He's stiff at first but then seems to melt at my affection. Soon, his fingers run through my ponytail in an absent way. His lips press to the top of my head—a sign that everything is going to be okay.

I believe him.

He's sweaty and smells a little rank from all the hard work in the late May afternoon sun, but I inhale him and memorize his scent. Not many things comfort me, but my Dad is one of them. His heartbeat is loud with my ear pressed against his chest. I love to listen to the strong cadence of it. When I was younger, I used to make up songs that went with the beat.

"Everything's going to be okay," I vow and squeeze him tighter.

He lets out a heavy sigh. "Promise, Pip?"

"Pinky promise."

Mom has slept all day in the back. Normally, it hurts my feelings, but today feels different. Today we find our new home. Dad and I are on an adventure.

I steal a glance his way. His aviator sunglasses sit perched on his nose and his shoulders are relaxed. A half smile plays at his lips. He's excited just like me. The scruff is beginning to grow on his jaw. It gives him a rugged appearance. Before we left San Francisco, he playfully teased he would grow out a beard. I can't help but grin imagining my dad's normally clean shaven face full of wiry hair like Mr. Bobbitt, my old chemistry teacher.

"What are you smiling about?" he asks, turning his attention briefly from the road to glance over at me.

I shrug and kick my bare feet up on the dash. "Just thinking about getting to our new home. I'm looking forward to it."

He reaches over and takes my hand. I get a quick squeeze of assurance before he releases me. The road seems to end and Dad drives slower than usual. When we emerge from the trees, we come upon a small clearing on the top of what feels like a mountain.

The road simply ends.

"Dad!" I screech and point through the windshield. "We made it!"

He's just as eager as I am. Both of us bolting out of our doors as soon as the RV is parked. Dad reaches the edge of the cliff first. I approach slowly behind him. The edge drops off at least two hundred feet straight down into a gorge. A rushing river winds through the trees down below.

"It's beautiful," I gasp, my hand clutching my chest. "The pictures didn't do it justice."

He pulls me to him and we hug. "We're here, Pip. Finally." Hope tinges his words. Hope that we'll all go back to normal. After all this time, we'll be a family again.

I get a kiss on the top of my head before he releases

me. Walking over to the edge, I point down. "How do we get down there? I want to go down there."

"I'm not sure, but we'll devote the morning looking," he promises. I don't need his pinky to know he'll be good on his word. "I'm going to move the RV parallel to that area." He points along the edge. "That way, we can block the northerly wind if we want to have a fire tonight. What do you say, Dev? S'mores? Might be the last time you ever have them until we visit your grandparents."

My stomach groans with hunger. "Yes!"

I help direct Dad while he moves the RV where he wants it. It takes some maneuvering, and at one point he curses up a storm when he gets one of the wheels stuck, but we eventually get it the way it needs to be.

While Dad messes about outside, I run inside to break the news to Mom. I find her staring out the side window in their room that overlooks the gorge below. No smiles. No excitement. No anything.

"Mom…"

She shoos me on. "Devon, my head is killing me. Go help your father."

Tears of rejection fill my eyes and I nod. I obey and go help my father.

We cook hot dogs on the open fire and then indulge in s'mores. Mom stays in the bedroom.

"It's cold." I tuck my hands into the big pocket of my hoodie. "It's practically summer. Why is it cold?"

Dad chuckles and takes a long pull on his beer. "Earlier you were complaining it was too hot. Which is it, Pip?"

I stick my tongue out at him but hold my feet out toward the fire.

"Come here." He pats his lap like he used to do when I was a kid.

With a silly grin on my face, I leap at the chance to sit on my dad's lap. He's warm and cozy. Strong and protective. He wraps me up in a hug and I rest my ear to his chest. The familiar cadence of his heart thrums in my ear, drowning out the forest sounds. He pets my hair and then kisses the top of my head.

I must fall asleep because I wake as he carries me inside. The fire has long since dwindled. He sets me down on the sofa bed and then covers me up with my favorite quilt. His fingers stroke along my cheek before he gets up and darkens the RV. Despite being sleepy, I feel my ears perk up at every sound.

The sliding of the partition as he shuts it.

The jangle of Dad's belt.

Murmured voices.

And then the grunts.

Heat burns through me as the RV rocks another night in a row. Mom seems to participate because she lets out a moan. I'm embarrassed when heat begins to pool in my lower belly. I kick off my quilt and shimmy out of my jeans.

Grunt. Grunt. Grunt.

More murmured voices. The words belong to Dad. He sounds angry.

A slap.

And then the RV really starts shaking.

More slaps as she calls him every name in the book.

He bellows something unintelligible to her.

Then I hear what sounds like smacking sounds.

They're kissing.

A flare of jealousy flits through me and I'm immediately horrified by it. It just upsets me that she ignores us all day and then gets his undivided attention and affection. She doesn't deserve it after the way she treats him.

Another loud groan.

Shame ripples through me the moment I slip my fingers down between my thighs. I've touched myself before, but I'm not very good at it. All I know is it feels good when I touch a certain spot. Greedily, I rub at that spot. I'm craving the relief it will give me. Relief I've found before on occasion. It's always been difficult to get there and sometimes it never happens.

My ears ring and drown out their sounds as I furiously rub at myself. I'm no longer staring toward their partition door but am instead giving in to the electric sensations burning through me. I'm hot and sweaty. Quickly, I tear off my hoodie and then get right back to rubbing myself. I let out a choked sound the moment pleasure steals me from this reality. A loud sigh escapes me and I blink my eyes back open.

Light.

It shines from the bathroom out into the hallway.

Dad stands there in just his jeans glaring at me. When our eyes meet, he shakes his head in disproval before storming into the tiny bathroom. He slams the door shut.

Tears prickle my eyes. Shame courses through me tainting my recent orgasm. How am I going to explain that to him? He looked so pissed. I start to cry and quickly drag the quilt up my body even though I'm sweating. When Dad finally emerges, I pretend to sleep. I can feel him watching me in the darkness for a few moments before he retreats to their room.

I'm sorry, Dad.

I wake with a start.

I heard something.

Fear clutches my heart and I slip out of my bed hurrying to my parents' bedroom. Dad snores softly and Mom seems to be asleep too. Like I did when I was a little girl, I climb in between them. I slide my arm around Mom's middle and bury my face in her hair. She pats my arm absently in her sleep. The small moment of affection sets my heart on fire. I'm just relaxing when Dad rolls over and hugs me from behind. I retreat from my mother and seek his safety. Dad is strong and solid behind me. His arm curls around me and his lips find my hair. It grounds me.

Nothing will get me with him having my back.

He's still breathing heavily in a deep sleep, and it drowns out what I now realize is thunder. The RV shakes from the wind. Soon the rain starts to pound. A chill ripples through me. I start wiggling to get under the covers with them. Eventually, I manage to slide beneath their quilt. Dad's warm chest pressed against my back through my T-shirt heats my chilled body.

I manage to doze off but wake up again because the storm is going crazy outside. Lightning cracks every few minutes and the wind threatens to rip the top off the RV. I'm distracted, however, when Dad hugs me tighter. As though, even in sleep, he knows I need comfort.

I wiggle up against him again, and something hardens from behind me. His snores continue on but his penis presses against my butt through his boxers. My entire body stills. The storm is nothing in comparison to the way my heart jackhammers in my chest. I've never seen or felt a penis in person. The one poking into me is intimidating. I start to move away but he lets out a big snore like he might wake soon. His palm slides under my shirt. Skin against skin. Heat burns through me at a rate I can't compute. I know he'd have a conniption fit if he woke up right now and found us this way. And yet I can't bring myself to move away. His touch comforts me like no other person can. When his palm slides up to cup my small breast, my breathing stops altogether.

I want him to touch me everywhere.

The thought—so sudden and fierce—has a low, embarrassed sound escaping me. His thumb brushes against my nipple causing it to harden and me to shudder. I've never been touched by a boy and yet here I am at second base with my dad.

My skin is on fire now.

I should be moving away.

I definitely shouldn't be wiggling my butt again just so he'll stay hard. It fascinates me that a man can have an erection in his sleep.

"Sabrina," he murmurs, his voice thick with sleep. He's trapped within the dream world and he thinks I'm Mom.

I don't wake him or correct him.

I bite my lip and revel in his soft, possessive touch. The way his hips have begun slowly bucking against me. His hand abandons my breast, and I almost pout, but then my flesh ignites as his palm slides along my toned stomach to my panties. They're soaked and I'm horrified how turned on I am right now. The moment his fingers rub me in the spot that feels good over my wet panties, I jerk in his arms.

Explosive sensations shoot through me, far more powerful than the lightning and thundering outside. It feels a thousand times better than when I touch myself. My body is squirming and moving against his touch, desperate for more. More of what? I'm not sure. I just want more.

His breathing is quiet now and I realize he's awake.

I had my chance to move away but now he's awake and will flip out once he realizes what is happening. Still, I can't be the one to break the spell.

He kisses my neck and murmurs my mother's name as his fingers slip past my panties.

"So wet, Sabrina," he breathes against my flesh.

My eyes roll back in my head the moment he begins pushing his finger between my drenched folds seeking entrance to a place that even I haven't touched. Fire blooms deep in the pit of my belly. As he enters my body with just one of his fingers, the burn is almost too much to bear. I let out a whimper as a tear leaks out, but I don't want him to stop.

His entire body goes completely stiff and still. Slowly, he pulls his finger away. I feel him pat me and then pat my mother.

"Fuck!" he snarls in the dark. "Fuck!"

Mom stirs from her side of the bed but I can't move. I'm too horrified by his reaction. I attempt to pretend to sleep.

"Devon." His voice cracks and I swear he's going to cry again. Like those early days after Drew had died.

A sob escapes me and I roll over to face him, seeking his comfort. I bury my face against his chest, reveling in the way his hot flesh is sweaty against my bare stomach now that my shirt is pushed up. The connection sends fire surging through me once again and his erection bounces against me.

"Fuck," he growls and pushes me away.

He climbs out of bed and starts jerking on clothes. I can't stop crying. I don't understand why he's so mad. I mean, deep down I get it. He just touched his daughter in the dark. But it wasn't his fault. He thought it was Mom. I'm the sick one because I let it happen.

"Dad—"

"No, goddammit!" he barks out, waking my mother. "I need to think."

He yanks the partition closed and starts slamming things around in the kitchen. I snuggle close to my mom, my tears freely falling.

"Everything okay, sweetie?" Her voice is soft and real. Like the one I remember before we lost Drew.

"Momma," I sob.

The camper seems to move. Is Dad driving us somewhere?

Cracks and hisses and crushes.

My belly seems to float right out of my body as I fly out of the bed, my head cracking against the ceiling.

What's happening?

chapter three

REED

Fuck. Fuck. Fuck. Fuck!

I didn't just touch my daughter.

Did.

Not.

Fucking.

Happen.

Hysteria rises in my chest and I gag. Hot, furious tears sting at my eyes. I just ruined all of our lives in the blink of an eye because I thought it was Sabrina I was touching. I should have known my goddamned wife wouldn't respond to my touch.

Bile rises in my throat.

That means my daughter *did* enjoy it.

I snarl out a string of furious curse words.

I've probably just fucked up her head royally for the rest of her life over one stupid moment. I start slamming cabinets on a search for some hard liquor. I need a fucking drink so I can think of how I will fix this.

the wild

I.

Will.

Fix.

This.

I have to. That's my baby girl.

The storm is violent outside, and it matches my raging heart. Everything rattles and shakes. My daughter sobs from the other room causing my heart to shatter into a million pieces.

Don't worry, Pip. I'll make it right again. Just let me cool the fuck off.

A loud, earthly groan is the only warning I have that something is seriously off. And then I'm free falling. My shoulder slams against the ceiling before I get tossed across the room.

Crunch.

Smash.

Rip.

The yelp of our dog.

So many awful noises I can't make sense of anything.

Pop! Pop! Pop!

My head slams against every surface and all I can think about is *thank God* Dev and her mother are safe in the bedroom. It's my last thought before everything goes black.

Black.

Black.

And still falling.

I think I'm tumbling straight to hell.

After what I did, I deserve to go there.

But they sure as hell don't.

Black.

Screams.

Loud, ear piercing wails.

Devon.

She and Drew are out in the backyard. By the way she's screaming as though she's trying to wake the dead, I know she's in severe pain. I charge down the stairs knocking a few frames off the wall as I tear along toward her. My bare feet hit the cold marble floors and I skid to a stop long enough to shove my feet into my boots. Then, I'm running through the house and out the back door. The screen door slams behind me as I sprint toward the edge of the woods behind the house. Long ago I built her and Drew a treehouse.

What if she broke her arm?

Worse yet, her neck?

Bile rises in my throat as I run.

My first inclination is to blame Sabrina. I was buried in paperwork while she did God knows what. She's probably fucking napping. So help me if something happens to Devon...

I find her standing in the clearing, her blonde hair wild. Her face is bright red as she sobs. Rushing over to her, I pull her into my arms and then start assessing her for damages. I kneel down and take her small face in my hands.

"Where are you hurt, Pip?"

Her face crumples as she sobs and points up at the treehouse. My heart ceases to beat.

"It's Drew?"

She nods.

"Stay here," I instruct as I scale the small ladder up the tree.

Her wails are all I can hear.

A sound so devastating I'm not sure I'll ever get it to leave my memory bank. It'll probably haunt me until the day I die.

My head is throbbing.

Screams.

It only intensifies my headache, but it does pull me from my fog a bit. I absently pat at my forehead above my right brow. The skin is split there and hot blood rushes from it spilling over my eye. Using my palm, I press it to the wound to keep it from bleeding and try to make sense of what just happened.

I'm still in the RV.

Everything is mangled and crumpled and broken.

The RV is on its side, and I'm lying along the wall in between the cabinets and the stove.

"Devon," I croak out. "Sabrina."

My voice can barely be heard over the howling wind and torrential rains that still rattle the camper. I groan as I try to pry myself from my position. Nothing feels broken. My head just fucking hurts.

"Daddy!"

The scream, so sharp and terrified, jolts me completely out of my daze. It reminds me of that day when I thought she was hurt. And just like then, I scramble to find her. Her hysterical sobs are coming from the bedroom where I last left her.

Where you had your finger inside her...

I grit my teeth and push that into the recesses of my mind. I have more important things to worry about like my wife and my daughter's safety. The trek to the back where her cries haven't lessened is difficult. The RV is torn to shreds and rain pours in through a hole right before I get to the bedroom. I manage to yank the partition door up so I can squeeze through.

Lightning flashes and I get a sense of where Devon is at. Over and over the lightning illuminates the sky, allowing me to see fairly easily.

What I see nearly has me vomiting.

A tree has come through one window, a long and slender pine, and gone through the other window. Like a toothpick right through a sausage. My daughter's legs dangle from the upper window. A thin branch from the tree has impaled her on the side. Each time she wiggles, she slides further against the branch.

"Devon," I bellow over the storm, finally finding my voice. "Don't move."

"Daddy!"

Despite my orders, she kicks her legs frantically. I clamber over to her and let go of my forehead to grab her legs in a bear hug so she'll stop moving. She's sobbing so hard that her body trembles. I kiss her flesh and then try to inspect the branch stabbing her.

"Listen to me, Devon. I need you to calm down. I'm going to get you out of here." My gaze scans the small ruined room and Sabrina is nowhere to be found. Sickness roils in my belly. "Baby, can you see your mother. Tell me what you can see."

"It's raining too hard," she screeches. "I can't see anything. Lightning is going to strike me!"

Gritting my teeth, I lift her by her ass. She starts screaming in pain.

"See if you can climb up some," I holler. "I need to get this branch out of you."

I help her put her foot on my shoulder. Quickly she understands what she's supposed to do and kicks against me. Her howls are enough to crush my heart but my strong girl manages to slide off the branch. When she's free of it, I grab it and break it. Then, I slowly ease her back down into the camper with me. As soon as she's free, she latches onto me bawling her eyes out.

"Dev, I need to stop the bleeding. Let me see your wound." My voice is hoarse from exertion. We've fallen back against the mattress that is standing up since the RV is on its side. I don't have the energy to move. Blood rushes from the gash on my forehead and our bodies are slick against each other from the rain and blood from her stomach.

"I-I'm t-tired, Daddy." Her teeth are chattering wildly. I think she's going into shock.

I jerk my eyes open. I'm tired and dazed, but I can't just lie here. Sabrina is missing. Both Devon and I have wounds that need tending. And yet I can't move. Blindly, I reach for the quilt and try to wrap it around us. Devon is shivering so badly that I think warming her up is the first order of business. She burrows against me as though she's trying to crawl inside my skin. I hug her to me and kiss the top of her soaked head. We slump down—me falling on my ass and her nearly strangling me so I won't let her go.

She cries and cries.

I have to be strong for her.

My eyes droop and my muscles feel as though they weigh a ton. I can't seem to find the energy or strength to do anything else. Her fingernails dig into my chest. As my eyes start to close, I have the forethought to maneuver her so that her wound is pressed against my stomach. Hopefully that's enough to stop the bleeding.

"Rest for just a bit, Pip."

"Daddy."

The voice is soft and sweet. I don't walk toward it but I run for it.

My eyes crack open, and I'm blinded by a sunray that's shining in on me. It takes one horrible second to remember the chaos that happened last night. When I start to frown, something tugs at my forehead. I try to rip at it, but someone grips my wrist and pulls it away.

"Don't touch it. I bandaged you up," Devon whispers softly. A sob tears from her. "Buddy has vanished."

I tilt my head to the left to avoid the bright sun and stare at my daughter. Her blonde hair is wavy, damp, full of leaves, and caked with blood. The dog is probably smashed under the RV.

"He'll turn up." Lies. "Your stomach," I croak, my hand fumbling across her chest.

She lets out a whimper when I yank the fabric up to see. Her entire chest is scratched up like she took a slide face first down hot concrete. Both of her small breasts bore the brunt of the attack. But what has me most worried is her stomach. She seemed to have found the first aid kit because her abdomen is bandaged up too. Blood stains the gauze. I'll probably have to stitch her up soon.

"Have you been outside? Have you seen your mother?" I'm still frowning at the scratches on her breasts and stomach when she slowly stands letting her shirt fall back down.

"Dad…" Her bottom lip wobbles. "Let's just stay in here. I'll find you something to eat."

I close my eyes. The horror in her eyes is all I need to see. Sabrina is gone.

"Help me up," I grunt.

She grabs my wrist and helps me to my feet. When I sway, she hugs my waist. "I think you have a concussion," she whispers against my bloody still-bare chest.

I swallow and stroke her matted hair. "I'll be fine. We need to figure out what happened."

Her head tilts up to regard me. Fresh new tears well in her eyes making her blue eyes seem like lakes. "The cliff gave out. Washed away right underneath us last night. Must have been all the rainwater and the weight of the RV."

Guilt claws its way up inside me. "This is all my fault."

She shakes her head in vehemence. "No."

I clench my jaw and give her a clipped nod. She releases me and clumsily starts ambling out of the room and down through the camper. I follow after her, my head throbbing in pain. She's barefoot and wears nothing but a T-shirt and her bloody panties. I'm stuck in a pair of jeans but still shirtless and shoeless. We're a mess. I'll need to find us clothes, but first I need to find Sabrina.

The window that used to be beside the table has been smashed out. As if she's done this once already, Devon grabs the edge of the window, uses the bench seat at the table for leverage, and hoists herself out. Her legs flail as she tries to climb through. I grab her slender thighs and push her through. The metal of the RV groans as she walks along the outer side. My head hurts like a motherfucker but I easily hoist myself through the opening as I'm taller and stronger than my daughter. The moment I'm out of the hole, my breath catches in my throat.

We fell.

RV. Trailer. Everything.

At least two hundred feet down the side of the cliff. Trees, along our path of descent, are destroyed. Just the one tree seems to have impaled the RV. All of our belongings and tools and food are scattered over trees and along the forest floor. When I look to my left, I'm sickened to see some of it floating down the river.

"Where is she?"

Devon points through a few trees but doesn't look. As soon as I see Sabrina, I wish I hadn't looked. She hangs upside down from a tree by her foot that's caught on a branch. Her arm—Jesus fucking Christ—has been torn from her shoulder and dangles in the wind, barely held on by some muscle. Her other leg hangs off to the side in an obscene way. Her eyes remain open and her tongue hangs out.

Fuck.

Fucking gruesome goddamned shit.

"Daddy…"

"Stay there," I bark as I slide down the side of the RV to the muddy earth. A stick stabs my foot but I ignore it. Hobbling over to my wife, I pray it's just a figment of my imagination. That she's not dead. Simply passed out.

"Sabrina," I call out as I rush over to her.

So much blood.

While I was trying to save our daughter, she was out here bleeding to death. I didn't look for her. I just held our daughter and fell asleep. What the fuck?

I run my fingers through my hair and roar at the top of my lungs.

This was supposed to be our new life.

Our motherfucking happiness.

Not this.

It was never supposed to be this.

Falling to my knees, I let out a choked cry. "S-Sabrina. I'm s-so sorry."

Devon, despite being told to stay, squeezes me from behind. Her thin arms hug my neck as sobs make her entire body tremble. I stand back up and shake her off me.

"Go back to the RV," I snarl. "I need to take care of this."

"N-No, Dad. I'm going to help."

I glare at her, but she lifts her chin in defiance. I want to scream at her that now's not the time to back talk. She needs to fucking listen. But she looks so goddamned brave and fearless right now. Her mother is hanging dead from a tree like something out of a horror flick and she's begging to help.

"We need to find you clothes." My throat aches with emotion. There is so much that needs to be done to take care of her. I'm fucking overwhelmed. I don't even know where to start. But I hate that she's standing there in a torn shirt and panties, covered in blood.

"We can look for some after we help Mom," she whispers. "I promise."

With my jaw clenched, I reach forward and offer her my pinky. She hooks hers with mine and then we release our hands. I break away from her sad gaze to try and grab onto Sabrina's good arm. I'm about four feet too short.

"Put me on your shoulders. I can pull her down," Devon says as she comes to stand in front of me.

Since it's the quickest solution, I kneel down. She slides her thigh over my shoulder and then the other. I grip her legs so she won't fall as I rise. We wobble as she reaches for her mother.

My sweet, brave daughter has to tug her dead mother from a damn tree.

chapter four

DEVON

HER SKIN IS COLD AND HARD. A SOB CATCHES IN my throat but I refuse to let it escape. Dad is exhausted and about to lose his mind. The last thing I need is to give in to hysteria. Last night was the worst night of my life. When I woke up half sticking out of the RV with a branch stabbing me, I'd freaked out.

But he saved me.

I knew he would.

This morning, I was scared to death when I woke up. Dad was out of it and too pale. It took some hunting but I found the first aid kit in the bathroom still intact. He didn't rouse or anything when I bandaged him up. My biggest fear was that I'd lose my parents and I'd be all alone. Even my dog was missing, although I had a sneaking suspicion we'll find his bones one day beneath the RV or trailer. My heart aches for all the loss.

Deep down, I knew Mom was gone before I even

discovered her body. I just felt it deep in my soul. And as devastated as I was, all I kept thinking was that she was happy with Drew now. Mom could finally be at peace.

It's chilly this morning, especially after the storm, and I shiver as I attempt to pull Mom down by her good arm. The branch groans but doesn't release her. Dad grunts from exertion as he tries to hold me upright. For several long minutes, I pull and pull.

"Time to come down," he utters. "This isn't working."

"I can do it," I argue, lifting my entire body off his shoulders in an attempt to use all of my weight to bring her down.

A sick cracking sound is my only warning before I go crashing at least ten feet to the forest floor. Dad tries to catch me but he isn't quick enough. My ankle turns in a painful way and then my mother's cold body lands on top of me.

"Get it off!" I screech.

He grunts and pushes her body off of mine. Red hot pain radiates from my ankle and I grab it tenderly, fresh tears streaming down my cheeks. I stare up at him helplessly.

"We're going to die out here." My lip wobbles.

Fierce determination glints in his chocolate brown eyes. "We are not going to die, Pip. Don't talk like that."

I swallow and nod as he kneels to inspect my ankle. Gently, he takes the back of my calf and brings my foot into his lap. It's already swelling quickly. He presses in some places and moves it in ways that make me scream. Then, he brings my foot up and kisses my ankle bone. It's something he's always done. Kissed my ouchies. This time, after everything that happened last night, feels awkward.

Heat once again prickles at my flesh.

Embarrassment floods through me and I look away.

"I need to do something with…" he trails off and his throat bobs. "Then, I am going to start collecting everything that is strewn about. We need to salvage what we can."

"What should I do?"

He helps me to my feet, his strong hands gripping my elbows. When I put weight on my foot, I cry out in pain.

"You're going to stay inside and rest."

Before I can argue, he scoops me into his arms and begins the trek back to the demolished RV. I cling to him and wish this was all a bad nightmare. That maybe I went to sleep too upset last night about the accidental touching, and I'll wake up soon to Dad making pancakes.

But I don't wake up.

The chilly air makes me shiver.

Reality is cold.

He hugs me closer to him.

"I don't think I can get you back inside. I'm going to try and pull out one of the tents from the storage bin. That part of the RV looks intact, so hopefully we can have some sort of shelter tonight." He sets me down on a rock before sauntering away. The sun beats down, but it isn't warm. Cold air blasts me from the north every few minutes making my teeth chatter. I rub my arms and watch Dad as he hoists himself up on the side of the RV. His back muscles flex as he pries the hatch open.

"Fuck yes!" he hollers before pulling the bagged tent from the compartment and holding it above his head like a prize. His bicep flexes, and I find myself staring at it.

In fact, I must be in total shock because I stare at my father like he might disappear at any moment. I catalog his every expression. The sound of his voice. Each time he assures me everything is going to be okay.

Within fifteen minutes, he has a tent erected. Then, he disappears back into the RV. When he comes back, he's carrying some blankets that were folded and stored in a cabinet that must have survived along with two pillows.

"Can you make our bed?" he asks as he holds out the blankets.

I try not to blush. Our bed. I'm so stupid. It reminds me of last night in their bed.

"Y-Yes."

"As soon as you get it made, prop that foot up," he instructs. "I'm going to go…" His gaze drifts to where Mom's body remains unmoving a few yards away. "Bury her."

I shake my head. "Don't, Dad. The ground isn't deep here with all these rocks. You'll use up all your energy. Just…" Tears well in my eyes and I point at the river that rushes by. "Just let her go."

His features darken, but I can tell he's considering my words. He reaches forward and strokes my hair out of my eyes. "Everything is going to be okay, Pip. We can do this. Make smart decisions. Be strong. We've got this."

I smile and nod.

He storms off to deal with Mom. He didn't pinky promise.

"Wake up, Devon. You need to eat and drink something."

I jolt awake and look around me in confusion. The sky is dark and I can see a fire going just outside the tent.

"How long did I sleep for?" I rasp out.

His face is shadowed in the dark tent. I can't make out his features. "I'm guessing around twelve hours."

"Dad!" I cry out, horrified that he's been dealing with this mess alone. "Why didn't you wake me?"

"You needed the rest and I had it handled. Eat this," he instructs, handing me a warm can with a spoon sticking out of the top.

Chili.

I hungrily devour the chili. He watches me the entire time. It's then I realize he's cleaned up some and found a shirt.

"Did you find our clothes?"

"I did. I put them in the other tent for now with the other supplies I thought needed protecting from the elements and critters." He reaches over into a bowl and wrings out a wash cloth. "I also found the soap." His grin in the darkness seems to light up the space. "Lie back and let me look at your stomach."

I hand him the empty can and fall back against the blankets. A shiver ripples through me when he pushes my shirt up past my breasts. My breath hitches but he doesn't seem to notice. He peels away the bandages and groans. Soon, a flashlight clicks on and he puts it between his teeth. I sneak a peek down at my abdomen. The wound still gapes. In a clinical way, he sets to scrubbing at all of my scratches on my torso with the warm soapy rag. It stings and I whimper, but he doesn't stop. When the rag runs over my breasts, my nipples harden. I let out a sharp breath that has his hand stalling. He cleans each breast well and then the rest of my torso before inspecting the gash.

"I'm going to have to stitch it up," he tells me once he plucks the flashlight from his mouth. "It may hurt, Pip. Can you be brave for me?"

I nod. Tears already stream from my eyes. This whole situation is painful. What's a little bit more? He has the first aid kit handy. With the flashlight once again in his mouth, he threads the needle and then sets to stitching me.

"Owwww," I complain, my hands fisting the blanket.

"Don't squirm."

I clench my eyes closed and try to breathe calmly through my nose as he carefully closes my wound. Each time he pours alcohol in it, I scream. Eventually, he gets it stitched and rewrapped in bandages.

"Take your clothes off," he orders before exiting the tent.

I'm so shocked that I don't move until he returns carrying my hoodie and some yoga pants. Sheepishly, I tug off my soiled shirt and hand it to him. He waits, his flashlight blinding me, for the rest. My heart is hammering in my chest as I wiggle out of my panties. I can't see his face as I hand him the panties.

"Use the rag to clean up. I'll bring you some water and some Ibuprofen in a minute." He disappears once again.

Quickly, I give myself a sponge bath and wish I could wash the blood and dirt from my hair. Once I'm clean, I pull on my warm clothes. All of the movements have left me exhausted. Dad eventually returns with a bag. He drops it just inside the tent along with a shotgun. Then, he takes the water bowl out with him.

When he returns, he stumbles.

"Are you okay?"

"I'm just tired," he says in a thick voice as he zips up the tent behind him.

Our tent is small, meant for just me, but we make it work. The other tent my parents were supposed to share. He kicks off some shoes he found, and I wait until he's settled on the pillow beside me before I grab the blanket to draw it over us. I curl up against his warm body and hug him tight.

"I'm scared," I admit in a whisper.

"Me too."

"Are we going to die?"

He strokes my matted hair and kisses the top of my head. "Pip, we're going to live. Day by day. We'll do it. Be strong for me. Promise me that."

I lift my pinky and he takes it. We link them but this time we don't let go as we fall fast asleep.

Something grunts outside our tent in the middle of the night. I can hear it snort as it sniffs around. Just when I think it will rip open our tent and attack us, its heavy footsteps retreat. The temperature has dropped and I'm freezing. I snuggle closer to Dad for warmth.

"Dad," I whisper. "I'm cold."

He rouses and his hand absently strokes my cheek. "What, baby?"

"I'm cold."

"Take off your hoodie." His voice is thick with sleep. Surely I misheard him.

"No, it's too cold."

He lets out a tired sigh. "Body heat. I'm fucking cold too." He sits up and tugs his shirt off. "Pip, take it off."

I nod and reluctantly peel it away. Before I can even complain about the cold, his arm wraps around me and he spoons me from behind. His arm is hot against my cold flesh and he splays his palm out over my chest bone. Soon, his breathing evens back out but my heart is still hammering in my chest. Thoughts from the night before keep replaying. The way his thumb brushed over my nipple. How he urged his finger inside of me. I don't even realize I'm wiggling with need until I feel his hardness against my butt.

I freeze and listen for his snores but he's quiet. He doesn't move away like last night. Instead, he keeps me locked in his grip.

"I'll keep you safe," he whispers, his hot breath against my neck.

My entire body relaxes at his words. "Thank you."

Sleep must steal me away because I wake at some point overheated. We're facing each other and a tangled mess of limbs. While he sleeps, I explore his hard chest with my fingertips. My fingers continue their trek to his sculpted shoulders and then up his throat. I touch his scruffy cheek and then his soft lips.

"Go to sleep, Pip." His voice is a deep rumble as he

grips my wrist and tugs me against him. My breasts smash against his hot chest.

"Okay."

He has a death grip on my wrist but the moment he starts softly snoring again, I hike my thigh up along his toned leg. My breath hitches when my knee rubs against his erection. I'm going to combust. The thoughts and feelings surging through my mind are sinful and wrong but I can't stop thinking about the way he touched me last night.

I'm losing my mind, clearly.

My mom was brutally killed. I've yet to mourn her. It's like my mind has shut off that reality. When I shudder, he hugs me tighter. My thigh is pressed against his hot erection through his jeans and I keep wiggling against him as if to seek relief from the friction.

"Please go to sleep, Devon. Please." His voice is so pained, so raw, that I can't help but obey.

"Okay."

And I do.

chapter five

REED

I WAKE WITH AN EMBARRASSING HARD-ON. MY daughter is clinging to me as if I'll leave her at any moment, half naked I might add, and my dick is hard.

It's just morning wood.

That's what I tell myself.

My body's natural response.

I'm dreading the day ahead of me. So much needs to be done. Yesterday I gathered our shit to the point of exhaustion. Today, I can hardly move.

Devon's palm slides to my lower stomach and I hold my breath. I know she's asleep. The sound of her breathing is rhythmic. Unlike last night.

Heat bubbles up inside of me. Angry heat. She's getting confused and I don't know what to do about it. Her life was literally turned upside down. She's clinging to whatever she can. I'm all she has left. I wish I knew how to undo what's already been done though. The parts where I accidentally touched her and how she thinks she can freely touch me now.

I'm not a sicko.

I'm not a motherfucking child molester.

Her knee bumps my dick and I groan. I have to get out of this tent. With a grumble, I slide out from beneath her and grab my shirt. I'm sitting on my knees putting it on when I feel her staring at me. Stupid me chances a glance her way.

She lies there with her arm curved above her head. The blanket reveals her scraped up left breast, the nipple peaked and at attention. Her pouty lips are parted and she stares at me with a look I don't understand from her.

She's fucking with my head.

"Get dressed," I snap and then charge out of the tent before she can see my erection.

When I hear sniffling, I ignore it before I do anything more stupid than I've already done, like go back to her and console her.

There needs to be boundaries.

Now.

It's been five days since we tumbled off the side of the cliff. Devon can't walk yet, her ankle still too weak, so I have her do tasks she can manage while sitting. Sorting through piles of collected stuff. Meal prep. Inventory.

Meanwhile, I have been obsessing over building us a home. The tents are fine for the summer but I need to get some legitimate shelter in place before the winter gets here. My chainsaw survived the accident but I don't have much gas left for it. I'll have to reserve it for special uses. All of my other hand tools and nails were recovered though. It will take some hard, manual labor, but I'm going to build us a home if it's the last thing I do.

"I'm going to explore," I call out as I pick up my ax.

Devon lifts her blue eyes to meet mine and frowns. "Without me?" The hurt written all over her face is enough to crush me. Sure, I've been avoiding her as much as possible. She still clings to me like a spider monkey in the middle of the night, but so far we've managed to not have any touching mishaps. We haven't talked about what happened though. Eventually, I owe it to her as her father, to try and talk her through the confusing feelings she's having.

"You can't walk."

Fire flashes in her eyes and she stands. She's wrapped her ankle in one of her mom's old scarves to help support it. Her movements are slow but she hobbles my way, determination driving her forward. I can't help but smile at her.

"You going to bore me with useless information the whole time?" I ask as I grab a couple of water bottles I've recycled and toss them in my bag.

She rolls her eyes. "My useless information will save us one day. I'm going and you'll have to endure my chattering."

I hold my hand out to her and she clasps it with hers. Together we begin a slow trek through the wilderness. We walk for what feels like hours until Devon whimpers each time she puts pressure on her foot. The forest is thick in these parts, but I can still hear the river rushing by.

"A cave!" Devon shrieks, her voice reminding me of when she was small.

"Stay here," I instruct. "Sit."

She plops down on a fallen log and watches me as I explore the crevasse in the side of the mountain. When I peek my head in, I frown at seeing some bats. But other than that, the crack is about three feet wide and nine feet deep. Too small for bears and there isn't any animal dung to indicate anything lives here. I reach in and touch the smooth stone surface. Cold. It would be a great escape this summer when it gets hot and perfect for storing things in the winter.

I survey the land outside the cave. It's relatively flat and close to the river. The trees are plentiful here so I'd have plenty to work with and wouldn't have to drag them very far. I grab a fallen limb and scare all the bats from the cave. Devon squeals from behind me and I laugh. Once I deem it safe, I saunter over to her and scoop her into my arms. Her smile is brilliant and full of love. This is the daughter I know. We can fix the little bit of damage we've done. I just know it. We'll go back to the way things used to be.

I set her on the ledge of the small crevasse and grin at her. "What do you think?"

"It feels good," she exclaims as she lies back on the cool stone floor. "Soooo good."

I laugh and climb in next to her. There's bat shit everywhere but neither of us care. It's cold and refreshing this hot day. She grabs my hand and threads our fingers together.

"It's kind of small but I love it." Her gaze darkens. "Mostly I can't see all the wreckage."

"I like it too." I lean forward and kiss her forehead. "I'm going to build us a house up against this crevasse."

She beams at me and I vow right then I'm going to make her smile like this more every day. "Thank you."

My heart clenches in my chest. "It's my job to take care of you."

Her palm touches my cheek and she gets that dreamy look in her eyes again. "I want to take care of you too."

The spell is broken as shame creeps up my spine. "Let's get back." My tone is gruff as I pull my hand from her grip.

"Can we go swimming today?"

I regard her over my shoulder as I scoot out of the cave. "I don't think it's safe yet for you."

She frowns. "I want to wash my hair."

The very idea of bathing with her in the river has my hair standing on end. But it is my duty to make sure she bathes. I can't keep her at arm's length forever.

"Fine, but you're not walking back." I flash her a smile. "Piggy back?"

Her bright grin is back and it's a motherfucking salve to my bleeding heart.

I shed my T-shirt and jeans but leave my boxers on. My gaze remains on the ground as I see her clothes drop on top of my pile. With a bar of soap in her hand and a bottle of shampoo in the other, she hobbles into the icy water.

"Shit! It's cold!" she complains.

Laughing, I turn to watch her ease her way into the

water. From behind, she doesn't even look like my Devon. She's only wearing a skimpy pair of pink panties. No shirt. Nothing. Her ass is too round, too fucking womanly. I'm glad she'll die a damn virgin. She'll be safe from dipshit college boys forever.

"Oh!" she cries out as she slips.

I lunge for her and hook her around the waist before she goes floating down the river. Ignoring the blood rushing down my body, I dip into the water with her in my arms.

"Do your washing. I'm not about to lose you too," I grumble.

She lets out a sigh but sets to soaping her body down while I hold her shampoo bottle. Her skin is slippery but I don't let her go. I find a place for us to sit. With her wedged between my legs and my arms gripped around her, she's not going anywhere. She wiggles and soon her pink panties are in her grip. My gaze is fixated on them as she scrubs them with the soap. When she finishes, she twists them around her wrist so they don't float away.

"Do you want to wash?" Her words are breathy and soft.

"Not if I have to let you go."

I wince at how those words could be misconstrued. She twists in my arms and settles on her knees in front of me. The water laps at her breasts, a distracting sound that I desperately try not to focus on.

"I'll do it for you."

My grip tightens around her. I close my eyes as she runs the bar of soap over my chest. When she moves her soapy palm down my abdomen and her fingertips brush against the waistband of my boxers, I growl.

"Devon." It's a warning.

She plays innocent and sets to washing my shoulders. When she finishes, we trade the soap for the shampoo.

"I have to get my hair wet," she murmurs. Her legs wrap around my waist so she can hold on and she floats back in the water.

For one moment, I'm mesmerized. I can't tear my gaze from her nipples that stick out of the water as she wets her hair. And what really fucks with my head is the fact she's naked with her legs spread wide open right against my cock. As if I called it to action, I grow embarrassingly hard against her soft body.

"Devon, hurry," I snap through gritted teeth.

"Okay," she breathes as she scrubs at her hair.

I close my eyes and try to think about anything to make my erection go away. I'm surprised God hasn't struck me down right here in the river.

"Let me wash yours," she says, causing me to jerk my eyes open.

She's clean and too damn pretty with the river water dripping from her dark lashes. I let out a groan but lean back to wet my hair. Once I sit back up, she squirts some shampoo in my hair and begins scrubbing. It feels good to be tended to. For so long Sabrina denied me something as simple as affection. Devon's soft touches soothe my battered soul.

"Rinse," she orders.

I smile and lean back. Her breasts press against me as she leans forward to help me get the soap out. It's easy to confuse who we are in this moment. With the sun baking down on us and the water rushing by, it's easy to pretend we're just a man and a woman in the wilderness.

She's sixteen.
And your daughter.

I sober up quickly and stand up with her in my arms. My dick is still rock hard. I'm sure she can feel it but neither of us speak of it. I carry my naked child to the river banks.

"Tonight we need to talk," I snap as I deposit her on her ass.

She yelps and stares up at me in confusion. "Am I in trouble, Daddy?"

I look up at the clear blue sky and pray to God for strength. This whole ordeal is too hard on my psyche. I'm cracking. Just like the hole in the side of the mountain. I'm widening and splitting right down the middle until the only thing that fits is she and I.

And that can't fucking happen.

Ever.

She watches me over the fire, fear dancing in her eyes. We've yet to discuss things but I'm waiting to get a little braver. And with one of the bottles of Jack I found on one of my scavenging hunts, the liquid courage is beginning to surge through me. I take another long pull on my bottle. She bites on her plump bottom lip and flashes me another worried look. Her hands busy themselves with braiding her long golden blonde hair.

She's so fucking pretty.

I close my eyes and shake my head.

Focus.

"That night should have never have happened. I need to apologize." My words are hoarse as I rip off the proverbial Band-Aid.

"Dad…"

"No," I snap. "We're discussing this." I scrub at my face and pin her with a hard glare. "I'm your father. Not your boyfriend." My words are mean and harsh and I instantly wish I could retract them.

Her full lips part open and tears well in her eyes. "I didn't say that," she whispers.

"But you're thinking it. Whatever romantic notion is running through your head ends tonight. Are we clear?"

She swallows and nods. "I just…"

"No."

"But…"

"No."

"Dad…"

"Jesus Christ, Devon. I said fucking no. Do I need to whip your ass to get that through your thick goddamned skull?"

She jerks her head my way and glares at me. "I hate you."

"Go to bed," I snarl. "Get over your fucking self and go the fuck to sleep."

Tears streak down her cheeks and she all but runs to the tent. I stay back and drink myself stupid. Hours ago I should have gone in and apologized to her but I don't trust myself. Lines are blurred and fuck if it isn't confusing for me too.

When I finally stumble back to the tent, she's crying softly. Guilt surges up through me. I kick off my boots, undress down to my boxers, and fall into bed beside her. Her back is turned to me. It breaks my heart that I've done this to her. Crushed my sweet happy girl.

"Come here," I order.

"No. I hate you."

"Come here!" I bellow. "I'm fucking sorry, okay?"

I reach for her and she elbows me. Undeterred, I hook my arm around her waist and haul her to me. It's fucking cold and she'll freeze without my body heat. She struggles against my hold. When she turns toward me and slaps the shit out of me, I lose it. I grab her by the throat and pin her down.

"Calm the fuck down," I growl.

I can't see her in the dark but I can bet she's glaring at me. Leaning forward, I kiss her forehead except it's not her forehead, it's her lips. Fat, swollen lips. I kiss them again. Her body relaxes and my grip on her throat falls away.

I want to taste her.

The thought disgusts me but I want it nonetheless.

"You confuse me," she whispers, her breath hot against mine.

My palm slides up to cradle her soft face. "I don't know what's happening to us. Everything is tearing apart. I just want us to be the way we used to be."

I press one more kiss to her mouth before falling on my back. I pull her over to me and lock her in my grip. She's no longer trying to get away. We mold together like every night.

"I'm sorry, Pip."

"Me too, Dad."

chapter six

DEVON

I CAN HANDLE A LOT OF THINGS IN THE WILDERNESS but my period is one that kills me. We've been here for two months. Each time I get my cycle, I am miserable to the point I want to die. Sure, I have a small supply of tampons but I'm bloated and uncomfortable and bitchy as hell. Plus, it's almost August and unbearably hot during the day. I spend more time in the cave than anywhere else during shark week.

My hormones are also out of control.

I sit up on my elbows and watch Dad work on our new home. He's downed twenty-six trees. I've watched him over the weeks bulk up from the manual labor and I can't stop staring at him. He walks around shirtless with his jeans low on his hips revealing muscles that seem to point right to his cock and it drives me mental.

Ever since the night we fought, I've tried hard to go back to the way things were. Dad has tried even harder. But we're strained. It's in the back of both our minds, I know this without doubt, but we both ignore it. And at night, we cuddle like two related people shouldn't.

I crave him.

Badly.

More so than chocolate or any other thing I no longer have access to.

I don't want any of it.

I want him.

I want to run my fingers through his thick beard and kiss his perfect lips.

Shame causes my skin to heat up and I grab my water bottle in irritation. My belly growls and I wonder if I should scavenge for some berries. They are plentiful and I'm trying to figure out a way to preserve them for the winter. Dad has built some traps to save his ammunition. We've feasted on squirrels and rabbit. Aside from the forbidden tension between us, life is kind of nice. Sometimes late at night we talk about how much we miss Mom and Drew and Buddy, but mostly we just hold each other and find solace in the only other person on this earth we have left.

"I think I'll make the door face east. Once we get the cabin erected, I'm going to start cutting off metal from the RV to use for the roof," he says as he hefts his ax in a log. He lifts his muscular arm to swipe sweat from his brow. His bicep bulges and his abs flex.

Oh, God.

My entire body feels as though it's buzzing with electricity. I have no way to expel the energy.

"Sounds good," I tell him absently. My gaze falls to his

butt when he bends over to pick the ax back up. The boys in my old neighborhood never looked this good. Strong. Muscular. Sweaty.

I'm going to combust.

I peel off my tank and lie back on the cool stone. It works wonders to cool me off.

"Put your shirt back on," Dad says, his voice close.

I shield my eyes from the sun to find him standing right in front of the cave opening. His gaze shamelessly rakes down my bare chest.

"I'm hot," I pout.

His jaw clenches and he tears his gaze away. "I need you to check the traps near camp. Skin anything we catch. I'm going to work on clearing the brush for the foundation a little more. Soon I can start on the frame."

I sit up on my elbows again. My breasts are swollen since I'm on my period and I'm happy they're a little bigger than usual. His gaze falls on them again. When he licks his lips before turning away, my heart flutters in my chest.

"Shirt. On. Now."

Rolling my eyes, I pull the shirt back on before climbing out of the cave. I stomp back to camp. I've only made it a few hundred yards away when I realize I forgot my knife. With a huff, I turn on my heel and head back. Dad is nowhere to be found. When I approach the cave, he's lying inside with his legs dangling out. His jeans have been pushed down his muscular thighs. My jaw drops to see that he's fisting his thick cock. I'm enthralled by the way his veins on his tanned forearm bulge with each time he jerks at it.

It's the hottest thing I've ever seen.

He fists it harder and harder until he groans in

pleasure. When my name is whispered from his lips, I freeze fearing I've been caught watching. Then I become mesmerized at the thick ropy cum that shoots up his bare hardened abs. He starts to sit up and I run.

This must be hell.

Hot and miserable.

Teased with what you'll never be able to have.

Anytime Dad sends me away to run errands for him, I always sneak back to see if he touches himself. Often, he goes back to work. Sometimes, though, he yanks his cock out and whacks off until his release is spent. I feel dirty watching him but I can't help it. He's my addiction. We're well into September now and our warm days are behind us. The nights are too cold. We spend far too much time snuggled together for body heat.

"We can always add on," Dad says, his hands on his narrow hips.

I walk around our cabin that doesn't have a roof yet. I love that it's pressed against the side of the mountain and we can keep our cave. "Seems plenty big enough to me. My favorite part is the porch."

He winks at me and saunters into the structure. "I'm going to make us matching chairs and a little table so we can sit out here and eat breakfast each morning."

"I can't wait."

His gaze stalls on my lips so I lick them. I find myself desperate to drive him as crazy as he makes me.

"Get back to work," he barks out and gives me a playful swat on my bottom.

I roll my eyes at him despite the fire raging within me and set to scraping the bark off the inside of the cabin walls. I'm distracted though when he starts cutting wood he plans to use on the roof. Muscles upon muscles. Dad never had those before. I mean, he was cut and lean but I never knew he could look like this.

"Take a picture, it'll last longer," he teases.

Heat flashes across my skin. Is he flirting with me?

"You look sweaty. Maybe we should go swim and I'll wash you." I quirk up an eyebrow in challenge.

"Bad girl," he mutters before going back to his project.

I grin because I feel like I won this round.

Today is moving day. It's freezing and I'm tired but our cabin is ready. I'm dying to get out of the tent. And yet here I am, curled under the blankets dreading all the hard work ahead of us today.

"Pip," Dad chirps as he unzips the tent and sits on his knees beside me. His grin is infectious. "I have a surprise for you."

I sit up and rub sleep out of my eyes. "Show me."

His laugh is warm and rich. It heats me from the inside out. "Come on, pretty girl."

I melt under his flirtatious compliment and accept his outstretched hand. Once I'm dressed, we walk hand in hand to our new home. As soon as it comes into view, my heart swells. We built it together. Dad did all the heavy lifting but he let me help a lot. I'm proud of it.

Tears well in my eyes. It's constructed with pride. Dad didn't cut any corners. The porch is a lovely touch and our table and chairs are perfect. The roof had given him hell but he made it work. It's pitched with logs but he used the metal from the RV to fashion a roof that should remain leak free. The extra pieces of metal, he lined the inside of our cabin for insulation against the cold. Together, we'd taken apart one of the bench seats in the RV and made a couch for our living space. The cabin is spacious. There's a bedroom, a living room, and a small kitchen area. It's perfect.

"Close your eyes," he murmurs as he tugs me closer to our home.

I close them and let him guide me up the steps onto the porch. He pushes open the fancy door he made and we step inside. It's warmer than the chilly air outside and I smile. I'm scooped into his arms and I squeal. When he tosses me, I cry out and then gasp when I land on a soft surface.

A bed.

He told me the mattress was ruined inside the RV, yet here it is with my favorite quilt spread over the top.

I burst into tears.

"Shhh," he coos and sits beside me on the bed. I'm pulled into his warm arms. "I thought you'd like it, sweetheart."

I sob but look up at him. "I love it, Dad."

His brown eyes light up and he leans forward. When his lips brush against mine, I nearly melt. He pulls away and smiles. "Happy birthday, Devon."

I blink at him in confusion. "It's my birthday?"

"I've kept up with the calendar. You're seventeen now."

"I feel forty," I joke.

He strokes my hair out of my face and regards me with a tender expression. "You've grown into a beautiful woman."

Heat coils in my belly like a snake. "Thank you." I blush under his intense stare. Eventually, he breaks our gaze and stands.

"Let's move in. I'm ready to start preparing for winter and settling in."

"Me too."

Since it's cold outside, we curl up on the sofa and enjoy our new space. Our first night at our home and my birthday.

"The legal drinking age is twenty-one but I'm pretty sure I'll have burned through all the alcohol leftover before then. If you have any chance of crossing this off your life bucket list, we better do it soon. And what better time than your birthday?"

He pours some liquor into a coffee mug that survived the crash. I pull it up to my nose and crinkle it up in disgust.

"Ew. How do you drink this?"

"It'll put hair on your chest, that's for damn sure."

I laugh and shake my head. "I'm not sure if I want hair on my chest. I kind of like it the way it is."

His gaze darkens. "Just drink, Pip."

The first swallow feels as though I've swallowed fire. It burns me from the inside out. I cough and glare at him. "Gross!" But then heat spreads through my chilled bones and I decide I like that warm feeling. "Fine. I'll drink it but only because it warms me up."

"I promise I'll always keep you warm," he murmurs. His pinky hooks with mine and we leave them conjoined.

We grow quiet as we drink and the sun sets, leaving us in the darkness. Each of us are lost in our own thoughts. Mine are of the dirty variety. I have no idea what he's thinking. I can't read him like I used to before this trip. A storm always brews in his eyes. As if he's battling a war within myself. I wish he could find peace.

"I think that's enough for one night," he grunts, taking my now empty mug from me.

I whine but he simply chuckles at me. When I attempt to stand, I stumble. Lightning quick, he rises and steadies me with his hands on my hips. The jeans and hoodie feel like too much.

"Time for bed, Pip."

I peel off my hoodie and shirt. It takes longer to remove my jeans. I climb under our mountain of covers now that we've taken them from both the tent and the RV.

"Are you coming to bed?" I ask as I stretch out. I don't know how he wrangled the mattress all the way here by himself but I'm in heaven.

His belt jangles and my ears perk up as his clothes hit the cabin floor. When the mattress sinks with his weight, my heart rate spikes. I wrap my nearly naked body around his and let out a contented sigh.

"Did you have a good birthday?" he murmurs.

"It was the best. I wanted this one little thing though." My voice is a whisper but I'm dead set on saying it. The liquor encourages me.

"What's that?"

I tilt my head up and run my fingers through his wiry beard. Our hot breaths co-mingle, spicy from the alcohol. "A kiss."

He laughs. "I kiss you all the time."

I run my thumb over his bottom lip. "A real one."

Dad doesn't answer. Rejection makes me nauseous.

"I'll never get to kiss a boy for the first time. I'll never go to college. I'll never have a normal life. I just thought—"

I'm silenced when his hot mouth presses to mine. Soft. So soft. My heart is pattering in my chest and it feels as though butterflies dance in my belly. His strong hand grips my jaw and he pulls down so that my mouth parts open. I let out a surprised moan when his warm tongue brushes against mine. It feels weird but I like it. He starts to pull away but I'm not done. I thread my fingers in his long brown hair that hangs in his eyes lately when we go too far between haircuts. I grip him and urge him to keep kissing me. With a groan, he gives in.

We kiss like this for what feels like hours.

I want his mouth all over me but I settle for it on mine for now.

His cock is hard against my thigh. I'm trying to summon up the courage to touch him through his boxers but keep falling short.

"Devon," he rasps against my mouth. "That's enough. You got your birthday wish. Time for bed." Guilt laces his tone.

I don't want him to feel guilty. It's just the two of us. Nobody is judging us.

"Please," I beg as I try to kiss him again.

He turns his head away as he rolls onto his back. "No. Bed. Now."

I'm not afraid of his fatherly authoritative tone. Tapping into my bravery, I reach down and grip his erection through his boxers. I expect him to let me stroke him like he does himself.

"FUCK!" he snarls. "What the fuck, Devon?!"

He shoves me away from him and my pride is instantly crushed. Undeterred, I reach for him again. I shriek when he grabs my arm and drags me across his lap. His cock pokes painfully into my ribs as he rips my panties down my thighs.

"What—" My words give way to a scream when he spanks me. I try to scramble away, but he pins me in his strong grip.

Smack! Smack! Smack!

I sob and wiggle—anything to escape him spanking me. I haven't been spanked since I was ten years old.

Smack! Smack! Smack!

He spanks me so hard that I know I'll be bruised. Over and over again until I throw up all over our new floor. I'm tossed into the floor as he stands and stalks out of the cabin in nothing but his boxer shorts.

Confused and hurt, I crawl into the bed and bawl my eyes out until I pass out.

I've never felt so alone in my entire life.

chapter seven

REED

I COULD WRITE AN ENTIRE BOOK ON ALL THE WRONGDOINGS I'm guilty of since we made the trip to Alaska. Every single sin was committed against *her*. My girl. The only person I have left in this world. The one I love with my entire soul.

She won't speak to me.

She won't eat.

All damn day, she sleeps in our bed. Just like her fucking mother.

It kills me.

I shouldn't have kissed her. Fueled by the liquor, I gave in to the sinful urges. Her lips were sweet and perfect. I wanted to do it all night. But then she sent me over the edge. Touched my cock and drove me mad. I lost my fucking head and beat my daughter.

It's not her fault. She's young and confused. Fuck, I'm old and confused. I don't understand how to navigate this new world where we're the only people in it.

"You need to get out of bed today," I bark out from the doorway.

She doesn't flinch. With a sigh, I close up the cabin. I want to present her with another gift I scavenged but something tells me she won't care. Lighting a candle that I'd found in one of the boxes, I set it down on the end table I made beside the bed. The glow flickers off the walls. My gaze falls to her blonde hair that's spread out over her pillow. She's wearing one of my sweatshirts and I decide I like the way it looks on her.

"Pip?"

I shed my shirt and jeans before climbing into bed. When I curl up against her, she pretends to sleep. I miss her voice. Her smiles. The fucking light that radiates from her.

"I'm sorry," I murmur for the thousandth time since I spanked her a week ago. "Please forgive me."

I'm so lonely. It's as if I'm in hell without her. She's here but she's not. I fucking hate it. I'm craving her hot skin against mine. The need is overwhelming. My lips find her neck just below her ear and I kiss her softly. I want to bring her back to me. Her body responds to the simple touch and it lights a fire inside of me. I slide my palm to her hip and then turn off my brain as I slip it up her flat stomach before stopping to cup her small tit. Her breath hitches.

"It's cold," I murmur. "We need body heat."

The wind chooses that moment to howl outside as if to plead my case for me. She sits up and peels off the sweatshirt. Then, she pushes down her yoga pants. With more bare skin available to me, I kiss along her neck to her shoulder. I pull her onto her back and continue my kissing along her collarbone.

"Tell me to stop, baby. My head is all fucked up right now because I missed you so goddamned much." My hot breath against her sensitive flesh makes her shudder. "I want to do things no father should ever do with his daughter."

"Kiss me," she pleads. "I missed you too."

I don't wait another second before I devour her pouty lips. She moans against my mouth, her tongue just as greedy for me as I am for her. We kiss desperately. I pinch her nipple and then soothe out the pain with gentle touches.

"Dad…"

I close my eyes. "Call me Reed in our new house. It fucks with my head too much if you don't."

Her fingers thread into my hair. "Reed. I want to touch you."

I nod against her lips. She slides her palm down my tight abs and plunges her hand into my boxers. When she grips my aching cock, I nearly come right then. My breath hisses against her mouth. For someone with zero experience, she strokes my cock like a pro. I nearly black out from the intense pleasure. When I think I might come in her hand, I grab her wrist and pin it to the mattress.

"No."

Heartbreak flashes across her features. The flickering candle light makes her seem so fucking sad.

"No, baby." I kiss her mouth. "I just…I'll come and I'm not ready yet."

Her body relaxes and we start to make out again.

"Can I kiss you here?" I squeeze her perky tit.

"Y-Yes."

She lets out a low moan when my mouth finds her nipple. I suck on the tender flesh softly at first. Then, I nip at her with my teeth. She tastes good enough to eat. When I'm sure I've given equal attention to each of her tits, I lift up and give them a break. Her eyes are hooded as she regards me with a sultry look—a look I've never seen before but it speaks to the animal inside of me. I want to see this look more often.

"I know you touch yourself," I murmur, my eyes locked on hers. "How often?"

She chews on her bottom lip. "Sometimes when you fall asleep."

"Does it feel good?"

"I wish it were you instead."

My dick throbs in my boxers. "Do you want me to touch you there?"

She nods. "Please."

I kiss down her stomach until I reach the top of her pale pink panties. I press a long kiss to her clit through the fabric and inhale her sweetness. She lets out a soft moan when I sit up and urge her panties down her thighs. After I toss them aside, I clutch her knees and pry them apart. Her pink pussy glistens with arousal. Since she's a blonde, the hair is practically non-existent there and it's almost as though she's shaved. It turns me on so fucking badly.

I run my finger along her slit and revel in the way she jolts in pleasure. I'm going to blow her fucking mind. With our eyes locked together, I ease a finger in her tight channel. It's been months since I've been laid. My dick practically sings with the prospect.

"I'm going to kiss you there." My finger slides in and out of her wet pussy making obscene slurping sounds that set my blood on fire.

"Please do it, Reed."

I flash her a wide grin, silently thanking her for keeping me in this moment. When I lean forward and my breath tickles her, she moans loudly. Slowly at first, I start tonguing her clit. She cries out in pleasure, her fingers latching on to my hair. It's been seven years at least since I last did it. Once Drew died, Sabrina wouldn't let me pleasure her anymore. I worry I'll be out of practice but Devon has no complaints.

"Oh, God," she whimpers. "This is intense."

I'll show her intense.

I suck on her clit while curling my finger up inside her. My fingertip rubs against her G-spot causing her to make a choking sound. When I introduce my teeth to her clit, she cries out. Her pussy clenches around my finger. She's close. I attack her pussy with everything I've got. My mouth sucks and bites and licks her until she's screaming in pleasure. Her body shudders for a good thirty seconds before she calms. When I slide my finger out and lift up to look at her, her eyes are wild.

"I need…"

"More?" I quip with a lifted brow.

She nods. I'm glad she's my partner in crime here. If I think about all the wrong we're doing, I'll flip the fuck out. So instead, I just focus on the girl I love.

"I want to make love to you," I tell her, my voice raw. "But it's a big deal, Devon."

She frowns. "I want it. I want you. I'm too lonely

without you. I don't like when anything stands between us."

I clench my jaw. "It's going to hurt, baby."

"Like the day you spanked me until I threw up?" she challenges. "I think I can handle it."

A growl rumbles from me and I pounce on her. My dick strains against my boxers as I dry hump her. She's so wet she soaks my underwear. Our mouths meet and it's easy to get caught up in our love.

"Please," she begs. "Reed, I want you inside of me."

Her words drive me right over the edge of sanity. I reach between us to shove my boxers down and pull out my aching dick. When I tease her slick opening, she whimpers. At this point, if she told me no, I'm not sure I could stop. I'm so far gone into the deep end.

But because I love her, I give her one more chance.

"Tell me to stop. It's not too late. All of this can end now, baby."

"I don't want it to ever end."

Her words snap the last thread of control I had. Not so gently, I push my thickness into her tight virgin pussy. She squeals in pain but it's going to hurt no matter what. Doing it quick is the best thing for her. I buck my hips hard against her, destroying the last of her innocence. Her scream is otherworldly. I don't think she realizes she's clawing the shit out of my shoulders.

"Baby…" I kiss her mouth but don't move.

She starts to cry. "T-That hurt."

I stroke her hair away from her sweaty face and kiss her soft lips. My dick is about to explode with the need to come but I don't dare move. She's upset and I don't want this to feel like rape or some shit. I want her to enjoy it as much as I do.

"You're my pretty, brave, smart girl," I coo, my lips worshipping hers. "I lose my head around you and I don't even care anymore. I just love you in a way I can't even begin to describe."

Her body relaxes beneath me. Our mouths mate. Nipping and sucking. Desperation in a kiss. After several minutes, she starts wiggling. I know when my girl wiggles It means she wants me. Slowly, I start sliding in and out of her. I kiss her hard while I find her clit with my free hand. She lets out a moan when I massage her sensitive place.

"You're perfect," I praise. "So fucking perfect."

"Oh God," she cries out, her body getting snatched by a fierce, sudden orgasm. Because she's so tight, her body constricts around my dick in a way that nearly blinds me. I'm spilling inside of her before I can even stop myself. I thank God she just finished her period. Otherwise, I'd probably knock her up or some shit. I'll have to get a handle on this for next time.

Next time.

I'm still fantasizing about that when my cock finally drains the last of my orgasm. I nuzzle my nose against hers. "That was better than I could have imagined."

"Really?"

"Was it okay for you?" I ask, a half grin tugging at my lips. She nods. "It was mind-blowing."

I slide out of her body gently as not to hurt her sore insides and then tug her against me. I turn my head and blow out the candle, shrouding us in darkness.

"I love you," she breathes, her grip tightening around me.

She sounds so fucking happy. All it took was to plunge into sin with her. I'm sure this will all feel different in the morning but for right now, I'm going to enjoy it.

I love this girl.

She's mine in every sense of the word.

And no matter what happens, I'll never let her go.

I wake up colder than fuck. Devon feels like ice burrowed against me. We're still naked. I clench my jaw as reality sets in.

I fucked my daughter.

Jesus.

Guilt infects me.

Out here in the wilderness, my mind is slipping. I'm not millionaire Reed Jamison, global real estate mogul. I'm not husband and father.

I'm just a man.

Brutal and savage.

An animal.

I take what I want. Last night, I took her. My sweet, beautiful Devon. It's as though someone shoves a straw into my chest and sucks my heart out. I'm hollowed and empty. Full of regret. Hate festers deep inside of me.

But I don't know how to turn off the animal side of me. Even as I nearly choke on self-loathing, I'm stroking her soft blonde hair. Pressing my lips to her head. I can't be two people. I don't know how.

I want her with every ounce of my being.

When I just think about her and me out here alone, it all makes perfect sense. A taboo fantasy come to life. When I allow my real world self to dwell on what I've done, I can't help but consider how this would look to an outsider. Back in California, the police would be banging my door down. Not only did I sleep with an underage girl, but she's *my* girl.

They'd scream incest.

It would be a media sensation.

Real Estate Tycoon Corrupts His Young Teenage Daughter.

Bile creeps up in my throat. If Sabrina were here to know what I've done, I'm sure she'd try and kill me. Her children were her everything—even if she did abandon one to perpetually mourn the other.

"Good morning, Reed," Devon says, her voice breathy and sleepy.

And just like that, my animal rips off the head of the old man inside of me. The animal within moves his hand to cup her breast and nuzzles his nose against her hair, inhaling her sweet scent.

"Morning, beautiful."

She lets out a contented sigh. My head may be a fucked-up mess right now but she calms those thoughts. "It's cold out today."

Our mouths meet and we kiss. Soft. Simple.

"I'm going to make us a wood burning fireplace to heat our cabin," I tell her. "There's plenty of metal leftover. I think I can use the oven from the RV and use the muffler to ventilate the smoke out of the cabin. I'm not going to promise it'll work but I want to try."

She grins up at me. "That would be wonderful. This cold is the worst."

"Devon…"

Her brows crinkle together. "Yeah?"

"What happened last night…" I swallow and tear my gaze from her adoring one. "You know this isn't right."

She clutches my cheek and turns my head to look at her. "It felt pretty right to me."

I clench my jaw. Getting lost in her stare is easy. She looks at me as though I'm everything she's ever wanted out of life. "It's illegal."

A small chuckle escapes her. "Maybe you should turn yourself in."

"Smartass," I growl and tickle her ribs.

She squeals and then we're wrestling in our bed. I tickle, she screams. This goes on until the blankets are kicked to the floor and I have her pinned by her wrists to the bed. I fixate on her crimson cheeks and parted pouty lips. We stare at each other. She's different from the way she was back in California.

Wild.

Free.

Uncaring of consequences.

Oh, to be young.

"Are you still sore from last night? My question comes out as a rasp.

She nods. "But I like the sting."

My dick thumps against her flesh. Triumph glitters in her brilliant blues.

"I want to watch as you slide inside of me," she breathes.

I close my eyes. She's learning how to drive me straight into madness. Easily. With few words. She makes them count.

"Baby…"

She lifts her hips and wiggles her thighs. Like the brainwashed bastard I am, I allow her to slide her legs out so she can wrap them around my waist. My dick is throbbing against her soft pubic hair. I'm aching to slide inside of her but my brain is still at war this morning.

"Just rub it against me," she says coyly. A wicked gleam dances in her blues.

And because I'm finding it increasingly difficult to deny her a thing, I grip her wrists tighter and start rubbing myself against her sensitive pussy. She whimpers and moans and fucking begs. I have to close my eyes because she's so goddamn hot I feel like I'll nut all over her just from looking at the way her lips move to say my name.

"Fuck me, Reed," she orders, her tone bossy as hell.

I snap my eyes open and glare at her. "Don't say words like that. Your mouth is too pretty to let dirty things like that come out of it."

She licks her pink lips and taunts me more. "You could always put something in it to shut me up."

Her words have me going mental. I start rutting against her, rubbing the outside of her pussy raw with my stone-hard dick. She whimpers and pleads for more.

"I want your big cock inside of me. I like the way you stretch me and fill me with you. It feels good. It feels like I'm whole. Fuck me. Fuck me. Fuuuuuck—"

She doesn't get to finish her words because I slam into her so hard she screams at the top of her lungs. Her hands struggle beneath my grip but I hold her still as I fuck her like she wants. Nothing soft or gentle about this.

I'm an animal.

She fucking provoked the beast.

Her eyes are feral as she stares me down while I own her with my cock. I'm still not used to her tight little body because the need to come is overwhelming. I release one of her hands so I can grip her jaw.

"Make yourself come, Devon," I growl. "I'm about to come all over your flat stomach but I want you to get off too. I can't fucking wait any longer."

She nods and forces her hand between us. I groan as she works herself up while I tear her still so pure body apart from the inside out. It's only fair as she's the one who ripped my mind right from my skull and fucking fed on it.

With my fingers digging into her jaw, I lean forward and kiss her like a savage. As though I'm trying to eat her mouth. I bite her. I make her cry out. I taste blood. She's killing the man that I've grown to know and freeing the beast inside. When she comes with a jolt and bites my bottom lip, I explode. I should be pulling out but I'm too wrapped up in the way her body contracts around mine and the trembling of her orgasm seems to vibrate through my dick. My heat surges deep inside her. And when I spend the rest of my release, I collapse on her thin body.

Our hearts are hammering together as one.

She's mine.

The only one who ever could reach inside me and free the wild.

We are one now.

More than family.

Everything.

"I love you," she purrs, her lips kissing the top of my head.

I love her more than words can fucking express. I don't understand this love. It's some brutal smash of history and past ground into raw, feral need. It's man and woman with the connection of two best friends bound together by trag-edy. It's confusing as fuck and I don't even want to try to comprehend it.

I just want it.

I just fucking want it.

chapter eight

DEVON

I FOLLOW BEHIND DAD—er, REED—AS HE CARRIES the heavy oven from the RV. The reason it was so cold last night is that we had our first heavy snow. We've bundled up but the wind is brutal. We need this to work desperately. As we walk, my mind drifts to last night and earlier this morning.

We had sex.

Last night we made love and this morning we fucked.

There is a huge difference and I love them both equally.

But dear God am I sore. While he worked on pulling the oven out of the RV earlier, I packed some snow in my glove and held it against my sore sex.

"If we get this thing made, I want to make some stew," I tell him as we trudge along.

He looks over his shoulder and grins at me. It effectively chases the chill from my bones, replacing it with heat. "Rabbit?"

"And before it snowed, I found some edible plants that I put away in the cave."

"Sounds good, baby."

My cheeks warm at the endearment. He calls me baby more and I don't think it has anything to do with me being his daughter. Back when things were good, he used to call Mom "baby." It's how he shows affection for the woman he loves.

He loves me.

I swear my heart flutters in my chest like a bird in a cage. I don't want to free it. I love how it goes crazy inside my rib cage any time he looks my way, smiles, or touches me. He owns that little bird and I'll be damned if I let it go.

Once inside our cabin, he gets to work. I try to assist but he's happy doing all the grunt work himself. And then I get a show when he gets hot and strips down to his jeans. My sex stays wet because I can't stop thinking about him pressed against me and inside of me.

"I'm going to go scavenge since you don't need my help," I tell him, my voice breathy. Really, I just want to cool off before I get too weird and start touching myself on the bed while he works. He grunts his approval but doesn't look up at me. I run my fingers through his sweaty hair before slipping out of the cabin.

On the way back to our old campsite, I wonder where I'll look this time. He's picked a lot of the RV apart to use for stuff but there are still parts inside of the mangled covered trailer that we haven't been able to get to. I'm sure there are things we could use if we could just get access.

I'm smiling when I hear it.

Snorting.

Loud and feral.

And so close.

When I look up, I'm staring down the path at a giant grizzly twice my height not a hundred yards away. He has to weigh six hundred pounds easily. All the crap I learned from the brochure flies out the window. It's hard to remember the rules when you're staring down a beast with claws as long as your hand.

I take a step back and the crunch of my boot has the bear jerking his head toward the sound. A guttural growl rumbles from its chest as it rises to its full height. It makes a sound that echoes off the trees and chills my bones.

Please go away.

It growls again before falling back down to all four paws. I stay incredibly still hoping it will turn and walk away.

But it doesn't.

It trots toward me, not a full run but certainly in a hurry, and all I can think of to do is screech. "Daddy!"

As soon as it nears, I crumple to the earth and roll into a ball protecting my neck with my hands. A heavy paw swats at my back and the fabric of my coat rips. My heart is sputtering in my chest and I'm afraid it will give out. The bear seems to grab at my side and his claws puncture my coat poking right through my flesh. A gut-wrenching scream escapes me.

And then I mentally check out.

"When I grow up, I'm going to be just like Dad," Drew tells me, a wide smile on his lips.

"Me too."

He snorts and throws a twig at me. "You can't be like Dad. You're a girl. You have to be like Mom."

I frown. I don't want to be like Mom. She's quiet and sleeps a lot. When she's happy and smiling, she's pretty. But when she's sad, she ignores all of us. One time I asked Dad what she's so sad about. He told me life. I didn't get it. I still don't get it.

"I don't care. I'm going to be like Dad. He's strong and funny and is good at cheering us up," I tell my twin brother with a huff.

"But you have boobs," he argues.

I gape at him in horror and cross my arms over my chest. "I do not," I grumble.

"Do too."

"Do not."

He reaches up into the tree to break off another twig. When Dad is working and Mom is sleeping, Drew and I like to hang out in our treehouse.

"You're mean," I say, my lip pouting out.

He grins at me, his blue eyes twinkling. "I'm just kidding. I'd rather be like Dad if I were you too." His features fall and he stares at me sadly. "Does Mom not like us?"

I scrunch my nose up. "She loves us."

He blinks and reaches up to grab at another twig. "There's a difference, Dev. She loves us because she has to. But she doesn't like us like Dad does. She doesn't play with us."

I don't like talking about it so I change the subject. "Want to go ride bikes?"

He grins at me with his hand reaching up. "Yeah—ow!"

His hand jerks down and he inspects his wrist. "I stabbed myself on a stick!"

Laughing, I stand and hold my hand out to him. "That's what you get for destroying Mother Nature's pretty tree."

"It's hot," he complains and ignores my offered hand. "We'll go in a minute."

With a frown, I plop back down and pick up my book. He curls up on his side. We both grow quiet for some time as I read and he rests.

"What book are you reading?" His voice is a whisper as he lies on one cheek and stares at me with droopy lids.

"The Boxcar Children. They are homeless and live in a boxcar. I like how they scavenge for things and take care of each other."

"Devon," he rasps out. "I don't feel so good."

His skin is pale and he's sweating.

"Get up and we'll go back inside."

He closes his eyes. "I…"

"Drew?"

I toss my book down and crawl over to him.

"Drew?!"

Everything happens so fast. One minute he's fine. The next he's sleepy and pale.

"Are you sick?" I demand, clutching his hand. I frown when my palm touches something wet. When I look at his wrist, I don't think it looks like he was stabbed at all. It appears to be a snake bite.

A quick glance into the tree Drew had been messing with, and I see it wrapped around the branch.

I scream. I scream at the top of my lungs because I'm

afraid it is going to bite me too. Letting go of my brother, I scramble to the hatch and hurry down the ladder to go find Dad. Guilt consumes me because I left him up there with it.

With tears streaming down my face, I scream again.

Pop!

I'm dragged from my horrible memories of the day we lost my brother by the sound of a gun shot. I'm no longer in the hot treehouse but instead curled into a ball in the cold snow.

The animal grunts but it crunches away from me, a roar escaping it.

"Devon!"

I start sobbing and sit up on my knees. I watch in horror as the bear runs full speed toward my dad.

Pop!

Pop!

Pop!

He's holding out a handgun and unloading in the bear. Each hit makes the bear stagger. It's moving so quickly still though. And when it lunges at my father who is wearing nothing but jeans since he ran straight from the cabin, I scream.

A disturbing cracking sound has bile rising in my throat. I'm going to be sick. The bear is on top of my dad. I scramble toward him, ignoring the searing pain from where the bear's claws got me, and look for a big stick to hurt the grizzly with so he'll get off my dad. When I approach, I can see Dad attempting to move but the bear is too heavy. At least the bear isn't moving though. Blood is everywhere and I pray it belongs to the grizzly.

"H-Help m-me get th-this th-thing off m-me," Dad rasps.

I grab onto the bear's massive arm and start pulling. Tears stream down my face as I exert all my strength to pull the bear.

"He's too heavy!" My voice is shrill and panicked.

Dad doesn't respond.

Oh, God.

What if the bear bit him? What if he's bleeding out as we speak?

I abandon the bear and find Dad's leg. With all of my strength, I tug on his leg. Over and over. He moves little by little but it's better than nothing. My entire body is trembling from the cold and fear but I can't leave him under that thing. I can't be alone. I can't. I need him. Eventually, I free him with one last hard yank. I go flying back and hit my head hard on a tree trunk. It dazes me and I have to blink away the urge to sleep. When I crawl back over to Dad, he lies there with his eyes closed. He's covered in blood. A sick wheezing sound is coming from him.

"Daddy!"

His eyes crack open but he doesn't say anything. Just reaches for my hand. I clutch onto it as I sob. It's too cold out here for him to be in the snow shirtless and hurt. I have to get him back inside. When I stand and grab his arms, he lets out a raspy groan of pain. He's injured and dragging him back to the cabin won't work. I don't want to hurt him worse. With a choked sob, I abandon him and run all the way back to the cabin. I rush inside and rip a piece of the metal RV sheeting from the wall. Then, I run back. Getting him on the metal is tricky and at one point, I slice my hand right open but adrenaline fuels me on. Once he's secure on it, I start dragging the metal with him on top along the snow-covered path.

Twenty long minutes of this and I get him to the cabin steps. I can't figure out a way to move him without hurting him. So with a deep breath, I grab him under the armpits and pull him up the steps. He moans in pain and it breaks my heart but I need to get him inside. I manage to pull him in and shut the door behind me to keep the elements out.

"I-I need to s-see where you're hurt," I chatter out. Blood drips from my hand as I rake my palm over him. His breathing scares me. It's noisy and rattled. I attempt to calm down and assess him. Before this trip, I read up a lot on first aid. With the bear's weight landing on top of him, there's a good chance he broke some ribs. My stomach bottoms out. If one of those ribs punctured his lung, he'll die out here.

Please, God, don't let him die.

"I'm going to clean you up," I tell him, my voice firmer than before. I can't break apart. I need to keep my head about me so I can look after him. Running back outside, I poke at our fire and boil some water. Then, I fetch a recently cleaned rag and settle back beside him. Cleaning him will allow me to take stock of his injuries. Carefully, I wash him from head to toe. He has no actual cuts or bite marks that I can see which is good, but his awfully loud breathing means something happened inside of him which feels worse. I can't see inside of him to fix him. Quickly, I clean up my own hand that hurts and pour some alcohol into the wound. Then, I use some gauze from the first aid kit to wrap it tightly. The pain on the side of my back from the bear's claws niggle at me and needs cleaning but it can wait.

"Wake up," I urge, my voice soft. "I need you to promise me everything will be okay." Hot tears spill down my cheeks and splash on his chest.

He doesn't speak but he does wiggle his pinky. I sob as I grab onto it. It's a promise.

I wake with a start, groggy and confused. I'd managed to cover us with a quilt as I curled into his side. His breathing is still rattling and noisy. But when I look up he's staring at me.

"Reed!" I promised I'd call him by name in our cabin. I don't break my promises either.

He attempts to smile but then winces. It shatters my heart.

"Shhhh," I coo, my fingers running through his beard. "Let me take care of you. Can you sit up? I want to move you to the warm bed."

He nods.

Progress.

Pushing away the quilt, I straddle his waist careful not to hurt him. Then, I hook my arms under his armpits and struggle to stand. He's super heavy and is now cursing like a sailor in a hissed voice, but then his feet work with me and he goes up the rest of the way. The trip to the bed isn't far and I manage to get him situated on the soft mattress. The rattling sound is louder than ever and it scares me.

I set to bundling him up with covers. Then, I stroke his long hair from his eyes and kiss his mouth. "Tell me what hurts."

He groans. "I think I cracked my ribs."

My heart rate quickens. "Okay, so we can do this. Cracked ribs are better than the horrible scenarios running through my head. Those can get better with rest. Remember the time Drew cracked one of his when he fell out of the treehouse?"

His lips quirk up on one side at the mention of my brother. "Rowdy."

I smile too. "He was."

His eyes find mine. "Are you hurt?"

Lifting my bandaged hand, I nod. "The metal got me," I admit, shame in my tone. "I haven't looked at the bear's damage on my back yet."

"Take your coat off and let me see," he rasps.

With shaking from my cold fingers, I unbutton my coat and toss it away. My hoodie gets pulled off next. Dad lets out a sharp exhalation and then starts coughing. It sounds awful.

"Are you okay?" I ask over my shoulder.

His gaze is on my back and tears are in his eyes. "It hurts to breathe deep but I remember the doctor telling us to make sure Drew took deep breaths every hour when he was hurt. Help me remember." His fingertips touch my spine. "Baby, your back is fucked up."

I sit up straight and shake my head. "I'm fine."

"You're not fine. Go get the first aid kit. I think you need stitches."

Reluctantly, I climb off the bed to hunt for it. Once I return, I soak a new rag in alcohol and hand it to him. He dabs at the wounds that most definitely do hurt. While he does that, I thread the needle. It takes forever but he manages to stitch me up.

"I'm so tired but there's so much to do," I tell him, my voice shaky with unshed tears.

"Rest, baby."

I curl up next to him, my bare breasts pressed gently against the side of his arm. Leaning up, I kiss his mouth. Soft at first but then I kiss him desperately as though he might disappear at any moment. When he starts wheezing again, I whimper and pull away.

"Rest, baby," he murmurs again.

With a choked sob, I obey.

chapter nine

REED

EXCRUCIATING PAIN RADIATES ACROSS MY RIBS. Breathing is a sonofabitch but I can do this. I remember what the doctor had said when Drew cracked his rib. We were told he needed to breathe deeply—even though he cried every time—so he didn't develop pneumonia. And that is exactly what I do. I take deep breaths even though I prefer the shallow ones. I can't get worse out here. She needs me. The healing time on this shit is like six weeks. In the wilderness, I can't let her do everything by herself for that long.

When I look down at her sleeping face, my heart aches. She's so beautiful. Her dirty face is tear stained and puffy. Her wild, blonde mane is a mess. But she's as pretty as an angel sent just for me. I'll be damned if I ever leave her.

That bear pawing at her scared the ever-loving shit out of me. It was the same ear-piercing scream she used when we discovered her brother had been bitten by a venomous snake in the treehouse. Despite the rush to the hospital and the anti-venom, his heart stopped and my little boy died in the emergency room. When I saw the bear, I couldn't help but fear I'd lose her too. She wasn't moving and he was so fucking big. I pulled my .45 caliber pistol from my jeans that I keep on me at all times and unloaded. The minute that fucker crashed into me, I thought I was a goner.

But my girl…

My sweet, brave as shit girl, yanked me out from beneath that heavy ass bear. She was clever and managed to haul me back to the cabin. Then, she cleaned and took care of me.

The least I can do is pull the fuck out of this.

It's been three days since the incident. I've shown her how to chamber a bullet on the .45 and now she keeps it with her when she goes outside to do chores. I feel like an invalid. She helps me piss and shit in a bucket since I can't move very well. She feeds me—literally spoon feeds me like a child—every meal. And she bathes me. I wish I had the strength to do more.

What surprises me the most is she skinned the bear and harvested the meat.

"This morning, we're having bad bear soup again," she says as she sits up, the quilt falling away from her naked body.

I reach forward and brush my fingertip across her nipple. It hardens under my touch and her cheeks blaze pink. I can't help but smile at her. "Bad bear soup is my favorite. Do you have to go yet?" I pinch her nipple and she lets out a gasp.

"I'd much rather lie in bed with you," she admits. "But no rest for the weary."

I slide my hand down to her panties and massage between her legs. "I miss touching you, baby."

She moans. "You shouldn't be moving. You're hurt."

"You could always straddle my face and let me kiss your pretty pussy."

Her mouth drops open. "You're dirty."

"You'd be the one making my face all messy," I smirk at her.

She slides her hand down to my erect cock and strokes it. "I could kiss yours too." Her words are breathy and embarrassed but it turns me the fuck on. Especially when she darts her tongue out and licks her full pink lips. I have a quick fantasy of those perfect lips wrapped around my dick.

"Let me kiss you first. Then you can have your turn," I concede, my dick jolting in her grip.

Her eyes twinkle. "I have a great idea. I'll let you put your mouth on me but I'll get on all fours backward and kiss you too. At the same time. It will feel like..." she trails off and blushes. "Like when we have sex."

I've fucked her twice and I'm dying for more. I don't tell her they have a name for her suggestion—sixty-nine—because I love keeping her as innocent as I can. She's mine. All of this is hers to discover on her own.

"That's a great idea, baby. Now sit on my face and let me taste you."

She lets out a low moan of embarrassment but sheds her panties. Then, carefully, she straddles my face. Her familiar musk sends desire shooting straight to my cock. Her round ass and pink pussy are right in my face as she assumes her position.

"Have you ever..." I trail off. I'm about to ask my daughter-turned-lover if she's given head before. Thankfully she stops me.

"No, but I promise to make you feel good."

I grip her fleshy bottom and run my tongue along her slit, enjoying the whimper she makes. "I had no doubts, baby."

When I start eating out her delicious pussy, I groan the moment her tongue teases my tip. I can't see what she's doing but her tiny tastes and little licks are driving me insane with pleasure.

"Put your sexy mouth all the way around my dick. Fuck it, beautiful," I instruct, my voice strained.

Like the good girl she is, she obeys and soon she's sucking my cock with vigor. I devote my attention to sucking on her clit and fucking her tight hole with my thumb. Her body trembles above mine. I'm sure it's awkward for her to maintain the position as not to hurt my ribs, but this girl has already proven to me she's strong. Her body is small but she's developed some sexy as fuck muscles since our crash. Slurps and moans from both our ends are enough to have my balls seizing up.

I'm trying to hold out until she comes. She's close, based on the way she trembles. I slip my thumb from her pussy and probe the tight ring of her ass hole. She cries out when I start pushing inside of her.

"Oh God," she garbles out around my cock. I've barely started fucking that hole when it clenches tight around me. She screams in pleasure. Her arousal from her cunt drips down into my face and I lap it up, greedy for every drop. When my dick hits the back of her throat and she relaxes it, I lose control. My cock throbs out my violent release and I nearly black out when she swallows me. She fucking swallows my dick. My orgasm shoots down the back of her throat that has me in a hot, tight grip. She eventually gags and pulls away from me, her slobber and some missed cum dripping down onto me.

"That was…" Her body trembles and clenches.

I ease my thumb out of her and press a kiss to the inside of her soaked thigh. "Perfect. That was perfect, baby. Now make us some food, woman," I tease and slap her ass.

She squeals and scrambles off me. When she turns to regard me, I'm stunned speechless. I've never seen something so goddamned beautiful in all my life. Her hair is wild just like her blue eyes. Her mouth is puffy and red and wet as fuck. Her tits are swollen and nipples are erect. Her pussy is bright red and soaked.

I wish I were well because I'd bend her over the mattress and take her rough if I were. I'd tangle my fists in her gorgeous mane and fuck her so hard from behind she'd scare away all the bears.

"You're hard again," she says, pointing at my relentless dick.

I grin at her. "As soon as I feel better we're going to do something about that."

Her eyes darken as she bites on her lip. "Pinky promise?"

"You better fucking believe it."

Three weeks have come and gone. I literally have cabin fever and it's driving me fucking crazy. At least once a day, my sweet Devon straddles me and we trade orgasms. It's the most amazing feeling but not satisfying enough. I want her. I want to sink my cock deep inside of her and come with her tight pussy clenching around me. Don't get me wrong, the girl is becoming a master at sucking my cock. I just want to be inside of her.

"Today, I'm making the fireplace. Just tell me what to do." She's all smiles as she dusts snow off her jacket.

I grumble in protest. "I can do it. Just get me my—"

"Reed," she says in exasperation. "No. I can do this."

Reluctantly, I concede. We spend hours as I walk her through constructing the fireplace. My girl is clever and so fucking smart. And capable. I watch in absolute awe as she builds this thing every bit as well as I could. Thank God my tools survived the crash. Without hammers and saws and nails and every other tool imaginable, we'd have had a lot harder time surviving out here.

"The most difficult part will be sealing those holes so smoke doesn't escape into the cabin," I say thoughtfully.

Undeterred, she hammers out metal to make v-shaped corners to fit in the gaps. She uses too many nails but she's making it pretty airtight. I don't criticize her or tell her how to do it. Devon is smart and has a plan in her head.

Hours later, once she's cut a hole in the cabin so the muffler pipe can stick out that's also attached to the back of the oven-turned-fireplace, she dusts off her hands and grins at me. "Time to test it out."

She disappears but then comes back with some wood she no doubt chopped herself. I watch with pride as she makes a fire—just as I've taught her—inside the contraption. Once she's satisfied, she sits back and watches it. Amazingly, the damn thing works. Heat billows from the open oven door but all the smoke is flowing into the muffler pipe and outside.

"You're fucking brilliant," I praise.

She beams at me as she takes off her coat. "Now we can roast bad bear steaks right from our bed if we want. How romantic," she sighs playfully. God, she's so damn cute.

"I know of other ways we can be romantic…"

As if catching my drift, she begins a slow strip show that has my cock aching beneath the blanket. When she's fully naked, she crawls in bed beside me.

"Sit on my cock, Devon."

Her eyes widen. "But you're still hurt."

"My dick is perfectly fine," I argue.

Our eyes meet in challenge. I pin her with a glare that leaves no room for argument.

"Fine," she huffs, clearly not happy about it.

"It's no different than when you suck me off, baby. At least this time I can look at your pretty tits while you bounce on me."

My words turn her on because she gets that look in her eyes—the look that says she wants to fuck desperately.

Slowly, she straddles my thighs and takes my dick in her hand. Then, her eyes dart to mine. "I don't know how to do this."

"Just get on and ride."

She laughs but carefully guides my throbbing cock to her soaked pussy. With a gasp, she slides all the way down.

"Wow…"

"What?"

"It just feels bigger like this. Like it's poking stuff inside of me."

"Does it hurt?"

"No…just feels weird. I like it." She bats her eyelashes at me.

"I'm going to touch your clit but I want to watch you play with your sexy tits," I tell her as my fingers begin massaging her between her thighs.

She moans and nods. Her palms go to her breasts and she slowly slides up and down my shaft. At first, she's rigid and clinical. But after a few moments, she loses her mind to the ecstasy. She bucks against me like a wild woman, greedy for release. Seeing her so free and lost to the pleasure has my nuts drawing up eager for release. To my horror, I begin spilling abruptly inside of her—before she orgasms. But thankfully, it seems to set her off because her pussy clenches hard around me with her release. Our bodies make slurping sounds as she continues to fuck me. When the last of my seed pours inside of her, I take a moment to stare at her while her eyes are still closed.

Serene.

Happy.

Mine.

"We need to be careful," I tell her, making her eyes snap open. "The last thing we need out here is a baby."

Her mouth parts. "Okay. How?"

"We just need to communicate. When I get ready to come, I'll tell you. It's called the pullout method," I tell her with a smile.

As much as the idea of her with a rounded belly turns

me on, I can't fathom if something went wrong. She's only seventeen and she's tiny. All sorts of complications could arise from pregnancy and giving birth. In the old days, women died from childbirth all the time. And I'd go mental if I lost her over something stupid like that just because she feels too good wrapped around me when I come.

"The pullout method. Got it," she assures me. "Now are you ready for some steak, Mr. Romantic?"

I tickle her sides. "Feed me, woman."

She swats away my hands and lifts a challenging brow at me. "Woman? Are you a cave man now?"

Gesturing to the crevasse, I flash her a wolfish grin. "Technically yes. But I'll make sure to fuck you in there soon just so we don't have any confusion."

chapter ten

DEVON

I T'S BEEN SIX WEEKS SINCE THE BEAR ACCIDENT. Dad—*Reed*—is better. He walks around, chops wood, hunts, and does a million other chores. And then when we fall into bed at night, he relentlessly makes love to me. We're careful to always pull out, aside from the one or two accidents in the beginning.

I'm so thankful he's back to normal though because lately, I'm exhausted. Winter is harsher than I could have imagined. The wildlife is plentiful here but I'm dying for something besides meat. We try not to touch our canned foods we have from the RV and trailer but twice now I've begged—and offered sexual favors in exchange—for a can of fruit.

My stomach grumbles at the thought of more peaches.

When I roll over onto my stomach to silence my grumbling belly, I'm sad to see Dad is already out of bed and nowhere to be found. I get a whiff of the meat we've stored in the cave and it turns my stomach. Gagging, I clamber out of bed and grab the bucket just in time to expel my guts.

I'm sitting there feeling sorry for myself when a thought occurs to me.

I haven't started my period.

Counting backward, I realize I've gone nearly two months with no cycle.

Oh, God.

And I'm nauseous this morning.

Oh, God.

My boobs are sore and I'm incredibly fatigued.

Oh, God.

When I bring my palm to my stomach, I notice that it's slightly swollen. I'd not paid much attention before but now I'm cataloging everything.

I'm pregnant. I have to be. At seventeen.

Instead of fretting like a normal human would, my heart swells with happiness. A baby. We made a baby. Out of love. It won't be just us two all alone. Happy tears stream down my cheeks. I want to tell Dad but I'm afraid of how he'll react. He's been grumpy lately and I don't know why. I think he's stressed about something but I'm not sure what. I'll have to tell him next time he's in a playful mood.

When I hear his boots clomp up on the porch, I let out a squeak and quickly snag a hoodie to pull on over my head. He steps inside, a cold rush of air sweeping in with him, and regards me with a frown.

"What?" I sound guilty and desperately try to hide it. I'm glad the bucket is in the corner. I'll have to get rid of the puke when he's not watching.

"Bears. I saw two more while out."

Panic rises up in my chest. This place is crawling with bears. "Do they smell the skin of the dead one?"

He rolls his eyes and my chest clenches in pain. "They don't give a damn about the hide drying out in that tree. They're curious about our cabin though. I found claw marks near the door like one was trying to figure out how to get in."

Terror skitters through me. "What do we do?"

He frowns. "I'm going to have to fortify our home better and set some traps." His eyes are tired and he looks older today as if he badly needs a nap. "Are you going to lay in bed all day like your goddamned mother or help?" he snaps.

I gape at him in confusion. What the heck is his problem today? "Reed—"

"Just put some clothes on and help me. There's a ton of shit to do," he barks out and storms from the cabin.

I burst into tears.

"I'm tired," I whine, my arms weak from holding the heavy pine tree on one end.

He ignores me as I trudge through the snow behind him. It's been a week since I figured out I was pregnant. Each day is the same. Morning sickness. Fatigue. Sore breasts. Cravings for that stupid fruit. But what's the worst is that I cry at the drop of a hat. This seems to make Dad mad every time. He hasn't touched me in I don't know how long and I spend my nights sniffling in the darkness. I don't know what to do.

"Put it down," he barks out when we're near the cabin.

I drop the thin tree on my end and dust off my gloves. He drops to his knees and whips out his knife. Just like he's done the other twelve trees so far, he starts carving one end into a sharp point. He's driving each one into the earth, braced by a fence-type thing he made and pointing the sharp end away from the cabin. His theory is that if a bear comes up, they'll impale themselves on the wood long before they ever get to us. The spiked trees are horrifying to look at—like we're in the middle of a zombie apocalypse or something. Dad doesn't care though. He throws himself into his job.

While he works, I let my mind drift to the past. When he never looked at me with angry eyes.

Snakes.

Everywhere.

Eating me alive.

It's the same nightmare I've had for four years, ever since my brother died from a snake bite.

"Daddy!"

Mom told me last time I screamed for her during a bad dream that I was too old to be having nightmares. So now I just call for my dad. He always comes. He always saves me.

I hear his bedroom door bang against the wall as he runs from his room. Heavy footsteps make their way quickly to my room. The door gets flung open and soon he's sitting on the edge of my twin bed.

"Everything okay, Pip? Snakes again?"

I start to cry because the nightmares remind me of my brother. Dad grabs the blanket and lifts it so he can join me in the bed. As I sob, he pulls me against his warm chest and holds me. Each kiss on the top of my head warms and soothes me.

"I'm sorry I woke you up," I whisper.

He strokes my hair. "I'll always come for you. No matter what. If you need me, I'll be there. I love you, Devon. It's my job as a parent to protect you."

Bitterness creeps up my throat. "Mom doesn't like it when I have the nightmares."

He lets out a soft sigh. "I know. Your mom is dealing with her own issues that don't involve you. Sometimes, she takes them out on you and it isn't right. I'm sorry."

"Sometimes I wish it were just us," I whisper, mostly to myself. It's the truth though. Dad and I have more fun without Mom. When she's smiling, I love it. But she hardly smiles or engages.

"Don't say stuff you don't mean," he says firmly, his body tense.

I sniffle. "I do mean it though. She's not like the other moms. It's embarrassing."

He takes my hand and we thread our fingers together. "She has her reasons."

"What reasons?"

I can hear his teeth grinding together. "Nothing you need to worry yourself over."

I can't fathom what her reasons could be for treating her surviving child and husband as if they are a bother to her.

"I wish she was like you. You're the best."

He snorts. "Hardly, Pip. I'm a very flawed individual."

"Lies," I say, laughing.

"I'm serious. I put on a good show for you but I'm far from perfect. I'm a moody bastard and I lose my temper."

"But I never see it," I argue.

His hand squeezes mine. "Because I do my very best to keep that from you. You don't need to see my bad days and when I lose control. I keep things to myself to protect you because I love you. One day, you'll understand this."

I drift off thinking he's yanking my chain because to me, he's perfect.

I sniffle as the memory fades. Maybe he's hiding something to protect me. He'd warned me long ago that he had his own fair share of issues. I just wish he'd talk to me. I'm frowning when I swear I hear voices. Dad is grunting as he shaves the wood and is making all kinds of racket. I stand and walk away from him to get a better listen. My ears are perked up trying to hear.

"Jesus Christ, Devon," Dad growls. "There's too much shit to do to be standing around. Go make yourself useful."

My jaw drops as I stare at him. His back is turned to me and he's tense.

"I think we should talk," I murmur.

"Goddammit, go inside before I get my belt."

Hot tears well in my eyes and I run toward the cabin. When I see the bear hide that I've been working on for weeks, washing and oiling, I decide it's good enough. With a huff, I yank it down from the side of the cabin and haul the heavy thing inside. I have to pull out my knife so I can cut it to fit the space. I make sure to put the longest, thickest strip between the mattress and the fireplace. Then, I use the extra pieces to cover other parts of the cabin floor. After kicking off my shoes, I almost shout out with excitement that we officially have carpet. I want to holler at Dad and make him come look but he's too pissy. Once I shimmy out of my jeans, I put my yoga pants back on and settle for one of his warm sweatshirts. My stomach growls. Since I'm in trouble anyway, I sneak into the cave and steal a can of peaches from the back. It has a pull top so I rip off the lid and gobble down each peach before slurping down the juice. When I hear him coming, I hide it away in the back of the cave.

The door bursts open and I swivel around, a guilty look on my face.

He sniffs the air and I know I'm busted. "What are you doing?"

"Nothing."

"Don't lie to me, Devon."

Anger rises up inside of me. Screw him for treating me like this with no explanation. I lift my chin. "I ate a can of peaches."

His features darken and he stalks over to me after he shuts the door. He strikes out at me with his strong hand to grip my jaw. With each breath he takes, his nostrils flare. "Got something else to tell me?"

I swallow and shake my head. Now is definitely not the time to tell him I'm pregnant.

He scowls. "I can't take you fucking lying to me."

"And I can't take you acting like a giant asshole," I snap back.

"Don't you dare take that tone with me, young lady," he snarls in his most authoritative dad voice.

I scoff at him. "Really? Now you want to play the part of daddy? I bet you want to spank me again too."

"Maybe you need your ass whipped!" he roars, his grip on my jaw tightening.

I shake him away and slap his face. We both stare at each other in shock. He growls and it pisses me off so I slap him again. Over and over until he grips my shoulders and turns me around before pushing me face first into the cave. I struggle but then he's pulling my pants down. His belt flies off with a swoosh and he whips me with it. Fire slices across my bottom and I scream. He hits me again.

"I hate you!"

"I wish you actually did!"

I'm sobbing when the belt gets tossed to the floor. He shuffles behind me and then his cock is pressed between my thighs. With a rough thrust, he drives deep inside of my sex.

"Oh, God," I whimper. I look over my shoulder and stare down my feral man. Heartbreak shines in his eyes and I don't understand it. I cry harder as I try to touch him. "I love you, Dad. Please don't be mad at me."

His touch is soft as he wraps his arms around my middle and lifts me. Our bodies are flush and he leans me against the cold stone wall. He kisses me hard on the neck and I turn my head in desperation to meet that kiss with my mouth. Our mouths mate in a wild way as he bucks against me. His hands are all over me. My stomach. My breasts. My clit.

I cry out when my orgasm hits. He sucks on my tongue and drains himself inside of me. Does he know? He's been pulling out each time. The moment we come down from our high, he pulls out and scoops me in his arms. I'm carried over to the bed where he sets to stripping me the rest of the way down. His mouth worships my body while I sob. When I chance a look at him, his eyes are red and teary as he splays his palm over my stomach.

"I was so mad when I realized you were pregnant. I counted the days. Watched the signs," he breathes against my flesh. "I can't lose you, Devon. I can't fucking lose you."

I sob so much I think my chest will explode as I finger his overgrown hair.

"I want to have this baby with you," he chokes out. "So bad. But so help me if you die, I'll shove my .45 into my mouth and take my life. I can't do this without you, baby. I can't fucking do this."

We spend the rest of the day curled around each other making sweet love. He apologizes over and over again.

"Your mother saw me lose my cool plenty of times," he tells me, his voice sad after supper. "I'm moody when I'm pissed. Unfairly, I took it out on you."

"It's okay, Reed." Earlier I slipped up and called him Dad.

"It's not okay," he breathes. His mouth trails down my throat to my collarbone. "You're too sweet and perfect to deal with that. I fucked up."

"Isn't that what couples do? Fight and then make up?" I ask.

He lifts his gaze and smiles. "I suppose so. The makeup sex was pretty damn hot, I'll admit."

It was angry and animalistic.

Brutal and fierce.

I came so hard I saw stars.

"It was," I agree. "But next time you're mad, talk to me. It's too lonely out here to be alone. You're the only other person I have. When you don't talk to me or you yell at me, I feel so lost. Please promise you'll try."

He kisses his way down to my stomach. "I promise to you and our little baby here that I'm going to be the best dad ever."

I hold out my pinky and he takes it.

He always does.

chapter eleven

REED

CRUNCHING IN THE SNOW WAKES ME FROM A DEAD sleep. It's early in the morning and the sun is just shining in. When Devon asked for a window, I found one of the only unbroken ones, a small one that had been over the RV sink and brought it back to the cabin. I cut a hole near the ceiling above the table on the east side so the morning sun would shine in and warm our bed. After I installed the window and braced it with wooden strips, Devon made curtains from some of the torn sheets from the RV. It warms my heart that she's made this place her home.

I listen for the sounds. My fence isn't complete. I'm hoping to finish it in the next few days. Until then, we're vulnerable to bears. She sleeps soundly beside me. Her naked body pressed against mine is warm and soft.

Fuck, I was such an asshole to her yesterday.

I knew, deep down, she was pregnant and I flipped my

shit. Horrible scenarios where she bled out in each one trying to deliver our baby replayed over and over again like a record in my head. In my fear of losing her, I was pushing her away.

I reach over and run my thumb over her plump lip. She's so innocent. So fierce and loving. I don't deserve her, but I don't care. She's mine to love forever. Leaning forward, I palm her stomach that holds our child and kiss her cheek.

Crunch.

My body stills as I listen. Slowly, I creep out of bed and pull on my jeans. If there's a bear out there rooting around, I plan on shooting the bastard before he gets a chance to get inside of here. I pull the .45 out of her jeans pocket and sheath my knife in my belt. Jerking on a shirt, I make my way to the table to stand on and look out the window. I'm just hiking my foot up when I hear it.

Voices.

Before I can comprehend if they're real or not, our cabin door flies open. An older man with salt and pepper brown hair and missing teeth grins at me holding a sharpened piece of wood in his hands.

"What the fu—" I start but then he's lunging at me.

The guy is taller than me but I have more weight on him. He manages to tackle me but I quickly overpower him. I punch him hard one, two, three times in his ugly face until I knock his ass out.

"Papa!" A deep voice hollers from the doorway. Fuck, there're more. At this point, Devon sits up in bed and screams. The creep in the doorway can't be any more than Devon's age. When his predatory gaze lands on my daughter, I launch myself at him.

Another guy bigger than him charges into the cabin and whacks me over the head with a rock. I crumple to the floor, grunting, trying desperately to keep from blacking out.

"Daddy!"

Her scream jerks my eyes open. The big guy kneels with his knee in my back and a blade pressed to the back of my neck. I watch helplessly as the kid advances on my daughter.

"She's yours, Nathaniel."

The fuck she is.

"Run, Devon!"

She screeches as she attempts to run naked past the kid but he grabs her around the waist. The guy pinning me down is laughing and cheering on the kid as if this shit is fucking funny. I try to reach into my back pocket for my gun but he stabs me in the arm.

"She moves too much, Ezekiel," Nathaniel grumbles.

"Make her stop," Ezekiel challenges.

Fuck.

I struggle and roar to no avail. I watch in horror as Nathaniel begins slinging my daughter around. Slamming her head into the side of the cabin, hitting her over and over, kicking her. She screams and pleads. And then the unthinkable happens.

He pins her to the bed face down. The motherfucker pulls his dick out and pries her thighs apart despite her struggling. I know the moment he starts raping her because the blood-curdling scream makes my heart turn black with rage.

"STOP!" I bellow this order out on repeat but it goes ignored.

Helplessly, I have to watch as he slams into her over and over again. Her sobs tear out pieces of my soul and toss them all over the cabin. I can't watch and yet I can't allow her to be alone through it. Our eyes meet and I beg her to stay focused on me.

The kid grunts out his orgasm within seconds. Then he's standing and walking over to Ezekiel.

"My turn," Ezekiel growls.

"No!" I shout.

He kicks me hard in my still sore ribs and I howl in pain. The kid takes his place but he's not as strong. As soon as Ezekiel mounts my daughter, her screams are louder than before. He's hurting her worse than the kid. I go black with rage and I shake off the piss ant despite the blade sticking out of my arm and the pain in my side. I yank my gun from my pocket and put a bullet right through Ezekiel's face. He grunts and collapses on Devon whose screams are on repeat. Next, I put a bullet through the skull of the unconscious man on the floor. Then, I turn around but the kid is already bolting. I storm outside after him. He runs away from me quickly. I manage to pop off two shots that hit him in the shoulder and back thigh. His howls of pain fuel me on but Devon is crying out my name.

"Daddy! Daddy! Daddy!"

As much as I want to go after the fucker, I can't leave her in this state. I rush back inside and go to her. The guy is still on top of her. When I push him off, I'm enraged to find he was in her ass. Blood is everywhere. She's shuddering so hard I think she's going to vomit. I drag him and the other guy out of the cabin so she doesn't have to look at them. Then, I'm back inside pulling her into my arms.

She's sobbing so much and I can't fucking fix her.

My shaking palm smoothes over her silky hair and I kiss her so many times. I promise her everything will be okay. She trembles out of control. I don't know what the fuck to do. All I can do is clutch her pinky.

And then it happens.

A low, guttural howl rips from her chest. "Noooo!"

Hot liquid soaks the thighs of my jeans. Jesus. Fuck. No.

"Noooo!" she continues to screech, her head shaking back and forth.

I squeeze her tight. "Baby…fuck…baby…"

"Noooo!"

Her tears soak my chest and I soon realize I'm crying along with her. In one moment, our world was completely destroyed. Those men stole so much from my daughter. They fucking raped her and hurt her bad enough that she's losing our child.

"I'm so sorry," I choke out. "Pip, I'm so sorry."

I want to go after Nathaniel. I want to gut him like a goddamned fish and make him eat his entrails. I want to shove my knife so far up his ass that he can feel it in his throat. I want to cut out his eyeballs and offer them to my daughter so she can crush them in her fist.

But I do no such thing.

Yet.

She needs me.

I spend an hour cleaning her body and checking over

her wounds. Her ass only bled a little from the intrusion so no major damage. But her pussy was brutalized. It was all the blood from the loss of the baby that had my heart breaking into a thousand pieces. She mentally checked out. Passed out from shock and exhaustion.

Once she's clean, I observe her. Her abdomen is already heavily bruising where that motherfucking kid beat her up. My poor sweet girl. I'm sick and raging and losing my goddamn mind.

I don't leave the cabin to check my traps or work on my stake fence or anyfuckingthing. I stay at her side. Whispering assurances. Spoon feeding her. Making her drink water. Tending to her needs. My arm hurts so fucking bad where he stabbed me but the best I could do was clean it and wrap it in gauze.

After a tiring day, I curl up against my girl. She shudders even in her sleep. The nightmares will be back. And just like before, I'll hold her through them.

For an entire week, she sleeps. Every second of every day. I'm weary and going mad but I don't dare leave her yet. I'm desperately trying to bring her back to me. I've brought her cans of fruit that go untouched. I've tried telling her stories about Drew. Nothing makes her engage.

It's so reminiscent of Sabrina I could throw up.

I refuse to let Devon be defeated. She's so much stronger than her mother.

"When your mom had her first miscarriage, I learned

firsthand what depression was," I murmur against her shoulder blade as I tenderly rub her bare belly.

She stiffens but doesn't reply so I continue.

"Everything was fine. We'd only been married for one summer and she turned up pregnant. She was so fucking happy. We both were. But then one day when we were driving home from dinner, she cried out. I remember to this day the look on her face. Absolute horror. And then it was followed by a gut-wrenching sob." I swallow down my emotion. "We went straight to the hospital. She lost the baby at thirteen weeks."

Devon starts to cry and I hug her tighter.

"For an entire year after that, she was broken. It happened once more and it crushed her. But then you guys came along." I smile against her shoulder and kiss her softly. Skating past that entire story, I fast forward two years later. "When you both were around four, your mom got pregnant again. She was so afraid of losing it. Obsessively went to the doctor. Everything was fine. Until it wasn't. At the dreaded thirteen-week mark, she lost that baby too."

Devon's entire body trembles as she cries.

"Jesus, was she ever fucking depressed. I wanted to take care of her but I didn't know how. After her losses, I laid in bed with her just like this. Kissing and hugging her. But with the last one, I had to take care of you and Drew. I couldn't lay in bed with her. I think this made her sink into a deeper depression but I didn't know what to do about it."

"Why didn't you ever tell me?" she whispers.

I nuzzle against her hair. "I told you I wanted to protect you from the bad stuff."

"I grew up being so angry at her..."

"Shhh," I coo. "It's okay."

We stay cuddled together for a long while before I speak again.

"She lost another baby right before your tenth birthday."

Devon tenses in my arms. "I feel so bad for her. I…I'm devastated and it was just the one baby."

"You're going to be okay, Dev. I promise. You're going to pull out of this and one day we're going to have the family we deserve. But until then…" A growl rumbles in my throat. "I won't sleep until I've hunted him down."

She relaxes her body and turns to face me. Her palm goes to my bearded cheek and she smiles for the first time in a week. "I want him to suffer."

I grab her pinky with mine and kiss her knuckle. "That's something I can deliver, sweetheart."

chapter twelve

DEVON

WHILE DAD WORKS ON HIS FENCE, I WHITTLE a small branch. I'm making a cross to hang on the wall beside our bed. For Peach. I don't know if our baby was a boy or girl but I feel like it was a girl and I named her Peach. It's been two weeks since we lost her. I sit for hours working to make it perfect. I even carve her name into the branch. As soon as I hang it, I cry so hard I eventually pass out.

"You need to eat something."

I blink away my sleep and scrunch my nose in confusion. It's dark outside. How long did I sleep for? I accept the steaming bowl of stewed bear that no longer turns my stomach. My stomach grumbles and I gratefully eat it.

I steal a look at Dad as he undresses after a hard day of work. He strips down to his boxers and I can't help but roam my eyes over his perfectly sculpted body. All of the physical labor has molded him into an Adonis. My heart seems to pump blood for the first time. I watch him as he strolls over to the door and slides the heavy branch into the slot. It's durable and keeps any would-be predators out.

"Fence is finished," he says as he roots around in the cave for something.

I take another bite of my stew and then smile. "Really? That's great news. The gate too?"

He nods. "Bears aren't getting in." He doesn't mention people and it wipes the smile from my lips.

When he returns, he's holding one of his few precious liquor bottles he has left. I devour the rest of my stew while he adds some logs to the fire. He takes my empty bowl and sets it on the table. Then, he saunters over to me. The fire casts delicious shadows all over his body. His black boxers stretch over his impressive cock that isn't even hard right now. Heat floods down south and I blush. The last person who'd been inside me was Ezekiel. A shudder ripples through me.

"What's wrong?" he asks, concern written all over his handsome face. He swallows back some liquor.

I hold a shaky hand out to him. "I was just remembering how Ezekiel…" I trail off and tremble.

"Drink, baby."

Our eyes meet and I sip down the liquid fire. It burns me all the way to my hollow stomach. Just above where I'm not carrying my baby anymore. This thought has me drinking again. And again. And again. The bottle gets pried from my grip. Dad drinks greedily from it as he towers over me, his gaze glued to my bare breasts.

I reach for the bottle and he relinquishes it. We pass it

back and forth until my entire body—no my whole soul—
is blazing.

"I don't want him to be the last thing I remember," I
blurt out, my eyes teary.

He polishes off the bottle and tosses it onto the bear
carpet. With haste, he pushes down his boxers and his
heavy erection bobs out. I lie back on the pillows and
open my body to him. He settles on top of me but doesn't
make any moves to enter me yet. Instead, he kisses my
throat.

Possessive.

Hungry.

Feral.

As if he's trying to mark me with his teeth.

I whimper and my body thrums with the need for
him to slide into me and erase the horrors. His cock rubs
against my clit dizzying me. Our mouths finally meet and
he kisses me as though he requires me to breathe.

My dad, my best friend, my lover pushes into me
suddenly. No warning. Just one thrust, driving home. We
fit. Perfect and whole. I claw at his flesh as I kiss him in
desperation. His powerful hips thunder against me as he
fucks away the heartache and pain. Nothing else exists in
this moment except us.

He flows through my veins hotter and more fervent
than the alcohol I just consumed. With him, it isn't one
sensation, it's *all* of them.

Love. Lust. Darkness. Light. Right. Wrong. Sadness.
Happiness. Anger. Everything.

When his fingers move to touch my clit, I shake my
head. "Just fuck me."

He growls. "Hell no. You're getting off, baby. I'm not playing this game again."

I have no idea what he's talking about and the moment he touches my clit, I don't care. He knows me better than myself. I need to disappear from reality for a moment. His fingers are experienced at touching me and I soon lose control. My back arches up off the mattress as I cry out in pleasure. The orgasm is intense but it chases away all the evil that seemed to be haunting me. His teeth sink into my throat and he bites me hard enough to remind me that I'm alive. When I moan, tears of joy sliding down my face, he comes with a groan. Hot, explosive cum jets deep inside of me. And selfishly, I pray for another baby. I don't want to replace Peach but I want a family with Dad.

Once he's done coming, he pulls out and lays beside me. His fingers trace patterns all over my breasts and stomach. I stare at his handsome face that's relaxed and happy.

"Do you love me like you loved Mom?" I ask, my voice but a whisper.

His thumb runs across my lips. "I loved your mom a lot in the beginning. But over time, I fell out of love with her. We just didn't connect anymore. I wanted to love her. I forced myself to love her. But I wasn't in love with her." He leans forward and kisses me. "But you? I fucking love you more than words can describe. It isn't a feeling—it's like a storm that crashes into me and obliterates me. I can't stop it. I wasn't prepared for it. I just know that it's the best thing and scariest thing to ever happen to me."

I frown at him. "Why the scariest?"

His palm slides down to palm my breast as he frowns. "Because I've never felt like I couldn't live without someone.

the wild

What we have makes no sense outside of this cabin. It defies the rules and logic we were forced to learn. Laws are being broken—all of them I'm guilty of. Despite the chances we're taking to be together, I'm diving headfirst. I don't stop to think about repercussions or reality. All I know is I want you. If that means keeping you here forever all to myself, I'll do it. I don't want to return to society if it means what we have is seen as disgusting or wrong. And that scares the hell out of me. When I truly think about the fact that I'm a forty-year-old man who is sleeping with his seventeen-year-old daughter, it fucks with my head. I live every day with this battle of morals. The fact that I'm easily cutting out the part of me that cares what people would think says that I'm losing myself. I'm not the man who drove that RV out here. I'm some beast the wilderness created. I take what I want and that's you."

Tears slip out of the corner of my eyes. "You didn't have to take me. I gave myself to you. I'm yours. Here or out there. I always was."

He smiles and leans forward to kiss my nipple. His breath is hot against me. "Tomorrow I'm going to hunt down that motherfucker. Then, I'm going to come back and make love to you until you're pregnant again. I won't let anything happen to you. So help me, I'll kill every fucker on this planet before I let another person even look at you. You're my secret. My everything. Nobody deserves to be in your presence. Mine."

His possessive words aren't playful. He's dead serious. Just the thought of seeing anyone frightens me. I feel safe when it's just me and Dad locked away by ourselves.

"Promise?"

He grabs my pinky with his. "On my life. Because if anything comes between us and hurts you, my life doesn't matter anymore."

Dad works on packing a bag. Food. Weapons. Other supplies he needs for his hunting mission. Once he's got one ready, he takes me back to our first campsite. He rummages through the RV looking for things and I work on the mangled trailer. A lot of stuff is smashed and destroyed. It's been picked over by animals. With the patience of a saint, I slowly pull everything out. There's more stuff toward the back of the trailer. The trailer was nearly smashed in half but once I move stuff around, I am just small enough to squeeze through the dented metal. It's dark aside from a few holes in the side of the metal that allows sun to shine in. One of the first plastic tubs I open up has clothing in it. I pull out a piece and hold it to the light. I immediately recognize it as one of the frilly dresses I wore as a baby for our three-year-old pictures. Tears well in my eyes. Mom kept this. Despite her detached personality, she was determined to take these memories with her. Memories of Drew and I. The dress is so pretty. It would have been perfect on Peach.

A sob catches in my throat, but I swallow it down. I stuff the dress back in the tub and seal the lid. One day I'll pull this box out and properly look through it. The next box I open has books and notebooks in it. It's my box. I let out an excited shriek as I pull some novels into my lap. I find a pencil bag and one of my notebooks I'd planned to write in. Greedily, I stuff my arms with them before sealing the lid. I'll come back for the rest later.

It takes some maneuvering but I eventually squeeze out with my haul. Once I'm out of the trailer, I find Dad sitting on a rock starting to skin a rabbit.

"Can you try and save the pelt?" I ask as I approach. "I think I can use them like I used the bear skin."

He looks up at me, blood running down the back of his hand from the rabbit and grins before nodding. Out here in the wilderness, with the snow as our backdrop and him looking positively feral as he skins the game, I feel my heart rate quicken. He's the kind of handsome you'd see on the cover of a romance novel or some Alaskan hottie calendar.

And he's mine.

"You're blushing."

I bite on my lip and shrug. "Just thinking about how hot you are."

His dark eyebrow lifts. "The feeling is mutual." He winks and the bird inside my ribcage flutters. "What do you have there?"

I smile and sit down beside him on the rock. "Some books to read and a notebook. I'm going to write."

He leans over and kisses my temple. "You're glowing. Are you happy?"

"Right now, like this. I'm happier than I thought I ever could be."

"Good. Me too."

Eventually he finishes with the rabbit and we head back to the cabin. He hands over the pelt and I set to washing it. I'll need to stretch it and oil it with the leftover bear fat but I'm excited to start collecting the soft furry pelts. It will be perfect for when we do have a baby to line the bed with. I'm sitting in the chair singing an old song Mom and I used to sing on the radio when I feel as though Dad is watching me. His features are dark as he cuts the rabbit meat for our meal.

"What?" I ask, heat creeping up my neck. He's been inside of me more times than I can count and I still get all heated and embarrassed when he stares at me as though he wants to devour me.

"I love when you sing."

I smile and continue with my task making sure to sing every song I can think of since he loves it. Once we're both done with our tasks and eating, he boils some water.

"Before I leave tonight, I want to bathe you." His voice is husky and raw. It sings to the woman inside of me that can't get enough of the beast inside of him.

While he finishes with the water, I peel off all my clothes. His gaze is greedy as he roams it over my bare flesh. He sits in one of the chairs and places the steaming pot on the table.

"Come sit, Pip." He pats his knee.

I walk over to him. He helps me sit on him so that I'm straddling his thighs. My sex feels open and exposed. It makes me want to ask him to put his fingers inside of me to fill the space. These thoughts make the blush spread down to my breasts.

"Are you embarrassed?" he asks as he sweeps my hair around to one side. He combs through the knots with his fingers, a brow lifted in question.

"I'm turned on," I admit.

His smile is predatory but I'm not afraid. "I'm always turned on around you." He grips my wrist and guides my palm to where his erection is stiff and throbbing inside of his jeans. "See."

Instead of touching me where I want, he sets to getting the rag wet and wrung out. Slowly, he runs the scalding hot rag along my flesh. I hiss because it burns but it feels good because he's the one doing it. Quickly, it cools. He runs it along my breasts and my nipples become hard pebbles. Leaning forward, he flicks his tongue out and tastes one.

"Your little nipples are my favorite things to put in my mouth," he breathes hotly against my breasts.

I let out a whimper and run my fingers through his unkempt hair. He has me lift my arms where he washes underneath them and then he moves down to my stomach. My heart catches in my throat when his fingers linger on my stomach, both of us having a moment of silence to acknowledge our loss. Hot tears spill down my cheeks and splash his arm. He sets the rag on the table and takes both of my cheeks in his palms. His lips press to mine and then he licks away my tears like a lion would lick the face of his lioness. I tilt my head back slightly and let him clean away the hurt. When I'm good and dry, he continues licking to my jaw and down to my throat. His palms roam my body in a way that feels halfway between him marking his territory and checking for ailments. Concern and possession. Equal parts obsession.

"Mine," he murmurs and then his fingers are right where I want them as he kisses my throat. One finger pushes inside of me followed quickly by another. The heel of his palm grinds against my clit as he uses his fingers to fuck me. "Always so wet for me. Good girl."

I whimper and rock against his hand. The pleasure sensations rippling through me are intense and overwhelming. I love how he plows through me every time we connect. He ruins me. Destroys me. And I love the feeling as he desecrates me.

His hand gropes my small breast while the other works me from the inside. Reality abandons me as I lose myself to the moment. I come hard and with a shriek when my orgasm strikes. I'm weak and dizzy and in near tears from the pleasure as he stands with me in his arms. He carries us to our bed and lays me out before him. I stare greedily at him as he rips off his shirt and bares his stone chiseled chest at me. His pectorals twitch and his abs ripple with movement. My mouth waters to run my tongue along the solid V-shaped muscles that point straight to his cock that owns me.

I'm spread open and waiting. My arousal dripping as the need for him becomes almost unbearable. He's quick with his movements in undressing but not quick enough for my liking. The moment his jeans and boxers are gone, I stare at his cock that points right at me. Long. Thick. Veiny. I know from experience that it feels like velvet in my hand. Soft and pliable on the outside but hard and unbreakable beneath. He tastes of salt and musk and him. My stomach practically growls for him.

He grabs my ankle and kisses the bone. Then, he slowly trails hot kisses along my calf and to the inside of my knee. The moment his beard hair tickles along my inner thigh, I let out a moan. He kisses the entire journey to my clit.

There, he kisses me in an obscene way that would probably make people blush. Desperate and hungry. Sucking as though he wants to pull it right from my body and devour it for a snack. I'm still so sensitive from my last orgasm that I come with his name on my lips. And then his kissing continues along my stomach, between my breasts, and then to my lips. His tongue dives inside my mouth the exact moment his cock pushes inside of me. I moan in surprise at the intrusion but he doesn't give me a chance to recover. Like a wild animal, he thrusts against me. Words of praise and vows of love are murmured against my lips as our bodies mold together as one.

I'm everywhere all at once.

I'm nowhere but here.

My mind is a cacophony of thoughts and out of control sensations as he shows me what it feels like for two souls to bind.

Threaded together. A tight braid of man and woman. A link that cannot be severed. We're beyond the thrill and needing to feel good. We're in love. Madly. Deeply. Desperately. Sickly.

I'll die without him.

I understand his words from before.

One cannot survive when the other half of your heart bleeds out. They're connected, which means you bleed out too.

He grunts out his release. The heat burns me from the inside and, once again, I pray for a baby. When love is this intense, this explosive, this real, miracles happen.

I want my miracle.

chapter thirteen

REED

SHE SOBS FROM THE PORCH AS I WALK BACKWARD away from her in the dark night. I don't want to fucking leave her but I have no choice. The motherfucker who beat my daughter and then raped her, causing her to miscarry our baby, still lives and breathes somewhere out there. I will track him down and I will kill him. I've armed her with a shotgun that she's to use first and then ask questions. Nobody will touch her. She has enough food and firewood to keep her safe in the cabin until I return.

I will return.

"I love you," she calls out.

"I love you too." I wave one last time and turn away. The echo of the door closing shut and the branch locking her in calms my erratic heart. Leaving her is so fucking hard.

The pack is heavy on my back and the .45 stays in my

grip ready to fire. If I see any bears, I'll kill them with a quick pop to the head. But if I see Nathaniel, I'm going to incapacitate him before taking my time murdering the sick fuck.

As I trek through the darkness, my ears are aware of all sounds, my mind drifts to earlier. With each passing moment, I fall deeper in love with Devon. It's an infinite fall with no bottom. Just gets deeper and deeper. I can't explain how fucking terrifying the feeling is but I'm obsessed with it nonetheless. I'm madly consumed by her. I'm not fulfilled unless I'm buried inside of her. I'm not whole unless our mouths are mating like our bodies do so well. I'm not happy unless she's happy. Her smiles are my sustenance. I don't need food or water. I just need to see her blue eyes shining with love and adoration and joy.

They raped her.

Stole so much from her.

Her sense of security. Her child. Her mind.

And yet she wades through that darkness and finds me. Unlike Sabrina ever could, my strong, fierce girl finds me. Seeks me out as though she thirsts for me. I'm fucking ravenous for her too.

Each day out here in the wilderness, I feel my sanity slipping. We grow up learning norms and behaviors that are deemed acceptable. Yet when all of life's easiness is stripped from us and we're thrust into something arduous, those norms get forgotten. They get shoved to the side as instinct guides the way. The mind is no longer needed. A useless organ. It's the heart that grows wild. It forges the way. It makes decisions that defy reason and instead break rules that don't exist out here.

The heart becomes a hungry, selfish beast.

It devours the mind and feeds the desires.

My heart is free.

No longer caged by the world but released by love.

I'm not sure how long I've walked for, but I can no longer see or smell the smoke from our cabin. If I had to guess, it's been a couple of hours. The wind picks up and I got a whiff of smoke. I clench my jaw because I'm close. I can practically smell the enemy.

People.

They are my nemesis.

This shack may not hold the rapist but it holds others who may try and steal what's mine. And for that, they will pay with their lives. No one will come onto my property and touch my love.

Something growls and I halt. My eyes dart over to the shadows. It could be a wolf—the sound is most definitely of the K9 variety.

"Easy there," I mutter as I lift my .45.

The animal stops growling and whimpers. The sound is familiar and niggles at my long shut off brain. Now curious, I approach the shadows. The whines grow louder. I kneel down and pat my thigh.

"Come here," I order.

With his head lowered and a rope tight around his neck, my goddamned dog Buddy creeps out toward me. I'm so overcome with joy that I leap forward and hug the dog. He licks my face as if he's happy as hell to see me. I quickly cut through the rope around his neck with my knife and massage away the dent in his skin from how it gripped him. He practically attacks me. His tail wags as he licks my face all over. When his nose nuzzles against my hand and he lets out a small bark, I know he smells Devon.

"She's back at the cabin, boy," I coo. "I'm going to take you back home. Just gotta take care of something first. I'm going to make him pay."

The dog, loyal as fuck, runs a circle around me. When I point back toward the cabin, he looks that way and sniffs the air. I let him go as he starts sniffing along the pathway I've come from. The scent of Devon has him eager and on the hunt. I stand and make my way to the front of the shack.

I push the door open slightly and notice a fire going in crumbling river rock fireplace. Sleeping on the floor in front of it are two guys close to Ezekiel's age. Bearded. Toothless. Dirty. They're ruffians with dicks in their pants. Dicks that could guide them to my daughter. I suppress a growl as I pull out my knife. The stink of sex is thick in the air. In the back room of the shack, I can hear sounds. Fucking.

I kneel down beside the bigger guy and dig my blade deep into his throat before slashing past his carotid. Blood spurts out, spraying my face, and then he's gurgling, eyes wide in confusion as he clutches his throat. The man beside him stirs and I attack him next. He rouses just as I slash for him and blocks my hit. His eyes are filled with terror and surprise. He's weak compared to me and I pin him down quickly. The knife plunges into his fat vein. I rip it back and forth destroying it, soaking myself with more blood, before I yank it out. My heart hammers in my chest.

Nathaniel.

I know he's in there. I can practically feel it.

The door creaks open when I push through it.

"Not now, John," Nathaniel grunts, his bare ass flexing as he drives into someone. "You promised she was mine tonight." Another fireplace is in this room lighting it up for me.

His thigh has a red gnarly scar from where I got him with the bullet. I bare my teeth before pouncing. Grabbing a handful of his greasy hair, I yank him away from his fuckfest. His dick pops out with a vulgar noise. One quick glance at the makeshift bed and my heart stills in my chest. A girl with wild, messy brown hair and tears streaming down her face lies there with her legs spread wide open. She has no tits to speak of and is bare between her thighs. If I had to guess, she's no older than eleven. Twelve max.

"Don't hurt my sister!" he pleads, dragging me from staring at the horrific scene.

I snarl with rage and slam him to the floor. He puts up a fight. Just a fucking youngster but filled with so much evil. In another life, a kid like this could have been friends with my Rowdy. But in this life, he's the villain. The fucking monster.

I stab him in his chest hoping I hit a lung. He doesn't get off easy like those other fuckers. I stab him again, this time lower in his fleshy abdomen. Gurgles and screams escape him. I snarl at him and plunge the knife into his side. He howls and cries and fucking begs like a pussy.

When he was making my daughter scream as he raped her and stole her baby, he didn't award her a pardon. He just took and fucking took.

So I take and fucking take.

His blood soaks my hands and I slash him over and over again against his chest. I want to steal his heart like he stole hers. I want the motherfucking thing in my fist. The girl on the bed sobs and I briefly wonder if I should kill her too. But then I recall the terror and despondency in her eyes. She didn't ask for this. They took from her too.

He stops squirming as he vomits up more blood that makes him choke. I can't stand the look on his face. So goddamned helpless. With rage that consumes me, I drive the knife into his face.

Again.

Again.

Again.

My knife gets stuck between bones in his face and I yank so hard I hear his neck snap. I manage to free my knife and land on my ass with a thud. When my gaze sweeps over him, peace settles around me like a refreshing fog. The one who hurt my baby is dead. Brutally ended.

I smile.

Like a fucking maniac.

The girl whimpers and I stand to my full height. She scrambles far away from me. My knife is clutched tight in my grip. I should just cut her throat and put her out of her misery. Her lip wobbles as she drags the blankets to cover herself.

"Thank you." The whisper from her lips has my soul calming.

"Can you survive on your own?" My voice is gruff.

She nods.

"I'm taking my fucking dog," I snap.

Her body trembles and she nods once more.

"If you so much as come near my home and try to steal from us or hurt us, I will gut you like a goddamn fish."

She widens her eyes as tears spill out.

"But if you need help," I growl. "We can help."

Her head shakes back and forth. "I-I don't need help."

I grunt because I don't believe her.

"They deserved it," I mutter. "They hurt my girl."

Tears stream down her cheeks. "I'm glad you killed them."

I reach into my pack and pull out a can of fruit. A whimper escapes her when I kneel beside her and place it on the floor next to her. I pat her head and then stand again. Before I've even left the room, I can hear the can rip open and slurping behind me.

That girl will be dead by the end of the week.

I'm almost to the cabin when Buddy trots over to me. I forgot about the spiked fence and gate. He waited patiently until I got back. His tail wags wildly as I approach.

"Good boy. Your momma is going to be so happy," I tell him as I scratch behind his ears. I open the gate and walk onto the porch. "Devon, it's me!"

I hear footsteps inside and the lock slides out of place. She answers wearing nothing but my sweatshirt. Her long bare legs are on display and fuck how I've missed them.

"Oh," she gasps as her mouth parts upon seeing my gruesome appearance. I'm covered in other men's blood. For her. Always for her.

132

Buddy pushes past me and a scream of surprise escapes her. But the moment she realizes it's her beloved pet, she falls to her knees sobbing. I think she's more excited to see the dog than me. He kisses her all over and she squeezes the life out of him. In this moment, I'm transported to the past.

"Who's a good dog?" Devon coos as she holds up a treat.

Buddy whines but remains seated. He knows the drill.

"You're a good dog," she praises and gives him the snack. He chomps on it and happily runs off to one corner of the backyard to eat it. When she stands up, her hands on her narrow hips, I frown.

"Did you leave work early to come swimming?" she asks, her smile wide. I can't see her bright blue eyes behind her glasses but I know they're shining with hope. I can hardly deny her a thing.

"I came home early so we could take Mom to the movies but..."

She lowers her head and frowns. "She doesn't want to go."

I clench my teeth and nod. "Did you want to call some friends over?"

"Seth asked if he could come over but you said no boys, right?" Her teeth bite down on her bottom lip.

My gaze rakes down her too-womanly body in a black bikini. The triangles barely cover the small swells of her breasts and her tiny nipples are erect beneath the wet fabric.

Her bottoms are even smaller. She has hips that flare out and a narrow waist. Every teenage boy's wet dream. Hell, she's cost me one friendship already because I overheard one of my golf buddies talking to another guy at the club that he'd like to be her sugar daddy.

Boys are a bad idea.

The only man she gets is me because I can protect her from them.

"No boys," I agree with a growl.

She laughs. "I heard Seth was a bad kisser anyway. You just saved me, Dad."

"I'll always save you," I vow.

I get a sweet smile before she turns and gets ready to dive in. I was right. The material barely covers her ass. Anger swells inside of me that men and boys everywhere are beginning to notice my sixteen-year-old daughter. Soon we'll be off to the Alaskan wilderness and nobody will look at her.

She leaps into the pool and submerges her body under the water. Effortlessly, she swims to one side of the pool. I'm still staring after her deep in thought when she climbs out on the other end. Water sluices off her body as she makes her way over to the hot tub. After the helluva day I've had, including the part where I yelled at Sabrina just now for being a selfish bitch, I could use to unwind in the hot tub.

I quickly head upstairs to change. Sabrina lies in bed naked, a silent invitation to make up, but I'm too angry still. I ignore her like she always ignores me and put my swim trunks on. Before heading outside, I grab a beer and make my way over to the hot tub.

Devon is singing with her back pressed up against the jets. She's so fucking cute with her wet hair now piled up *messily on top of her head. Her head moves to the beat that plays in her head as I climb into the hot water. Once I'm seated, I tilt the beer back and take a cold swallow.*

"No fair," she pouts as she makes her way over to me. I don't even argue when she takes the bottle and drinks a swallow. She's been stealing drinks of my beers for as long as I can remember. "Do you think we'll swim a lot in Alaska? Doesn't it, like, snow all the time?"

I laugh and take the beer back. "What? Miss I-Know-Everything hasn't checked the temperatures?"

She sticks her tongue out. "I did. Summers can be warm there. I just want to make sure. I love swimming."

When she reaches for my beer again, I switch hands and hold it away from her. She's playful as she lunges for it. Her breasts brush against my chest and I freeze. No dad wants to feel their daughter's tits. I'm still so weirded out that when she grabs the bottle, I release it. Instead of moving away, she settles in my lap. Like a thousand other times. But unease flits down my spine this time. Maybe it's the fact that we're both in our swimsuits. Maybe it's the fact I was just worrying over the fact that she looks like a woman now. Whatever it is, I'm afraid to move. I don't want to hurt her feelings. She's so sensitive because of her mother's blatant neglect. We've always been close. I've never pushed her away. I'll be damned if I start now.

"I read up on how to tan pelts. There are oils and stuff you can buy but you can use nature's supplies as well. I wonder how Buddy will feel if we ever skin an animal around him." She laughs and sips the beer. "I bet he'd think we were barbaric."

I laugh, my arms wrapping around her middle like

always. "You think you're going to be out there tanning hides? What in the world would you ever need animal furs for?"

She shrugs and leans against my chest. "To pet."

Snorting, I steal my bottle back and take a long pull. "That's silly. That's what you have Buddy for."

"But rabbits are so soft," she says, a smile in her voice. Then she looks up at me. When the hell did she grow up on me?

"They are. Are you really ready to leave all this behind? No more hot tubs or pools or bad kisser Seths." My growl at the last part makes her giggle.

She takes the beer and downs the rest. Then she wiggles her ass against me as she leans forward to set it on the ledge. The movement causes a physiological reaction that I wasn't expecting.

A motherfucking erection.

I shove her away from me and clear my throat. "I have to get another beer since you drank mine." My voice is husky and I feel as though my face is red with embarrassment.

She stands up out of the hot water and puts her hands on her hips again. Her swimsuit is slightly off kilter on one side and the pink of her nipple is showing.

Tearing my horrified gaze away from her, I rush out of the hot tub careful to keep my stupid, disgusting erection away from her line of sight. "I'll be right back," I bark out.

I don't fool with a towel, just rush into the cold house. My dick is throbbing and I'm pissed about it. This is all Sabrina's fault, I decide. Had she just gone to the movies with us, I wouldn't have had a creepy moment with my daughter. Fucking sick.

I storm through the house ready to give Sabrina a piece of my mind. When I barge through the bedroom, she's still lying there like a lazy ass. Naked. With a growl, I shove down my wet shorts and prowl over to her. I smack her thigh causing her to yelp. Then, I grab both ankles and drag her to the end of the bed. She cries out when I flip her onto her stomach. My erection is aching for release. I slip it past the crack of her ass to her cunt. With one hard thrust, I drive into her. Reaching forward, I tangle her hair in my fist. I fuck her hard and without apology. Several times, I slap her ass so hard she screams. When I get ready to come, my mind slips from this moment. To a tiny sliver of forbidden nipple. I nearly gag in disgust at myself. And yet I come harder than ever before. Pulling out, I shoot my cum all over Sabrina's now red ass.

"That was so good," she moans from the bed.

"Are you going to come to the movies with us now?" I bark out, anger still surging through me.

"You exhausted me," she says with a small laugh. "I'll sit this one out."

I grit my teeth. I want to slap the shit out of her to knock some goddamn sense into her. She's singlehandedly destroying her family.

"Of course," I snarl.

Once I'm showered and dressed, I come back outside. Devon perks up when she sees me. She climbs out of the hot tub and saunters over to me. Jesus. Who taught her to walk like that—hips swaying and shit? I'm irritated at myself for being weak. Infuriated at Sabrina for giving up. And bothered by Devon that she's seducing male parts of me that are strictly off limits to her.

"Are you mad?" Her bottom lip pouts out. "It was only a few sips, Dad."

I scrub at my smooth jaw and shake my head. "I'm not mad at you, Pip. Let's go see a movie just you and I."

She beams and stands on her toes to plant a wet kiss way too close to my lips. "You're the best. I'll be ready in thirty minutes."

With shame surging through my veins, I watch as her ass bounces away toward the house.

I'm losing my damn mind.

chapter fourteen

DEVON

"**I**'M SO HAPPY!" I CRY OUT AS I STAND AND search Dad's eyes. He's frowning and his scowl is in place. As handsome and as fierce as he looks with blood splattered all over his bearded face, I like him better clean so we can kiss. "Go sit in the chair."

He blinks away his daze and offers me a small smile before doing as he is told. With haste, he strips out of his outerwear and sweatshirt until he's wearing nothing but his jeans and socks. I feed Buddy some leftover rabbit pieces and make him a bowl of water. He seems content to lie on the bearskin rug, gnawing on the meat.

When I turn to look at Dad, he's seated wearing a predatory glare that makes me shiver. I boil some water and then prepare to clean him. My eyes skitter over his chest every chance they get. His muscles are a work of art. I set to washing the blood from his face and hair. His dark brown eyes bore into mine. He's extra intense tonight. I mean, he did kill someone. I'm guessing that would make anyone intense. Instead of feeling frightened, I feel relieved. He's living up to his promise to protect me no matter the cost.

"Do you remember the last time we planned to go to the movies before we came out here?" His voice is strained. Hoarse.

I stroke my fingers through his hair. "Of course I do." It was one of the first times I'd felt unusual hormonal sensations surging through me. With my dad of all people. As I clean him, I think back to that day.

I've never been on a date. I'm not old enough Dad says. But every time he and I go out together, I pretend that's exactly what it is. He always dresses nice—a lot nicer than the dumb guys I'm friends with who live in the neighborhood. I'm proud he's at my side. And I always go the extra mile for him too. Since Mom won't go with him, I think he deserves someone pretty on his arm. Someone womanly. Tonight, instead of my usual jeans and T-shirts, I chose a powder blue sundress that compliments my eyes and hair. I coupled it with strappy tan sandals and straightened my hair smooth. When it's soft like this, Dad absently touches it a lot. I like when he touches my hair. Normally, I'm not one for a lot of makeup but tonight I doll myself up for him. Earlier, in the hot tub, he seemed angry with me. I don't want him to be mad.

Once I spritz on some perfume, I grab a small clutch

and hurry down the stairs. He's waiting, looking young and handsome, in a pair of charcoal slacks and a white button-down shirt. The shirt is ironed crisp and he's left the two buttons undone at his throat. He's also rolled up his sleeves revealing his toned forearms. I smile because he looks really nice.

When our eyes meet, his eyes quickly roam down the front of my body before he shakes his head. "No."

Hurt clutches my heart and I frown. "No?"

"That dress…" His jaw clenches and looks away. "It's too…fancy."

I look down at the summer dress with the plunging neckline. Sure it's fitted and silky but not fancy. "Dad," I pout. "I like this dress."

"The dress isn't the problem," he grumbles. "It's how people will react when they see you in it."

I smile. "You afraid I'm going to find a boyfriend tonight?"

He doesn't laugh like I expect him to. Instead, he frowns and his fingers run through my smooth hair. "You're too pretty."

My heart does a little flutter at his words. "So protect me from those creeps," I tell him, beaming. "That's what dads do." I grab onto his forearm and he tenses. All I get is a clipped nod of agreement. It's enough.

Thirty minutes later and we're zipping through town in Dad's black sports car. We pass by the movie theater and I frown in confusion. He drives us all the way out to where the piers are and parks along the side of the road. As soon as I step out of the car, I can smell seafood and my stomach growls.

"I thought we'd have dinner instead. That dress is too nice to waste in a dinky theater," he says gruffly.

My heart blooms like a flower. He takes my hand and I don't feel like his young daughter. I feel like a beautiful woman on the arm of a handsome man. These people don't know us. They might assume we're a couple. The thought is a dangerous one but it's not unwelcome. It sends tingles of warmth trickling through me. He squeezes my hand and I grin.

"We'd like an outdoor table that overlooks the bay," Dad tells the hostess.

The hostess smiles and shows us to the table. I can't help the embarrassed blush that creeps up my neck when Dad pulls my chair out for me. His fingers run through my silky strands for just a moment causing me to shiver. Then, he sits across from me, his brown eyes darker than usual.

"When you're eighty and allowed to start dating," he teases with a wolfish grin that turns my insides to mush. "You set that man straight on how you're to be treated."

I nod and smile. "I'm taking notes."

He smirks which causes foreign heat to flood through me. His leg brushes against mine under the table and it sets my nerves alive. We order our food and Dad asks for a bottle of wine. The server doesn't question my age. Simply brings out the expensive bottle and pours it into our glasses.

Dinner is fun. We laugh and talk and enjoy our food. We're both excited about our upcoming Alaskan adventure. I can see the delight dancing in Dad's eyes. He's ready for this next step. I'm ready too. Selfishly, I'm looking forward to more time with him. He works so much that I feel like I never see him. As the alcohol buzzes through my system, I find myself *accidentally brushing against his legs more often. His eyes are positively manic as he stares at me. I don't understand the look but it seems to make my heart thunder in my chest.*

After dinner, he guides me into a bar where people are dancing. He orders shots but only lets me have one. I pout and he laughs. His fingers, as if having a mind of their own, toy with a lock of my hair. I'm not sure that any date will ever be able to top this one with my dad. When the alcohol has him loose and laughing more often, he whisks me into the crowd of sweaty dancing bodies. The music is fast and we both start moving to the beat. He's all smiles and I like when his hands keep touching my hips. It feels as though he burns me each time he does it. At one point, I'm dancing in front of him with my back to his chest when his palm rests against my stomach. Burning desire surges through me. His other palm slides down my ribs and I let out an embarrassing moan that is thankfully covered by the music.

I'm drunk.

The feelings creeping through me are because of the alcohol.

His fingers slide further down my stomach. I don't think he realizes his pinky is touching my pubic bone. I'm so aroused that I'm dizzy. My panties are soaked with desire and my dress is drenched in sweat. When my knees buckle, he grabs me suddenly, his strong forearm just under my breasts.

"What's wrong?" he demands, his voice panicked against my ear. "Are you sick?"

"Dizzy. I'm just dizzy."

He pulls me to his side and guides me away from the dance floor. Once outside of the busy bar, he finds a sole chair on the corner of the deck. The wind is cooler now that the sun has set and it chills my skin. He sits in the chair and pulls me into his lap. Our bodies are sticky with sweat but the wind makes me shiver.

"Just let the alcohol wear off. I shouldn't have let you have that shot," he says, shame coating his voice. His fingers run through my hair and my belly seems to flop.

I snuggle against him for warmth. "I'll be fine in a minute. I just got too hot. Now I'm freezing." I laugh at the silliness of it.

His arms pull me tighter to him. Dad is warm and safe and strong. I start to drift off. His palm is rubbing circles on my lower back but eventually he stops and lets it rest on my butt. I don't think he realizes where he's touching me, but I don't correct him. I like his hand there.

I wake up later to him carrying me to my bed. I don't remember much but I'm eager for sleep. He removes my shoes and then covers me up with my quilt. I'm quiet as his fingers stroke my hair. His lips press to my forehead and he whispers something I almost don't hear.

"I promise I won't allow myself to have another selfish night like tonight."

My heart sinks because his selfish night was the best one of my life. But when he stalks away, I can't help but smile in the dark.

He didn't pinky promise.

"I wanted you that night," I admit, my voice shaky.

His dark brown eyes sear into mine. "You did?"

"You were angry with me after the hot tub and I wasn't sure why. I just wanted to please you. That's why I dressed so pretty. For you." I smile as I set the rag back down on the table.

His features are wild. An animal behind his eyes. "I wasn't angry. I was disgusted at myself. You rubbed up against me. It made my dick hard. I thought I was a sick fuck."

I frown and shake my head. "You're not sick. You were never sick."

He scowls. "Took it out on your mother." Shame flickers in his gaze. "But I wasn't satisfied. Something forbidden was festering inside of me. I wasn't sure how to turn it off. That night, I selfishly wanted to pick at that internal wound if only for one night. I wouldn't have done anything to cross the line but I just needed…"

I look at him from under my lashes, a shy heat burning across my cheeks. "I was dizzy on that dance floor because of the way you were touching me. I wanted more. I wanted it all. I wasn't sure how to process that thought. Your fingers were so close."

He growls and rubs at the back of his neck. "I almost touched you that night. The alcohol confused me. My eyes were closed. I was lost in the moment. If you wouldn't have spoken, I'm afraid I might have rubbed my fingers against your clit right then."

All this talk of that night has my panties wet. I peel away my sweatshirt and reveal my bare breasts to him. Breasts that he once thought were off limits. They were never off limits. Here or there, I'm sure I'd have offered them to him at one point regardless.

145

"I would have let you," I admit with a whisper. "I'd have let you finger me then. In front of everyone. I wanted your touch." I reach for his hand. "I still want your touch."

He rises and towers over me. When I get twisted in his grip, I let out a shocked whimper. His hips start moving to an imaginary song. I bite my lip when I feel his erection poking into me. Two hands whisper over my bare flesh, recreating that night. The one at my side tickles but the one dangerously low on my stomach has me seeing stars. I close my eyes and I'm back at that night. His fingers moving under my dress. Slipping into my panties and searching my heat. Thick fingers pushing inside of me. Owning me. I cry out in pleasure. My arousal drips from me like never before. He pushes my panties down my thighs and they fall to my ankles.

"Bend over," he demands, his voice husky.

I reach for my toes, offering my bare body to him. His jeans and boxers hit the floor before he starts rubbing his hot erection against my slick sex.

"Would you have let me fuck you right there on the pier if I'd asked?" His voice is feral and deep. I wince when his powerful fingers dig into my hips. "Tell me, baby girl."

I whimper at his sexy voice and words. "Yes. I touched myself that night. I imagined it was you. Sometimes I would pretend to have nightmares so you'd come into my room wearing nothing but boxers. I liked the way our bodies fit together. How you were so strong and virile. I was small and vulnerable. When in my bed, you kissed and held me like a lover would. Possessive and protective. You'd pet my hair as if I were yours and only yours. So many times, I wanted to straddle your thighs once you started snoring and—"

I scream when he slams into me with a harsh buck of his hips. My body trembles as if I might collapse, but his death grip on my hips prevent me from falling. He fucks me hard. So hard our skin makes a loud slapping sound. So hard the dog whimpers. So hard I know I'll be bruised everywhere.

"Harder," I beg.

I want him to split me in two and own me from the inside. His hips piston in an erotic way that has me wild with lust. I come with a violent shudder. He pulls out suddenly and I expect cum. Instead, he presses against the tight hole of my ass. Terror climbs up my throat but before it can escape, he runs his fingertips along my spine.

"I want him gone from there," he growls.

I know exactly what he means. Ezekiel was the last person to touch me there. Suddenly, despite the pain, I want it too.

"Yes," I choke out. "Gone."

He pushes in slowly and fire rips through me. I nearly suffocate on a sob I was attempting to stifle. Dad doesn't ram into me like that rapist. He's gentle but possessive. I can barely hold myself up and I'm thankful when he sits back down in the chair with me impaled on his cock. The fire inside of me is raging but I trust him. He wraps his muscled forearm around my middle and pulls me flush against him. I tilt my head back to rest on his shoulder.

"Put your feet on my knees," he orders, his hot breath tickling my neck.

I assume his desired position and am thankful it seems to lessen the burn inside my ass. My sex feels open and exposed. And like a dog sniffing a bone, both of his hands explore me there. He rubs against my clit while he uses three fingers to push into my still dripping sex. The intrusion hurts but when I clench in response, pleasure zings through me. I'm so full of him. Everywhere. He fucks me with his fingers as if it were his powerful dick. I am so lost to all of the sensations that I feel as though I'm stepping outside of my body. His teeth ravage my flesh everywhere he can reach and I'm helpless. He's devouring me bit by bit and I'm elated.

With a soul-shattering scream, I come. I orgasm everywhere. I don't understand it. I can't describe it. I just simply explode. My body seizes in his grip and I black out as I shudder. The burn in my ass intensifies as his cock seems to expand. Then, hot cum is jetting inside of me.

I'm being consumed and swallowed whole.

I come again.

And then I pass out.

chapter fifteen

REED

I GRIP MY GIFT TO DEVON IN MY POCKET. I'VE BEEN carrying it around with me ever since I pulled it from where I found it. It's time. I want her to have it. It's been nearly three months since I slaughtered those men. Guilt should live inside my heart that I left a small girl with no one. But nothing exists inside my hollow chest but Devon. Always Devon.

Sniffing the cool air, I can't help but notice that the weather doesn't feel as cold. Spring will be here soon and will melt all this away. My darling girl will be in her element again in the river and hunting for berries. I can't wait to see her wearing less clothes too. When at home, we remain naked. Our stove is warm and it keeps us cozy. But after seeing the fireplaces at the shack, my brain has been whirring with new plans for our home. I want to move the fence out on one side and extend it. And when I do, I want to build an actual fireplace with a chimney to keep her warm.

I pick up the two dead rabbits at my feet and head back to the cabin. Devon will like the size of these animals. She's become obsessed with collecting their pelts. It's fucking cute how she yells at me if I don't skin them just right. God I love her.

"Honey, I'm home," I playfully sing as I clomp through the front door.

She's sitting cross legged on our bed. Naked of course. Her long blonde hair is clean and brushed smooth. It hangs down in front of her small tits. A smile plays at her lips as she uses her mother's old sewing kit to stitch together the animal pelts. The blanket is getting bigger each day when I bring home more rabbit.

She lifts her gaze to mine and flashes me one of her smiles that lights up the room. "That didn't take long."

"I was gone hours," I say with a chuckle as I close the door and lock it. "You were just lost in your task."

She yawns and moves the blanket and sewing supplies to the floor. I pull off my coat, my eyes never leaving her, as she stretches out on the bed. Her hair falls away from her breasts that are slightly swollen. I don't miss the tiny pooch on her stomach. This time, instead of jumping to conclusions or freaking the hell out, I pray for a baby. I don't deserve it but I want it anyway.

"You look tired," I observe as I undress. There's a shit ton to do but right now I just want to lie with my woman.

Her eyes are a soft blue as she regards me. Once I'm naked and stretched out beside her, she takes my hand. She guides it over to her stomach and rests it there. A serene smile plays at her lips.

"I think I'm pregnant." She bites down on her bottom

lip, worry flickering in her eyes. I was such an asshole last time I found out, I can understand her reaction.

"Really?" My grin is wide as I lean forward to kiss her mouth.

"Really."

I devour her lips and kiss her hard hoping she'll feel how happy I am about this. After the loss of Peach, I've never wanted anything more. This baby is ours and nobody will hurt it. That vow is one I can feel deep in my soul.

Pulling away from her, I war internally with whether she'll like her gift. I kept it all these months for her. In the beginning, it was for other reasons. Now, it means something completely different.

That is, if she'll accept it.

"Stand up," I order.

She arches a blonde brow but obeys. My girl always fucking obeys because she trusts me completely. I reach into my jeans pocket and pull out my gift. Still on my knees, I take her hand and look up at her.

"Devon Abigail Jamison. I know you won't have a normal life but I'm asking you to live this life with me. Forever. Just us and the lives we create. Be my wife, baby. Please." Her eyes are wide and shimmering with tears. I kiss her belly when she nods. Then, I take her hand and hold up her mother's wedding band. "She would have wanted you to have this one day. I know it. I don't have anything to offer but this. If you'll accept it."

Tears snake down her cheeks and her hand shakes. "Of course I accept it, silly. I love you. We belong together."

I pull her down into my lap and we kiss hard.

We kiss until the sun goes down.

And we kiss until it comes back up again.
We. Just. Kiss.

"Pepperoni pizza with mushrooms," she says groaning. "That would taste much better than rabbit."

She's definitely pregnant. Two months ago when I asked her to be my wife, we'd assumed she was. But now there's no denying it. Her tits are bigger and delicious as fuck. And, Jesus Christ, even her belly is a turn on. Small and round but most definitely carrying a child. She gets sick often and sleeps a lot but it all feels normal. The cravings though are hard. I hate denying her but I also don't want to burn through our supplies in case of emergencies.

"How about green beans?" I ask as I saunter over to the crevasse.

She claps her hands. "Really? We can really have some?"

I nod as I fetch the can. She's thrilled as hell over a can of green beans. It makes me feel guilty that I can't give her all the foods she wants all of the time. But I do sneak her a can of something—either fruits or vegetables—at least once a day because I know she needs the extra nutrients and meat isn't enough for our growing baby.

Once I cook the beans and offer her the entire pot to eat, she chirps happily about things she wants to make for the baby as she inhales the green beans. I don't focus much on what she's saying but how she's saying it. Her eyes are lit up with joy. A permanent smile is affixed on her pretty face. She's so fucking happy. I've never seen her this way. So free and in her element.

"You're beautiful," I blurt out, interrupting her.

Her cheeks burn pink. "Thank you."

I reach forward in my chair and finger her long hair. "I mean it. I can't stop looking at you."

She laughs. "You're not so bad to look at either."

When she launches into how she wants to lug some boxes back from the trailer, I get lost in staring at her. My mind drifts off to when we were packing that trailer.

"I'm bringing this." Sabrina drops a plastic tub in front of me. Her eyes are flickering with life for once.

"What's in it?" I ask, frowning. We're supposed to be bringing less junk and more supplies.

"Some memories of when the kids were small. Important papers. Stuff like that."

I want to tell her no but she hasn't asked to take any-thing. If this is important to her, we'll make room. It can col-lect dust in the wilderness like it collects dust here.

"Okay," I concede.

She leaves me and flits through our now nearly-empty house, back to bed no doubt. I'm loading the rest of the trailer tonight and we set out tomorrow. We didn't pack any furniture. Our plan is to live in the RV until I get the big cabin built on the top of the mountain. Once it's finished, I'll take the RV and trailer back to town to buy furnishings.

I put the plastic tub in the trailer along with about fifty other tubs. After I lock it up for the night, I head back inside. I'm sweating like a motherfucker so I peel off my shirt and head for the shower. Soon, showers like we're used to will be a thing of the past.

Music plays from Devon's room so I sneak up to check on her. I lean against the door frame and watch her. Her room is now empty aside from her bed and dresser that we've sold with the house. She's reading a survivalist book and twirling a lock of her blonde hair. I can't help but smile.

"What are you doing?"

She sits up and tosses the book onto the bed. "Learning how to suture wounds and which plants are poisonous. Question is, what are you doing?" Her gaze skims over my bare chest and I instantly regret taking off my shirt. Things have been weird since a few weeks ago when I took her to dinner. I lost my head that night and I'm desperately trying to regain control.

"Packed up the last of the boxes in the trailer. Got anything else that needs to get packed?"

She smiles. "Just me. Don't forget about me."

"I could never forget about you."

Both of us are silent for a moment.

"Dad..."

"Yeah?"

"I'm really excited about this." Her brows furrow together as she climbs out of the bed. "You're doing the right thing. For Mom. For us."

I hate that my stupid eyes skim over her nipples that poke out of her silky night shirt. Gritting my teeth, I force my gaze up to meet hers. She hugs me and doesn't even complain about my sweaty flesh.

the wild

"I love you," she tells me, her hot breath tickling my chest.

I let out a deep breath and stroke her silky blonde hair before kissing the top of her head. "I love you too, Pip."

"The wild. We're really doing it."

I hug her tighter. "We really are."

"Reed!" Devon screams from inside the cabin.

I abandon the wood I'm chopping and run inside, Buddy right on my heels. When I burst in, expecting the worst, I find her standing naked on the bed with both palms on her big round belly. We've guessed her to be about five or six months but we're not sure.

"Come feel," she tells me, her face bright and excited.

I stalk over to her and place my hands on her hard flesh. I'm frowning when something inside of her bumps my hand. Our eyes meet and I swear my heart stops beating in my fucking chest.

"Was that the baby?"

"No, it was the alien that took over my body," she teases.

I laugh but don't take my hands from her. I want to feel it move again. "This is the most amazing thing I've ever felt."

She stares at me thoughtfully. "Even more amazing than when you felt Drew and I in Mom's belly?"

Her words, so sudden and confusing, startle me. I step away as if my hands have been burned. Running my fingers through my hair, I back away from her.

"What's wrong?"

"I-I just remembered I never brought those boxes to you. I'll go fetch them now."

When she frowns and her lip wobbles, I stalk back over to her. I take her face in my hands and kiss the hell out of her. "I love you," I assure her. "I love our baby too. That was amazing, Dev."

Her smile is back but it doesn't reach her eyes. I wave to her and bolt outside. The warmer temps have melted off a lot of the snow. I'm boiling from the inside out. I tug off my sweaty shirt and tuck it into the back of my jeans as I stride back toward the trailer. It takes three trips of carrying two tubs each trip before I decide that's enough for the day. Devon is no longer sad as she excitedly points at where she wants them. I've been building her shelves and a cabinet to store things. We're quickly outgrowing our small space. Now that the warmer temperatures are here, I'm going to start on the extension.

I grab the big bucket we use for water and set off toward the river. It's the same trip I make at least once a day. I've worn a path down to the river banks. One day I'll build a small pier out here so we can have picnics and enjoy the sun without having to stay in the dirt. I'm just headed back and step into the clearing of our house when I hear it.

A voice.

Deep and manly.

A predator.

A motherfucking rapist.

Slinging my water bucket down, I grab the handiest object I can find which is my knife on my belt. I'm ready to gut the fucker.

"Whoa, fella. Calm down."

The voice is familiar. My eyes bore into the stranger. He pulls off a beanie and his obnoxiously long golden light brown hair tumbles out. Jade colored eyes pierce mine.

"Reed Jamison?"

I stiffen, searching for my long-slaughtered brain to slot the final piece into place. "Atticus Knox."

He lets out a slow breath, nodding. "Almost didn't recognize you there, man. The beard and shit." His eyes remain fixated on the knife that I've yet to put back into its sheath. Despite knowing the guy, my hackles are raised. I trust no one. The only person I trust is my Devon.

He's a bigger guy than me and that sets my teeth on edge. Back when I bought this land, we shared a few beers after the closing. Nice guy. Mid-thirties. Played football in college. Family owns more acreage in Alaska than all the other families combined.

But now…

He's a threat.

They all are.

"I just came out to check on you now that the snow is melted off some. You never showed up in town. I was sure you'd be back for supplies or something. Had my friends at the hardware store and the grocery store keep an eye out. Worried about you guys all winter. When I pulled up and saw what happened, I just knew you guys had been killed. But then I hiked down to the gorge and evidence was all over someone had been here. I'm so glad you made it," he says, his tone genuine.

Anger surges through me. "My wife was killed on impact."

Sorrow flickers in his eyes. "I'm so sorry. Your daughter?"

I clutch my knife tighter. Jealousy and protectiveness

explode inside of me. I don't want him asking about her or saying her name. "She's fine."

He lets out a breath of relief and scratches at his scruffy jaw. "You okay, man?"

Gritting my teeth, I shake my head. "You lied. You said no people were here. People. Are. Here."

He takes a step back. "Calm down now, Reed. That was something I came to warn you about. On my land we found at least fifty squatters this winter. Some are violent. They're fucking inbred." The word on his tongue has him making a sour face. "Did they hurt you?"

My jaw clenches. "They hurt *her*."

Understanding dawns on him and his face crumples. Sadness plagues his features. So maybe he isn't the enemy. "Fuck, man. How can I help?"

I swallow and shake my head. "I killed them. I fucking killed them."

He nods in approval. "Nobody cares about them. You won't go to prison."

Like I give a shit about prison.

"What do you want?" I ask, my tone harsh.

He's still staring at me as though I'm a wild bear that he needs to calm. "I just want to help you guys. Do you need any supplies? Medicine? Food?" His gaze flits to the cabin. "I see you were resourceful in making shelter."

My thoughts flip to Devon. With her having a baby soon, we will need supplies. I can't be stupid and run off my only tie to the outside world who can help us. Reluctantly, I nod. "Actually, we could use some things. You staying for supper?"

He smiles, his teeth perfect and white, unlike those fucking savages. "Of course."

chapter sixteen

DEVON

I GET LOST IN GOING THROUGH MY BOX OF BOOKS. THE heroes on the covers are all handsome but not as intense or soul-burning hot like Dad. Still, I'm eager to read them. There isn't much to do out here for fun. Reading is fun and I can't wait to pass that down to our child. I'm a little saddened I don't have any books for the little thing. Perhaps I'll write my baby some stories.

I pick up my notebook and write a children's tale about a fierce man who battles scary bears. The man's name is Reed and he saves the princess in the end. I'm smiling as I scribble down the story. That is until I hear it.

Voices.

Panic clutches my throat and I whimper. It's too dangerous to climb onto the table to look out the small window in my very pregnant state. Dad's voice is one of them and he doesn't seem alarmed or afraid. Still, I am worried. Quickly, I pull on my yoga pants I have to wear low on my hips—they're one of the few pieces of clothing I can wear—and then hunt for one of Dad's shirts. Everything of mine is too tight. Once I'm dressed and have my boots and coat on, I snatch up the shotgun and then I slowly open the door. With the quietness of a mouse, I creep around the side of the house. Dad stands with his back to the cabin talking to a man.

The man has wild golden brown hair and smiles as he talks to my father. He's not holding any weapons. I'm still afraid because he's taller and wider shouldered than Dad. If he wanted to hurt him, I'm afraid he could.

Chick-chuck!

I load the slug into the shotgun, ready to fire.

Dad jerks around and the guy gapes at me.

"Wh-What do you want?" I demand, my voice wobbling with fear.

"I'm not here to hurt you," the man says, his palms up. "I came to see if you needed any supplies."

"This is Atticus Knox. The fella I bought the land from," Dad says in a soothing tone. It calms me marginally so. But the fact Dad still has the knife in his tight grip doesn't chase away my fear completely.

"Supplies?"

"Anything you need. I can fetch it and be back in another week or two," Atticus assures me.

"Why would you help us?" I question, anger and distrust dripping in my voice. "What do you get out of it?"

"Money," Dad answers for him. "I have some in the safe that survived the crash in the trailer."

"If I get you a list, you'll get me what I need?" My mind begins to whir about all the things we'll need for the baby.

So maybe I shouldn't shoot this man. He doesn't look like the rapists from before. I shudder and meet his gaze with a feral one of my own.

He swallows. "Anything. Devon, right?"

My nod is clipped. "If you try to hurt us, I'll shoot you," I threaten.

Atticus smiles and it's warm. "I understand. I only want to help."

Despite the warmer temps, it's not completely spring yet. A cool breeze from the north whips at us. The sun will set soon and I know it'll be cold tonight.

"Are you staying for dinner?"

Both he and Dad nod.

Then, Atticus speaks again. "I thought I'd stay for a few days. Show you both some things about surviving out here that will be useful. Then I'll be on my way."

I finally lower the gun. "Okay."

Dad winks at me and my heart warms. I beam back at him.

Atticus is impressed with the inside of our cabin and the fact that we utilized the cave as well. He marvels over the fireplace we made and the furniture. The bloodstains on the quilts make him look away though. For me, they're a constant reminder of Peach, who I refuse to forget.

I stay bundled up in my big coat despite the warmth. My baby is safe from his leering eyes. But eventually I start to sweat. He and Dad chat easily sharing a bottle of whiskey Atticus brought with him. Every so often, Atticus regards me with soft, sad eyes. I don't want his gaze on me.

"You hardly touched your stew," Dad observes, a frown marring his handsome face.

"I'm not hungry."

His jaw ticks but he says no more on the matter. I continue to write down my list of things I need while they chat and laugh. It irritates me that this man is in our home. I don't want any man besides Dad here.

"There's one can left of the mixed fruit you love so much with the extra maraschino cherries," Dad says, his face still frowning. The worry is written all over his features. He wants me to eat for the baby.

With a sigh, I toss down my notebook and shed the hot coat. When I stand to go fetch the fruit—because just talking about it has my stomach growling—I catch Atticus staring at my pregnant belly.

Horror.

That is the only way to describe the look on his face.

I clutch it protectively as I pass by him to the cave. I can feel his unwanted eyes on me as I grab my fruit. When I pass back by him, he's frowning.

"I'll need stuff for the baby," I tell him pointedly.

He swallows and nods. "Write down what you need."

I burrow under the covers to hide and eat my fruit in peace as I scribble down items. Eventually, I fall asleep because Dad won't let that man hurt me. But just in case, I clutch onto the shotgun behind me.

I wake with my heart in my throat as someone kisses my bare stomach. My body relaxes to find Dad's warm brown eyes staring down at me. He helps me pull off my shirt and then removes the rest of my clothing. His mouth finds mine for a chaste kiss and I can taste the whiskey on him. I want to suck it off his tongue.

"Did he leave?"

My eyes dart to the door and I relax seeing our lock in place.

"Camping in his tent outside just inside the fence," he tells me, his mouth kissing down to my much larger breasts.

Desire pools in my core and I whimper when he sucks my nipple hard. My belly is large and in the way but it never stops him from getting what he wants. Me. He's clever about positioning me in ways that aren't awkward or hurtful.

His palms rub over the swell of my stomach in a possessive, reverent way. He kisses the flesh and whispers to our baby. My heart melts each time he does it. By the time his mouth latches onto my clit, I'm so horny I can't think straight. Being pregnant means I want sex all the time. Dad is happy to oblige.

He sucks and nibbles and teases until I'm thrashing with need. I grip his hair and beg for more.

"Please…" My moan is loud. "I need you."

"Come for me, baby. I'll fuck you as soon as you come."

His words have their intended affect because I start trembling. When he sucks one last hard time, I lose myself to a glorious orgasm. I've barely quit shaking when he sits back on his heels. He grabs my hips and hauls me closer.

"You're so beautiful," he murmurs, his palm rubbing over my stomach. "I love you."

I smile, ready to return the sentiment, but then he's driving into me at this odd angle that only seems to work well when pregnant. His cock hits me deep and shudders wrack through me.

"Oh, God." I'm helpless as he holds my hips up and bucks against me. All I can do is sit up on my elbows and watch him. I can't see where he's entering me because of my large stomach but I can see the way his chest muscles flex with each movement. I lick my lips and practically drool over the way his biceps bulge as he holds me up. His dark hair hangs in his eyes, dripping with sweat, and his full lips are parted as he fucks.

He's my beast.

Delicious and gorgeous and wild.

At this angle, I lose control and orgasm without warning. This causes him to grunt out my name before draining his own release inside of me. He pulls out and stares at me with a domineering glint in his eyes.

I am his.

He owns me.

And I'd never argue that because I love being his.

I'm safe with him.

Always.

The next morning is awkward. Atticus is no longer looking at me in a sad way but instead with pity. I watch him, his jaw tightening, as if he's physically keeping words in. It makes me curious. Why the sudden change?

Since the weather is nice, we all three go down to the river. Atticus has a net and he's convinced he can catch us some fish. The water is icy-cold but it's Dad who wants to use the net. We stand on the river banks watching my father wade out into the chilly river cursing about how cold it is.

"You're pregnant." Atticus's words are clipped and low.

I frown and look over at him. "I am."

"How old are you?"

Glaring, I huff. "Seventeen. How old are you?"

"Thirty-six. Can I ask you something?"

Nervously, I twist my wedding band around my finger. Something tells me I won't like his line of questioning. His jade-green eyes dart to my fingers and he curses under his breath.

"Is Reed the father?" he asks, his voice husky and disgusted.

"He is. Do you have a problem with that?" I challenge.

Our eyes meet and he frowns. "That's incest, sweetheart."

My lip curls up. "It's none of your business."

He grumbles and crosses his giant arms over his chest. "It is my business if I think you were coerced. I think you're a little brainwashed, Devon. Last night, I heard you two. Fucking like wild animals. That's not normal." He swallows and shakes his head. "Sleeping with your father is not normal. Not to mention, it's highly fucking illegal in the state of Alaska."

Dad hoots that he almost caught a fish. I beam at him and hold my thumb up before regarding Atticus.

"The laws don't matter here. We love each other. This is our home." I clutch my stomach and smile. "This is our baby. We're happy."

"You'll be happy until the moment that baby comes out," he tells me in a low voice. "Don't you know what incest does to people?"

My blood runs cold because I don't know what it does to people. "What do you mean?" I hate that I'm entertaining him by asking questions on the matter.

He scrubs at his cheek. "Birth defects."

Panic nearly stops my heart in my chest. "Wh-What?"

"Blood relatives who reproduce are extremely likely to give birth to a child with issues. Most of them mental issues but some can be physical. I've lived out here in the wilderness long enough to see firsthand what incest does to families." He pauses and looks at me with sadness flickering in his eyes. "The squatters who hurt you, did they seem normal?"

I shiver and stare down at the rocks at my feet. They were wild and lost. No humanity in their eyes. Madness lived within them.

Will my baby be mad too?

Bile rises in my throat and the world seems to spin. Atticus clutches my elbow.

"Are you okay?" he demands, concern in his tone.

"I think I'm going to be sick."

I've barely spilled the words out before Dad comes splashing back. With cold, wet arms, he scoops me into his grip. Tears burn in my eyes as he carries me back to the cabin. Atticus stays outside as Dad helps me undress and puts me under the covers.

"What can I do to make you feel better?" he questions as he strokes away the hair from my clammy forehead.

Tell me everything is going to be okay.

Pinky promise that we're not going to have a baby with problems.

A sob catches in my throat but I swallow it down. I don't want him to see me upset about our baby. Despite the worry niggling at me, I still want our baby. We made this baby together out of love.

"Get some rest, Pip," he says, a soft smile on his lips.

Two long weeks pass by with Atticus overstaying his welcome. Sure, he's great at teaching Dad some new survival techniques and they're quite chummy which warms my heart to see Dad happy, but I'm unnerved. I can't stop obsessing over my child. As Dad chops firewood, Atticus takes the moment to talk to me again. I've been avoiding him so the fact that we're alone stresses me out.

"What?" I snap.

He sits at the table and reads through my list. "Do you want me to bring a book about inbreeding?"

A choked sound escapes me. "No."

"Look, Devon. If you want to leave, I can get you out of here. All you have to do is say the words. I'll go back to town and get the police involved. You're underage. They call that statutory rape. Are you familiar with that term?"

I scoff. "He did not rape me!"

He holds his hands up in defense. "I understand how

you, having gone through what you did, would see it that way. But he did take advantage of you in the wilderness. He shouldn't be having sex with you every goddamn night." He grits his teeth together as if he's disgusted. "He shouldn't have gotten you pregnant."

"Just leave us alone," I beg. "Don't get anyone involved. It's our business. We're happy."

He frowns. "I'll be back in about two weeks with the supplies. I'll bring you some reading material on the subject. When I come back, all you have to do is give me the word. We'll leave and I'll get you the help you need. There are therapists who can help and—"

"Get me my stuff but I don't need the other things you speak of. If my baby has problems, I'll deal with it then. You're overstepping, Atticus. Now please back the hell away from us." My gaze is venom-filled.

He sighs and nods. "It's never too late to change your mind."

"Duly noted," I seethe.

chapter seventeen

REED

WITH ATTICUS GONE, I CAN BREATHE EASIER. I didn't like the looks he gave me when he thought I wasn't aware. Disgust and disapproval. He knows my daughter and I are having a baby. That we have sex and love each other. But with my warning glares, he knows not to involve anyone. I'll kill anyone who tries to take her away from me, and that's a motherfucking promise.

He's been gone for days now. When I told him about the girl at the shack, he wanted to go check on her. I gave him directions and that should be the last we'll see of him until he returns with many much-needed items.

Devon is in a weird mood—has been ever since he showed up. I'd thought she'd snap out of it but she's lost inside her head. I've given her time but I'm losing my patience.

"What's wrong?" I ask after a long hard day of building the frame on our cabin extension.

She furiously stitches on another pelt to her baby blanket. "Nothing."

Liar.

When she was a kid, I always knew when she was lying. Her lips would twitch on one side. With a sigh, I peel off my shirt and kick off my shoes. I'm sweaty and in desperate need of a bath. As if sensing this, she abandons her blanket to prepare some water for me. I sit in my chair and she silently begins washing me.

"Why won't you look at me? What's going on in that pretty head of yours?"

She shrugs and runs the rag low on my stomach. It irritates me that she's blowing me off. I grip her wrist and haul her to me so that our faces are close. Her blue eyes are wide with surprise.

"Sit down and tell me what the fuck is going on," I demand.

She swallows and throws the rag into the bowl with a splash. When she attempts to primly sit on the edge of my knee, I growl before pulling her to straddle my hips facing me. The shirt she's wearing stretches over her stomach that has our growing baby inside. Her legs are bare and her pussy is free. Just the way I love having her. A shiver runs through her when I tug off her shirt so I can see all of what's mine.

"I love seeing you pregnant with our child," I praise as my palms cup her big tits and even bigger stomach. "It makes me want to put many more babies inside of you."

When I lift my gaze to grin at her, she's frowning.

"Atticus told me incest could lead to birth defects," she blurts out. Her bottom lip wobbles and tears well in her eyes. "What if something is wrong with our baby?"

Anger surges inside of me. I didn't realize that mother-fucker put horrible ideas inside of her when I wasn't paying attention. If he were here right now, I'd run my fist right through his nose. He's causing problems that aren't his to worry about.

"Our baby will be fine," I vow as I try to take her pinky.

She swats it away. "But how do you know that?" Furious tears roll down her pink cheeks and splash her tits.

"Because we've endured too much to have something ruin our happiness. Our baby will be just perfect. You shouldn't worry about that shit," I snap.

Her lip snarls up in fury. "I have to worry!" Her voice is shrill and on edge. "This is our baby! Don't you fucking care?!"

I grab her jaw in my brutal grip and jerk her to me so that our noses touch. "I. Fucking. Care. Don't ever accuse me of not caring, goddammit. I've cared for you since the day I held you in my arms. Why the hell would I stop now?" I seethe.

She sobs as she tries to break free from my hold. I'll be damned if I let her go. "You knew this could happen," she accuses. "You fucked me knowing we could have a messed-up baby."

"Do not talk to me that way," I spit out. "This wasn't some goddamn plan to ruin your life. Jesus, Devon! Who the hell do you think I am?"

She's pissed and hysterical. Her fingernails claw at my wrist until I let her jaw go. Then, she beats me with her tiny fists. When my lip splits open from her knuckle, I've had enough. I reach behind her and whip her round ass. This only makes her lose her shit more.

"I hate you! You did this on purpose! You knew!" Her sobs are maniacal as she slaps and claws at me.

I smack her ass again. "I didn't do anyfuckingthing on purpose!" I roar. "The only damn thing I'm guilty of is loving you when I shouldn't!"

She falls against my chest, her entire body shaking as she cries. I wrap my arms around her and kiss her hair. Our sweet, perfect baby rolls in her belly between us. Pride surges through me.

This.

Baby.

Is.

Perfect.

I feel it down to my toes.

"I swear to you that everything is going to be okay, baby," I whisper.

She sniffles as she holds out her pinky. I grab it without hesitation and I hold onto it. My promises don't break.

Not to Devon.

Devon is my everything.

"I don't like him," Devon tells me as she helps me collect river rocks to use for the fireplace I plan on building. Buddy has gone exploring—hunting if I had to guess—so he's nowhere to be found. That dog gets braver by the day.

"You don't have to like him, Pip. But he's bringing us supplies we'll need for the baby. Have you thought of any names?"

Her head bows and she shrugs. "Maybe. I don't want to get too excited."

Reaching forward, I tilt her chin up with my fingers. "Why not?"

"Because…" Her nostrils flare and her lip wobbles. "I don't want to have named it and then it have something wrong with it. If this baby dies too, I won't be able to take it, Reed."

I clench my teeth. When Atticus comes back, he and I are going to have a long discussion about him filling her head with all this stupid shit that worries her from sun up to sun down.

"Our baby is safe and healthy. We feel it moving around all the time. It won't be long and I'll prove it to you," I assure her.

She's frowning when she freezes. "Dad…"

Slowly, I turn around and a bear swats at the water trying to catch a fish not fifty yards away. I pull out my .45 and point toward the cabin. "Devon, go."

Her fingers clutch at my shirt. "No. I won't leave you."

With her big belly brushing against my back, I'm overwhelmed with the desire to protect her and our child at all costs. We remain still and quiet as not to alert the bear. But after some time, it stands on its hind legs and sniffs the air. It turns and sees us, a low growl in its throat. This time, I don't wait, I stalk it. With my arm raised and unmoving, I fire at it.

Pop! Pop! Pop!

All three shots pierce its skull. The bear collapses into the water. It's then, I see two cubs playing in the trees beyond the shore.

"Devon, you need to go home. I need to do something you're not going to like," I mutter before gritting my teeth.

"What—" Her breath catches when she sees them. "No. Dad, no. They're little. We can keep them as pets and teach them."

I turn and clutch the side of her neck. My lips find hers and I kiss her softly. "I'm sorry, baby, but no. It doesn't work that way out here. These are wild animals."

She starts to cry but I don't have time to coddle her. These animals, if let go, will grow into beasts that will hurt my girl and our baby.

I stride over to them and with two pops, I end them.

I'm sorry, Pip.

The days turn into weeks and Devon and I are both on edge knowing Atticus will arrive soon. With his return, it brings both excitement and stress. If he sells us out, he might even bring the law.

I hope they bring firepower because I will not go down without a fight.

This life is ours.

We do what we want.

Devon's stomach is gigantic. Tiny silvery marks line the sides like someone painted stripes on her. She's never been one to be vain and hasn't mentioned them. But I love looking at them. They're evidence her body is stretching and expanding to accommodate our child. She's tiny and there's no doubt this kid is going to be big like his father.

This worries me but I vowed to her that I wouldn't let it consume me. We'll deal with it when the time comes. Until then, we cherish each day together.

Each morning, I laze around later and later because it's the time of day when our little cub is the most active. Her stomach bulges and moves while she sleeps. It's our quiet moment, just me and the baby, alone. I tell the little angel what a great mother Devon will be. How she's fierce and brave and beautiful. And that they will be smart just like her.

"My back hurts," Devon murmurs, her voice thick with sleep.

"Sit up and let me massage it."

It takes some effort but she manages to pull herself upright. She sweeps her long messy hair to the side and bares her naked back to me. From behind, you'd never be able to tell she was pregnant. With firm motions, I knead her lower back muscles. Carrying this child is hard on her body. I do my best to alleviate her pain whenever possible.

Soon, the massage turns sexual as it always does. When we touch, our bodies seem to thrum with an electric pulse that draws us together. Her head tilts back and she leans against me. I wrap my arms around her to touch her breasts that are large as they prepare to feed our baby. Her nipples are erect and sometimes leak with a liquid that I think has something to do with breastmilk. We aren't for sure but I like to taste it. I like to taste all of her.

Sliding my hand along her ass crack, I cup her from beneath. My fingers slip easily into her wet pussy. It feels hotter and tighter than usual. She must enjoy her body's new physiological changes because as soon as my fingers are inside her, she starts whimpering and shaking. I fuck her hole with two fingers until they're soaked with her juices. Then, I urge her to lie back down on her side while I continue to massage her insides with my hand. The moment she comes, soft and breathy, I slide my fingers out and guide my cock inside of her. Her body grips mine in a way that has me losing all sense of reality.

"I love you," I murmur, my hot breath on her shoulder.

"I love you too." Her words are garbled and stolen by her pleasure.

I slip my wet finger between the crack of her ass and tease her puckered hole. She's used to me taking her here often and her body is relaxed as I push one and then the other finger inside her. I like when she's filled up with me in every way possible.

"Oh, God," she whimpers.

"Come all over my cock, baby girl. I want you to make such a fucking mess."

My words, like usual, turn her on. Her body trembles and quakes. I know the moment she loses herself to an orgasm because hot juices soak my cock. Now that she's pregnant, her body gets so much more aroused and she drenches me every time. The first time it happened, she was embarrassed, but when I licked it all away and praised her on how delicious she was, she stopped worrying.

My nuts seize up in pleasure and I groan as my cum surges inside of her. Her body is tight around mine and she's still moaning. I buck against her until my cock is drained and softening. Then, I slip my fingers out of her before easing my cock out. We make a mess and I love it.

"I think I'm going to go down to the river and haul some more rocks up here," I tell her, my lips pressing kisses on her shoulders. "Then I thought we could—"

Bang! Bang! Bang!

Buddy barks from the corner of the cabin he'd been sleeping in and his hackles raise as he growls at the door.

I jolt up, my dripping dick flopping against my leg and lunge for my shotgun. I push it out in front of me and point at the door. "Who's there?" I bellow.

Chick-chuck!

I load the shotgun and then someone speaks.

"Whoa, Reed. Don't go blowing off my head. It's me, Atticus."

Buddy starts wagging his tail and barks happily. I look over my shoulder at Devon. Her brows are pulled together in a frown.

"Get dressed and eat breakfast, baby," I say to her and then to him. "I'll be right out!"

I kneel before her and kiss her mouth hard. "Don't let it bother you. It's you and me. Nothing will tear apart our love, okay?"

She swallows and nods, her eyes flickering with trust. I grab her pinky with mine and she smiles. Once I'm dressed, I trot outside. Buddy follows after me and runs off into the thicket, no doubt after his breakfast. Atticus leans against a tree wearing a scowl.

"Supplies are up there. It's going to take us all day to unload the trailer and haul each item down here," he says, his jaw clenching.

"Let's get on it then." My tone is frigid.

He hands me a protein bar. Instead of eating it, I run

it inside to gift it to Devon. I steal one more kiss. "We're going to unload. You rest, beautiful."

When I get back out, he shakes his head and hands me another bar. "Eat this one," he grunts. "You'll need your energy. We have a long day ahead of us."

Together, in silence, we hike up the side of the mountain about halfway between the cabin and the shack where I left the girl. The trek isn't as steep through here but it's still one Devon would never be able to make in her pregnant state. When we finally reach the top and I see his big Ford-250 with a trailer attached, I can't help but smile. It's filled with supplies we desperately need. More ammunition and guns. Dishes and silverware. Medical supplies and medicines. Baby items. Books. Food. So much stuff that it's going to be difficult getting it all down. But the look on Devon's face will be worth it.

Before we even start, I cross my arms over my chest and level him with a glare. It's not even noon and the sun is hot today. I could probably even take Devon swimming for a bit if she were up to it.

"We need to talk."

His brow lifts and he leans his hip against the truck. "About you fucking and knocking up your daughter. Let's talk."

I grit my teeth and fist my hands. "It's not so fucking black and white."

He grunts. "Whatever, man. It's your business. As long as she's not here as your fucked-up prisoner, I'll do my best to ignore it. But know that it doesn't sit right with me. When we met at the closing, all you could do was talk about how proud you were of your daughter. How she was going to go off to college in a couple of years and was going to do great shit. The look on your face was one a normal father should look like when talking about his daughter. Fast forward to now…" He shakes his head and his nostrils flare. "She's pregnant with your kid. Scared of her own shadow. And you two fuck all hours of the day. It's sick, man. Not just illegal but fucking immoral. You've taken advantage of the fact that she's young and doesn't know about this shit. *But I know*. I know that incest can fuck up your kids."

I growl and he shrugs.

"I'm just telling you my stance. But so help me if she even shows an inkling of wanting to leave here, I'll snap her up and haul her back to town. Drop her confused ass on Child Protective Services' doorstep. I'll send the cops back to deal with you." His green eyes narrow at me. "The only reason I haven't done that shit is because she seems happy and severely dependent on you. I'm not a home-wrecker. The last thing I need on my conscience is de-stroying a family that wanted to be together."

"You take her and I'll hunt you down," I vow through gritted teeth. "I'll fucking gut you and slit the throats of anyone who tries to take her from me."

He shakes his head and opens the back gate of the trailer. "I get your need to protect her. She's your daugh-ter. But I'm just warning you that I'll take my chances with your psychotic ass if it means protecting her from some-thing she doesn't want."

I grab a crate of canned goods and level him with a serious stare. "And I'm just warning you that my psychotic ass will protect her from anyone who thinks they know what's better for my daughter than I do. Things are different out here, Atticus. I'm not the man you sold this land to. I am not your friend. The only friend I have is the one carrying my child down there. So don't get any wild ideas. I will stop at nothing to protect her. Fucking nothing."

chapter eighteen

DEVON

THEY KEEP BRINGING MORE AND MORE STUFF. So much stuff we have nowhere to put it. It gets stacked on top of the tubs in one corner that we'd brought from the crash site. I don't like Atticus in our home, nor do I like the way he tries to pass on secret messages with his eyes. I simply don't like him trying to mess up my happiness. When he drops a box down in front of me full of new books I haven't read, a squeal of excitement escapes me. They head off to unload more crap and I dive into my box marveling over the new romance stories. I pick up one book and frown in confusion. It doesn't look like romance. As soon as I read the title, my heart rate thunders in my chest.

Incest in the Wild.

I throw it away from me as if it's covered in poison. Hot tears well in my eyes and on instinct, I clutch my huge stomach as if to protect my baby. For what feels like forever,

I sob as I stare in horror at the book. When my tears finally dry, anger takes over.

How dare he keep sticking his nose where he shouldn't?

With a choked, furious sound, I snap the book up and ready myself to throw it in the fire. But before I can fling it away, a festering begins deep inside of me. Maybe I should read it just so I know what I'm up against. What to expect. I'm going to love this child no matter what but I feel like I owe it to him or her to see what we'll be dealing with.

I swallow down bile in my throat as I open the book.

Page after page, I greedily read up the knowledge. What I learn disgusts and terrifies me. I'm afraid, more so than before. So many complications. So many potential mental problems.

When the door flies open, I screech and guiltily toss the book back into the box. Dad takes one look at my tear-stained face and rushes to my side. His arms are sweaty but protective. He searches my body with his palms as if he can find what's hurting me.

It's my heart.

It aches and bleeds for our future.

He can't fix it.

Only God can.

And for the terrible things we've done, I'm afraid God has turned his back on us.

"Baby," he coos. "Tell me what's wrong."

I accept his deep kiss and my heart calms some. Dad will do anything to protect me and the baby. He loves us deeply. I'm letting Atticus and his stupid book get to me. Together, Dad and I can make this work, no matter what happens.

"Nothing. Pregnancy hormones. I think I'm just too hot and sweaty," I say with a ragged sigh.

His mouth finds my neck and he kisses me. "I'm going to take a break to take you swimming. As much as I'd love to see you naked always, I don't want that motherfucker seeing you. Can you wear your black swimsuit? You know I love that one on you. I always have."

I turn to meet his heat-filled gaze. He admitted to being aroused by me before we left to come out here in our hot tub. It makes me wet thinking that he got an erection simply from looking at me. When he was married to Mom. When those thoughts were a lot more dangerous there than here.

"Okay," I agree with a smile.

His eyes burn with need—a need I wish I could fulfill, but we have a stupid, nosy visitor.

Twenty minutes later, we're headed to the river. Unfortunately for us, Atticus tags along. I think he's watching and waiting for an opportunity to talk to me alone again. I refuse to let that happen. As Dad carries me into the river wearing boxers only, I cling to him. Maybe if we ignore Atticus, he'll go away.

"Oh my God!" I shriek. "It's so cold!"

It's freezing, but my pregnant self is already so hot all the time and it's barely spring. We dip under the rushing water and I moan in relief. After an entire winter of sponge baths, it's nice to get submerged. We bathe at first with some soap and shampoo. Then, we spend hours lazing in the river. Atticus eventually sits on the river banks and rummages in his backpack.

"I need you," I whisper to Dad as I wrap my thighs

around his waist. My belly is squished between us but I can still kiss him.

He doesn't argue as we make out. Simply pulls his hard cock out. I help him by moving my swimsuit to the side. When he pushes into me, I cry out in pleasure. Atticus shakes his head and refuses to look at us. I float back with my legs wrapped around Dad and lose myself to the sensations. His palms greedily tear at my top until I'm free for him to maul. My breasts are soon in his mouth as he sucks and bites at the flesh. It makes my pussy clench around him, desperate to come.

Like animals, we fuck in the river.

Two savages.

Wild and free.

Bound by love and our growing offspring.

"What are you going to do with those three bearskins?" Atticus asks as we roast some hot dogs he brought in his ice chest. Their savory scent has my mouth watering. After nearly a year of meat and the occasional canned fruit or vegetable, I'm ravenous for the stuff he brought. Something as simple as the grapes in his pack seem too good to be true. Both men laughed when I claimed the bag for my own.

"Devon wants to make more carpet for the expansion," Dad tells him as he pulls my hot dog off the stick and presses it into a bun. He hands it to me and I don't fool with condiments. I simply devour it.

"I could help you with the extension," Atticus tells him. "With the two of us, it shouldn't take any more than a couple of weeks."

They lose themselves to conversation about measurements and design but I frown as I eat the rest of my food. I thought he'd deliver our supplies and then leave. Unfortunately, he's back to wearing out his welcome. He's long since stopped side-eyeing me. Ever since Dad fucked me in the river within earshot, Atticus has seemed to give up on his quest to save me from a situation I don't need saving from. I'm thankful for the supplies he brought us but I still am unhappy about the book. So when he suggests sleeping in the cabin with us, I screech in protest.

"No," Dad tells him firmly. "You have your tent. I'm sorry but she doesn't feel safe around men."

Atticus shrugs as if it doesn't bother him. He didn't want to sleep in the cabin. He just wanted to stress me out.

"What happened today?" Dad asks. "I know something happened."

Guilt rises in my throat and I try to turn away from him. "It's stupid. Nothing."

He pulls me onto my back and hooks his thigh over mine to keep me from rolling away. His massive palm covers my lower belly. The baby nudges him and we both smile for a moment, distracted from our conversation.

"It was Atticus. He said something to you, didn't he?" His brows are furrowed together in concern. Sometimes I try to remember him back at the house in San Francisco. Was he always this good looking? Without all the facial hair and feral glares, was he still hot?

My mind drifts to one of the nights leading up to our arrival here. When we camped out somewhere in Canada along the way.

"Your turn," Dad says as he draws a card. It's pouring down rain and I wish we could go to the campground pool. Instead, we're stuck inside while Mom sleeps. We've played more card games than I can count. With a yawn, I stretch my legs out under the table and rest them on top of his thighs.

I frown at my cards as I decide what I'm going to play. Dad sets his hand down and starts massaging my bare feet in his lap. I bite on my bottom lip as I try to focus on what cards to put down but I can't ignore the way excitement seems to pulsate from how he's touching me. It kind of tickles when he kneads the bottom of my feet but mostly it feels good. I like that his hands are giant compared to my small feet. He leans his head back while he waits but continues to rub my feet.

I take the moment to stare at him over my cards. His Adam's apple protrudes from his throat with his head leaned back. The grey T-shirt he wears fits him well and showcases his lean yet fit body. His dark hair is wild and messy on top of his head.

A smile plays at my lips.

We're finally headed to the great outdoors. We'll get to

do this stuff all the time. No stress. No school. No work. No worries. Normally, I detest my mother's behavior but right now I'm thankful she gives us so many moments alone.

"Mmm," I let out a surprised moan. His hands on my feet feel too good.

His head jerks back up and his stare bores a hole through me. I frown when he clenches his jaw as though he's angry, but he doesn't let me go. It's awkward staring at him but I refuse to look away. I love his undivided attention. When his fingertips slide up from my feet, brushing along my ankle bones under the bottoms of my jeans, I gasp in surprise. It feels intimate with his fingers on my lower legs beneath my jeans.

I'm still staring at him, admiring his ruggedly handsome face when he clears his throat.

"I need a beer. You want anything?"

I pull my feet away. "I'll get it, Dad. Stay put."

He flashes me a relieved smile that I don't understand when I bounce off to get us something to drink. I pop open a beer for him and set it on the table. And then, not-so-innocently, I walk over to my bag on the sofa and rummage around for some more comfortable clothes. I can feel his stare on me as he sips his beer.

I unbutton my jeans and push them down my thighs. Over my shoulder, I flash him a smile. "I need my yoga pants," I tell him as if that's the most normal reason in the world for a girl to undress in front of her father.

He takes another swallow and gives me a nod. His gaze tears from mine but as soon as I turn back, I can feel it on me. I'm slow in my movements as I kick off my jeans and then bend to pick them up. My panties are wet and this is probably sick but right now I'm pretending this trip is just for us. I always feel so safe and connected to him.

"Actually," I say with a breathy laugh. "It's hot. I think I'll wear shorts."

I peel off my hoodie and toss it away. I'm standing in a tank top and my panties in front of my dad. He doesn't argue or get on to me. He doesn't say a word. My nipples are hard because this feels dirty and wrong but I like it. I find the shortest pair of skintight cotton shorts I own and slide those up my hips. Once I'm dressed, I turned to catch him averting his gaze. I walk over to the fridge and grab myself a beer too just to rile Dad up.

When I return, we're quiet as we finish our card game. I prop my right foot back on his thigh and he absently rubs at it and my leg as far up as my knee. I'm so turned on by Dad's innocent touches that I know I'm going to get off to-night once they've gone to bed.

The hours tick by and we play a card game neither of us are interested in. He eventually gets up and rolls out the sofa bed for me. I stare at his lean body as he moves. I'm becom-ing unhealthily obsessed with staring at him.

"Don't go to bed yet," I murmur as I stand. I'm desper-ate to keep him here with me. "I'll read to you. Alaskan wil-derness boring facts. It'll be fun."

He turns and glances toward his room before looking down at me. Indecision wars in his eyes. A month ago, he'd have sat down without hesitation. Something is up with him.

"Please," I beg. "I'm bored. You entertain me."

A smile tugs at one corner of his lips. "Fine. Bore me until I fall asleep."

He stretches out on the bed and pats the blankets. With a grin that matches his, I crawl in next to him. He lies on his side and I stay on my back. I grab the book from the floor and begin reading out loud to him. His breathing eventually evens out as he falls asleep. I turn toward him and selfishly stare at him. While sleeping, he's younger than his forty years. He could easily pass for thirty. I let my fingertips whisper over his shoulder and up to his jaw. Dad and I have always been affectionate but this feels different. Taboo, maybe. He doesn't know I'm touching him in a wanting, intimate way. If he woke up, he might be angry. Eventually, a big yawn has me sleepy. I curl up against his warm chest and nearly squeal with delight when his arm wraps around me in a possessive sleepy hug. I fall asleep almost instantly.

"Devon, baby, talk to me." His voice is exactly the same. Concerned and caring. Full of love. We're the same two people—just a whole bunch of crap happened between then and now.

I open my eyes, blinking away my memory, and smile at him. "I love you."

His features soften and he kisses my mouth. "I love you. You know this."

"Before we ever came on this trip, my feelings for you had started to evolve. More than how a girl adores her father. Deeper. Darker. Forbidden. Do you think had we not come out here it would have happened anyway?" I ask, my voice soft.

189

His eyes narrow as he considers my question. "I don't know."

Lies.

The guilt on his face tells me it would have.

"Dad," I smirk. "I mean, Reed. Tell me. Would it have happened?"

He swallows and stares off in a daze. "I was pretty horrified when I touched you that night. But the more I thought about it, the more I was secretly glad it happened. I imagine that at the rate we were going, something may have happened between us. Your mother was pushing us together whether she realized it or not. We were both desperate for her love and affection and when she denied us, we turned to each other." He grunts and meets my gaze with shame in his eyes. "It's horrible, Devon. We were having the beginnings of feelings no father and daughter should have for each other. Had they been one-sided, it would have been easier to deny. But we both were falling in too deep. I'm sorry I'm a pedophile of a father but I'm not sorry about us. This baby. Our sexual relationship. Our love. All the components make for one messy design but it's one I'm happy with nonetheless, no matter the consequences."

His ability to throw everything out the window for me warms my heart. Decision calms me to my core. I sit up and rummage through the box. When I hand him the book, he growls. I turn to face him and straddle his hips.

"I want to burn it."

His features darken. "You sure?" I can feel him growing hard between my legs.

"Now."

Without hesitation, he tosses the book straight into the fireplace and together we watch it catch fire. I lift up and accept his thick cock into my receptive body that belongs only to him.

While we fuck like father and daughter shouldn't but do, we watch the damn incest book burn to dust.

chapter nineteen

REED

ATTICUS, WHILE I WAS PISSED AT HIM AT FIRST, HAS become a good friend. I know he hates what Devon and I have. In fact, he strongly advises against it any chance he gets. But he also helps us. Instead of dumping the supplies and leaving, he's stayed for nearly three weeks helping me with the addition. With another strong, able body, we're able to fly through it. Each day Devon grows bigger and more miserable. At one point, she dragged everything from the cave and now spends a lot of time lying on the cool stone. We don't have a good timetable but we know she could give birth any day. I'm thrilled and fucking terrified.

"I'm going to go check on Eve and then I'll come back in a month to check on you guys. I'll bring stuff you might need and if you need more, let me know then." He shoulders his backpack and scrubs at his face.

"Eve?" a growl rumbles in my chest. "Who the fuck is Eve?"

His jaw clenches. "The girl. In the shack."

I'm surprised she's still alive.

"You're going to take her to town? Call Child Protective Services?" I ask.

He frowns and shakes his head. "I offered to take her to town last time. She nearly gutted me with a shiv. Demanded fruit. So, I'm bringing her fruit."

"She's only what twelve? Thirteen?"

"Something like that, but you know how it is out here in the wild. You get used to it. The outside world seems too big. Too loud. I just…" His features darken. "She reminds me of my little sister. And since she has no family to look after her, I feel like I ought to at least check in on her."

I let out a frustrated sigh. "Tell her she is welcome to visit us if she wants. I know Devon would like to talk to another girl. I was too upset back then but I wouldn't hurt her now."

He nods as if he approves of my words. "I'll pass it along. And Reed?"

"Yeah?"

"If you're going to be having babies, you're going to need something a little better constructed than your cabin. I can put together some plans to frame out a real house up top." He points above the tree line where our original home was supposed to be. "I know you have the money and I can get the tools and supplies. It might take a year if we have help. Longer if just the two of us."

I cut him off. "Just us. I'm all about building a safer structure for my family but I don't want anyone on my land but you and the little brown-haired girl. I'll put a bullet through the skull of anyone who trespasses."

He nods and holds out his hand. "Good luck. I'll see you soon."

I shake his hand and then he's off.

Once I can't see his retreating frame any longer, I go back inside our much bigger cabin. We cut into the far wall where our bed normally is and made that the opening into the new space. Our bed has been moved to the farthest corner beside the river rock fireplace we built. We'll still keep the RV oven fireplace for the front room but this one will work nicely for the back. It's much larger and can hold a bigger fire.

Devon is busy organizing our cabin. She sits on the bed, that now is about two feet higher off the ground since Atticus and I built a frame for it, and folds baby clothes. A smile has her full lips turned up and she's at peace. With my hands on my hips, I stare at her. Boxes and tubs are everywhere but she seems happy to be unloading everything.

"He's gone?" she asks when she notices my presence. Our eyes meet and hers twinkle with love.

"Off to see Eve."

"Eve?" Her nose scrunches up.

"The girl at the shack."

She presses her lips together and nods. "If she's safe, I don't mind us looking after her."

"I think she's safe but she's a loner. Atticus says she prefers to stay at the shack."

"Okay, then. Maybe we should bring her some food or clothes. I feel bad she's out there all alone," she says. She abandons the clothes and eases out of the bed. Her palms clutch onto her giant stomach that is covered in her new

194

summer maternity dress Atticus bought. She prefers being naked but since we had a visitor, she had to remain clothed. I'm dying to rip it from her ripe body and kiss her bare belly.

"We can do that," I assure her.

We hug and I inhale her hair that smells like apples after our most recent river bath. I could devour this woman from sun up to sun down.

"I've been reading a lot in the book Atticus brought," she murmurs.

I grab her jaw and tilt her head up. Her brows are furled together.

"Another incest book?" My jaw clenches in anger.

"No," she breathes, worry flickering in her eyes briefly. "The one about at-home natural childbirth. It's scary."

I kiss her supple lips. "Don't be afraid. We've got this. You're strong and capable. I won't let you die on my watch, Pip."

Her nostrils flare and the tip of her nose turns red. "I wasn't worried about me. I was worried about the baby."

"The baby will be fine. People had babies in the wild all the time before modern medicine."

She swallows. "And if it has something wrong with it…complications…from the incest…" Fat tears spill from her eyes. "Promise me you'll put it out of its misery. I won't be able to. I'm too selfish. You'll need to be the one to do it."

My chest aches. "Devon. Listen to me. Nothing will be wrong with this baby. Trust me. The incest scare is nothing but bullshit. Shouldn't even be something for you to worry about. When have I ever steered you wrong?"

"Never."

"I always promised I'd protect you no matter what. You have to trust that. Everything I do is for your well-being and the sake of keeping your heart intact. If there was something to worry about, I'd be the one doing all the worrying. I'm fine. Excited and slightly nervous but that's because I haven't held an infant in so long."

She smiles. "Since me and Drew."

My stomach does a flop inside me. "We're doing this. We will continue to do this the rest of our lives. We are a team. We've been that way for as long as I can remember."

A long sigh escapes her. "You're right. I'm done worrying over it."

"Good. Now take off your clothes and let me see your pretty pussy."

She squeals but my good girl always obeys.

"So. Many. Boxes." Sweat sticks to her face as she hobbles around the space trying to organize shit. From what I read in the pregnancy book, she's nesting. It means the baby should be here soon. My heart leaps at the thought of holding our infant in my arms.

Every night I pray to a God, who has probably forsaken me, that she and our baby will be okay. I hope he loves the innocent—and she and our baby are definitely innocent—because I won't survive if anything happens to them.

I need them to be okay.

"Tomorrow we should start tilling for the garden," she

tells me as she bends over to rummage in a box. I'm beat after a day of hard labor and am content to watch her cute ass as it jiggles each time she moves.

"We can do that. Atticus brought enough seeds for us to plant from here to Seattle," I say with a laugh.

She turns and smirks. "I'm excited for a garden. Fresh tomatoes and cucumbers. Oh God, that sounds like heaven."

My cock twitches at hearing her moan in delight. "You're cute as fuck all domesticated."

Her cheeks burn bright red and she gives me a shy smile. "You're handsome as hell all barbaric."

We both laugh.

Eventually, I drift off to sleep as she hums while she works.

This really is heaven.

"Nothing," she pouts and then winces.

"It's been four days, baby. Plants don't grow overnight."

She hobbles over to the bed and eases herself down. "My back is killing me."

"Rest."

"I need to get to the pile of boxes over there and—"

"Devon, rest." My tone is firm and leaves no room for argument.

"Okay, *Dad*," she smarts off.

It makes me want to stick my cock in her mouth.

"You know the rules," I growl.

"Soon I'll get to call you Daddy all the time in here," she teases, her eyebrow arched.

God, she's so fucking hot when she gets mouthy.

"Keep it up," I warn.

"Or what?"

"Or I'll shut your pretty mouth up with my dick. What do you think about that, bad girl?"

She starts laughing and her tits bounce with the movement. "If I could get down to my knees without all this pain, I'd gladly suck you off, *Daddy*."

"Lie down and rest," I bark out, my cock painfully hard in my jeans.

Obeying, she stretches out and rests her hands on her stomach as she watches me stalk across the cabin over to her. She bites on her bottom lip when I unzip my jeans and pull my dick into my hand. With our eyes locked, I stroke myself with my left hand. With my right, I massage her slick pussy. She whimpers and mewls and squirms. I love how wet and turned on she gets by my fingers. I know that her back hurts, so sex is out of the question, but we can both still get off.

"Oh, God, Reed," she breathes, her eyes fluttering closed. "Yes!"

Her body jolts with a seismic orgasm just from me touching her clit. It sparks my own release and I come with a grunt. My ropy cum jets out all over her big tits, marking and claiming her as mine. It satisfies me to see her wet with me. The dirty girl runs her fingers through my spent orgasm and brings it to her plump lips. Her blue eyes blaze with lust as she sucks off the cum.

"Yum."

I smirk. "Plenty more where that came from."

the wild

"I can't do this by myself, Sabrina." My chest aches and I'm exhausted. Purely fucking exhausted. The twins are difficult as I knew they would be. Nothing prepared me for having to do it virtually alone though.

She speaks through the pillow that covers her head. Her voice is ragged and I know she's been crying all day. "I can't do this at all."

With a sigh, I sit down beside her on the bed. The miscarriage—again—was not only the worst possible timing ever, but it's only made her sink deeper into her depression. I want to help her but I fucking can't this time. I have two little mouths in there that need feeding.

"Can you try? For me?" I beg, my own voice choked.

She rolls away so that her back is turned to me. With hot, furious tears in my eyes, I leave her all alone with her despair. I'm just headed to my office for a drink when Devon calls out to me from the nursery.

"Da."

My heart stops beating in my chest. Drew says words all the time but Devon has yet to speak one. I storm into the bedroom, swiping away my tears as I grin at her.

"What is it?"

"Da." She whimpers and holds her hands up. Her blonde, fuzzy hair is cute all messy from sleep. Drew sleeps like the dead but Devon wakes up in the middle of the night if she hears me up and about.

Our lives have recently developed this pattern.

She wakes up. Cries for me. And I carry her around the house while I do unimportant shit. Once she falls asleep, I tuck her back in.

"Hey, Pip."

She beams at me, all sleepy-eyed and toothy, and my heart melts. I scoop her up and carry her to my office. Unlike her rowdy brother, Devon doesn't run around the house and get into shit all hours of the day. She's happy to sit in my lap and mess with whatever I'll let her play with on my desk.

I plop down and hand her a pen and paper. Once I help her grip the pen, she scribbles on the paper, her squeals of delight a salve to my burned heart.

How can Sabrina lie in bed and ignore all of this?

How can she throw away our opportunity to finally be parents down the toilet?

Sure, she's fucking hurting. Well, so the fuck am I. But how in the hell can she blow off these two miracles?

"Da-da-da-da!" Devon chirps as she destroys the paper. At just two years old, she's able to climb inside my heart and latch on.

People had their advice.

How to handle our situation.

And at first, I wondered how you could love someone you barely even know.

But all that gets washed away the moment a blue-eyed, smiling toddler falls asleep on your chest. You inhale the baby shampoo and count your blessings.

I wish Sabrina would wake the fuck up.

These are our children.

We're supposed to love them.

I sure as hell do.

the wild

Fast and sudden and unexpected.

But I do.

Fuck, how I do.

"Da!" Devon throws the pen before leaning back with a cute sigh.

Smiling, I press a kiss to her soft head and wiggle my fingers at her.

She latches onto my pinky with her tiny hand. "Da."

I wake in the middle of the night, the old memory tugging at my heart. It makes me wonder if our baby will have blonde hair or brown. Blue eyes or brown. Either way, I know it will be beautiful and happy.

Devon sits at the table in the other room with a plastic tub at her feet. She's flipping through papers and reading them. I stare at her for what feels like hours until I drift back to sleep.

Life is perfect.

So fucking perfect.

chapter twenty

DEVON

REED IS AMUSED BY MY NESTING. I'M NOT AMUSED. I feel unsettled. As if I don't get everything unpacked and put where it goes, it'll never get done. I want everything perfect so that when the baby comes, we can relax.

Nervousness causes my stomach to rumble. We may never relax. If there's something wrong with the baby, we may have to move back to town. What if it needs a hospital or extra care?

Another sharp, aching back pain slices through me. I read that it could be labor pains. But I also read it could be false labor. Once my water breaks, I'll know the baby is coming. Until then, I'll wait through the pains.

Reed's snores are comforting. He works so hard each day. The house. Food. Everything. By the time he falls into bed, he passes out. I want him to rest more. Now that the cabin extension is finished, maybe he can.

I yelp when another pain snags me in its grip. It makes Buddy whimper in concern. I let out a swoosh of breath and pet him with my bare foot. "Shhhh."

He settles and I flip through pictures Mom had saved. One of Dad holding me at two years old has my heart warming. He looks so young and terrified. It melts my heart. I hunt through the pictures searching for ones when we were infants. I come up short. With a frown, I dig deeper into the box. At the very bottom, I find a sealed yellow envelope that says: Private. Do Not Open.

Curiosity gets the better of me. My eyes flicker to Dad and he still sleeps soundly. Dragging my eyes back to the envelope, I quietly tear it open. Inside is a manila envelope filled with court documents. Clipped to the front, I find a picture of a pretty blonde young teen—no older than fourteen or so—holding two baby twins.

She has my eyes.

The thought hits me hard and my heart stills in my chest.

I pluck the picture off and set it on the table. Tears well in my eyes as the betrayal sinks in. He lied to me. He lied about everything.

Adoption papers.

Loads of them.

All mumbo jumbo but in a nutshell, Abigail Hunter, gave away her rights to us to my parents.

I'm going to be sick.

Bile rises up and I quickly swallow it down.

This can't be true.

Every single worry about what incest does to babies didn't matter. Reed isn't my biological father. A pained moan rips from my chest that causes him to stir but not wake up. I feel as though my heart has been torn from me. Tears travel down my cheeks and drip down onto the papers.

No wonder Mom didn't like us.

We weren't hers.

My body trembles as I throw on my dress and stuff my feet into my boots. The pains that keep slicing across my lower back and wrapping around to my stomach are nothing in comparison to the searing, hollowing, soul-crushing pain in my heart.

I don't know where I am going.

I don't care.

But I can't stay here with him.

He's not even…we're not even…

I heft the lock out of place and push through the door. The night air is frigid and it cools my heated flesh. With sobs choking me, I push through the gate and run. I don't know where I'm going but it's far away from here and the wreckage of our lives. My boots crunch on the forest underbrush and my cries are so loud. Buddy dutifully runs ahead of me as if to kill anything that might step in my way.

I've been running for at least ten minutes when I hear it.

Pain.

Sorrow.

Devastation.

Rage.

The roar is half-man, half-animal.

It echoes through the trees and haunts me.

And it's coming for me.

It will stalk me until it captures me.

I don't want to be captured.

I want to be free.

Hate and fury and the sickening feeling of being duped my entire life fuels me on. A sharp pain hits me so hard, I stumble and nearly fall. I have to hold onto my stomach and suppress a scream until the pain passes. Once I can move again, I trudge forward although I'm much slower than before. My body trembles with my sobs.

"Devon!"

The way he says my name is a claim. A promise. A vow to love and cherish and protect. I hate the way he says it. He has no claim to me. I don't belong to him. I never did.

Our relationship was built on lies.

He let me think the most awful things about me, about us, about our baby.

"Devon!"

Another pain renders me immobile. I fall to my knees. The pain is unbearable and blinding. I'm lost to the absolute severity of it. He's closer now. I can hear his grunting. Cursing. Begging. Pleading. Crying.

Closer.

And closer.

The pain subsides and I stand on shaky legs. Step after step, I move myself forward. I've barely made it three when the slice across my midsection strikes again. Once again, I drop to my knees. I'm sobbing and desperately clutching at the earth as I crawl away from him. Every nerve ending in my body is alive and exposed and thrashing. The pain is too intense.

I'm going to die out here.

And worse yet, he's getting closer.

"N-No," I choke out as I crawl. "S-Stay away from me."

But I'm too late. Not quick enough. Like a viper, he strikes. His fist is in my hair and he's mauling me much like that bear once did. Nothing is gentle or curious. He's rough and territorial and demanding.

I cry out when he lands on the dirt behind me and jerks my head back. His strong arm wraps around my middle above my protruding belly in a possessive way. In his arms, I feel both safe and suffocated. My mind is warring with itself. I want him but I hate him. I love him but I can't stand to be touched by him.

"Mine." His growl is fierce and intimidating. More frightening than any forest animal. "Mine."

"No!" I screech and wiggle in his grasp.

His cock is hard and intrusive against my back. I hate it. I love it. I don't want it. I do.

"Mine!"

"No!"

I'm shoved forward and I barely have a chance to steady myself with my hands before he's shoving my dress up my hips. With a rip, he tears the fabric down the back and it falls to the dirt at my wrists. I scream and kick but he's strong. Determined. Undaunted.

Another slice of pain steals my breath and my sanity. He takes this moment of weakness. Fucking takes it like it belongs to him. Like he owns every part of me. His cock rips through me as he brutally shoves his way inside. This isn't rape like those bush people—because despite my screams of horror—I still want him. This is a hostile take-over. A reminder of who I belong to.

"I hate you!" I scream but I've stopped fighting. I fall to my shoulder with my ass up in the air.

"I fucking love you!" he roars, his hips slamming hard against my backside. "You can't ever leave me! Ever!"

I sob and scream and curse him. Another painful explosion rips across my abdomen making me black out for a second.

"Mine, Devon! You're mine, goddammit! I don't give a shit about those papers!" He's crying behind me. Furious but crying. "Y-You were mine the moment she handed you to me." His voice cracks and his brutal grip on my hips lessen. He runs a gentle palm up my spine. "I don't understand it but you burrowed your way in my heart at just two years old when we got you."

We're both crying and he's fucking me slowly.

"Y-You l-let me b-believe s-something could b-be wrong w-with the b-baby," I accuse, my words garbled and messy.

He fists my hair again and jerks me upright so that his hot breath is in my ear. Everything hurts but I need him like I need air. I hate him. I love him.

"Because I wanted to protect your goddamn heart. I knew it would fucking crush you, baby. Please understand that every single damn thing I have ever done has always been for you." He twists his grip on my hair so that our mouths meet. With an intensity I never knew existed, he devours me with a claiming kiss. His cock is deep inside me, I'm turned at an uncomfortable angle, and everything hurts like hell. And yet I'm kissing him back just as hard.

"I hate you," I sob.

Thrust. Thrust. Thrust.

"I hate you…"

"I love you, Pip."

"I hate you…"

Thrust. Thrust. Thrust.

"I love you so goddamned much," he breathes against my mouth.

"I hate you." Another sob as pain so intense ripples through me. I'm going to die. Right here. Right now. On the floor of the forest with a dick deep inside me.

And he won't know.

He won't know those are lies.

"Daddy," I choke out. "I love you."

"I know, baby. I fucking know."

The pain that sears through me has my insides contracting so hard I think I'll puke. Behind me, Reed comes with a feral grunt.

"Fuck!"

He's barely pulled out when a rush of warm heat gushes out with him. We're both stunned and I start to collapse but he grips me.

"A-Are you fucking having the baby?!" He yanks up his jeans with his free hand.

I cry in response.

"Fuck! Shit! Oh, God!"

He scoops me into his strong arms and all I can do is shake uncontrollably. I never hated him. I'm so upset and confused but I could never hate him. He's mine. We're cosmic and untouchable together.

I'm so dazed as he runs through the forest. My eyes are half-lidded and swollen but I soon see a shack. He charges up to it and with a powerful kick, he blasts the door off and into the house.

A girl shrieks from the back but he doesn't seem

bothered. He lays me down on some blankets that are in front of the fireplace.

"Eve!" he roars. "Help!"

He kneels in front of me and urges my thighs apart. When he looks down between them, his eyes widen in horror.

"What?!" I demand, my voice shrill. Terror overcomes me and I try to look past my stomach to see.

"Lie back," he orders, his tone abrupt. "The baby is coming. Just lie the fuck back, Devon."

A small girl stares at me in shock. Her wild brown hair is a mess and her eyes are wide. He barks out orders to her. Water. Towels. All sorts of things. He mentions the cabin. I lose sense of reality as another wave of pain crashes into me. The girl bolts.

"I-I can't d-do this," I choke out. "I'm going t-to die."

He glares at me. "The fuck you will. You're going to have this damn baby right now and you're going to be okay. I'm going to see if I can feel the head."

My eyes roll back when he begins pushing his thick fingers inside me. Immediately, he jerks them out and shudders.

"What?"

"The baby is breech."

Panicked, I let out a scream. "You have to turn the baby before it's too late!"

Sweat pours down his temples and his eyes dart all around as if he's coming up with a plan.

"Lie back and try to relax," he barks.

I do as I'm told and ignore the excruciating pain as he begins working his fingers and then hand inside me.

Slurping sounds can be heard as he moves it deeper inside me. He uses his free hand to push on my belly. The pain is too much.

"I need you to push right there," he grunts, his eyes manic. "We can do this but I need your help."

I gag as I press on my upper stomach on the right. Everything shifts inside me and I let out another scream. Another contraction rips through me as he pulls his arm back out.

I turn my head to the side and expel my dinner. The pain is too much to bear. His hands are all over my face assessing me and then he's back between my thighs. My energy is depleted and I feel overwhelmed. As though I truly will die on this floor. I just hope our baby lives.

"You have to stay strong, Pip," he chokes out, clutching my knee. "Stay with me. Focus. I can't get this baby out of you. You're going to have to do that all on your own. Would it help to get on your knees?"

I cry until another contraction steals my breath. Tears roll down my temples. I don't know what to do. I just want the pain gone. I want the baby out of me. I want to…

Push.

The urge is unlike any other feeling in the world.

It becomes my only thought.

Push.

I grip my knees and bear down, a guttural sound ripping from my chest. My eyes are closed but I can hear Dad praising me. The urge passes and I fall limp.

"You're doing well," he assures me. "Next time the pain hits, do that again."

We don't have to wait long.

the wild

The pain explodes through me again.

I bear down and keep my eyes on him. His eyes are looking down. When his face lights up, I gape at him in shock.

"I can see the head! We fucking did it! Baby, I can see the hair! Dark like me," he bellows.

I start laughing or sobbing, I'm not sure which, but I'm happy. Knowing the baby is so close—that it will look like him maybe—has me more determined than ever.

Over and over again.

I push and push.

"Oh, God," I scream. "It hurts!"

"I know, sweetheart. You're doing so well. Just keep going."

The next push, I feel some relief and Dad's eyes are wide.

"Holy fuck! The head's out. Jesus, Devon, the head's out!"

I don't have time to recover because another painful contraction tears through me. I bear down. Over and over until relief like I've never known slides out of me and into the arms of my father.

I black out.

For a moment.

But then my eyes are wide.

"It's not crying!" I shriek. "Why isn't it crying?!"

Dad's face is twisted up as he panics. He holds the limp baby in his arms and I sob at seeing it.

"Fuck!" he cries out. "Cry! Why the hell isn't he crying?!" Fat tears roll down my dad's face.

He?

"It's a boy?" I question, a sob caught in my throat.

He nods. "Fuck. Fuck. Fuck. What do we do?"

"I don't know!"

He grabs our son by the ankles and turns him upside down. I'm horrified by how brutal he's being. Then, not so gently, he spanks the infant's small bottom. I'm about to scream at my father when I hear it.

Choked at first.

Then louder.

His lungs. They're powerful.

"He's crying!" I exclaim. "Oh my God, he's crying!"

He cradles the baby in his hands and passes him to me. My arms protectively wrap around the child as I pull him to my chest. He's perfect. Dark hair, long skinny body. Perfect.

Mine.

Oh, God, he's mine.

I lie there crying in joy for what feels like forever. The baby is sticky and bloody pressed against me. He won't stop crying but I take this as good news. The umbilical cord is still attached to him and somewhere inside me.

Another smaller pain ripples through me. "I think the placenta is coming out."

Dad's face is frantic as he does his best to give birth to the placenta. It comes out easily. I'm shivering, my teeth chattering, when Eve runs back into the house, her arms full and a backpack slung over her shoulder. She brings me a towel and I wrap it around my son.

Blackness clouds my vision and I pass out.

chapter twenty-one

REED

FUCK. FUCK. FUCK.

Her eyes roll back in her head and I panic. "Baby! Wake up!"

She blinks her eyes open slowly. "I'm so exhausted."

Relief rushes through me. "Other than that, you feel okay?"

Her nod is slight.

"Go to sleep then. I'll take care of you."

The moment she passes out, I grab my knife and cut the umbilical cord. It hangs like a gnarly snake but I just need to clean her up. With careful movements, I scoop our son from her chest and wrap him in the towel. He kicks and squawks. I almost cry when I realize he has her nose. With a quick kiss to it, I smooth out his sticky hair and hold him up to a wide-eyed Eve.

"Can you hold him so I can take care of her?"

Trust is not something I hand over well, but she did

just run at full speed to help me. She looks terrified, not evil. Her features soften and she nods. Kid isn't much of a talker. I hand over the baby and she cradles him. My attention is back on my heart, my love, my motherfucking soul.

She's a mess.

I fucked her and she was in goddamn labor.

I'm disgusted with myself.

And yet, I know it had to be done.

She needed to be claimed and stamped and owned.

Mine.

Fucking mine.

The moment I woke up and discovered she was gone, I flipped my shit. The papers all over the table meant that she'd found my dark secret. A secret I worked so hard to keep from her.

She's my daughter.

The moment I held her, I knew.

I knew the moment she found out, if ever, she'd feel betrayed. But I told her. Fucking told her that I keep stuff from her if it meant keeping her heart safe. This was a secret that would destroy her. I just couldn't do it. Even when she was sick to fucking death worried over incest related problems, I couldn't tell her. This secret was worse than a little fear over birth defects. This secret had the potential to destroy her.

On autopilot, I boil some water and grab the first aid kit. Carefully, I wash Devon from head to toe. Her pussy is swollen and red. There is a small tear that I'm afraid needs to be stitched. I hate that she lies there, completely passed out, with her legs hung open. But at the same time, I need to take care of her without her moving. It takes some time but I manage to stitch her up and spread ointment over the parts of her pussy that look like they might hurt. Once she's clean and tended to, I cover her with a blanket Eve brought from the house.

My son cries and squirms. Eve seems terrified and gladly hands him back to me. I sit on the floor and lay him on a folded towel. The chilly air seems to piss him off and his screams get louder. Quickly, I wash our precious child. Everything about him is perfect. And his lungs are powerful. He reminds me of Drew by the way he hollers.

"You're a rowdy one, aren't you?" I coo as I wrap him tightly in a blanket.

His fist flies free and he suckles on it. I walk on my knees with him in my arms over to where Devon sleeps. It takes some maneuvering, but I manage to nestle him against her. His mouth opens as he searches for her breast. I cradle his tiny body in a way that soon has him latching on. His cries are silenced as he greedily sucks on her nipple. With tears in my eyes, I regard Eve with a grin.

"My family."

She smiles back. "Beautiful."

Eve lingers in the doorway of our cabin with my son wrapped tightly in her arms as I lower Devon into our bed. Once she's covered, I turn to accept my baby. It's been close to three hours since Devon passed out. I knew we had more to work with here so Eve dutifully followed behind me as I carried my love back home. I'm grateful to Eve in a way I can't explain. Without her, this would have been nearly impossible.

Once I settle my sleeping son onto the bed beside Devon, I turn to regard Eve. She lets out a squeak when I jerk her into my arms and hug her.

"Thank you."

Her body is tense but she doesn't fight against my embrace. When I pull away, she holds out her hand. "Fruit."

Smirking, I stroll over to a box with our canned goods. The girl is too tiny to carry it so I find the backpack and fill it with fruit cans. It'll be hard for her to get it back to the shack but she's fierce. I have no doubt she'll manage.

"If you see Buddy, will you bring him back?" I ask.

She nods as she shoulders the backpack.

That fucking dog bolted when I turned into an animal and brutally fucked Devon. I think I scared the shit out of him. He's yet to return.

"Come visit us," I call out to Eve. "Anytime."

Another nod.

Then she's gone.

I wake to a suckling sound. My back and neck are killing me. Sleeping in the chair beside the bed was a bad idea but I wanted to watch over my family.

And they are my family.

Devon is more than daughter and wife and friend.

She's laughter and life and love.

I'm grateful for the day that sixteen-year-old girl,

Abigail, agreed to adopt out her twins. She had struggled for nearly two years with trying to care for them. Having a baby at fourteen would be hard on anyone. This girl simply couldn't take it. Sabrina and I were thrilled because it meant we could finally be parents.

My eyes drift over to Devon as she nurses our son. Her eyes are soft as she watches in awe. He's beautiful. I love them both so fucking much.

Perfect.

With a smile on my lips, I think back to the day Abigail handed over the twins.

"Devon is the good baby," Abigail says, almost fussing over the toddler. "Sleeps well. It's that rowdy one over there you have to watch."

Tears well in her eyes and she lets out a choked sob.

Sabrina flashes me a worried look. Nothing feels real about this adoption. Not until we're at home with them will it really sink in.

"We'll take care of them," I vow, taking the young girl's hand.

"It's for the best, angel," Abigail's mom Patricia murmurs. "I can barely afford to feed the child I have, much less two more. Not after the divorce, especially."

Abigail stiffens. "I know, Ma." Then her blue eyes that sparkle like two lakes meet mine. "Can I talk to you for a second? About the babies."

Her mother stiffens but nods her approval to give us

some alone time. Sabrina and Patricia start discussing feeding routines while I slip onto the front porch with Abigail.

"What's wrong?"

"Promise me you won't change your mind?"

I gape at her as if she's lost her marbles. "I swear."

She swallows before throwing her arms around me in a tight hug. I can't help but embrace the sweet, sad girl in my arms. She smells like apples and innocence. I kiss her soft blonde head because it feels right.

"What is it?"

Her words are whispered but I hear them. My heart cracks open in my chest. The secret is one too deep and dark for anyone but the two of us to know.

"It was Daddy."

I swallow and stroke this poor teenage girl's hair. "What was Daddy?"

She shudders and nearly collapses but I keep her from falling. "H-He used to come into my room when he'd b-been drinking too much. I didn't want it but it happened..."

"I'm so sorry."

She shakes her head. "I'm not. There is nothing wrong with them. They deserve to be loved. But not here..."

Her head tilts up and fire blazes in her eyes. "I need to get away. To escape. I can't do that with them. Ma has blinders on. Daddy left us not long after I got pregnant. I lied to Ma. Said it was a boy from school. If she knew..."

"I won't tell a soul," I vow. That promise burns deep inside my heart.

"Thank you. They're smart babies. Sweet and interactive. I just want them to be loved. I'm afraid I can't give them what they deserve."

"I'll love them as though they are my own."

"Thank you."

"I think you should go to the police though and report him," I say softly.

She pulls away and lifts her chin. "No. I don't want anyone to ever know or to have an inkling. Please."

With sadness in my heart and for the future of those two babies, I nod in agreement.

"I promise."

She gives me a wide, toothy teenage grin. "Pinky promise?"

I laugh and offer her my pinky.

My heart is heavy as I remember Abigail. We'd only had the babies two weeks when I learned the teenager died of an overdose. I didn't realize her escape meant death. It haunts me to this day.

But her secrets of how my Devon and Drew were born of incest stay locked away in my heart. Devon will never know. Never. She's smart and beautiful and fucking perfect. I don't want her to ever doubt that. One day, when she's ready, I'll tell her how sweet and loving her biological mother was but that's it. She'll never know that she was born of rape and incest.

"I'm so happy," Devon rasps out as our son nurses.

Her blonde hair is dirty and knotted but I've never seen her look so serene and gorgeous.

"Me too, baby."

"What should we name him?" she asks.

He loses his grip on her nipple and hollers. We both laugh as she helps him latch back on.

"He's a rowdy little thing."

Her blue eyes find mine. "Rowdy has a nice ring to it. After his uncle."

My heart swells. "I love it. Rowdy Andrew Jamison."

"Thank you."

I laugh and come to sit beside her on the edge of the bed. My fingers stroke through her messy hair before I settle my palm on our baby. "What are you thanking me for? You did all the work. You did this, Pip."

She shakes her head as tears spill out. Her lip wobbles madly. "Thank you for loving me. From day one, whenever that day was, until now. Our love has grown and morphed into something nobody else on this planet has. We're special."

Rowdy opens his mouth as his eyes fall shut. Who knew infants were so fucking adorable? I missed all of this with Drew and Devon. This moment, admiring my newborn son, is a moment I'll never forget.

"I'll get started on breakfast," I say with a sigh. "No rest for the weary."

She pats the bed. "We'd rather you stay here with us. The food can wait."

I'm exhausted and sore.

The idea of sleeping with my family is one I can't refuse.

I undress to my boxers and crawl in beside her. With my arm wrapped around them both, I fall into blissful, peaceful sleep.

I'm home.

We're finally home.

epilogue

DEVON

Two years later...

"ROWDY, NO!" I SQUEAL AS HE RUNS AT WARP speed toward the fireplace. My belly is giant and all I do is waddle these days. Thankfully, Reed is faster than the both of us. He scoops our son up and tosses him into the air.

Rowdy shrieks with glee and hugs his daddy's neck.

"We need to build a fence and lock him in it," I complain and blow a strand of hair from my sticky face. "The terrible twos are worse than terrible."

Reed turns to grin at me. He's not wearing a shirt and his muscles are bulging. My hormones, just like with my last pregnancy, are buzzing out of control. I want to put Rowdy down for a nap and climb my husband like a tree.

"You're giving me that look, Devon," Reed growls.

"What look?" I feign innocence.

"The fuck me in the ass look."

I scoff which makes Rowdy giggle. He has no idea what he's laughing about which makes Reed and I both laugh. "I do *not* want it *there*."

"Is that so? You weren't complaining when I had you on your knees buried to the hilt last night," he challenges.

My throat blazes with heat. I rush over and pluck Rowdy from his grip before taking my little monster to his crib. Thankfully, he loves his naps and his rabbit pelt blankie I made. The moment I lay him down, he snags the blanket and starts sucking on his thumb, his eyes heavy with sleepiness. When I turn around, Reed is undressing. The moment his rock-hard cock bobs out and he's completely naked, a whimper escapes me.

"You drive me crazy," I complain.

He smirks and jerks his chin up as to call me over to him. Like the obedient wife I am, I find myself drawn to him. I toss aside the maternity dress along the way and lose my panties. His wolfish gaze devours my naked pregnant body. I love that he seems to appreciate my body's changes. I never feel less than in his eyes.

Always more than.

Always.

"Did you bring Eve some fruit when you were out hunting?" I ask when my belly brushes against his toned abs.

I feel bad for her. She helped us when we needed her to but other than that, she doesn't visit. Sometimes I can feel her eyes in the forest watching us but she never engages. Rowdy loves the presents she leaves for him on the porch though. She's always making him toys.

"Yeah. I told her she needs to come see her nephew or I was going to haul her over my shoulder and force her to come anyway." He chuckles. "She tried to shiv me."

I wince and shake my head. "Maybe with time."

"Maybe. She's wild though. Don't get your hopes up."

"When is Atticus coming back?" I ask, my palms rubbing up over his sculpted pectorals.

His hands grip my hips. Not soft. Possessive and harsh. It reminds me that I'm his.

"He had to fly out to Seattle for something but he'll be back next week. It's coming along pretty nicely. We'll work on the roof some more once he gets back."

I grin up at him. They've been working on the house for two years. It's framed—a giant monolith on the mountain side about a half mile from the wreckage site. They've worked hard on it but it's taken them forever. Reed thinks in another two years we can move in. Until then, we keep filling up our tiny little cabin.

"Lie down, Daddy," I purr as I reach down to grip his cock. It jolts in my hand. "Mommy wants to do the driving."

His smoldering grin nearly melts me to the floor. Like the obedient husband he is, he lies back on the bed. I waddle my pregnant butt over to him and straddle his thighs. With our eyes locked, I sink down on his throbbing length. We both hiss out in pleasure. His palms roam my belly and we both laugh when this kiddo rolls against his touch. Then, his fingers are at my breasts teasing me.

"You just going to sit there, woman, or are you going to fuck me?" he murmurs, his hips thrusting up.

I moan and lean forward resting my palms on his shoulders. Slowly, I begin rocking against him. Love, brilliant and deep and powerful, shines in his eyes. It burns me. Scalds me. Imprisons me. Suffocates me.

But it also fills me.

Fuels me.

Frees me.

His fingers are at my clit and he's thrusting hard from beneath me. My husband is an animal through and through. Even from the bottom, he dominates and controls. With a flutter of my lashes, I give in. I lose myself in the way he owns me.

We both come with sounds that are straight from the forest. Not sounds two humans should make. His cum jets up inside of me and I clench around him with the after-shocks of my orgasm.

"Promise me it will always be like this," I whisper.

His brown eyes are hard with feral emotions that all lead back to loving me. He grips my pinky with his and draws me closer to him. Even with my giant stomach wedged between us and his cock still deep inside, we manage to kiss.

"Pinky promise, Pip."

And I believe him because this man will do everything in his power to make that happen.

Lie. Steal. Murder. Cheat. Destroy.

All in the name of keeping my heart safe.

I couldn't ask for a more dedicated love.

He's mine.

All mine.

Five months later…

I watch as Rowdy and Reed throw snowballs at each other. Rowdy has a good arm on him despite being a toddler. Ronan screams from inside, awake from his nap. I flash Reed a big smile as I go inside to tend to our little one. When I make it over to his cradle, he's kicking and trying to eat his fist. These boys are always hungry.

He stops fussing when I sing to him. They all do. All three of them love when I sing. His blue eyes are wide as I scoop him into my arms and sit on the bed. He latches onto my breast with vigor.

My babies are gorgeous.

Reed and I make beautiful children.

I wonder if the next one will be a girl. I haven't told Reed that I'm expecting again. He'll be thrilled, I'm sure. They still haven't finished the house but it won't be long. By next summer, we'll be ready to move in. Not everything is done but we can still live there. And by then, we'll have a fifth member to our growing family.

Joy overwhelms me.

Sometimes I wish Mom were here to see them. I wonder if it would unlock her from her spell. Drag her from the darkness. Reed assures me it wouldn't. That depression is an illness that isn't easily cured by cute babies. He reminds me that she had Drew and I and still stayed trapped inside her head.

Other times, I wonder about my real mom. Reed burned up the adoption papers because he said we were family bound by heart which was better than blood or laws. A weight lifted the moment the papers were incinerated. I kept the picture of my birth mother though. It amazes me how much she looks like me. When I ask about my biological father, Reed shrugs and says he doesn't know. I guess it doesn't matter. All of those moments lead to this one.

"Momma!" Rowdy cries out when they walk inside. He runs over to me and gets me wet with the cold snow.

"Hey, baby," I tell him and ruffle his dark hair. He looks so much like Reed it makes my heart stop.

Reed walks over to me and kisses the top of my head. "How are my beautiful wife and baby boy?"

"He's hungry and I'm tired." I give him a weary smile.

His gaze narrows as he lowers his eyes to my breasts that are engorged with milk. "Are you…are we…"

My smile is wide and tears prickle my eyes. "We are. Are you happy?"

Rowdy grunts as he tries to rip Buddy's hair out. Buddy rolls over onto his back and licks our wild son in the face until he lets go.

"Devon," Reed growls as he tenderly strokes my cheek. "You make me happy every single second of every single day. These kids. You. The damn dog. All of it is my happily ever after."

I tilt my head up so he'll kiss me. "Spoken like a true romantic."

"I'll show you romance once these kids go to sleep."

"It's on, big daddy," I tell him with a saucy grin.

He nips at my bottom lip and growls. "Promise?"

"Pinky promise."

THE END

Dear Reader,

Thank you so much for going on this *wild* adventure with me! I know sometimes my stories are way outside the box but I can't thank you enough for always seeing it to the end. Please, as you review, keep your spoilers to a minimum. I'm afraid that some folks might miss out on an unconventional, but beautiful love story, if they knew what sort of taboo element they were looking at before diving in. Once you're in though, it sort of hooks you, which is what I hope to do for future readers! I appreciate you keeping that tidbit to yourself!! Thank you so much!

I'm looking to take you all on more *wild* journeys very soon!

Sincerely,
The *Wild* One
aka K Webster

PS – You can join the spoiler group to talk about The Wild here: www.facebook.com/groups/799341853554457

PPS – If you spoil it, I'll send Eve with her shiv after you…
PPPS – I mean it.
PPPPS – Kidding…or am I?

playlist

Listen on Spotify.

"Tainted Love" by Marilyn Manson

"Oh My" by Big Wreck

"Blown Wide Open" by Big Wreck

"Wild Horses" by Bishop Briggs

"Way Down We Go" by Kaleo

"I Put A Spell On You" by Annie Lennox

"#1 Crush" by Garbage

"Fade Into You" by Mazzy Star

"Game of Survival by Ruelle

"Ain't No Sunshine" by Bill Withers

"Time of the Season" by The Zombies

"How's It Going To Be" by Third Eye Blind

"Run, Run, Run" by Tokio Hotel

"Black Gives Way To Blue" by Alice in Chains

"Behind Blue Eyes" by The Who

"Say Hello 2 Heaven" by Temple of the Dog

"Can't Help Falling In Love" by Elvis Presley

"Cumbersome" by 4 Seven Mary Three

"In The Meantime" by Spacehog

"We're In This Together" by Nine Inch Nails

"The Sound of Silence" by Simon & Garfunkel

"Lovesong" by The Cure

"Foolish Games" by Jewel

"Head Over Feet" by Alanis Morissette

"The Morning After" by Meg Myers

"Someone Like You" by Adele

"The House of the Rising Sun" by The Animals

"Take Me to Church" by Hozier

"No One's Gonna Love You" by Band of Horses

"Ways to Go" by Grouplove

"Sail" by Awolnation

"To Be Alone" by Hozier

"Stubborn Love" by The Lumineers

"Alive" by Pearl Jam

acknowledgements

Thank you to my husband…you listened to my wild idea and encouraged me to write it. That kind of support is the best kind. Thanks for always being my number one cheerleader. I love you.

A huge thank you to my Krazy for K Webster's Books reader group. You all are insanely supportive and I can't thank you enough.

A gigantic thank you to my betas who read this story. Elizabeth Clinton, Ella Stewart, Misty Walker, Shannon Miller, Amy Bosica, Brooklyn Miller, Robin Martin, Amy Simms, Jessica Viteri, Amanda Söderlund, and Tammy McGowan, you all helped make this story even better. Your feedback and early reading is important to this entire process and I can't thank you enough.

Also, a big thank you to Ella Stewart for proofreading this story and reading it as I went along to make sure I was on track!! You're a great friend who always looks out for me. Your unconditional love for taboo is inspiring to me. Love you!

A giant thank you to Misty Walker for stepping into my life and helping me do all the hard stuff that I can't do. You encourage me daily and make me laugh. I can always count on you to say the things I need to hear and recommend a good horse book when I'm in a slump. My life would be NEIGHthing without you. NEIGHthing. Love ya, girl!

A big thank you to my author friends who have given me your friendship and your support. You have no idea how much that means to me.

Thank you to all of my blogger friends both big and small that go above and beyond to always share my stuff. You all rock! #AllBlogsMatter

Ellie at Love N Books, thank you SO much for saving my ass and editing this book. You're a star and I can't thank you enough! Love you!

Thank you Stacey Blake for being ninja queen as always when formatting my books and in general. I love you! I love you! I love you!

A big thanks to my PR gal, Nicole Blanchard. You are fabulous at what you do and keep me on track!

Lastly but certainly not least of all, thank you to all of the wonderful readers out there that are willing to hear my story and enjoy my characters like I do. It means the world to me!

the free

To my husband,
Thank you for loving the wild within me.

To my wild readers,
Your unconditional love for forbidden romance, specifically *The Wild*,
has inspired me, changed me, and driven me to keep writing from the heart…
even if not everyone understands, likes, or approves.
It's easy to be brave when my readers are even braver.
For your fearless willingness to explore the wildness in my mind, I'll be forever grateful.

"Maybe some women aren't meant to be tamed.
Maybe they just need to run free until they find
someone just as wild to run with them."
—Carrie Bradshaw

He took me from the wilderness.
I was all alone and death was near.
His plan was to heal me and then let me go.
A reprieve from my harsh reality.

Food. Warmth. Safety.
Just us.
It's temporary and one day I'll be forced to go home.
But I don't I want to go back.
I want him to keep me. To tame and love me.

Freeing the wild comes with grave consequences.
He thinks they'll cage him for being with me.

Our love's not right.
They won't understand it.
Forbidden. Immoral. Perverse. Vile.

I don't care what they think.
It should only matter to us.
We are innocent and beautiful and worthy.

Love is wild.
And we're going to set it free.

prologue

EVE

The Past...

MY EYES WELL WITH TEARS AS JOHN AND EZEKIEL dig a hole for Esther. My sister wasn't but three years older than me and we were close. The boys—Ezekiel, John, Solomon, and Nathaniel—all had Papa. Mama passed on two winters ago when illness struck. So Esther and I only had each other.

Ezekiel took the only thing I had in this world away from me. I knew it was him. He's the only one who could make her scream that way. As if he could reach inside her tiny body and steal her soul. My brother stole everything from her, including the light in her eyes.

"You're the woman of the house now, Eve," Papa tells me, his squeeze on my shoulder gentle. I'd seen him touch Esther in ways I never wanted to be touched. I've always been the baby. The one nobody ever paid any attention to. I don't want to be the woman.

The moment Esther began bleeding between her thighs, the men in our family started stalking her much like the mountain lions do when they're hunting. Papa began teaching her how to be a wife. She never shared what those teachings were, but they took place in his bedroom and she cried the entire time.

I'm all alone.

It's my turn to cry.

Ezekiel doesn't appear to be upset as he rolls Esther's cold, stiff body into the hole. This is all his fault. Had he not carried on his own teachings, she'd still be alive. His teaching had been too brutal and he'd somehow hurt her inside of her body. All I know is the blood was coming from someplace it wasn't supposed to. She and I'd sobbed until she turned pale. Until she stopped moving. Until she left me.

"I'm going hunting with the boys," Papa tells me, his voice gruff. "Since you're the woman of the house now, you get to sleep in my room. Tonight, we'll begin your teachings on how to become a wife."

A hot tear rolls down my cheek and I nod.

Once Esther is buried, they take off with their weapons. The wind is brutal and unforgiving. I shudder and walk into our home. It's quaint—only the two rooms—but the fireplaces are warm. I remember being a little girl and curling up beside Mama in her room she shared with Papa. She'd show me pictures of her and Papa. When they were small too. Back when they lived in town with my grandparents. Mama and Papa were brother and sister too. But Papa wasn't ever cruel to Mama the way Ezekiel was to Esther. I'm worried Ezekiel will hurt me too.

I slip into my new room and worry about what Papa will teach me. Esther was never happy about it. My heart aches because I miss her terribly. Sometimes I wish I could just run far, far away from here. That a nice bear would befriend me and let me live in his cave. I smile as I pull out the pictures of my parents when they were kids from the small tin can on one of the river rocks on the fireplace.

My brown eyes are the exact shade of my mother's. Esther had her mouth. Mama was pretty when she was younger before her teeth began falling out. I can't help but run my tongue over my teeth. I've lost them over the years, but mine always grow back. I wonder why Papa's and my older brothers' teeth never come back.

After I've looked through all the pictures, I stuff them back into the tin. I'm just dozing off when I hear voices. Heavy footsteps thunder my way. When Ezekiel pokes his head in, I glare at him.

"Papa spoke to me while hunting and he believes he's too old to be a husband any longer. Since I'm the eldest, he wants me to teach you how to be a wife." His dark brown eyes narrow to slits as he regards me. "You're nothing but a kid, though. You haven't even started bleeding yet."

"I hate you." My hissed words seem to infuriate him.

"Esther used to say the same thing and sounded just like you," he snarls as he stalks into the room and leers at me. "Maybe you're not a kid after all."

I hug my knees to my chest and pray Papa will make Ezekiel go away. I start to shudder when he takes another threatening step toward me.

"Ezekiel," Papa barks out as he enters the room, his Bible clutched tight in his grip. "What's going on in here?"

Ezekiel has the sense to look shameful. "Nothin', Papa. I was telling little Eve how wonderful it was that she's a woman now."

Lies.

Papa frowns at him. "Go on, boy. Eve and I need some time alone."

Reluctantly, Ezekiel leaves and closes the door behind him. I remain frozen in fear. Papa begins undressing until he's naked. His manhood isn't hard like I've seen my brothers'. It remains small and limp amidst a bush of white hair. Papa isn't bronzed and sculpted as if from stone like my brothers. His skin hangs from his bones and brown spots litter his flesh.

"Take that smock off and come sit." His dark brown eyes flicker with anger as he sits and pats the furs beside him. "Our teaching begins with Genesis 3:16."

I'm afraid, but him educating us with Bible passages isn't anything new. I tug off my garment and toss it to the floor. My skin burns with embarrassment. I don't want him to see me like this. To my surprise, he doesn't look. Simply holds his hand out to me. I take it and sit beside him. His soft, wrinkly skin is warm against mine as he hugs me to his side.

"I named you after Eve in the Bible," he explains softly. He begins telling me a story where she was tempted by a snake and lured Adam to partake in the forbidden fruit alongside her. "Soon you will understand your namesake," he tells me and then begins reading a passage that makes my skin crawl. "I will greatly multiply your sorrow and your conception; In pain you shall bring forth children; Your desire shall be for your husband, And he shall rule over you."

He sets the Bible down and grips my jaw, forcing me to look up at his bearded face that has white curls—that match the ones surrounding his manhood—mixed in.

"I'm your husband now, Eve. There are no other wives left for me to take but you. And while you're young and not ripe for childbirth, you're still very much female. Soon, your body will change and adapt to satisfy your husband. To satisfy me." His fingertips are brutal as they dig into my flesh. A tear leaks out, but he's not bothered by it. "Tonight, I will begin my rule over you. To teach you how to please your husband."

I cry out when he easily pushes me down onto my back. Papa is giant in comparison to my small body. Like a mountain lion trying to mount a fox. It doesn't work. It's not right.

"Papa," I choke out. "Please. I'm afraid."

He wrenches my thighs apart despite my struggling and settles himself against me. His manhood is no longer soft. The wiry hairs that surround it tickle my bare flesh. I don't understand what's happening. Does it please him to rub his naked flesh against mine? Is that how females please males?

My questions only seem to multiply when he spits in his dirty hand. I stare down in fright when he gets his hard length wet with his saliva. Over and over again he does this until it easily slides up and down in his grip. Then, his terrifying glare is on me. I've never seen Papa with such a ferocious look in his eyes. Like when a bear once attacked my brother Solomon. Hungry. Territorial. Fierce.

"Your screams will lessen with time," Papa tells me.

That's the only warning I get before excruciating pain

assaults me. Papa is entering a place I had no idea existed. He's ripping me apart with his manhood. Stabbing me the same way Ezekiel plunges his knife into the animals he attacks. Deep and unforgiving.

My screams don't lessen.

They grow louder with each passing moment.

Louder.

Louder.

Louder.

Until I can't scream any longer.

chapter one

ATTICUS

The Present...

I'VE GOTTEN USED TO REED AND HIS FAMILY. AT FIRST, I was resistant. I'd wanted to get the police involved, but I'm not a fucking home-wrecker. Devon, while slightly brainwashed looking, was happy.

Happy then.

Happy now.

And their kids…

Jesus Christ, I love them like they're family.

I remember asking Reed not long after I discovered they'd had the accident and were surviving with the barest of essentials if they wanted to go back to town. *"They won't understand or approve of our love. Our only chance for survival is here. The love we have is wild and that's where it belongs."* At the time, I'd been rather annoyed that he'd chosen to keep his daughter out in the wilderness, but I'd respected their decision to stay. It wasn't until a few months ago when Reed and I had a little too much to drink that he blabbed about Devon not being biologically his. I wanted to slap that motherfucker upside the head for not telling me the minute I warned him of incest. I'm still a little pissed that he let me think the worst. He's still technically her father as far as legalities go, and that's still fucked up, but the possibility of birth defects evaporated and a weight lifted from my shoulders.

"Rowdy," Devon hollers from upstairs. "Can you bring Mommy Ryder's blanket?"

Rowdy—the kid lives up to his name, I swear—continues to throw punches at me like he's some tough little badass. At three and a half, he has more energy than all the adults combined. Reed smirks at me. Ronan, around a year old, is passed out in his arms.

"Boy," Reed finally grunts. "Better go help your momma."

Rowdy whines but runs off.

"When I get ready to build again," I tell my friend, "your old ass better be ready to help me."

He snorts. "City life getting boring?"

"I hardly call where I live city life."

He rolls his eyes and kisses the top of his son's head. My chest aches. I'm almost forty and I've yet to find a good woman to settle down with. The ones outside of the city are too wild. The ones in the city aren't wild enough. But Devon and Reed have me longing for what they have—aside from the creepy father-daughter shit.

"Have you seen Eve lately?" I ask as I pull my overgrown hair into a man bun that Reed likes to give me shit for.

His brows furrow together. "Ran across her before winter when hunting. Gone by the shack a few times, but she wasn't there. I don't know where she's gone to."

We're both somber for a few moments. If she's out there away from her shack, there's no way she can survive the elements. Eve reminds me of my sister Judith. Our family almost lost Judith under my watch. I was twenty and she was ten. I'd been stalking a fox when I heard the splash. She'd fallen into the river and got swept off. It happened so quickly and had I been near her, I could have snatched her right up. Instead, it took my family and me almost two days to find her. We were sure we were looking for a body. Eventually, I found her in a small crevasse in the mountain on the brink of death. She doesn't remember it to this day, but Mom, Dad, and my two brothers all remember.

And me?

It haunts me.

Fucking plagues me.

All it took was a second.

"Devon's pregnant," Reed says abruptly, pulling me from my thoughts.

I shake my head at him. Those two fuck like bunnies and keep pumping out these damn kids at every turn.

"She just had Ryder like three months ago!" I exclaim.

He smirks and shrugs. "When you live in the wild, you don't have birth control."

I roll my eyes at him. "I put a box of condoms in each of your Christmas stockings."

His laughter is infectious. "Rowdy uses those as water balloons."

"Ridiculous," I grunt.

We launch into a discussion about a treehouse he wants to build for the boys, when Devon tiptoes downstairs. She's all smiles as she kisses Reed and takes the sleeping toddler.

"You guys keep it down. I got both boys asleep upstairs."

I tip my head at her and Reed winks. Once she's gone, he rises and heads over to the kitchen. Everything is rustic in their home, but I brought them real shit to use. Couches. Beds. Sinks. They don't have running water, but Reed makes the painstaking journey each day to fetch it for them. Devon, the brilliant chick she is, has been reading up on water retention and purification. She's convinced by next summer she'll have figured out how to recycle snow and rainwater so Reed doesn't have to haul it in so much.

He snags a bottle of Jack—another Uncle Atticus gift—and fetches his coat. I grab mine and follow him outside. The winter air is frigid, but it doesn't bother us as we sit on the porch swing. We pass the bottle back and forth.

I'm about to take a swig when I hear crunching.

My eyes dart to Reed's in the darkness and he rises, pulling his .45 from his jeans pocket. I stand too and search the darkness. Despite the fence we built, it doesn't mean bears will stay out. It's always in the back of our minds.

We both suck in a sharp breath when the gate creaks open.

Familiar messy brown hair is what I notice first. I bolt from the porch and charge through the snow to get to her.

"Eve!"

Something's not right. She limps and a terrifying moan rips from her chest. And the blood. Fuck, there's blood all over her.

I jerk her into my arms and scoop her up. She won't tell me how old she is, but I'm guessing she's around sixteen now. The girl is short and nothing but bones. I think Rowdy weighs more than her. She sobs against my neck as she clutches my coat. Her tattered clothing hangs off her brutalized body. Once I get her inside, I carry her to the floor near the fireplace. Reed storms in behind me and I can hear him rooting around for the first aid kit.

"Look at me, Eve," I order, my voice tight with emotion. It's like when I found Judith. On the brink of death. Helpless. Broken. "Eve. Look at me."

Her brown eyes flutter open and they're sad. I feel like she's giving up. I stroke her dirty hair from her face and start ripping at the fabric to see where she's hurt. Once I tear apart her clothes, I can assess the damage. Blood coats her abdomen. Long, deep gouges slash across her flesh. Her breasts are so small and her stomach concave. Such a fragile little thing. The bones on her body protrude everywhere. There's no way a small girl like herself can survive such a brutal wound.

Reed kneels down beside me and starts threading a needle. "Clean her wounds," he barks out.

I shake away my daze and set to pouring alcohol on a clean rag. When I dab at the gash near her breast, she cries out, tears spilling from her eyes.

"Shhh," I coo. "We're going to fix you."

Reed's jaw clenches and I understand what he doesn't say.

She won't make it.

Fuck.

I need her to make it.

"Please be strong," I beg as I carefully cleanse her. "Please."

Her eyes roll back and she passes out the moment Reed starts stitching her up. He works quickly but not very neatly. I don't care, though, as long as he closes up those gaping holes in my little friend's body. We manage to get her to choke down some over-the-counter painkillers too. After nearly a half hour of stitching, he's done. I'm careful as I wrap her with gauze. Once we're sure she's not going to die on us, I scoop her in my arms and take her to the guest room Reed and Devon keep for me for when I visit. Reed yanks back the quilt so I can lay her down. I pull the covers back over her so she'll stay warm.

"We need to keep an eye on her. If she hasn't improved by morning, you probably should take her into town to the hospital," Reed utters, reluctance in his voice.

It's the last thing she'd want.

"She'll improve," I assure him, my teeth grinding to dust. "She has to."

He gives me a clipped nod before slipping out of the room. I undress down to my boxers and climb into bed next to her. Wrapping my massive body around her tiny, fragile one, I warm her. She's blue and icy to the touch. I just need her to get better.

Her breaths are ragged and raspy. I worry about her lungs and her heart and everyfuckingthing.

"Stay alive and I'll bring you all the fruit you could ever dream of," I vow, pressing kisses to her temple. "Stay alive, little one. For me."

She turns her head slightly and her eyes crack open. Her hand shakes as she touches my scruffy face. My heart leaps at her movements. I want to squeeze the life out of her, but one hug from me could probably do just that, so I refrain.

"Fruit," she rasps, her lips dry and cracked.

I kiss her right on the mouth because it's the closest part of her to me. "Yes, Eve, fruit. Just hang in there for me."

Her eyes flutter closed, but a smile quirks up her lips on one side. This girl never smiles except when fruit is involved. My little Eve. For three and a half years I've looked out for this girl. I sure as hell won't stop now. Not when she's out there all alone. I'll protect her. Eve needs me.

And goddammit, I need her too.

"Fruit," she whispers, and my heart leaps in my chest. "Atticus…"

chapter two

EVE

"Eve." The sound is rich and throaty. Like the sound of a bear grunting as he plays with his cubs. Deep and rumbly. Possessive yet loving.

In my dreams, I always ran away to live with the bear in his cave. He was a nice bear despite the claws and teeth. I could burrow up against him for warmth and he simply held me.

"Eve."

I crack my eyes open and a sharp searing pain rips across my chest. I'm thrust into reality where I remember that real bears aren't cuddly or sweet. They are ferocious. Feral. Hungry. And the bear I happened upon when I was checking my rabbit trap wanted to devour me. He was giant and determined. But I'm small and clever. The big beast managed to swipe his sharp claws across me, but I slipped away from him. Always quiet and light on my feet. I disappeared into the night.

"Eve."

The voice is familiar and relentless. Deep down, I know who it is. It was him I'd sought as soon as I knew my injuries were too grave to treat on my own. I wasn't sure he'd be at Reed and Devon's big home on the hill, but I'd hoped they would know how to contact him.

Atticus Knox.

I've hardly said more than five words to him in the past three and a half years, but I've come to know him as someone safe and trustworthy. In the wild, the people you come across aren't always that way. They steal from you or hurt you. They try to own you.

I belong to no one.

Reed Jamison made sure of it the day he ripped my brother Nathaniel from my body and slaughtered him in front of me. I was certain he'd kill me too, but he didn't. And while he frightened me, that all changed when Devon gave birth to Rowdy in my home. The way he treated her and loved her was something I'd never experienced before.

Reed didn't rule over Devon.

If anything, it was as if she ruled over him.

It made no sense and went against everything Papa and my brothers taught me about marriage. When Papa and Ezekiel were killed, John claimed I was his wife, but he let Solomon and Nathaniel take turns. I hated my father and brothers with a passion. When Reed murdered them all, I felt free. No man would ever lay claim on me again.

"Eve."

I'm exhausted and my chest is on fire. My toes still feel frozen. And I'm in the warmest, softest, best smelling bed I've ever been in. I'm not eager to wake from this dream.

To wake up all alone, cold to the bone, in my little shack. I shudder at that thought.

"Eve."

My stomach cramps and I'm reminded that my cycle is due. I remember heavily menstruating the night Devon had her son in my home. I was terrified Reed would notice. That he'd try and mount me like my father and brothers had. But he never did. His eyes only ever saw Devon, which was fine by me.

When Atticus came along, I was terrified. I even tried to stab him. He'd been gentle with me, though. Regarded me with the kindest eyes I'd ever seen. All my fears lessened when he smiled. He had teeth. Bright, shiny, white teeth. A mouthful of them. Prettiest mouth ever. It wasn't until he began dropping in on me from time to time that I began to trust him. Fruit. Always fruit. Eve was tempted by fruit in the Bible, so it's fitting I'm the same way.

Sweet. Syrupy. Delicious.

The best thing I'd ever tasted.

My stomach groans.

"Fruit," I croak, my voice sounding foreign to my own ears.

I manage to open my eyes and two glittering green orbs bore into me. Like the hot summer days when I lie on the riverbanks and stare into the sky. The sun is severe and blinding but warms me to my core.

Atticus's eyes are that way.

They soak into me. Heat me. Burn me in ways that feel good.

I like his eyes on me.

"How are you feeling, little fox?" His voice is deep and it seems to rattle the bed.

My cheeks heat under his intense gaze. *Better now that you're here, big bear.* I don't say those words, though. I don't say anything. Instead, I study his face. Something about his face is hard to look away from. His hair is the color of honey straight from the combs. Rich, golden, perfect. He sometimes pulls it out of his eyes in a silly knot on the back of his head. It fascinates me. I want to tug the band that holds it in place away so I can run my fingers through it to see if it feels as soft as it looks. Unlike Reed and my family, Atticus's face has less hair. The hair is clipped short so you can still see the bones in his face. His jawline is sharp and his cheekbones pronounced. The nose on his face is strong but has a slight bump in the middle. I want to touch that too.

But I don't.

I never touch him despite my cravings.

He's a man.

What if he wants to make me his wife?

A shudder ripples through me. Atticus is larger than Reed or Ezekiel. His shoulders are every bit as wide as the bear that attacked me last night and he's nearly as tall. Muscles upon muscles are what make up Atticus Knox. He's both beautiful and terrifying all in one breath. If he wanted to mount me and teach me how to be his wife, he could. Easily. After three and a half years of being free, I'd belong to someone again. The pain would come back.

Another shudder.

"Eve," he coos, his voice soft like the underbelly of a rabbit. "I'm here. I will protect you and look after you."

His warm words calm my stuttering heart. He isn't touching me in any awful ways, so I greedily steal the moment. Sometimes, from afar, I watch how Reed strokes his fingers along Devon's cheek. How she leans into his touch and meets his gaze with a smile. I've watched them for years and I've never seen him hurt her. The sounds that come from their cabin when he mounts her are ones of pleasure. Like when you sink your teeth into a juicy berry and a moan slips out.

Just. Like. That.

Warmth curls deep in my belly despite my injuries. I can't say I hate the feeling. It's a tingly feeling that seems to ripple through my body.

"You have to get better," Atticus murmurs. "For me."

My gaze falls to his full lips. They're pink and look soft. Without thinking, I bring my fingers to his mouth and touch them. His breath hitches and he regards me with a frown. Perhaps he doesn't like it. Feeling chastised, I pull them away. He presses a kiss to my nose and a strangled sound escapes me. Papa and my brothers would kiss me often, but this doesn't feel like punishment. It feels like a reward. Before I can consider his actions, he climbs out of bed.

I've never seen anything so mesmerizing.

I knew he was muscular, but I hadn't seen him without his clothes on. Now, he's wearing nothing but some tight black underwear. His back has artwork drawn all over it and a pang of jealousy cuts through me as I wonder if his wife drew it on him. I never considered that maybe he has a wife. It would certainly explain why he didn't mount me.

He jerks on his clothes as if he's angry, with his beautiful back to me. Eventually, his art becomes hidden when he pulls his shirt on. When he steals a glance at me, his eyes seem worried.

"I'm sorry, Eve," he says, his throat bobbing. "I'm going to have to do something you're not going to like."

Terror wells up inside me. It doesn't make any sense. If he's going to mount me, then why did he put his clothes back on? Where is the hunger in his gaze like Papa's and my brothers'? I'm confused when he leaves the bedroom completely.

I try to sit up, but it hurts too much. Hot tears roll down my temples.

Beyond the walls, Atticus and Reed are arguing. These walls aren't thin like the ones at my shack. I can't hear like I want. Why are they angry?

A few moments later, Atticus storms in with a scowl on his face. Reed follows behind him, his nostrils flaring. Panic assaults me and renders me immobile. Are they going to take turns mounting me like Nathaniel and John used to do?

"P-Please…" I choke out.

Reed glowers at Atticus. "She doesn't want to go."

Atticus growls like the bear that attacked me. "Goddammit, Reed. She's feverish. I've waited for four fucking days for her to get better, but it's not."

Four days? I thought it was one.

He continues, "There's infection, I'm sure of it. She needs a doctor."

Most of his words are gibberish, but I get the gist. He wants to take me away.

"They'll put her in child protective services. Eve can't survive in that world," Reed bellows. Despite the sharp tone, I feel like he's trying to protect me.

"She'll die if we don't do something. I can't…" Atticus

pinches the bridge of his nose and closes his eyes. "I won't let her die."

My panicked gaze dances back and forth between them. I nearly stop breathing when I see the resignation in Reed's brown eyes.

"Promise you'll bring her back the moment she's better," he pleads.

Atticus nods at him before turning his attention on me. He sits beside me and takes my hand despite my attempt to pull it away.

"You're not getting better," Atticus tells me, his voice firm. "I'm going to take you someplace where they'll give you medicine."

I shake my head. "N-No."

His jaw clenches. "I'm sorry, but I won't take no for an answer."

A screech rips from me when he slides his strong arms beneath me and lifts. The pain across my chest is intense. The more I move, the more it hurts. Defeated, I choke on my sobs as Atticus carries me through the house. I feel eyes on me—most likely Devon and the children—but I can't meet their gazes. I'm wounded and weak. I'm at this man's mercy. He carries me to his truck. It's big and black and terrifying. Papa used to tell me stories of his father's truck. A metal contraption that takes you to far places so you don't have to walk.

I don't want to go anywhere far.

I want to stay here.

But I'm powerless to fight against him. He lays me down in the back seat before he climbs into the front. The truck roars to life and within minutes we're moving. I try to sit up, but I can't move. All I can see are the trees rushing by at an alarming speed.

I want to claw at him and demand he take me back, but I'm too tired.

From the simple exertion of screaming, I'm depleted of my energy. With a sob, I close my eyes and hope that wherever we end up, no one tries to keep me as theirs. I don't want to be kept.

I want to be free.

chapter three

ATTICUS

EVE SLEEPS PEACEFULLY IN MY BED WHILE I PACE MY
bedroom and panic. Taking her to the hospital was out
of the question. They'd demand answers I didn't have
to give. And quite frankly, Eve would have been traumatized
as fuck. Which is why I called in a favor to a friend.

Suma Walkingstick and I go way back. My parents used
to hire the Native American woman to watch over us during
the summers when they'd travel to California. Suma is wise
and known for having remedies for everything. Even local
doctors have called upon her when modern medicine doesn't
do the trick. But it isn't her healer ways that had me dialing
her number, it was desperation. If anyone could help her and
keep it discreet, it was Suma.

"This paste will help the infection on the surface. The
elixir we made her drink will help beneath the surface," Suma
explains. Her dark brown leathery skin is a contrast to Eve's
pale white flesh. "The paste must be applied four times a day.

It will burn and itch, but it needs to be applied." She clicks her tongue in disproval. "The stitching your friend did isn't right, Atticus. It needs to be pulled out soon. Until then, keep the child comfortable."

I swallow and nod. "Is she going to be okay?"

Her black eyebrows furrow together as she regards me with the palest blue eyes I've ever seen. My brothers Will and Vic used to tease me that Suma was a witch. "The Wild burns in her veins. When we forced the elixir down her throat, I saw into the windows of her soul. She's untamed. The child doesn't fit in the world we know. Once she's healed, you need to free her."

I bristle at the thought of letting Eve go back out into the wilderness where she's practically defenseless. I'll cross that bridge when I get there. "Thank you."

The short old woman waddles over to me and takes my cheeks in her hands as she looks up at me. "Anything for you, son."

I lean down so she can kiss my forehead. Suma and I grew close after Judith nearly died. I blamed myself for not watching my sister. Even after she was fine and back home, happy as could be, I held onto that guilt. Suma taught me how to release that from my mind. Explained that the dark thoughts that owned me were evil in nature. That I was too good to allow the darkness to steal me. Eventually, I learned to work through that guilt with her help.

Leading her out to my porch, I watch with a frown as she climbs on her old bicycle and rides away through the snow. Suma lives six miles from me and refuses to let me drive her anywhere. That old woman will live to be a hundred easily. Nobody her age is in that good of shape.

An owl hoots in the distance. It will be dark soon. At night, the wilderness comes to life. I'm still twelve miles away from town. Close enough for amenities and to see my family, but far out enough that I don't hear the buzz of people. Trees surround my modest home. It's peaceful here.

I slip back inside and lock up. My home isn't large. I don't require a lot of space being that it's just me. I have a living room with a single recliner because I don't ever entertain guests. But what I do have, that I find difficult living without, is electricity. The television mounted on the wall looks ridiculous in the space when not turned on, but it's pretty badass when I can watch football in high definition.

Walking past the living room, I make my way into the small kitchen. A refrigerator, stove, and microwave are about it in here. I have a small table with two chairs in one corner despite always eating alone. I'm thankful to have the other chair because Eve will have a place to sit. I grab a bottle of water from the fridge and make my way back to my bedroom. The shower calls to me as it always does after spending time camping. It's one of the reasons I couldn't live like Reed and Devon. I love a hot shower more than anything in this world.

I rip off my clothes once I'm in the tiny bathroom and stare at myself in the mirror as the shower heats up. The scar on my right shoulder is a living reminder of why I live out here in the woods rather than in Colorado playing for the Denver Broncos. Gritting my teeth, I tear my gaze from the mirror and step under the hot spray. The water cleanses away the body odor and dirt buildup of a few weeks with Reed and his family. I scrub until I feel raw. And fuck does it feel like heaven to be able to wash my hair again. Once I'm good and clean, I stare down at my cock. Thick and limp.

I hardly get an erection anymore. The last two I'd had were when I was staying with Reed and Devon. Those two fuck all the time. And I'll be damned if hearing them have sex didn't make my dick hard. Embarrassing as shit having to whack off into one of my dirty T-shirts.

The water eventually grows cold and I climb out. I snag a plush towel and tie it around my waist. I'm just sauntering out of the bathroom, water dripping from my hair, when I notice Eve's awake. Her eyes are open as she stares up at my ceiling. Suma had rubbed the green paste all over Eve's chest wounds and ordered me to leave it open so it could dry the paste. My gaze falls to Eve's chest. Her breasts are small and her nipples are hardened pebbles. When my cock thumps against my leg, I tear my eyes from her and rush over to my dresser. *I did not just get a semi looking at a teenager's tits.* With a growl, I yank it open and locate a pair of loose boxers to sleep in.

When I turn around, she's watching me. Her brown eyes flicker with distrust and fear. I run my fingers through my wet hair and motion around me.

"This is my house. You'll be safe here." I point at her chest but don't break eye contact. "A nice lady friend of mine treated your wounds. We need to apply the paste four times daily so you'll heal. Are you hungry?"

She winces in pain and nods. "Fruit."

My lips tug into a half smile. Of course she wants fruit. Little Eve loves her fruit. Her only request ever. I stride through my house and set to pouring two cans of fruit into a Tupperware bowl. I snatch a fork and head back to my bedroom. Eve tries to sit up and I growl.

"Don't do that."

Her nostrils flare, but she obeys. When I sit beside her on the bed, she's tense. Using the fork, I cut the peach slices into bite-sized pieces. Then, I stab one before bringing it to her cracked pink lips.

"Open."

Her mouth parts and I feed the fruit into the opening. A sound of pleasure rumbles from her. Again, my cock thickens against my thigh. Ignoring the blood rushing there, I feed her until all the fruit is gone. Once I've put the bowl up, I assist her in sipping from the bottle of water. I can tell with every grimace that she hates accepting my help. Eve is independent and fierce. She must feel like a prisoner in her own body.

"Time to rest, Eve."

I flip off the lights before crawling in bed next to her. This will be the fifth night I've slept by her side. Ever since she collapsed in Reed's yard, bloody and on the brink of death, I can't bring myself to leave her side. I feel responsible for her. Eve has no one. She needs someone.

Her breathing is soft in the darkness. Despite the central heat that warms the space, her body is cool to the touch. The fever has let up, thank fuck. I wrap my arm across her lower torso and press my hot body against hers to warm her. The tension melts away as she accepts my gift of heat. Soon, we both fall asleep.

"More," the brunette begs as she holds onto the headboard. *"Please."*

Her tiny pale ass just begs to be bitten and marked. I give it a good slap before driving hard enough into her that my balls slap against her bare pussy, making a loud smack. I tangle my fist in her dark locks and yank her head back. She moans and soon her body is shuddering around my cock. My orgasm explodes from me with a groan.

I wake to the early morning birds chirping outside the window. Today, despite the hour, it's dark out, which means more goddamned snow. A yawn escapes me and I take stock of my situation. Bile creeps up my throat when I realize my boxers are drenched. I had a wet fucking dream. Came in my shorts like a damn teenager. All of that would be bearable if not for the fact my thigh is pressed against Eve's core. Her legs are parted to accommodate my big leg.

Fuck.

Fuck.

Fuck.

My heart is thundering in my chest. I'm a fucking pervert. I just came with my dick pressed against a teenager's hip. I'll be forty damn years old in April. What the hell is wrong with me?

She stirs and I remain still. I'm too horrified to move. If she falls back asleep, then I can creep out of here. I'm planning my escape when she starts clawing at the skin on her chest surrounding the gashes.

"Eve," I bark out suddenly, my voice hoarse from sleep. "Don't do that."

She ignores me and continues scratching. I snag her wrist and clutch it tight. When she starts in with the other, I grip it too. Pinning them both to the bed, I glare at her.

"I said no."

Her brown eyes flame with fury. It's the most life I've seen in her eyes since long before the accident when I saw her last. I try to ignore the fact that my wet boxers are smashed against her bare flesh.

"It itches," she hisses out, her nostrils flaring.

My gaze softens. "I know, but you can't scratch it. It'll hurt."

"Are you going to mount me?" Her words are but a whisper.

It takes me a moment to register what she's asking. I jerk away from her as though I've been bitten by a snake. In my haste to jump from the bed, I knock the quilt to the floor. Her naked body in my bed speaks to my cock, which doesn't understand rules. It rises of its own accord.

"W-What?" I demand. "No. I'm not going to…mount you." Even as I spit those words out in disgust, a quick image flits in my head. One where she's healed and I'm buried deep inside her. I'm sickened that I would think such a horrible thing about a girl. "Fuck. Fuck!"

She goes to claw at her skin again. It distracts me from the giant fucking boner I have going on and I once again pounce on her. If she reopens those wounds, it could be bad. She squirms against my hold. Using my body weight, I pin her to the mattress. Between us, her chest heaves from exertion. Like the stupid fuck I am, I glance down. Her tits are perky as ever and her nipples still hard. I close my eyes and attempt to shake away the vision.

"Are you going to mount me?" She asks the god-damned question again that has me going fucking mental. Instead of flipping out, I pop my eyes open and glare at her.

"No, Eve. I'm not some sick rapist."

She relaxes and her features soften. If she notices that my cock throbs against her thigh with need, she doesn't let on. "Thank you."

"You're welcome. Now can you hold still and let me apply more paste?"

She nods and bites on her bottom lip in a nervous manner. Fuck if that shit doesn't go straight to my dick too. I slide off the bed and throw some jeans on because I need more of a barrier between us than my wet boxers. Once I'm covered, I bring the quilt back over her thighs to her hips, averting my eyes from between her legs. My gaze dances across her nipples again and I want to punch myself in the fucking face for having zero self-control. I snag the bowl of paste from the end table and scoop out a glob on my fingertips. Her breath hisses when I begin spreading it across the gashes. My pinky brushes against her nipple and I have to close my eyes to stop any feral sounds from es-caping my throat.

What the fuck has gotten into me?

This is Eve.

Little fox.

Not some goddamned plaything.

Once I finish, I flash her a quick smile. "Rest up. I need to take a shower and then I'll get you some fruit."

Her entire face lights up as she smiles—wide, bright, beautiful. I don't think I've ever seen Eve smile like this. Fucking ever. I'm so taken aback by it that I stumble away from her. It isn't until I'm in the shower under the hot spray that I realize my obsession with her has bloomed into something forbidden. I lean my forehead against the cold tile and grip my aching cock. My eyes close as I attempt to bring forth the brunette I'd been dreaming about when I unexpectedly came. I jerk at my dick as I think about her ass and the bones on her spine. Her dark hair. I'm getting close when the girl in my vision turns around to look at me. Deep brown eyes. Soulful as fuck. Eve. With a choked grunt, I release my orgasm and my seed spurts against the tiled wall.

Fuck.

Fuck.

Fuck!

I start scrubbing my body forcefully as punishment to myself. The last thing I need is to be fantasizing over Eve. She's still a kid, for fuck's sake. Whatever stupid fantasies are in my head cannot leave this shower. They need to slip down the drain and straight into hell where they belong.

I can't think about her like that.

I can't.

I just fucking can't.

When I dry off and throw my jeans back on sans underwear, I saunter into the room, expecting her to be asleep. Instead, I find her staring at me. Her big brown eyes aren't angry or frightened. They flicker with curiosity. With a grunt, I make my way over to my closet and snag a T-shirt off the hanger.

"It's warm here," she murmurs.

I halt and turn to regard her. "Do you think you can get up today?"

She starts attempting to sit up, so I rush over to her. Together, we manage to get her into a sitting position. Her chest looks awful, but it's not half as angry as it was before. The paste is already helping.

"I need to…" Her cheeks burn bright red. "Go." Her gaze darts to the window. And by go, she doesn't mean leave. She needs to pee.

"Can you walk or should I carry you?"

"Carry me."

I ignore the fire burning through me as I scoop her tiny body into my arms. She weighs nothing. I bet she barely breaks a hundred pounds on the scale. A yelp escapes her when I sit her on the toilet.

"Cold!"

Laughing, I release her and take a step back. "It's a toilet. You relieve yourself into it. That's toilet paper you use to clean up with and then that little lever is to flush it all away."

Her eyes are wide and her lip is slightly curled up. "Where does it all go?"

"Through pipes to a septic tank."

"What's a septic tank?"

I'm about to open my mouth when I hear tinkling in the toilet. Like the sick motherfucker I am, I can't help but glance down between her thighs. Her urine streams out and my dick is fucking hard in my jeans again. I back out of the bathroom, clipping my shoulder on the frame before stumbling into the room.

"Call for me when you're done," I bark out and stalk away. I run my fingers through my still wet, wild hair. I'm losing my damn mind. Bringing her here, after going so long without sex or the touch of a woman, was a bad idea. I need to get her well and dump her ass back at Reed's. I start slamming drawers on the hunt for a T-shirt.

I'm still beating myself up when I hear the toilet flush. She lets out a choked sound, which has me rushing back into the small bathroom. Her eyes are teary as she stares at the mirror.

"Esther?" Her fingertips reach up and she touches the glass.

I come up behind her and frown at our reflections. "It's a mirror. Like when you see yourself in the river."

Understanding dawns in her eyes, but not before a tear snakes down her dirty cheek. I hand her the giant white T-shirt.

"Put this on and then we'll get some food in you."

She allows me to help her dress. I'm mindful of her gashes and keep my eyes diverted. Once she's dressed, I lock my arm around her tiny waist and slowly guide her to the kitchen. She's quiet, but I can see her taking everything in. Outside, the snow falls heavy and thick, but we're warm inside. I sit her at the table with a can of fruit and then start on making her something hot.

"I don't have many perishables since I've been gone for a while, but I'll pick some up next time I go to town. I hope you like oatmeal." She'd probably do better to have real steel cut oats, but all I have is the instant shit I loved when I was a kid. I choose the apples and cinnamon flavor for her and set to making it. Once I finish, I place the steaming bowl in front of her.

I make some coffee for the both of us. I'm not sure if she'll like it or not, but I think the caffeine could do her some good.

"What is this?"

I turn to see her devouring the oatmeal. Her eyes are bright and happy. It eases the tension in my shoulders. My T-shirt swallows her. Her skin is dirty and bloody—a stark contrast against the clean white shirt. I've brought the wild home and she stands out against everything in the clean, sparse home.

"Oatmeal. You like it?"

"More," she pleads, her voice a needy whisper. With her eyes on me like that, I go back to losing my damn mind.

I set a steaming mug of coffee, that I mixed in extra sugar and cream since she appears to love sweet shit, in front of her. "Drink this. I'll make you more oatmeal."

The sounds of pleasure coming from her as she sips the hot liquid warm me. It gives me satisfaction to show her new things. By the time I've made her a second bowl of oatmeal, she's downed the entire cup of coffee. Her eyes dart around all over the place, curiosity evident in her features.

"If you're feeling up to it, you're free to explore," I tell her. "Just stay inside. You're hurt and we need to get you well."

"Free."

I let out a chuckle when she starts inhaling the oatmeal. I'll need to add that to the grocery list since she's such a fan. Absently, she scratches at her chest and it reminds me that her stitches need to come out. The thought of seeing her naked again fucks with my head. When I go to town to get groceries, I'll have to find one of my fuck buddies to get my mind off this bullshit for a while.

"I need to clean your wounds," I tell her, my tone gruff. "Then maybe you could shower."

Her nose crinkles and I'll be damned if she hasn't ever looked cuter. "Shower? Like rain shower?"

I chuckle and take her empty dishes to the sink. "Something like that, but warmer."

After I grab my first aid kid and a giant bottle of rubbing alcohol, I set them on the table and kneel in front of her. "Shirt needs to come off."

Instead of removing it, she lifts her arms, her brown eyes boring into me. I grit my teeth but gently take her shirt off. With extreme focus, I begin cleaning away the paste and dirt and blood with the alcohol. She whimpers and cries but doesn't push me away. Once she's clean, I grab the small scissors and begin the tedious task of cutting out the stitches. It takes over an hour, but I manage to free her from them. Already, after one day of having the paste, her wounds are much better. Bringing her here so Suma could treat her was a good decision. Even if my dick keeps trying to make bad ones.

"Shower," she reminds me.

I smirk. "You're a woman who knows what she wants and isn't afraid to ask for it."

She reaches forward and touches my teeth. "How come your teeth don't fall out? Like Papa's or my brothers'?" I think this is the most I've ever heard her speak all at once.

I snort. "I brush them."

Her eyes widen in horror. "Will mine fall out?"

"If you don't keep them clean, it's inevitable."

She swallows. "Clean them in the shower?"

"It's a little more complicated than that," I say with a chuckle. "But nothing you can't handle on your own once I show you."

chapter four

EVE

THIS PLACE IS STRANGE. CLEAN AND WARM AND free of threats. It's filled with the most delicious foods and the clothing is soft. Best part is, Atticus is here. His scent is everywhere. He smells one part like the pine trees but also a scent I don't know. It smells good, though. His eyes are always on me. They flicker with fire—the same fire Papa and my brothers had sometimes. It makes me wonder if he wants to mount me and take me as his wife. The thought isn't a bad one like with my family. With Atticus, it makes my belly burn with want. It makes me curious to know what his mouth tastes like.

Just thinking about his mouth has me ashamed. He cleans his teeth, which is why they are so bright white like fresh snow on the first day of winter. I want mine to be clean too.

"I'll get you your own toothbrush," he tells me. "For now, we can share mine."

His strong grip is once again on my waist. The shirt he gave me hides my body from him. I don't like wearing it, despite it smelling like him, because he can't look at my body with that hungry stare I've come to enjoy. But having his hands on me, like now, is better than his eyes. I like the way he's gentle with me but powerful enough not to let me fall. We make it into the small room where the toilet is, and he once again stands behind me. Our gazes meet In the mirror.

Atticus is beautiful. His skin golden and his hair silky. Compared to my dark, matted locks, he looks like what I imagine the angels in Papa's Bible to look like. It embarrasses me because I don't look like him. Mud and blood are crusted on my face and in my hair.

His body is hard and hot pressed against my back. I can feel his manhood poking into me. My eyes meet his and I'm fascinated when his cheeks turn ruddy as though he doesn't want me to know his manhood is ready to mount.

"I'll go first so you can watch me," he murmurs, his voice husky and scratchy.

I pay special attention to the way he squeezes some blue paste onto a tiny brush. He brings it to his mouth and begins vigorously scrubbing. Foam spills from his mouth into the bowl under the mirror. He reminds me of the animals that sometimes get the madness. But he winks at me and it causes a flash of heat to course through me. He spits into the sink and then turns a lever. Water comes out and he rinses the brush. Once he's all clean, and his teeth certainly sparkle now, he hands me the brush. I hold it steady while he squeezes more blue paste out. Mimicking his actions, I start scrubbing. The paste makes my mouth cold, but I like it. Actually, I love it. I scrub and scrub until I'm foaming from the mouth too. I'm mad. Positively mad. I giggle and nearly choke on the foamy paste.

I spit and rinse like he did. My mouth feels clean and smooth and refreshed. "Can I do it again?"

He chuckles and it reminds me of how Nathaniel would laugh when he was a boy. Soft and playful and warm. "After every meal if you want. But now we need to get the rest of you clean. Just take the shirt off and bathe under the hot spray." He turns on the shower and then leaves me alone.

I'm not sure about this shower he speaks of, but I do as I'm told. I take off the shirt and pull the cloth to the side to peek inside. All white smooth rocks of some sort. Steam billows around me. When I reach out and the hot water pounds into my hand, I shriek.

Atticus storms back into the bathroom, the concern for me rippling from him. I'm comforted by his presence.

"I-I don't know what to do. Does it hurt? Can you teach me?"

His green eyes blaze with an emotion I don't understand, but finally he grunts in agreement. He stares at my breasts for a long moment before he shakes his head. "I need to find my swim trunks."

I frown in confusion. "Why? Are we swimming?"

"Actually," he grunts. "It's fine. Just…just don't look."

He unfastens his pants and they fall to the floor. His giant manhood springs to life. I watch in awe as it bounces out in front of him. Points at me as if it knows me.

It's on the tip of my tongue to ask him if he's going to

mount me and make me his wife. But earlier, he'd gotten angry. The thought that maybe I'm too dirty crosses my mind. For once, I'm disappointed to not be wanted. I sulk as I step into the shower. His massive body joins me and I'm forced under the hot spray.

I've never felt anything like it.

I moan as the heat rushes over my dirty skin. His manhood pokes against my hip. We stand there for a long moment, his body pressed against mine in the small space and the hot water cleansing me. My breath catches in my throat when he squirts something cool on top of my head. Then, his long, strong fingers are massaging it into my scalp. I moan in pleasure.

"I'm washing your hair," he explains, his voice but a whisper. "We might have to wash it a couple of times. You're lucky I have long hair. I only buy the expensive shit."

I have no idea what he's talking about and I don't care. All I care about is the way he makes my body thrum to life with just his fingers. He truly is an angel from the Bible. I'm completely lost in this wondrous dream as he tends to me. Scrubs and rinses over and over again. Eventually, he claims he's finished and hands me a slippery white block.

"Soap. Use it to wash away the dirt," he tells me.

When I frown at him, he chuckles. "Just rub it all over your body."

I bite on my lip but obey him. The soap smells good and I like how it feels on my flesh. His manhood is still hard and expectant. I wonder how it will fit. If it will fit. Will he be gentle like Solomon sometimes was? Will he be brutal like Ezekiel?

"You're crying," he whispers, his fingers lifting my jaw.

I blink away the tears. "Will it hurt when you mount me?" Boldly, I reach down and grasp his manhood. "It's so big and I'm so small."

He lets out a choked sound as he backs me against the wall. The fire in his eyes lights a fire within me. "Eve, baby, you can't touch me there," he growls. "Please." And yet his hips slightly buck against my grip as if my hand is the best thing he's ever felt.

"Will it hurt?" I try again. I'm fascinated with the way his manhood jolts in my grip.

He leans his forehead against mine and grinds his teeth. "It won't hurt because it won't ever happen." Slowly, he pulls away from my grip. "Fuck."

My chest aches in disappointment. "Why don't you want me to be your wife?" I don't understand the way I feel inside.

"You're like sixteen or some shit, Eve." He scrubs at his face with his palm. "I'm almost forty."

He's worried about my age? My family never worried about these things.

"But your body wants mine," I argue, my gaze falling to his manhood that is very much still alive. "Your manhood is ready for me."

"My cock," he corrects, "has a mind of its own. I shouldn't be showering naked with you, Eve. This is wrong."

He slips out of the shower and leaves me alone. The rejection crushes me. Tears, much hotter than the shower water, burn down my cheeks. I stand there silently crying until the water shuts off. Atticus, now fully dressed, pulls the cloth away and holds up a giant warm blanket. Reed and Devon have these same ones.

"Dry off. These are towels," he tells me, his eyes diverted to the floor. "Get dressed. I want to show you something."

After he leaves, I use the towel to swipe away the water droplets. I put on a new, clean shirt that smells like him. He's left more garments, but when I try to put them on, they swallow me and won't stay on. Eventually, I give up. When the steam melts away from the mirror, I'm shocked to see the woman staring back at me.

Clean.

Wide brown eyes.

Full lips.

I'm still amazed at how much I look like Esther. It's like she's here with me. Staring back at me. I hear sounds coming from the other room. When I enter, moving pictures are dancing across a black box on the wall.

"It's called a television. It's meant to relax and entertain you," he explains from his cushy chair. "Now sit and let me brush out that mess."

With my eyes glued to the television, I watch in awe as people move and talk. Everyone is clean and smiling. I'm amazed. Gently, Atticus begins brushing through the knots in my hair. It feels good—like when he scrubbed my scalp in the shower. I find myself drifting off while he brushes.

"Hey," he murmurs, waking me from my nap. "You're shivering."

He urges me into his warm lap. I curl into his bare chest and bury my nose against his neck. His giant arms wrap around me and I once again fall asleep.

the wild

I wake in his bed. He's nowhere to be found. It's dark outside now and a quiver of unease ripples through me. I can hear him making sounds in the other room. Clangs and rattles. My chest is wet with newly applied salve and my shirt is gone. Heat pools between my thighs as I imagine him touching me while I slept. Forgoing the shirt, I use the toilet like he taught me and brush my teeth. I love the cold, clean feeling in my mouth. I'm quiet as I creep out of the room. He's in the kitchen preparing food and it makes my stomach growl.

When his green eyes lift, they flicker with hunger. I love the feral look in them.

"Eve," he grunts. "Where's your shirt?"

"You took it off me."

His jaw clenches. "Go put it on."

"It irritates my wound," I murmur, the lie shaky on my tongue.

All I get is a grunt in return as he goes back to stirring. I'm curious, so I make my way into the room with the delicious smells. Foods I've never seen are boiling.

"Spaghetti," he tells me as if that strange word makes sense.

"Spaghetti," I repeat.

"Here," he says as he scoops some of the red sauce into a spoon. He blows on it and then offers it to me. "Taste it." His eyes bore into mine and I wonder why he doesn't like looking at my naked form.

I part my lips and accept his gift. I've never tasted anything like it. A low moan of pleasure escapes me as I devour the small taste. "This is extraordinary."

He smirks and gives me a half shrug. "It's even better with the noodles. Can you please wear something?" The strain in his voice has me wanting to look at his cock as he calls it. As if it calls to me, it bulges proudly in his pants. Since my nakedness seems to bring him physical pain based upon the frown on his face, I reluctantly go dress.

Once I walk back into the kitchen, I settle in the chair and watch him cook. It smells so good and my stomach grumbles loudly. His jaw clenches as he cooks quietly. I close my eyes and think of my sister and of Mama too. There was a time when I was happy. My mother would tell me stories of the city. Places called restaurants and movie theaters and malls. It all sounded so magical. Papa would always get stern with her and tell her she was filling our heads with nonsense.

I wonder if I'm allowed to talk about the nonsense with Atticus. Would he frown like Papa and tell me not to speak of it? Worry niggles at me. As soon as I am well, I will leave his home. Everything here is too unusual and I feel out of place. I don't want to say or do the wrong thing.

I just want to be free.

But you're lonely.

The voice within me mocks me and emotion quivers through me. My lower stomach is aching and I know I'll be menstruating soon. The sadness is always the worst during that week each month. Perhaps I should leave before I start. Tears fall and don't stop for days on end sometimes. I certainly don't want Atticus seeing me that way.

"Here you go, little fox," he murmurs as he sets down the mountain of food in front of me.

I lift my gaze to his and our eyes lock for a moment. My core clenches simply from looking at him.

Because he's so beautiful.

Blinking away that thought, I stare down at the food that steams. I wait for him to sit and eye my plate warily. When I kill rabbits or squirrels, I cook their carcasses over the fire and eat the meat from the bones. And the fruit I just gulp straight from the can. I'm unsure how to eat this…spaghetti.

He picks up a utensil and starts twisting. Then, he shovels in a bite, the red sauce splattering over his whiskers. It makes me smile. He freezes mid-chew and I wonder if I did something wrong. Quickly, I look down at my plate.

"My friend Suma Walkingstick will be by tomorrow to check on you," he says after he swallows his food.

I carefully pick up my utensil and attempt to mimic his actions. The twisting is difficult and if the food wasn't so hot, I'd settle for just picking it up with my fingers and eating it that way. I manage to get some of the food into my mouth but most of it falls back onto the plate. I let out a frustrated groan.

"Would you like me to cut it up to make it easier to eat?" he asks. Our eyes meet and his green ones sparkle with humor.

My cheeks burn in shame. I remember my brothers ridiculing me and this doesn't feel much different.

"Fruit," I snap and let out a huff.

"Whoa," he says, chuckling. "Calm down. I wasn't

283

insulting you. I'm just trying to help." His bare foot nudges mine under the table and it sends currents of excitement zapping through me. Instead of retreating, I rub my cold feet against his warm one.

"I don't eat food like this."

He lets out a sigh. "Which is why you're skinny as fuck. We're going to fix that, Eve. I'm going to teach you things."

The utensil falls to the plate with a clatter and I rise to my feet. My hands tremble with worry. "I don't want to learn," I rasp out. I cringe at the many lessons my father and brothers taught me.

Slowly, like I do sometimes when I'm sneaking up on an animal I need to kill for food, he rises. Both his palms are out and his brows are furled together.

"I won't ever hurt you," he rumbles, the vow thick in his voice.

Somehow, I believe him.

I've known him for years and he's not hurt me once. In fact, he's only tried to please me with gifts and kindness.

"I can't stay. I don't need a husband," I whisper.

His lips flatten into a firm line and he shakes his head. "Whoever hurt you from before…" he trails off. "I'm not like them." He tilts his head a little as he scrutinizes me. "I'm like Reed. I just want to keep you safe and well."

Slowly, I approach him and press my palm to his chest. His heart beats steady and strong inside. It makes me think of nights when I'd curl up with my sister and lay my head on her chest. She'd hum and stroke my hair. Hot tears burn my eyes and I turn on my heel.

I need to leave.

Being here with him, not worrying about constant

survival, it gives me too much time to think. The last thing I want to do is think about the past that hurts.

Rushing over to the door, I manage to fling it open and dart out into the night. I'm not sure how I'll find my home, but I'll try. As soon as my bare feet hit the snow covered landing outside the door, I let out a squeak. Atticus yells my name, but I can't stay.

I long for my boots that I took from my brother when he was killed. I'm not sure where they went or what happened to them. The snow bites into my flesh as I run out into the darkness. Sticks and rocks beneath the snow stab at the bottoms of my feet, but I don't stop. I run through trees, dodging them here and there. The licks of the branches hurt, yet I don't stop.

Eve! Eve! Eve!

My name is called out over and over again.

I'm running and running when I fall into an especially large snow drift near a big tree. My body sinks into the snow that's chest high. The chill works its way down to my bones.

Someone sobs, loud and ragged.

Defeated.

That someone is me.

And then two strong arms are pulling me out and into their warmth.

Atticus.

I cling to his shirt and sob against him. My entire body shudders. Will he whip me like Papa and Ezekiel would when I didn't obey? I cry harder and find it difficult to breathe. I don't want Atticus to hurt me.

"Shh, little fox," he rumbles as he moves swiftly back to

the home. "You can't run away like that. I was only trying to feed you, not insult you. Promise me you won't do that again. It's not safe."

I nod even though I'm not sure I can promise it. Anything to hear more of his soothing words. He's not angry. He seems sad.

"I'm c-c-cold," I chatter out.

"That's what happens when you run your near naked ass out into the snow." He chuckles and it has me relaxing considerably.

Once inside, he closes the door behind him. He carries me through the home back into his room. The heat feels good, but I already know what will feel better.

"Shower," I croak.

He shakes his head as he sets me to my feet. "In a little bit. You need to warm up first."

"The shower is warm," I argue. For such a smart man, he's not acting that way at the moment.

"Fine," he grunts.

"Fine," I mimic.

chapter five

ATTICUS

I CAN'T TELL HER NO.

When I try, she frowns and her swollen bottom lip pokes out. It fucks with my head because I want that lip. I'm not supposed to, but I do. I want a lot of things I'm not supposed to.

Walking past her, I head into the bathroom and start the water. By the time I turn around, she's naked, blue, and shivering in the doorway. My cock reacts. Again.

"I'll be in the kitchen," I say gruffly as I start to move past her.

She doesn't step out of the way and instead presses a palm to my chest. "Shower. You and me." Her wide brown eyes blink at me and her brows furl together.

"I can't." Because a man only has so much self-control and she's testing mine.

Her head bows as the rejection of my words stings her. My first instinct is to comfort her. I wrap my arms around her frigid body and hug her to me. She relaxes against my chest. I can't help but run my fingers through her soft hair.

"Just…just wash your hair like I showed you. I'll reheat our food."

I grip her shoulders and peel her from my body. She's still trembling from the cold and her teeth clack together. Poor Eve. Such a fucking mess. I scrub my palm through my short beard and shake away images of my assisting her in the shower.

She allows me to turn her and gently guide her into the shower. Like a fucking perv, my eyes skim down the bones in her spine and land on the two dimples above her ass. I quickly look away.

"Holler if you need anything," I say in a gruff tone.

Once I hear her moaning under the hot spray, I bolt out of the bathroom. I find a pair of my thickest socks, some sweats, and a hoodie. Maybe if she layers up in all this stuff, she'll warm up.

I head back to the kitchen and am just starting a pot of coffee when the house phone rings. As soon as I see who's calling, I smile.

Mom.

"Hey—"

"You were gone weeks, mister. Weeks! And I find out from Suma that you're back home! You didn't even call your own mother—"

"Ma, it's fine. Just been busy. I was going to come into town in the morning to see you. Scout's honor."

"Oh, don't you Scout's honor me, kiddo. I can tell when you're lying, remember?"

I let out a heavy sigh as I watch the coffee brew. "A friend of mine was hurt. Fuckin' bear."

"Lord," she breathes. "Is he okay?"

"Yeah, my friend is fine," I say, delicately dancing around the fact he's a she. If Mom knew I had a female friend, she'd sniff that one out until she made me crazy. "Suma patched things up as per usual."

"Do I need to stop by and bring some soup?"

"No," I say quickly. "I'll come into town for supplies and stop by."

"When your friend heals, I want you both home for dinner. Understood?"

"Yes, ma'am." Then, because I'm an idiot, I ask a question that usually leads to a lot of probing ones. "You seen Cassandra around?"

The line goes silent and I frown.

"Ma? Did we get disconnected?"

"Um, yes. I've seen her around. Still works at her daddy's bait shop."

I let out a sigh of relief. Cassandra is my fuck buddy. She's great in the sack and doesn't put up too much of a fight when I fall off the grid to do my own shit. It's like she's always waiting around for me. Hell, maybe I'm supposed to settle with a girl like Cass. It wouldn't be the worst thing.

"How's Judith?"

"Oh, she's Judith," Mom replies with a sigh.

"What now?"

"Dating some guy who's bad news. Your father wanted to throttle him at dinner the other night. She has some bruises on her arms. I asked her about them and she got angry. I don't know what's going on with her."

Typical Judith.

My sweet sister wasn't the same after her near death experience.

Another added layer of guilt on my conscience.

"I'll talk to her," I vow. "When I come to town, I'll visit with her and get to the bottom of it."

"You're a godsend. See you soon, sweetheart."

We hang up and I worry about Judith. Coffee and spaghetti don't exactly go together, but I'm too spaced out to figure something else out. My sister weighs heavily on my mind.

A prickle of awareness making my hairs stand on end has me swiveling around. Eve looks every bit of thirteen in my massive clothes. But she looks warm and that's what truly matters.

"These are too big," she says, pulling the sweats away from her body.

I step over to her and show her the inside where the drawstrings are at. Pulling as tight as I can make them, I tie the strings in a bow and then fold the top down to make them fit even more snug. When our eyes meet, hers seem darker than usual. Hardened. Angry.

"Did you have any trouble washing your hair?"

"I don't do it like you do," she says with a pout that makes me smile.

"I've had years of practice."

"I cleaned my teeth again." She bares her teeth like a mountain lion.

"Beautiful." As soon as I say the word, her bluish tinted cheeks flood with crimson.

Quickly, I tear my gaze from her and clear my throat. As though she were a child—I mean technically she is—I cut her spaghetti into small pieces so she doesn't have to twirl it around her fork. She seems pleased by this and wastes no time scarfing it down. I'm not even hungry, but I force food down so I have an excuse not to talk.

Everything I say comes out twisted.

All my thoughts are no better.

"Tomorrow, I'm going into town. Do you want anything?"

"Fruit," she chirps.

A smile tugs at my lips. "That's a given, Eve. What about chocolate? Cookies? Books?"

"Knife."

Right. This isn't some high school chick. No, this is Eve. Feral, wild Eve.

"Right, a knife. I'll find some better fitting clothes for you as well."

She nods, seemingly pleased by this as she holds her coffee mug. Her eyes close as she inhales the scent wafting from the steaming cup and then gingerly takes a sip.

"I love coffee," she whispers.

"As much as you like fruit?"

She glowers at me.

"Point taken," I joke. "I know you love canned peaches, but have you had a fresh one before."

Her head cocks to the side.

Desperate for something to talk about so I don't stare at her plump lips, I start blabbering. "Yeah, peaches. They grow in orchards. They're an orange color and have a slight fuzz on the skin. You can eat it. Most people eat fresh peaches like they would an apple. My ma loves to put it in peach cobbler—"

"Ma?" Her eyes water.

Fuck.

"Do you miss your mother?" I ask, my voice soft.

Her lips press together. "I ache for my sister."

It makes me think of Judith. Finding her cold, broken body inside that crevasse. Feeling the weight of responsibility crushing down on me like an avalanche. I reach across the table and gently pat Eve's hand. "I can't imagine losing a sister."

She jerks her hand back. "My brothers..." Violence gleams in her brown eyes. "They hurt her."

Pain lances through my chest. "A brother is supposed to look after his sister. It's his duty to protect her. I would do anything for my sister Judith."

A hot tear races down her cheek and drips from her jaw. "Is she your wife?"

Disgust roils through me. "Fuck no," I growl. "She's my sister."

"My father was my husband," she says, her voice growing cold. "My brothers wanted to be."

Jesus.

What is it about these woods and fucking incest?

This is a conversation Reed should be handling, not me.

"Whatever they did to you was wrong," I bite out. "Understand? Relatives don't..." They don't fuck or marry or whatever the hell was going on in those woods. "It's just wrong."

Her features lose some of their hardness as she regards me. "Wrong."

"Yes, wrong." Then I sigh. "Plus, you're too young for all that."

"All what?"

I rub at the back of my neck, trying to find the right words. "Bedroom stuff."

Her brows furl. "Sleeping?"

"Together."

"Like us?"

Fuck.

"We sleep in the same bed because I only have one and you've been injured. You need me to look after you." I shove the wet dream out of my mind.

"Papa kept me in his bed but…"

Goddamn, I don't want to hear this. "He hurt you."

She winces. "Teaching me."

"That's not education, Eve, that's abuse."

"Abuse?"

"When someone uses their power above you to make you feel powerless. To punish and torture you. What your father and brothers did is abuse. Sexual. Mental. Physical."

"You don't abuse me," she whispers. "We just sleep together."

God help me.

"We sleep in the same bed."

"Together."

I give up on this one. "Yeah, Eve. We sleep together."

She starts to scratch on her chest and it reminds me we need to apply more healing paste. I stand and motion for her to follow me to the bedroom. When I start for the paste, she lets out a heavy sigh.

"I don't like that."

"And I don't like seeing you hurt. The paste helps." I motion at her. "Lift your shirt."

She pulls off the hoodie and I'm once again forced to

stare at her chest. Her breasts, now clean, seem so soft and delicate against the harsh cuts on her chest. Thankfully, everything seems to be healing well.

"I think you can apply the paste now," I tell her, looking toward the window.

"I don't want to."

I shoot my eyes to hers and defiance shines in them. With an annoyed growl, I scoop up some of the paste and kneel in front of her. Her small hands go to my shoulders as I softly apply the paste to her tender skin. I can't help but glance at her small, peaked nipples. It makes me some kind of twisted to want to lick them. My dick's twisted too because I'm hard as fuck right now.

I need to get the hell out of this house.

Cass can suck my dick and make me forget all about these fucked up fantasies with Eve.

It's not fucking right.

Eve's just some feral kid.

And I'm not the man who's going to tame her.

chapter six

EVE

I WAKE UP DRENCHED IN SWEAT AND PAINS CRAMPING through my abdomen. In the dark, I can't make out my surroundings, but I smell *him*. Atticus. Not my father or my brothers, who always stank of their own putrid odors. Atticus smells fresh like pine and snow. His heavy arm is slung over me and he snores quietly. I take the moment to explore him while it's safe. My fingers dance along his hairy arm and slide along the strong curve of his shoulder. When I reach his hair, I run the silky strands through my fingers before bringing it to my nose to inhale.

His manhood—er cock—is pressed against my hip. It's strange that he doesn't ever put it inside me. I'd learned from an early age that when a man's body grows hard, he needs to be inside a woman to make it go away. But Atticus never needs me to make it go away. It just does after a while. In his sleep, he rocks gently against me. I'm not terrified of him like I was with my family or even Reed. He's the big bear from my imagination. The one who always looks after me. I'm fascinated by the way his breath hitches each time he ruts against me. How I can feel every curve and ridge on his cock through our garments. The more he rocks, the hotter I feel.

Warmth licks and lashes at me like when I'm standing over a fire. It burns from the inside out, though. Between my thighs, I throb with a craving I don't understand. My breasts feel heavy and achy—my nipples hard with this same need. To be touched. The throbbing pulsates until the need to rub at it and make it stop overwhelms me. It's an almost painful need. Like when I'm starving and my stomach growls desperately.

My heart races and then stops altogether when he moves in his sleep. His massive hand cups my breast over my shirt. When his thumb brushes my nipple, a thrill of exhilaration burns through me to my unfilled womb. The throbbing is driving me mad. Without considering my actions, I grab his wrist and pull it there. To the aching place. His fingers—of their own accord—rub at me there.

A moan escapes me.

It feels good.

Unlike anything I've ever experienced before.

Confusing but wonderful.

He's still sleeping, but his breathing is shallow. Like he might wake at any moment. He mutters a name—Cassandra—and an unusual feeling churns inside me.

"Eve," I croak.

All anger bleeds away when his hand slips beneath the pants. Flesh on flesh. His touch could create fire. It's brilliant and beautiful. I spread my thighs, desperate for more.

Rather than filling the ache within me, he simply touches a spot between my lower lips, buried in the hair there, and rubs it with expert knowledge. The sound that escapes me is one I've heard Devon make on many occasions.

Feral. Hungry. Eager.

His finger slides down, slipping in wetness that's leaking from me, and then he's back to rubbing that same spot. I lie there, helpless to the unfamiliar pleasure, as he introduces me into a world I've never been.

Glittering stars.

Bright lights.

Cries of need.

My body detonates. Every single hair on my body stands on end. A buzzing zings through every muscle, vein, and bone. And when it ends, I feel satiated and warm and tired.

"Oh fuck."

I stiffen at his gruff words.

"Fuck. Fuck. Fuck."

He jerks his hand from my pants and rolls away from me. I hear something heavy hit the floor on the other side of the bed. Then, bright light floods the room. I squint against the harsh lights to find Atticus standing beside the bed, half asleep and…terrified.

I look all around, searching for the threat. His home is safe, but could a bear get inside? A mountain lion? When I look back at him, he's gaping down at his hand. His fingers are covered in blood. My blood. It's then I realize I've begun menstruating.

"I hurt you," he chokes out, his face crumpling. "Oh, fuck, Eve. I'm so sorry."

Hurt me? He made me feel amazing.

"It's my blood," I whisper, "but you didn't hurt me."

His wild green eyes meet mine as he wiggles his fingers. "Then what do you call this?"

"My blood."

"Because I hurt—"

"Menstruation. It means my body is ready to bear children," I admit with a frown.

His gaze hardens, making me wince. "I can't sleep in here with you anymore. It's too…"

Too what?

Warm?

I like warmth.

"You're a temptation I don't need and didn't realize I wasn't strong enough to ignore." He growls and storms into the bathroom. I hear the sink turn on as he washes his hand.

Papa spoke of temptation in the Bible. Is that what I am? Cursed? Hot blood trickles from within me, leaking into my pants. Maybe I am cursed. I'm named after Eve, who wasn't exactly God's favorite.

With a sigh, I climb out of bed and rid myself of the soiled pants. If I were in my shack, I'd roll up some old, tattered strips of cloth and use them to soak up the blood. I'm not sure what to use here. Blood runs down the inside of my thigh, dripping onto the floor below. I stare down at it, pondering what to do next.

"I, uh, I don't have female products," he says with a cough, exiting the bathroom holding a small cloth. "Maybe clean up with this and I'll see about finding you some way of dealing with that."

That being the river of blood running down my leg.

He tosses the cloth at me and it hits the floor. When I make no moves to grab it, he strides over to me and kneels down. Then, he gently grabs my thigh and runs the hot cloth along my flesh.

"Damn," he grumbles. "It's really coming down. Is this natural? Does it always do this?" He looks up at me in panic. "My mom and sister used tampons, but like, I never saw how they put them in or anything."

I blink down at him. "Sometimes it's so heavy it attracts predators."

His eyes widen in horror. "Predators."

"They smell the blood. I use clothes to soak it up, but they still smell it."

"Jesus…fuck…Eve…"

He lets out a strangled sound and then quickly cleans up my mess. I'm pleasantly surprised when he cleanses my lower lips, though it doesn't bring me the same pleasure as before. Just a warm feeling inside my chest. That he's looking after me, but not trying to hurt me.

He hands me the cloth before walking over to his drawers. I admire his strong body as he roots around for whatever it is he's looking for. Eventually, he pulls out his black underwear.

"These are still too big for you, but we could roll up a towel and put it inside. Might soak the blood up while you sleep. I'll add tampons or pads or whatever to my run to town in the morning."

Once I'm cleaned up, dressed in his underwear and the towel is secured, I lie back down on another towel. I wait for him to join me, but his jaw clenches furiously.

"Eve…"

"Sleep," I bite out, patting the bed beside me.

"No. I'm sleeping in my chair from now on."

I glare at him. "You're warm."

"My house is warm enough that you don't need me." His green eyes flare with challenge. "You can sleep alone. Been doing it for years now, little fox."

A strange feeling tugs inside my chest. Sometimes, when I'm menstruating, I feel sad and lonely. So achy and desperate that death feels preferable. Hot tears well in my eyes. I also tend to cry more easily.

"I'm not mad at you," he chokes out, his brows furling together. "I'm mad at me. I…I touched you."

I don't understand his anger at himself.

"It felt good."

His nostrils flare. "That's beside the point. It can't ever happen again."

"What if I want it again?"

He pinches the bridge of his nose and sighs. "I'm sorry for what I did in my sleep. I didn't do it on purpose. But clearly, sleeping together is a bad idea. Please forgive me."

With those words, he slams the light off and stalks out of the room. I draw the covers up that smell like him and silently sob. I find one thing in my life that isn't about pain, survival, and terrible memories, but I can't even have it. Just a tease of something wonderful. A tiny taste of what Reed and Devon have.

I think about the way Reed cherishes Devon. Simple looks they share. The way he claims her with kisses she seems to love. How his touches are gentle but possessive. Nothing he does to her is even remotely like the way my father and brothers treated me. They both enjoy each other. I've silently watched them from the trees for years, so I know it's not something they only do in the presence of others. It's real. With Atticus, hope had started to grow inside me. That maybe I could have something like that.

He doesn't want me that way, though.

Atticus was clearly thinking about Cassandra while he touched me.

Is Cassandra beautiful like Devon? I thought my sister was beautiful, but Devon is like how I imagine the angels in the Bible to look like. Golden hair. Sweet smile. Ethereal.

How will a little fox claim a big bear if he has eyes for an angel?

Bitterness churns in my stomach.

A little fox has no place with a bear.

Foxes were meant for the forests. Running far, far away from others. Foxes do better alone. Alone hurts, though. It really hurts.

Another sob escapes me.

I cry all night.

chapter seven

ATTICUS

I'M SUCH AN ASSHOLE.

Worse than an asshole.

I'm a child predator like her father and her brothers. Fuck. This morning, I made her some oatmeal, turned on the television, and left her with the instructions to not leave. Then, like the coward I am, I bolted.

I need space.

Shame coats me like a drenching rain. I touched her. Made her orgasm. When I saw the blood, I nearly lost my shit. At first, I thought I'd hurt her. It sickened me. But then…

My dick hardens in my jeans, making me hate myself a little more.

Space.

Lots of fucking space.

I need to get her healed and sent back to the wild where she fucking belongs.

As though on autopilot, I drive into town, headed straight for the bait shop. Everything else can wait. I need to get laid and I need it now. Then, I can think clearly and stop looking at Eve like *that*. When I see Cass's white Chevy pickup in the front lot on Main Street, I park beside her and let out a relieved sigh. It'll be like old times. We can run upstairs, make it quick, and I can be on my way.

Hell, maybe I'll ask her out for dinner or something.

Cassandra is a good girl. I've known her since high school. She married right out of high school, but ended up divorced after their son was born. He's in high school now, but Cass still never settled.

I shut the truck off and fling open the door. Snow pelts my face, but I'm burning with the need to expel this sexual energy. I shut the truck door and trot into the bait shop. As soon as I walk in, the scent of familiarity hits me. It's a quaint shop filled with fishing gear and one I've shopped at often. This morning I'm shopping for a curvy brunette with a sweet laugh.

The moment I hear her laughter as she speaks to someone on the phone, my body relaxes. Yes. I need this. Desperately. Cass's dark hair hangs long down her back and she twirls the phone cord around her finger as she listens to the person speaking on the other line. Her dad's bait shop is the same as it was when I was a kid. Old but has a little bit of everything. I busy myself looking at the knives under a glass case at the register while I wait for Cass to end her call.

"Love you too," she says, "but someone just walked in. Okay, bye."

She hangs up and swivels around, a polite smile fixed on her pretty face. As soon as she sees me, it falls. "Atticus."

"Hey, Cass," I greet. "Long time, no see."

"Been about a year," she says, her voice tight.

"How've you been? Come out from behind the register and give me a hug."

Her lips purse together. "A lot can happen in a year."

I'm frowning as she walks around the corner. Her hand rests on her barely protruding stomach, an engagement ring glittering on her finger.

Oh fuck.

"You're pregnant?" I croak, shocked as hell.

"Frank and I are getting married."

Frank? One of our mutual friends? Last I heard, he left for California. Never knew he came back.

"Frank Jefferson?"

"Yes," she says. "He manages the bank now."

"Oh." I sound like a fucking idiot. "I, uh…"

"You have to find a new fuck buddy," she says, no warmth in her tone. "He put a ring on this one."

I wince at her harsh tone. Jesus. Was I really that much of a dick? I mean…I was coming here to fuck and run. Like always.

"God, Cass, I'm sorry."

"Most people say congratulations."

"No," I rush out. "Congrats on your life. I'm sorry I was such a dick to you. You didn't deserve that."

Her brows crash together. "You couldn't be tamed. Deep down, I knew that. You're meant to be out there." She waves her hand toward the window that overlooks the woods. "Free. Wild. Wherever it is Atticus Knox disappears to for months or even years at a time."

"I like to camp," I say lamely.

She snorts. "You like to be off the grid. It's fine. I prefer life in town and my fiancé spends every waking minute with me. Life is good for me."

I rub at my neck and sigh. "I'm glad to hear it. I'll, uh, get out of here then."

"Best you do. Frank won't be happy you came in."

"I meant no harm," I tell her. "Tell him I came in to buy something."

"Are you? Buying something?"

I see a small knife meant for a child. "Yeah. I want that knife right there."

"That one's sixty dollars. If you're buying one for a kid, there are some over here that are nineteen."

Eve, despite her age and her size, is no child. She's… something else. And a cheap knife won't do.

"I'll take the expensive one."

"Suit yourself."

I stare up at my parents' mammoth house nestled in the side of the mountain. Growing up, I loved our house. It was cozy and warm and I lived with two adoring parents. But I always felt freer outside of it. So many times I'd get my ass whipped for staying out past dark, playing in the woods. Dad would have to come find me every time.

Now, as the snow drifts heavily around me, I consider

bypassing the house and walking into the woods. Just walking and walking away from all the shit that's brewing in my
life. Never turn back. The idea is nice, but then it circles
back to Eve. She's waiting for me to return to her. To bring
her food and supplies. To take her back home eventually.

"I'm getting too old to chase you," Dad calls out from
the porch, startling me.

I shake my head and make my way through the snow to
the porch. "Hey, Dad."

He stands from his rocking chair and pulls me to him
for a bear hug. Dad is the one where the term "bear hug"
came from. Tall, broad shoulders, gruff. Dad is bigger than
any linebacker I ever encountered in the NFL. Bigger than
me and my brothers.

"Good seeing you, kid," he says. "Your mother has been
sick with worry. You know how she is."

I chuckle. I certainly do. Mom is the opposite of Dad.
Tiny and energetic and talkative. She buzzes around like a
bee on a hot summer day. They've always been an unusual
match to me, but they've been married forever, so they
clearly find a way to make it work.

"How's everyone been doing?" I ask, leaning against
the wood column on the porch. "Judith?"

Dad's face darkens. "Judith is Judith."

"She here?"

He looks at his watch. "It's not noon yet, so she's probably laid up in bed with a hangover."

"I'll talk to her."

He nods. "But talk to your mother first or we're getting our asses handed to us for lunch rather than the fried
chicken she's planning. Don't ruin my lunch, boy."

"Yeah, yeah," I grumble before heading inside. I shed my outerwear and lose my boots at the door so as not to track mud on the carpet. The house smells good. Mom's cooking is one I miss on the daily.

I find her standing over the sink washing her hands. She's barely five feet, but her attitude is fucking huge.

"Ma."

She whips around, grinning. "My baby boy!"

I laugh as she launches herself at me, squeezing the life out of me. She must have learned the whole bear hug thing from Dad. I hug her back and bend to inhale her familiar perfume I've always been comforted by.

This squeezing in my chest is why I've felt torn between two worlds.

My family means everything to me. But nature calls to me. It's why, even though I enjoyed playing football, I hated living out there. Beyond the safety of our small Alaskan town nestled in the snowy mountains and hidden in the trees. Playing ball for the Broncos was every man's dream. And for a while, I thought I wanted that dream. I injured my shoulder, though, two years in and the relief of coming back home was overwhelming.

"Smells good."

"Fried chicken. I knew you'd be around and it's your favorite. How's your friend? I tried to pry more information from Suma, but you know how that woman is. She just smiles. Doesn't answer a dang question. It's rather odd—"

"Ma. Chill," I say with a chuckle. "Everything's fine."

"Then you should have brought him by."

I groan, knowing I need to let her in on some of the

truth. Mostly, because I need female guidance. "Uh, ac- tually, my friend is a woman." Over exaggeration on the woman part.

She pulls away, her mouth agape. Her blond, curly hair has been pulled into a bun that resembles mine. Her green eyes glitter with shock. "Woman? You have a female friend?"

"Oh God," I grumble. "Don't start."

"Don't start? I most certainly will. I didn't start and you let sweet Cass slip away—"

"Thanks for the warning, by the way."

"And all I ever want is for my boy to settle down and have a nice family so he—"

"I'm gonna go check on Judith," I bark out and rush from the kitchen despite her chatter following after me.

I bound up the stairs and head down the hallway until I find Judith's room. Where Will and Vic moved out when they turned eighteen, Judith has never officially left home. It's like she never matured enough. Nothing is wrong with her mentally, but something keeps her from leaving the nest. I hate that I'm responsible for the girl she is today.

"Knock, knock," I utter, rapping on her door.

"Go away unless you have coffee."

"I'm not Mom or Dad, so that should at least grant me entry."

"Atticus!"

The door gets flung open and my sister flings herself into my arms. She's tiny like Mom, but has darker hair like Dad. Judith is every bit as small as Eve is.

"You have to hide me in here," I whisper conspira- torially. "Ma found out I have a girl who happens to be a friend and she's probably already started a Pinterest board for our wedding. Help. Please, sis."

She giggles and pulls me into her room. We flop onto her bed, both wearing matching smiles. Judith sits up on her side, regarding me with an impish expression.

"Spill. I may not be Mom, but I still want the juicy gossip."

I roll my eyes. "I'll spill mine if you tell me why you're being a brat to our parents."

"I'm not being a brat. They just think they can control me."

We grow quiet. I don't need to remind her it's because she still lives under their roof. She knows.

"They love you," I say instead.

"So does Joey."

I try to quell the irritation swelling up inside me. The protective big brother feelings will never be squashed no matter how old she gets. My sister may only be ten years my junior, but she's still just a kid in my mind.

"Joey sounds like an asshole," I grumble.

"He kind of is." She giggles. "Actually, not kind of. Joey is a *total* dick."

I pick up her wrist and inspect it for the bruises Mom mentioned. Sure enough, there are plenty of them. "A dick who puts his hands on you?"

"Not like that," she hisses, snatching her hand back. "It was all sexual shit, if you must know. He's a dick because once he gets laid, he doesn't need me anymore. Goes back to his stupid trailer and doesn't call again until he wants to fuck."

I wince at her harsh delivery because it's not unlike what I did with Cassandra. Men are such fucking assholes.

"Does Will know what a cunt this guy is?" I ask, feeling the urge to round up Will and Vic to beat some twerp's ass for hurting our sister. Like old times' sake.

"Oh, Will is very familiar with Joey. He's arrested him before. They don't like each other." Her nostrils flare. "But Joey is my decision. Not Will's."

"You deserve someone who will spend time with you, though," I tell her.

"Maybe. Now tell me about her," she says in a terse tone, changing the subject. "Your girlfriend."

"She's not my girlfriend."

"Oh, God. Another Cass?"

"No," I bite out. "Eve's…different."

She turns her wide eyes on me. "Different how?"

A fucking teenager for one.

"She comes from out there."

"Ohhhh…"

In this town, we're all far too familiar with the people who escape town life to live off the grid. We often run into them when they come to town for supplies or if we happen upon them while hunting or fishing or camping. They're all so feral.

"How did you befriend this wild one?"

"It's a long story," I say with a sigh. "I found her through a friend. She was all alone out there. Her family was killed. Recently, she was attacked by a bear. Fucked her up pretty bad. She needed medical attention. Suma came and helped me with her. Now she's just healing at my place."

"Is she hot?" She waggles her eyebrows.

"You're annoying."

"Am not."

"Lies."

She snorts. "Are you taking her back when she's better?"

"That's the plan."

"But you like her," she says, her green eyes gleaming with wickedness. "I can tell."

I grind my teeth. "Not like that."

"Why not? Did she lose all her teeth already? Stinky puss—"

With a growl, I cover my sister's mouth with my hand so she doesn't finish that question. "She's like fifteen or sixteen. Fuck if I know."

Her eyes widen and she stops squirming, so I remove my hand.

"Holy shit," she breathes. "My angelic brother has decided to break the law and fuck a teenager. Wait until Will gets a whiff of this."

"Stop." The last thing I need is my brother on my ass about this.

"I didn't say you actually did it. Just that you decided it."

"I didn't decide shit."

"Which means you're still thinking about it—"

"Judith."

"Just sayin', Atticus."

"Well, stop. Just let it go." I sigh heavily. "I need your help. Can we keep this discreet?"

Planning a secret mission behind our parents' back is exactly the type of thing Judith lives for.

"You betcha, bro. What do you need?"

"Panties. Tampons."

"You so nasty."

"Judith—"

"Right. I'm kidding. I'll get you the goods, but you must promise on Ma's Bible that you'll let me know the moment you fuck her."

"Jesus," I groan. "What makes you think that's going to happen?"

"Your stupid lovesick puppy eyes. You're totally gonna fuck her and when you do, I want details."

"I'll write you a letter from prison."

"Cool! If you see any hot guys while there—"

I shut my annoying sister up by tickling her until she cries.

chapter eight

EVE

I stare at the black thing Atticus used to make the pictures change on his box. The television is what he calls it. I had vague memories of my mother describing such things to me, but until my stay here, I'd never seen them.

It's loud.

Chaotic.

Unnerving.

I wish I knew how to turn it off.

Ignoring the loud talking, I make my way into the kitchen. Atticus didn't feed me anything but a little bowl of oatmeal before he left and now my stomach is growling. I find a couple cans of peaches, but without my knife, I can't figure out how to open them. His knives in the drawer all are too dull. In the past, the cans he brought me had a unique piece on top that you could lift and pull, but the ones in his cabinet are flat with no tab. I open the white box he calls "the fridge" and marvel over the chill coming from it. I could have really used one of these things last summer when I killed a deer. All that meat was wasted because I couldn't eat it fast enough before it spoiled.

The fridge is filled with little bottles of liquids. One is red, but I can't make sense of the words. At one time, my mother attempted teaching me to read. I wasn't interested and she eventually gave up. I wish I'd learned.

I pull out the bottle and pull off the cap. It smells sweet with a little tang. Opening my mouth, I hold it up and let it ooze onto my tongue.

Yum.

I pour until my mouth is filled and then gulp it down. It's the best thing I've ever tasted. I squeeze and squeeze until I've emptied the container that didn't have much in it to begin with. Once it's gone, I pout, but then abandon that bottle for another one. This one is in a yellow bottle. With a huge squirt, I eagerly taste the yellow sauce.

Yuck!

I spit it out and use my shirt to swipe at my tongue. This is vile. I toss it in the bin I've seen Atticus use to get rid of the things he doesn't want anymore. Rooting around in the fridge some more, I locate a jar filled with something green sloshing around in juice. I unscrew the lid and fish one out of the cold water.

Tangy and bitter.

But also very yummy.

I crunch on the little green things until I empty the container. Then, I gulp down the juice. Strange but tasty. The jar seems useful, so I set it on the counter to keep. I'm sure

Atticus won't mind. At the very back of the fridge, I find something in a tiny brown cup. It takes some effort, but I peel off the top to discover something sweet smelling.

I lick out the jiggly substance and moan in pleasure.

Now this is the best thing I've ever tasted.

Scooping out the brown stuff with two fingers, I suck down every last drop of it and even lick the cup. I'm still hungry, though. When I menstruate, it's like I can't get enough to eat.

When will he come back?

Will he come back?

He promised, but he seemed so eager to get away. Sadness prickles at my eyes, but I ignore it. I'll hunt some real food. I don't need him to bring his sharp knife and open my fruit. Fruit is nice, but what I need is rabbit or squirrel or something to not make me feel so dizzy.

After layering up with clothing that smells like Atticus, I steal some of his boots that are way too big, and then grab one of the useless knives from the kitchen drawer. Once I open the door, the icy wind hits me, making me want to retreat inside.

A few days here and I'm already afraid to go into the elements.

I need to get over that weakness right now.

Slowly, I walk out into the snowy wind and squint against the harshness of it. Finding game will be tricky, but it's not the first time I've had to hunt during a storm. I creep into the trees, careful not to fall into a deep snow drift. My ears perk, listening for animal sounds.

Cracking.

Something's running.

I hold my knife and press myself against a tree, keeping

my eyes peeled. Snarling. Wolves? My heart rate quickens. Wolves don't make for tasty meat and I don't think I'm hungry enough for that. I'd rather eat the yellow sauce out of the bin. Problem with wolves is, they'll eat you before you eat them. I make myself as small as I can against the tree as I wait it out.

A light brown rabbit darts through the snow toward me, so focused on outrunning the wolf it doesn't see me. With my lightning fast reflexes, I swing my knife down, making contact with the back of the rabbit. It lets out a strangled cry as blood bursts from it. I lose my knife in the process, but it rolls to a stop near a tree. Without hesitation, I pounce on it and bring it to my chest, pulling out the knife just as I hear the growl behind me.

Slowly, I turn to face my attacker.

A bear?

No, it's a dog. From time to time I see dogs in the woods. Once, several years ago, we had a dog, but then it turned out to be Reed and Devon's dog. This one is about that size but has fluffy, matted dark brown fur.

And no eyes.

It has huge, scarred claw marks down its face, no doubt having lost its eyes to a bear attack. My chest tightens and my eyes water.

"Blind bear," I murmur. "You hungry?"

It sniffs the air and whines.

Not so ferocious after all.

"Come here," I say, patting my thigh.

He gingerly trots through the snow toward me. I hold my hand out so he can sniff it. Once he deems me safe, he licks my palm and wags his tail.

"Let's get you some rabbit."

the wild

Blind Bear—the name I've taken to calling him—chews on one of the bones from the rabbit as we sit by the fire I started. It's cold out here, but sitting on a piece of wood with the heat flickering and chasing away the snowflakes as we eat our rabbit, it's not so bad. Feels more like home. And while the rabbit fills my belly as it should, I still crave more oatmeal or that brown jiggly sauce that was so good.

And Atticus.

I don't understand him.

I don't understand how I feel toward him.

With my sister, I loved her. She was my everything. I needed her by me always. Esther was everything good in my horrible world. When she died, I lost a piece of me—a piece I didn't realize was missing until recently.

Sure, Atticus came to visit and brought me gifts. And, despite my not wanting it to, I liked the way my heart would tighten in my chest whenever he'd show up. Something about Atticus has always felt warm and safe. I like Reed and Devon, but even they do not evoke this sensation Atticus does.

He's gone, though.

Left for supplies, so he says.

I'm still not sure if he's coming back.

He has to come back. I need things like a knife and something warmer to wear. I need him to take me back to my home because this new place is far from what I'm familiar with and it makes me uneasy.

Blind Bear whines and crawls closer to me. I hold out my hand for him. He scoots until he's close and then licks it. I scrub behind his ears with my nails, which he seems to like.

"How'd you lose your eyes?" I ask. "Big bear get you too?"

He barks.

I'll take that as a yes.

"Are you cold?"

Another bark.

I hate to admit it, but I am too. The idea of taking a hot shower is almost maddening. I'm irritated that Atticus has shown me something I thoroughly enjoy and will miss greatly once I go back home. I would've been better never being introduced to it.

I may not be able to take showers, but I will brush my teeth. The cool sensation in my mouth is something I'll never grow tired of. Not to mention, he says it keeps my teeth from falling out. All of my family lost their teeth except Esther and me. It made my brothers and father seem more frightening—not that they needed any help with that.

"Come, Blind Bear. Time to warm up."

He barks in agreement. I kick out the fire with snow and then walk back to the cabin. Once inside, I shed my wet clothing. Blind Bear wags his tail as he sniffs around, checking things out. He flops down on the floor in the bedroom, panting.

I strip off the rest of my clothes, frowning when I find the towel soaked with blood. I drop it in the pile of clothes before turning on the water. As soon as the hot water steams up the bathroom, I climb inside under the spray.

If heaven was a feeling, it'd be this. I just know it. I could take ten showers a day for the rest of my life and be thrilled. For the longest time, I just stand under the hot spray, letting it run down my body. I don't wash. Simply relax. Blood runs down my thigh and clouds the water at my feet. I'm reminded of how Atticus massaged me. Reaching down, I find the spot he touched. It throbs slightly beneath the pad of my finger. I never knew such a place existed on my body. A small place that if you rub it just right, it feels really good.

I press my finger down, applying more pressure, and rub circles. It makes my muscles tighten and small whimpers escape me. The urge to go faster is overwhelming. Over and over I move my finger until the pleasure explodes through me. I nearly lose my balance as I cry out. My heart races wildly in my chest. Whatever that is, I love it. I want them all the time, but they're exhausting to find.

The water eventually turns cold, so I shut off the levers. After drying off, I choose more of Atticus's clothes. I have to roll up another cloth to put into his underwear, but once I'm all put back together, I feel relaxed and almost happy.

Almost.

I'd be happy if he'd just come back.

"Blind Bear, let's go watch the noisy box. The people on there have shiny teeth and sometimes they talk about this thing called pizza that makes my stomach grumble. You will love it."

He barks in agreement.

Good boy.

chapter nine

ATTICUS

IT'S DARK BY THE TIME I PULL UP TO MY CABIN. I FEEL like a dick about that too. She's probably scared out of her mind. And I don't know that she would even remember how to make more oatmeal or coffee.

Fuck.

She's probably starving.

Guilt consumes me and I grab one of the bags in the cab before hopping out of the truck. The scent of fire makes my nostrils flare. I find remains of a recent fire near the cabin along with a bloody pile of bones.

Goddammit.

She was starving.

I swallow down the self-loathing. While I was out there trying to get my dick sucked and then having a nice lunch with my family, she was here hunting down food in her weakened state. I'm a monster.

The moment I push open the door, I hear growling. I pause. "Eve?"

Silence.

Did an animal get in? Is she hurt?

The door swings open fully, giving me a good view of what I'm up against. *Friends* on television. Eve curled up under a blanket on the recliner. And a goddamn mangy dog at her feet growling at me.

"Eve!"

She jolts upright and turns toward me. Her eyes are wild until she sees me and then relief flashes in them. More guilt floods through me. I close the door behind me and point at the dog.

"What is that?"

"A dog."

"I know that. But why is it in my house?"

"He was cold."

Only Eve could find some mangy Chow-Chow with no fucking eyes, befriend it, and move it into my house.

"Dog," I say lightly. "I live here."

His growling continues.

"Blind Bear, that's Atticus. It's okay." She scratches at his ears and his tail starts thumping.

I kneel. "Blind Bear, huh? Seems fitting. Come here, boy."

He sniffs his way over to me and when he deems me safe—probably when he can smell the lingering scent of fried chicken on my hands—he licks me.

"Good boy," I croon. I lift my gaze to Eve. "A dog, huh?"

She nods sharply. "I'm taking him with me when I go home."

Home.

The thought of sending her away, even though I was ready to moments ago in my truck, makes my stomach clench.

"Are you hungry?"

"Yes."

I rise and approach the recliner. "I'm sorry."

Her plump lips press together and anger flashes in her brown eyes.

"I shouldn't have left you for so long. I lost track of time."

"The cans are broken," she tells me, her words clipped with irritation.

I frown in confusion and then it hits me. The fruit. They don't have the pull tabs like the ones she's used to.

"Oh, shit," I growl. "Eve, I'm sorry."

She turns back around to watch the television. Ross is rubbing white shit all over his legs trying to get back into his leather pants under the guidance of Joey over the phone. I let out a sigh and walk into my kitchen.

What the fuck?

There's an empty pickle jar, an empty pudding cup, and an empty ketchup bottle neatly lined up on the counter. Droplets of what looks like mustard are everywhere. Did she seriously eat my condiments? Now I feel like the worst asshole on the planet.

I'll make it up to her.

"I'll be right back."

"Atticus," she shrieks as she clambers out of the chair.

Sad, pleading eyes. Trembling lip. Tears welling.

Jesus.

"Hey," I say softly. "I have some gifts for you in the truck. Let me grab them. I'm not going anywhere else."

Her eyes narrow as though she doesn't believe me. Gently, I stroke her cheek, pushing a wet strand of hair behind her ear. She flutters her eyes closed and leans into my touch. I stare at her dark lashes on her apple cheeks and her soft, pillow lips for a moment longer than I should before breaking away.

Fifteen minutes later, I've brought in all of my haul. She paces the kitchen, her eyes wide with anticipation, and the dog wags his tail.

"I got you a knife," I tell her, pulling it from my pocket.

She flashes me a half smile. "Your knives are useless."

"You're welcome," I tease as I hand it over.

"I went to my parents' house and Ma made me stay for lunch. But then, my sister Judith and I, we went to the store. Bought all kinds of stuff. Judith made it her mission to make you a care package."

Eve blinks at me and cocks her head slightly as I hand her over one of the sacks. Tampons. Pads. Chocolate. Even some makeup as if Eve would know what to do with it. I didn't stop my sister. Just let her do her thing. She pulls out a flashlight keychain. Eve pushes the button and exclaims with excitement. Another push of the button and it starts vibrating.

No, she didn't just give Eve a vibrator.

Eve stares at it in wonder, the cranks inside her head working as she makes sense of the object.

"Maybe you should give that to me—"

"Mine!"

I lift both my brows as she glowers at me, holding it to her chest. She mashes the button to turn it back off but doesn't relinquish it. Whatever.

"She sent a whole bag of her old clothes and picked you out some undergarments at the store. You should be all set in the clothing department."

"Food."

"Right. Your favorite."

I pull items out of the bag, secretly enjoying how she picks up each thing and curiously inspects them. She holds up a red package and sniffs it. Chewy Chips Ahoy. I peel back the top and offer her a cookie.

"I like the smell," she says, bringing it to her nose. Her pink tongue darts out to taste it. Brown eyes widen as she bites into it. Then, they flutter closed as she moans. My dick takes fucking note.

"Yeah, Judith said you'd love those."

She devours six in a row before I close the flap, earning me an angry growl.

"You can't eat too many or you'll make yourself sick. Especially since you haven't had a proper meal today. Luckily, my mom sent me back with some leftovers."

She roots around in the bags while I reheat the chicken, mashed potatoes, and green beans. By the time I finish microwaving it, both her and the dog are hovering. I toss him a piece of chicken and hand her the plate. Rather than bothering with a fork, she dives in, scooping it out with her fingers.

"Fork," I say gently. "In my house, we use silverware."

Her brows crash together and she makes a huffy sound before yanking open the drawer. She locates a fork inside. After stomping back over to the table with her plate, she sits and then loudly stabs at the green beans.

Hormonal woman.

Girl.

She's a girl, not a woman.

I fixate on the way she licks her juicy lips. I wish I were fifteen or however old the fuck she is so I could suck away that grease from her bottom lip. My dick strains in my jeans, desperate to join the party.

After she eats, I pull out the peach cobbler my mom made. Once it's reheated, I set it on the table beside her plate.

"Peach cobbler," I explain.

"Fresh peaches?"

I smile. "The freshest. I also bought some peaches for you." I dig around in a bag until I find them. When I show her, her head cocks to the side as she studies it. "See, it's fuzzy."

Her fingers reach out to touch it. A smile curves her lips up as she strokes the peach. "Soft."

"And juicy."

"Sweet?"

"Very." My voice is rough and I clear my throat. "I'll get this all put away. Then we can watch a movie or something together."

I busy myself with the groceries until she makes another moaning noise. I whip my head around to find her inhaling the cobbler. My mother's peach cobbler has that effect on everyone.

"Good?"

"Mmm," is all she says as she licks the container.

One thing I will admit to myself is I enjoy watching her try new things. I don't know what to make of my creepy fixation on Eve, but it's been there for years. Ever since I saw her wide, distrusting eyes behind her dirty hair. I wanted to earn her trust and friendship. Now, years later, something inside me aches for more. It's not fucking cool, but still there.

She puts the plate down on the floor and the dog takes to licking it clean. Her brown eyes lift to mine and gleam with something I've never quite seen. Happiness.

All I can do is stare.

chapter ten

EVE

H E HANDS ME THE SACK FILLED WITH UNFAMILIAR items. I'm careful to hide the light stick so he doesn't take it. Earlier, he looked angry about me having it. And the way it buzzed gave me an idea. One that I don't want him to know about.

I carry the sack and the bag filled with garments to his room. After setting them on the bed, I rifle through the bag until I find smaller underwear. Black and soft. I instantly like the way the material feels in my fingers.

"Do you, um, do you know what to do with that stuff?"

His voice from the doorway behind me makes me jump. I don't answer him. I just wait for him to explain what it is I'm supposed to do. With a resigned huff, he walks into the room and pulls out a box.

"These are tampons. They, um…" He stalls and scratches his beard. "They go inside you. To soak up the bleeding."

It sounds painful.

Like all the times my brothers and Papa were inside me.

Shuddering, I swat it out of his hand. "No."

"Okay," he agrees. "I wasn't exactly keen on explaining how to do that anyway. The pads are easier. It's like the towel, but you can throw them away." Then he smirks at me. "Like you threw out my mustard. Why did you do that anyway?"

"Yuck," I growl.

He laughs and it warms me to my core. "Point taken. Some of us like mustard. I put it back in the fridge. Keep it around for me, okay?"

I nod, though I don't understand how anyone could like such vile tasting things.

"Anyway, uh, let me show you how this thing goes on the underwear." He tears open the film on the pack and pulls out a yellow thing. "This is a pad. To open it, just pull back this tape." It all unfolds brilliantly and then he tosses away the yellow film. He picks up the black underwear. "Then, you peel off this part so that you can stick it inside your panties, er, underwear."

"Panties?"

"That's what girls sometimes call these."

"Panties." I smile. I like that word.

He shakes his head, chuckling. "So, yeah. You then put them on and—Jesus, Eve, I meant when I go in the other room." He quickly turns away from me.

I kick out of his pants and take the panties from him. They fit snugly and the pad seems efficient and less messy. I like panties and pads. I locate some thin pants that are red and black. They're soft like his bedding and it makes me want to wear them. I pull them on and am delighted to see they fit snugly without having them swallow me up like his pants do.

He peeks over his shoulder. "Warn a guy before you take off your clothes."

"You have seen me naked."

His cheeks burn red. "I know and that was a mistake."

Shame ripples through me. "Why?"

"Because you're young. It's not right."

I'm not sure why it makes me angry, but it does. I snatch the soiled clothes up and throw them in the clothes bin he has. Then, I grab my light stick and pocket it before heading to the bathroom.

"Eve…"

I stop in the threshold of the door.

"I'm sorry I'm fucking everything up. I am so out of my element right now." He approaches until he's near. "Your hair is tangled. Did you not brush it after your shower?" A shiver ripples through me when he lightly tugs at my hair. "I could brush it for you if you want."

I like his touch, so I nod.

"Where do you want me to brush it? In the living room again?"

"The black box is loud," I grumble.

"Television."

"It's loud."

"I'll show you how to work it so you can turn it off or down. We can turn on some music instead."

Music.

I have memories of my sister singing Bible songs and more recently I've heard Devon singing to her children. I like music.

"Yes," I agree.

He grabs the brush and we head back into the living room. After mashing buttons on the thing he calls a remote, he turns it to a station that plays music. Rich, vibrant sounds come out and my heart races.

"I like this," I tell him.

"Everyone likes Led Zeppelin." He chuckles as he guides me to sit in his lap. "I figure if you're going to listen to music, you may as well listen to what I like."

He runs the brush through my tangles. It feels good. Each little tug. My stomach is full, I'm warm, and I'm not afraid. Plus, Atticus is back and he's touching me. This feels like happiness. Once my hair is all brushed out, he sets the brush on the table beside his chair and pats my thigh. Rather than getting up, I lean back against him. He's stiff, but after a moment, he leans his head against mine. It feels nice. Warm and cozy.

"How's your wound?" His breathy words tickle the side of my face.

"It doesn't hurt."

"Liar."

"It doesn't," I argue.

"You just don't want more paste."

I turn to look at him. My nose brushes against his, but he doesn't pull away. "Do you want to put more paste on?"

His cock grows hard beneath me. The urge to rub against it is strong, but I refrain just barely.

"I think you can manage on your own," he whispers.

"Then, no."

He scowls. "Anyone ever tell you you're stubborn?"

I reach up and smooth out the wrinkle between his brows. "I like it when you touch me."

His eyes squeeze shut. "You make this really fucking difficult." His thumb rubs circles on my hip over my pants.

"What?"

"Being around you."

I flinch at his words. "Why don't you like being around me?"

"I didn't say that," he growls, his words rumbling through me. "It's just hard not to touch you when you're practically begging me to."

"I don't understand why you don't want to touch me anymore."

"Are we going to go round and round about this?"

I sit up abruptly, jerking away from him. He grabs my hip before I can get up. I freeze at his touch. Then, he slides his palm up to my stomach over my shirt and pulls me back to him. All tension bleeds away as I relax in his hold. He claims not to want to touch me, but he caresses my stomach in a way that makes me melt inside.

"You should go to bed soon," he says, his voice gruff.

"Only if you come with me."

"Stubborn."

"You are the same," I argue. "Same as me."

He chuckles. "Point taken. Fine, but we need to put a pillow between us. Last night can't happen again. I want you to feel safe here and if I can't keep my hands off you in my sleep, that's dangerous."

"Gentle bear," I murmur. "Not dangerous."

"Not very smart for a little fox to willingly go to bed with a bear."

"Bears are warm."

"Sometimes I feel like you use me for my body heat," he says, a smile in his voice.

"And your fruit."

This earns her a hearty laugh.

I've won our argument and it thrills me.

No. No. No.

My father sucks on my neck and I want to die. Right now. Just fade out of this world and find Esther. In heaven? I'd take hell at this point. Anything is preferable to the way he threatens to split me open with his manhood.

Every night.

Every single night.

More of the same.

Hot tears leak out, but I don't dare make a sound. Part of my training, I've learned, is that if I cry or fight it, I earn the switch. My bottom is still scabbed over from the last whipping. He fills me with his heat and then he's gone.

Just like that.

I let out a sigh of relief.

His snores soon fill the room and I make my escape. I've just exited the bedroom when two strong hands grip my shoulder. Ezekiel. I start to open my mouth to scream, but he's faster. Stronger. Meaner.

I pray for God to strike me down.

I can't take this anymore.

"Eve!"

I jolt, my body trembling in fear.

"Eve, it's me. Atticus. You're safe." His rumbled words in the dark calm me.

Rolling toward the sound, I clench onto his shirt, burying my tearstained face against his neck. He hugs me to him, running his fingers through my hair.

"Bad dream?"

"Memory," I murmur.

He tenses. "I'm sorry for what they did."

Why is he sorry all the time?

"I'm glad Reed killed them all."

"Me too," he murmurs. "Sleep now, little fox. I've got you."

I can't sleep, though.

Not when my dreams haunt me.

In the dark, I seek out Atticus's face with my fingertips. I touch his wiry beard and his smooth cheek above it. I can't see his eyes, but I feel them watching me somehow. Seeing me. Finding me like Blind Bear found me. Through instinct. Through smell. Through touch. I brush my fingertip down his nose and then gingerly touch his mouth. His lips pucker against my fingertip, making me smile. I withdraw my hand and find his mouth with mine. He starts to move away, but I latch my fingers in his long hair and keep him where I want him. I press soft kisses to his mouth. It's nice except he isn't kissing me back. The rejection stings.

And then it happens.

A pucker.

A kiss.

My heart flutters wildly in my chest.

It makes me want to taste him. To see if he tastes different than the monsters from my dreams. I lick his bottom lip, making him groan. Then, his warm, wet tongue lashes out, sliding against mine. We both make similar sounds of pleasure. I take advantage of his parted mouth and kiss him harder.

He curses and rolls onto his back, as though he's done with the kiss. I don't like how he tries to talk himself out of touching me. So, I take matters into my own hands. I straddle his waist and find his mouth again. His fingers bite harshly into my hips, but he doesn't pull me away.

The kiss heats me to the point I'm sweating. I pull away long enough to rip off my shirt.

"Eve." His voice sounds like a warning.

Ignoring the warning, I kiss him again. He's stiff at first, but then he gives in, offering me his tasty tongue. I run my own over his teeth, marveling once again at how perfect they are. His palm slides up my bare ribs, caressing me. I crave for him to touch me everywhere.

After kissing until the sun comes up, he finally breaks free and rolls us so I'm flat on my back. He keeps a protective arm around me and nuzzles his face in my ear.

"Go to sleep, Eve."

Exhausted and happy, I oblige.

chapter eleven

ATTICUS

I'M A SICK FUCK.

It's the only way to explain the fact I'm hard as stone right now. How I'm possessive as fuck with Eve pretty much smashed beneath my heavy limbs. The morning light pours in through the window, blanketing her half naked form. Her small tits are on full display. I could lie to myself and say I'm staring at her pink, pebbled nipples because I'm inspecting her chest wounds that are in fact healing nicely. But I can't lie. I'm fascinated by every part of her. And so is my dick.

Her mocha eyes flutter open and she stares at me, one corner of her lips turned up. With her clean brown hair spilled all over her pillow and an almost smile on her face, she's never looked so serene and peaceful. Every time I've seen Eve out in the wilderness, she was worried and fearful. Always scrounging for her next meal.

Here, she's relaxed.

This is how she should be. No teenage girl should have to live the way she does. Cold. Alone. Afraid.

"How are you feeling?" I ask, dipping my chin to indicate her chest.

"Good." Her stomach growls and I press my palm to it.

Brown eyes dart to mine, locking me in place. I run my thumb over her soft skin. "You want breakfast?" My words are rough and gritty.

"Oatmeal."

I slide my fingers up her flesh, careful not to touch the red, angry, puckered flesh that's healing from her bear attack. My fingertip brushes over her nipple. She bites on her bottom lip, her eyes intense as they bore into me. I give the nipple a little pinch before pulling away completely.

"Sorry," I grumble.

"I like when you touch me."

My cock jumps in my boxers at her breathy words. The little angel of morality that normally sits on my shoulder has disappeared. I keep wondering what Reed would say. Would he tell me to just follow my heart?

My heart's been following *her* for years.

Completely unacceptable.

Yet, I don't care in this moment.

Leaning forward, I lick the silky skin on her neck. Her fingers thread into my hair, tugging when I playfully nip at her flesh. I suck on her skin hard enough it will most definitely leave a hickey. The thought of seeing the purple mark has me nearly nutting in my underwear. I kiss down her neck to her collarbone, unsure what I have planned next, but it's nothing sensible, that's for damn sure. Her breath hisses when I avoid her wound and then flick my tongue out to taste her small nipple.

"Atticus," she hisses.

My name sounds good coming from her lips. I suck the tiny bud between my lips and then gently bite. A moan escapes her, making my dick leak with pre-cum. Fuck, I need to stop. I really should. She just tastes so sweet. I'm imagining what it would feel like to peel away her pants and panties before sliding into her tight, blood-soaked cunt, when Blind Bear starts growling and barking.

I'm out of the bed, my boner pointing the way, before I even take my next breath. I snag a Glock from my drawer and run to the front door. As soon as I see the face peeking in, my racing heart slows.

Suma.

I open the door, shivering against the cold, and usher her inside. "It's early, woman."

"I came to check on the child."

Child.

Between seeing Suma and that comment, boner officially gone.

"Right," I mutter. "Let me go wake her. Help yourself to some coffee."

Suma's eyes narrow, but I ignore her probing gaze of me in nothing but my boxers. I find Eve sitting up in bed, the covers pulled up, hiding her nakedness. Her brown hair is in messy disarray. Fuck, she does my head in.

"Suma Walkingstick is here. She's the one who made the healing paste. Can you get dressed? She's going to want to check you over again."

Eve's brows furl. "No."

337

I refrain from rolling my eyes. "No's not an answer I'll accept. Let her check you out and then I'll make breakfast. Come on."

Her nostrils flare and her brown eyes shine with anger. Well, she can get pissed off all she wants. When it comes to her health, I won't fucking budge. She throws on a shirt and then disappears into the bathroom. I dress in some sweats and a hoodie before making my way back to where Suma is standing in the kitchen. Wordlessly, we work together to make breakfast. I know Eve mentioned oatmeal, but I'll make her something she's going to love. Yesterday, I brought back stuff to make pancakes and bacon. I figure while Eve is here, she can taste the finer things in life.

We're just finishing up when Eve walks in, glaring at Suma with suspicion, her blind dog at her feet. She's wearing jeans that belonged to my sister, a pink, cashmere sweater, and green socks with frogs on them. I gape at her. She's never looked so…normal.

"Ahh, girl," Suma greets. "Let me look at you."

Eve takes a step back, her eyes darting my way.

"Maybe after breakfast," I tell Suma gently. "No one likes cold pancakes."

Suma shoots me a questioning look, but I simply shrug. We set to making our plates while Eve sits. I cut her food into bite-sized pieces before soaking them in syrup. Her eyes widen when I set the plate in front of her.

"You'll love syrup," I assure her.

She reaches for a syrup-drenched square with her fingers, but then picks up a fork at the last moment. After a stab and then shoving it into her mouth, her eyes widen.

A garbled "mmm" rattles up her throat as she starts inhaling the food.

"The child likes the syrup. Reminds me of another child long ago."

I stand at the counter, watching Eve eat while absently chomping on bacon. I toss pieces to Blind Bear, who seems pleased with the savory taste. Suma sits in the other chair, her eyes darting back and forth between us.

As soon as we're finished, Suma speaks up.

"Let us take a look," Suma says gently. She rises and motions for Eve to follow her.

"Atticus," Eve barks out, panic flashing in her eyes.

"Alone," Suma replies.

"No." Eve glowers at her as though she's the enemy.

"Just do it right here. She's nervous around new people," I explain.

Suma shoots me a frown. "Avert your eyes." Then she says to Eve, "Take off your shirt."

Eve bursts from the chair, nearly tripping over the dog, to cling to my hoodie. "No," she hisses.

Absently, I stroke my fingers through her hair. The urge to find the brush and comb through it is strong, and if Suma weren't here, I'd suggest just that.

Suma gives me a withering look. "I need to check the wounds, Atticus."

"Hey," I say to Eve. "Let's take off this sweater so she can look. I'll be right here." Gently, I turn her around to face Suma.

Eve makes a growling sound of frustration and then rips the sweater off her head, tossing it on the floor. Her body trembles with anger or fear, I'm not sure. I pull her hair off to one side and kiss her shoulder to calm her.

Suma clears her throat and I freeze, realizing what I've done. Losing my fucking mind is what. I start to back away, but Eve leans into my chest, her fists grabbing the bottom of my hoodie.

"They look much better," Suma says, walking slowly toward us. She squints as she inspects the claw marks. Eve flinches when Suma touches her skin with her weathered hands. "What's this?"

I peer down to look where she's pointing and notice the hickey. My cock hardens against Eve's back.

"Um," I mutter, clearing my throat. "Looks like a bruise."

Suma's eyes are sharp when they meet mine. "This bruise wasn't here last I checked."

Eve, having enough with Suma's probing, turns again in my arms, burying her face against my chest. I should be pushing her away, not holding her half-naked body against mine.

"If we're done here, I need to brush her hair," I say lamely. Anything to just get her out of my house. I don't like the way she's looking at the way I hold Eve. It's not like that.

Maybe it is, but it doesn't mean I want a fucking audience.

Suma bends to pick up the sweater and sets it on the counter. "How old are you, child?"

Eve ignores her.

"How old do you think she is?" she asks me this time.

"I don't know. Eighteen," I lie.

Suma snorts. "You will not hear it from me, but rest assured, you will hear it from someone like Will."

My brother.

The cop.

"Hear what?" I growl.

"You know what." Her eyes dip to Eve. "They put men in prison for these types of things."

Anger flashes hot inside me. "I haven't done anything, Suma."

"But you will."

With those words, she gathers her things and slips out of my house. Eve tilts her head up to look at me. Her gaze is soft as she regards me. I fucking love this look on her. How has she gotten me so twisted in a matter of days? I'm a wreck right now.

I'm not straddling a line between good and evil.

I'm simply holding good in my arms.

It doesn't feel fucking evil.

It feels right.

"I should brush your hair now," I murmur, my eyes locked on her plump lips. "Or I could teach you to do it yourself."

She growls. "You."

Stubborn girl.

"Uh, put your sweater back on. This is distracting."

Eve pouts, clearly annoyed, but slips the sweater back on. Once we're safe from my roaming eyes drinking up her tits, I can think better.

The kitchen needs cleaning. Chores need doing. My life needs sorting.

I ignore it all to guide her to my recliner and to pull her into my lap. She's relaxed as I start brushing. I take my time, enjoying the soft, breathy sounds that come from her. My dick is hard as stone, but we both ignore the way it presses against her ass. When her hair is silky smooth, I set the brush down and wrap my arms around her as she curls against me.

My heart beats louder when she's in my arms.

I like the cadence when she's around.

Hard, persistent, hungry.

One day she'll be gone and I wonder if it'll thump at all.

chapter twelve

EVE

I'VE BECOME COMPLACENT. WEDGED MYSELF INTO A routine that revolves around eating, cuddling, and being lazy. I like this little niche of the world with Atticus, but something inside me continues to gnaw. Feeding on me like a wolf as it devours a deer. Strip by strip, it breaks me down until I'm weak and useless.

Each night, Atticus holds me. Kisses me in the dark. Marks my flesh with his lips. Touches my breasts.

But that's it.

The need for him grows to the point I want to rage at him and demand he do something about it. I note that Atticus prefers the dark when we come together. He hides there. From me. From his self-imposed rules. From the memory of the look on Suma's face.

Irritation burns in my gut.

I saw the looks.

Suma didn't think I was good enough for Atticus.

Some wild thing who isn't worthy to have someone like him as her husband. I'd wanted to shove her out of the cabin myself. That was a full week ago and I still can't get her disapproving stare out of my mind.

I take a quick shower and am thankful I no longer have to wear the pads. Atticus has been busying himself chopping on a tree that fell when it couldn't bear the weight of the snow. I'd wanted to follow after him, but he told me I had to stay inside.

Why?

All I ever do is stay inside.

Shower. Eat. Watch *Friends*.

I think about how Chandler and Monica are together. It's so unlike what I remember with my own family. Monica has rights. She has a say in their relationship. She presses Chandler's buttons and he still has a goofy look for her by the end of the show when the words come on. It makes my heart hurt. It doesn't feel real, but it feels like something I want.

With Atticus.

Not some random man. Just him. He's good to me and sometimes he looks at me the same way Chandler does Monica. A half smile and glittering green eyes.

Knowing he won't be in for a while, I sneak out my light stick. Atticus hasn't asked for it since I hid it away. His sister sent it as a gift to me. While it's handy with the light that comes on at the touch of a button, it's the vibrating aspect I've been curious about. Now that I'm no longer menstruating and he's out, I decide to give it a try.

I take off my jeans and tear away my shirt. The panties I'm wearing are pink and silky. They're my favorites.

Atticus showed me how to run the washing machine and I wash them every day so I can wear them often.

Climbing onto the bed, I look down at my mostly naked skin. My wound is better and my usual bones in my ribs aren't protruding as much. I've put on a little weight this week because food is readily available. It's wonderful. My mind drifts to peanut butter and I just about moan in pleasure. This world is clever to come up with such things.

Focus.

I can think about food later.

Right now, I want to think about him.

His chest, bare and sculpted. Broad shoulders. Golden hair hanging down around his face. Mischievous green eyes. Heavily defined muscles in his abdomen that seem to point to his cock. And teeth. He has such lovely, white teeth.

I press the button on the light stick and it starts buzzing. Knowing exactly where I want the device, I rub it over my panties, right along the slit. My body lights up with anticipation. The nub is easy to find as it pulsates with the need for attention. I caress the area through my panties, letting the vibrations shoot spikes of bliss through me. It's an exhilarating feeling. I'm close to the edge of happiness when I hear the front door open.

I don't stop.

Not when I hear my name called.

Not when footsteps thump down the hall.

Not when I feel his heated stare on me.

My eyes drift to his. Shock. Anger. Hunger. His features morph as he processes what I'm doing. I bite down on my bottom lip to keep from crying out. My hips lift and rotate, seeking out the ultimate pleasure I know is coming. Through his jeans, I see the clear outline of his cock. Hard and at attention. I lick my lips, fixated on the size of it. I'm about to lose control when the buzzing slows.

Slows.

Slows.

Stops.

I growl and Atticus laughs.

My chest heaves with exertion and I frantically mash at the button.

"The batteries died. Those things are cheap," he says, prowling my way, an unreadable expression on his face. "I'll have to get you more batteries."

"Now," I order.

He laughs again. "Next time I'm in town. I don't have any of that kind."

A hopeless, horrified sound rattles up my throat.

His thighs touch the side of the bed and he absently runs his knuckle up my leg from my knee to my thigh. "I could help."

I sit up on my elbows, shocked at his words. "You will touch me?"

In this moment, there's no hesitation. It's like when we're in the dark. His eyes have a predatory glint that doesn't frighten me. It excites me. I start to push down my panties, but he halts me with a gentle pat to my hand.

"Keep them on. I need…I need insurance."

I don't know what insurance is, but I trust him. I give him a curt nod.

"Scoot to the middle of the bed," he instructs before peeling off his sweatshirt.

My eyes are glued to his muscular chest as I obey his command. He kicks out of his boots before climbing on the bed. I stare in awe as his muscles tighten and ripple with each move he makes. His large, powerful hands that are cold from being outside grip my knees and he parts me.

Before I can ask what he's doing, he drops close to my center and inhales me. A thrill shoots up my spine with anticipation. His nose rubs against my sensitive nub through the material. I arch my back, letting out a breathy moan.

"You smell good," he growls. His tongue darts out and he teases the nub with it. Even over my panties, it's the most wonderful thing I've ever felt.

"Atticus," I croak out, my fingers diving into his hair.

He nibbles at the nub and when he gets it between his teeth, he playfully tugs. Then, his tongue swipes back out, teasing the throbbing flesh. His finger hooks into the side of the panties and he pulls it aside. The moment his tongue meets my bare flesh, I squeal. Green, blazing eyes lock with mine, silently asking me questions.

Am I okay?

"Don't stop," I breathe. I know he needs the words and I'm not afraid to say them.

His tongue begins lapping at the juices leaking from my body. He sucks and licks and slurps, hungry for everything I have to give. I arch off the bed when he spears me with his tongue, much like a cock would. It's hot and wet and slippery—the most chaotic explosion of sensations I've ever known. His tongue drifts lower and he teases my other hole. Whiskers scratch and tickle my soft skin on my inner thighs. He'll make me raw with them and that's okay as long as he doesn't stop.

I lose all sense of reality as he devours each hidden part of me. My ache consumes me. I'm feverish with the need to be eaten alive by my big bear. He finds my nub again, greedy and ravenous. The tip of his finger teases at my slippery hole and then he slides it inside of me. He's thick and my body stretches to accommodate him.

I'm unsure why my body responds positively to him, but I don't question it. I live in this moment, giving him full control to bring me pleasure. His finger curls up inside me, pressing into a part of me that makes me see stars.

"Oh," I gasp out. "Ohhhh!"

He nips at my throbbing flesh, moving his finger with expert precision inside of me. Everything turns black before exploding with color. I scream out his name as I thrash in pleasure, my entire body convulsing from it. I'm still trembling when he pulls his finger out and rights my panties. Then, he presses a kiss on the nub before sitting up on his knees.

I'm about to pull him on top of me and let him do things I've never wanted before when he bolts off the bed. He nearly trips over his boots and then he rushes into the bathroom, slamming the door shut behind him. The shower turns on. I climb off the bed on shaky legs, trailing after him. When I try the door, I find it locked.

Hurt burns inside me. My eyes prickle with tears. I press my ear to the door and listen to the soft moans as he finds his own pleasure. Alone.

I would have given it to him.

He didn't have to shut me out.

Blind Bear whines from the corner of the room. Defeated, I push out of my panties and hunt down a new pair. I'll wear

Atticus down eventually. He won't have to train me how to be a good wife as I already know. With him, I want to be one.

I throw on my jeans and a black sweatshirt before finding some striped pink socks. I love the clothes Judith sent for me. The rags I wore before stank and had holes in them. These all feel so soft and fit me perfectly and have bright colors. I pull on the boots she sent and then locate the big black coat. Once I'm bundled up, I call for Blind Bear and we step outside. I shove my hands in my pockets to retrieve my gloves and then grip my knife inside.

The cold air bites at my face. It's harsh and unforgiving. Trapped inside with Atticus, I become some other girl. Not the same one who lived each day with one goal in mind. Survival. Now, I enjoy small moments, but something feels incomplete. Is it because he still pushes me away when all I want is to be wrapped around him? I still crave the exhilaration out there, but without him, it feels incomplete too.

I need to hunt.

Sure, I could go inside right now and eat macaroni and cheese. Another wonderful creation by the human race. It would be delicious and warm my soul. Atticus calls it comfort food and he's right about that.

Comfort makes you stupid, though.

What happens if he decides he no longer wants me in his home? When he deems I'm healed, will he take me back to my little shack in the woods and drop me off? I will be spoiled to the ease of town living and my survival instincts will suffer the blow.

I need practice.

I need to remember that I can still do it.

Step after step, I walk deeper into the snowy forest. It'll

be dark soon. I should turn back. Instead, I find a tree that I can rip the thin limbs from. Perfect length and width to make a trap. The squirrels and rabbits are plentiful near his home, and I could use some new pelts for when I have to leave.

I'd be foolish not to start collecting and stockpiling supplies for that moment. Shame burns in my gut. I've become complacent. No more. I'll start gathering and preparing for my departure so I'm not caught off guard.

Blind Bear whines as though he can sense my unhappiness. I bend to scratch him behind his ears.

"Don't worry," I coo. "I'm taking you when I go. You belong out there with me."

"Eve!"

Blind Bear whimpers, turning his head back toward the cabin.

"He won't come with us," I mutter, breaking the sad news to my dog. "Just you and me."

"Eve!"

Blind Bear, unable to ignore Atticus, barks and takes off running toward him. I follow him from the thicket, dropping a few of the limbs I collected at the tree line to grab later. Atticus stands on the porch, his hair still wet, and barely dressed. His expression is wild and worried. My stomach flutters.

"What?"

He frowns. "Don't what me, woman. Get back in the house before you freeze your ass off."

My brow hikes up as I drag my gaze down his front. He has a sweatshirt on and sweatpants. His feet are bare. His body shakes against the cold.

"I have a coat and shoes and gloves. You have nothing." I smirk at him.

With a roll of his eyes, he motions for me to come back inside. I follow after him and once the door is closed, I inspect the small cabin.

I feel trapped.

Like a small rabbit that ran into a shelter for the promise of food, only to discover there was no way out.

"I can't stay here any longer," I admit, tears stinging my eyes. "I can't."

He scowls and shakes his head. "We'll go into town. A nice change of routine will do you some good."

I would think he misunderstands me, but the intense, challenging glare states otherwise. He knows what I mean and doesn't want to hear of it.

"Atticus…"

"Is it because I touched you? Because of what we did?" His cheeks tinge pink and panic dances in his green eyes.

"I liked that." What I didn't like was that he ran from it.

He lets out a heavy sigh. "I liked that too." His palm scrubs down his face. "I'm out of my depth here, Eve. I want…I want things I shouldn't. I'm too weak to turn away from them. When I see you—kiss and touch you—I don't see the fact you're a teenager. I just see you."

"I see you too."

"How old are you?" he asks, his eyes pleading.

I don't know what the right answer here is, though. He seems to think there's an acceptable age I must be and if I haven't reached it, he doesn't want any part of me.

"Old enough to marry and bear children."

He snorts. "That doesn't answer my question. Sixteen?"

Is this the number he wishes for?

"Yes."

His body tenses, which means I've chosen the wrong number. I'm about to bark out some other numbers to see if those are the correct ones, but he stops me by pulling me to him for a hug.

"I can't…we can't do that stuff anymore, Eve. It's not right."

The finality in his voice makes my chest ache. I knew it was coming. I could feel it in my bones. Still, I wasn't ready for his words to feel so final and unbreakable.

"But I liked when your mouth was on my nub and inside me," I murmur.

His cock is hard between us. "I liked that too, but that was before I really knew how old you were. It was a mistake. I'm a fucking adult and responsible for you right now. I need to act like one." He pets my hair and kisses the top of my head. "No more of that stuff."

I tremble in his arms. "Do I have to leave now?"

He grips my shoulders and pushes me away to glare at me. "What? You think because I can't fuck you like I'm losing my mind to that I'll kick you to the curb? I may have crossed the line with you, but I'm not an asshole. Of course you're not leaving."

"Okay."

His gaze softens as he stares for a long moment. I stare right back, drinking up every lovely detail of him. When he's had his fill, he smiles.

"I'm taking you out. You need a change of scenery."

"Out hunting?"

"No, Eve. I'm going to let you be a teenage girl. Take

you out for burgers and a movie or something. Something normal. You need to experience the world some."

Normally, that thought would terrify me.

But boredom has me nodding my head.

This earns me a devilish smile that makes my knees nearly wobble beneath me.

"Be ready to go in ten minutes."

chapter thirteen

ATTICUS

SIXTEEN.

Sixfuckingteen.

The unknown was better. Then, I could pretend and deny the fact she was young. We never knew how old she was, but Reed and I had our own ideas. He thought she was younger and I thought she was older. The average age we came up with recently was sixteen. I'd hoped she was eighteen, but that hope was for nothing. And unlike Reed, I'm not all about fucking a teenager.

My dick jolts at the memory of how she whimpered and begged when I had my mouth on her cunt. So maybe I am all about fucking a teenager, but that doesn't mean I'm actually going to do it. I just secretly crave it. A fucking fantasy I'll never live out.

Focus.

She needs to get out of the cabin because she's going stir crazy. I need to get out of the cabin so I don't pounce on her and put my dick in her. We need space and normalcy.

"Will Blind Bear be okay while we're gone?" she asks, frowning as we trudge through the snow toward my truck.

"He looked mighty cozy in the middle of my bed," I grumble. "Besides, we can't take that dog with us everywhere we go in town. We'll only be gone a couple of hours. He'll be fine."

I open her truck door and then grab her tiny hips, hoisting her into the cab. She weighs nothing despite the food she's been inhaling all week. At least she doesn't look so gaunt and bony anymore.

After turning on the truck, I wait for the heater to blast. Once it's cozy, I hop back out to scrape the windows free of ice. It takes about fifteen minutes, but eventually, we're ready to go.

"Music?" I ask, reaching for the dial.

She nods. "Led Zeppelin."

"There's my girl." I wince at my words, but she doesn't seem to notice. I scroll through my satellite radio until I find a Led Zeppelin channel. "Whole Lotta Love" starts playing and I drum my fingers on the steering wheel.

Eve grins at me.

Fuck.

This girl is inside me now and I don't know how to get her out.

I have to get her out.

As much as I'd love to taste that forbidden fruit, I don't feel like going to prison over it. Suma was wrong. I won't cross the line.

The drive to town is long because of all the snow. We

pass by several shops on Main Street that are lit up. Her eyes are glued to the sights, drinking them all in. A flutter of pride flits through me knowing I'm giving this gift to her. The smile on my face falls the moment we pass by the police station. Will's truck sits out front. I haven't told Will I'm back in town, but I'm sure Mom passed on that tidbit of information. I'll need to call him just to keep him from dropping in for a surprise visit.

Suma caught me defiling Eve. With her, I got dirty looks. With Will, he'd put my ass in cuffs. Will doesn't play around with that shit. Brother or not, he'd lock my ass up.

"There's a great restaurant here in town called Muskies. Has a little of everything. Sound good?"

"Peanut butter?" she asks, her eyes wide and shining.

"Babe, peanut butter is so easy to come by, it's not even funny." I wince at the pet name. "Muskies has other good stuff. New stuff you haven't tried. I promise you'll love it."

"Yes."

I laugh. "Okay then."

The parking lot is nearly empty, which works for me. I wasn't really looking forward to an audience. This town is too small. Everyone knows everyone. I'd be hit with a barrage of questions I wasn't ready to answer.

We climb out and I place my hand on her back to guide her inside. I'm not familiar with the hostess, which makes me sigh in relief. She walks us over to a booth in a dark corner. Eve sits down on one side. When I start for the other side, she shakes her head.

"No."

"If we sit on the same side—"

"Here," she says in her bossy, stubborn voice, slapping the leather with her hand.

I start to put my foot down and tell her it wouldn't be appropriate, but then I see the slight tremble in her hand. She's nervous. And here I am wanting to abandon her ass.

"Right," I grumble. "As you wish, my queen."

Her smile is a breathtaking reward that I happily take. Once I'm seated, she scoots closer, resting her head to my shoulder. So much for boundaries.

"Hiya there," a waiter says as he struts over to our table. He doesn't look any older than my nephew Evan.

"Hey," I grunt out.

"What can I get you and your beautiful daughter to drink?"

I freeze at his words and snap my head up to look at him. The kid is staring goofily at Eve. Lovesick kind of goofy. Possessiveness coils around my heart and sinks its teeth in.

"She's not my daughter," I say in a low, threatening tone.

The kid, completely clueless, shrugs. "Cool. We have Pepsi products."

"What do you want to drink?" I ask Eve, not sounding unlike a father. That grates on my nerves. Eve's not some idiot kid like this one taking our drink order.

"What you have," she squeaks out.

"Two Mountain Dews. And some mozzarella cheese sticks to get us started."

The kid tips his head and saunters off. I crave to wrap my arm around her and pull her against me so he'll know she's mine.

She's not mine.

Still not my fucking daughter, though.

"This place is strange," Eve tells me. "He prepares the food for us?"

"Not exactly. He tells the cook what to prepare."

"Like I tell you when I want oatmeal?"

I chuckle. "Kinda like that." Then, because I'm curious about her reaction, I say, "That kid liked you."

Her brows furl. "Liked?"

"Has a crush."

"Crush?"

"Wants to kiss you and have all your babies," I joke.

Her features grow stormy. "I don't want him as a husband. He is weak and small. I want you as my husband."

For fuck's sake. Here we go again.

Thankfully, the kid returns with our drinks and appetizer. He openly gawks at Eve.

"Look elsewhere," she barks at him.

His cheeks turn red and he glances at me in confusion. "Uh, can I get your order?"

"She's never been here, so I want to give her the true Muskies experience. How about an order of chicken fried steak, mashed potatoes, and corn. Then, maybe the mushroom chicken with sweet potato fries, and fried okra. The fried green beans sound good too. Leave a dessert menu too."

The kid quickly scribbles down our order and rushes off.

"You scared him," I tease as I unwrap our straws. "Mean Eve."

Her lip curls up, venom in her glare. "I don't like him looking at me."

"I feel sorry for your future boyfriends."

"Boyfriends?"

I clear my throat as I grab a mozzarella stick. "Yeah. Guys who take you to dinner or the movies. Kiss you. Love you. That sort of thing."

"Like you." She smiles so sweetly it makes my heart ache. "Boyfriend."

"Eh, no, babe, er Eve. I'm nothing to you. Just your friend."

Her brows furl together. "Mine."

So she's a possessive little shit like me.

Wonderful.

"Right. So subject change. These things are fucking amazing. I like it in the red sauce. It's called marinara, but it's tasty in ranch too." I dunk my stick in the marinara and take a bite.

She watches with rapt fascination and then mimics my actions. Her groan of pleasure shoots right to my dick. I'm hard as fuck watching her eat a stupid cheese stick. She licks off a drop of red sauce and then double dips the stick. I don't correct her because it's not like we haven't already swapped spit before. Once she swallows, she eyes the straw in confusion.

I chuckle. "Like this."

She picks up her drink and wraps her plump lips around the straw. It doesn't help the state of my dick whatsoever. She sucks up the Mountain Dew and then makes a face.

"It burns!"

"It's just carbonation. It's good."

She sips again. And again. And again. As soon as she gulps it all down, she smiles. "It's good. I want more."

I pass her mine and set the empty glass out on the edge for the kid to refill. When he strolls back over, he's more confident than before.

"I thought you looked familiar, man. Are you Will Knox's brother?" he asks, grinning.

"Yeah," I admit.

"No shit! I'm friends with his son, uh your nephew, Evan. We both are seniors and play basketball together. I'm Rex." Then, he turns his attention back on Eve. "You go to school around here?"

"Look away," she hisses again.

"Eve," I growl. "You can't say shit like that."

Rex doesn't seem bothered and waggles his brows at me. "Don't worry. I like a challenge." He whistles as he bounces off.

"Listen," I say, patting her thigh. "Things are different than they are out there in the wild. You can't tell people to look away simply because you don't want to talk to them."

"Why not?"

"Because it's…I don't know…tacky."

"Tacky?"

"Rude. Mean. Cruel."

Her nostrils flare. "I don't like his eyes on me. It reminds me of the way my brothers looked at me."

Well, fuck.

"And how's that?" My voice is husky.

"Like I'm something they could have if only they could get me alone."

Protectiveness washes over me. Sensible me knows the kid is just flirting. But possessive me wants to carve his eyes out so he doesn't make her feel like she's something that can be conquered and owned.

"I'll protect you," I whisper, leaning in to kiss her head.

"Because you're a good husband."

And fuck if my dick doesn't jump at her fucked up words.

"I can't be your husband. You're sixteen, babe."

"I already know how to be a wife," she argues, sounding very much like the teenager she is despite the crazy words escaping her.

"I'm sure you'll make a great wife one day when you're older."

She opens her mouth, but I shove another cheese stick in it. Her brown eyes flare with irritation, but the greasy goodness wins over. We eat in somewhat of an amicable silence until Rex shows back up.

He sets all of our plates down and then plants his dumb ass in the booth across from us. Eve glowers at him, her hand curling around the steak knife sitting on the table. The kid is oblivious. He's the prey and taunting a fucking predator.

"So, Eve," Rex says. "Can I have your number?"

"Sixteen," she hisses hotly as though that is supposed to ward him off.

I guess, technically, it worked for me.

"Cool," he says with a chuckle. "I'm seventeen. I meant your phone number, though."

"She doesn't have a phone," I tell him. "Sorry, man."

"No worries. I could be a good boyfriend. Buy you a phone and shit. So we could talk every day." He grins at her. So naïve.

"I have a boyfriend." Her words bite out at him. "We talk every day."

"Lucky guy," he grumbles. "Do I know him? Shit, is it Evan? That fucker!"

"Atticus." She turns her pretty face to smile at me.

361

Oh, fuck no.

Rex's eyes widen. "Wait? Atticus? This Atticus? How old are you, dude?"

"I'm not her boyfriend," I attempt to explain.

"We sleep together," Eve reveals, her words dropping like bombs on our dinner plates.

His eyes dart back and forth, wide and confused. "Oh."

Yeah, oh.

Fuck.

"Listen," I tell him with a low growl. "She's not from around here. She gets her words confused and mixed up. We're not sleeping together in the way you're thinking. She's just sleeping at my cabin until I can get her back to her home. Nothing is going on."

The last thing I need is for him to blab that shit to Evan, who will then blab that shit to Will. Fucking hell no.

"None of my business," Rex says, his hand jerking in an awkward way as if to blow it off. "I hope you enjoy your dinner. I'll get out of your hair."

He stands and before he walks away, I grab his arm. "Kid, nothing is happening."

"Yeah, duh. Nothing." He pulls away. "I have other tables to check on."

Eve relaxes once he's gone and I'm all wound up.

"This was a bad idea," I grumble. "People are going to get the wrong impression."

She doesn't fucking care. Simply eats up the mashed potatoes like they're the best thing in the world.

God, I need to get the hell out of here.

And send her back.

That thought makes my chest ache, but it's a necessity.

chapter fourteen

EVE

"I NEED SUPPLIES."

He looks up from the sink where he's scrubbing a pot from lunch earlier and frowns. "Pads? Peanut butter?"

Well, maybe those too eventually.

"More knives. Boots. An ax. A pack like yours to store fruit."

His eyes bug out of his head. "Why?"

It's been a week since he took me to Muskies. Since then, we've been trapped in this house. But rather than us going back to the way things were, he avoids me. So I'm trapped with someone who doesn't want to be around me. He's even taken to sleeping in his chair. He won't kiss me. And he's certainly made no moves to touch my body.

I'm angry.

I want to slap and claw at him.

He thought I was cruel to Rex. Well, this is cruel to me.

To tease me with the idea of him becoming my husband only to rip it away. He wants me gone—back to my home in the woods—and I want that too. I've spent all week making traps and gathering supplies. Now, I want more. Once I have what I need, I'll go back.

"I want to go home."

His eyes flash with hurt, which makes no sense considering he's been ignoring me for the most part all week. "Already?"

"I'm healed," I bite at him.

He dries off his hands and walks over to me. "But it's not safe there."

"It's not safe here either."

"What? Why?"

"Each day I spend here, I grow weaker. I won't be able to survive out there if I don't leave soon."

"You're already surviving here. You don't need to go out there." His hand reaches up to caress my cheek. "Please, Eve. Don't go. Just stay."

Tears flood my eyes. "Why? You don't want me for a wife."

His gaze drops, as does his hand. "Can't you just stay as my friend?"

"Like Monica?" I challenge.

He snaps his head up. He knows what *friend* I'm talking about. "That's just a show."

"They're friends."

"It's different."

"Why?"

"Because they're both consenting adults!"

"You throw out these stupid rules that mean nothing to

me," I cry out, tears leaking down my cheek. "You look at me like Chandler looks at Monica. They are husband and wife. They're friends too. Why can't we be like them?" My bottom lip wobbles.

He pinches the bridge of his nose and is quiet for a long time. Then, he lifts his hardened stare and pins me in place. "I'll take you to get supplies."

I turn on my heel and run outside so he won't know he just broke my aching heart in two.

Neither of us speaks on the drive into town. He's gone silent and hasn't argued on the matter anymore. I feel defeated in ways I'll never be able to express. I'm just ready to get it all over with. Get away from him and the way he makes my chest ache sometimes.

"This is really the only shop in town to get good supplies. Be nice."

Be nice?

His comment rubs me wrong, but I ignore it. Not speaking to him has worked so far since we had our fight. I climb out of the truck and follow him into the shop. It's filled with more supplies than I could ever need. I go from angry to delighted within seconds. Rushing over to a shelf, I marvel at fancy metal hooks in wrapping with pictures of fish on them. I may not be able to read, but I know what they are. I've seen Reed fishing plenty of times to know. I'm definitely getting some of these.

I grab a handful and shove them in my pocket.

"Whoa," Atticus says. "You can't just steal them. I need to pay for them. Just put everything you want over there on the counter."

I follow where he's pointing and discover a woman staring at me curiously. She's pregnant like Devon. It only makes me hurt more knowing I won't be able to have Atticus as a husband and carry his children. I look away from the woman and start gathering all sorts of tools I think I might need. There's a pack that resembles Atticus's, so I grab it too. The more stuff I accumulate, the more I think I'll need two packs. I grab an extra just in case. I bet I could strap it to Blind Bear. He's a big dog and could probably handle the pack better than me. I'm just feeling some blankets when I hear giggling.

Snapping my attention over to the woman, I discover that Atticus is leaned against the counter speaking to her. No longer interested in my supply gathering. I watch the way they interact. As friends. But...she stares at him in a wistful way. As though she misses him.

I stalk around some shelves in the middle of the shop, silently getting closer. I'm good at sneaking up on animals. They never knew what hit them. I step to the side and she catches me.

"Hey, Eve, is it? I'm Cassandra. Nice to meet you, sweetheart. Atticus says he's looking after you for a friend. Glad to have you here and let me know if you need help finding anything."

Cassandra.

I take a threatening step toward her, but Atticus blocks me.

"Don't," he growls, no room for argument. "I know

366

what's going on in that little fox brain of yours and you need to quit right now. I'll buy this shit. Go sit in the truck."

I shove at his chest, but the big bear doesn't move.

"Now, Eve."

I'm embarrassed that he chooses her over me. Is she pregnant with his child? Is that why he doesn't want me? With hot tears in my eyes, I storm outside. The door barely closes behind me when I lose my footing on the ice and fall hard on my bottom. My wrist turns at an awkward angle, making a sharp pain shoot up my arm. The sob I'd been trying to hold in rips from me.

The door flies open and boots crunch behind me.

"Eve, baby, are you okay?" Atticus kneels beside me, his palm running over my head, stroking me.

"I fell."

"I see that."

Another sob chokes past my lips.

"Hey," he coos. "Are you hurt?"

I nod, swiping at my tears with my good hand. "I twisted my wrist."

His brows furrow with concern. "Let me get you in the truck and after I pay for that stuff, we'll take a look at it."

I let out a squeak of shock when he scoops me in his arms. He's warm and strong and safe. I nuzzle my face against his scruffy beard and inhale his scent. When my lips press to his jaw, he doesn't get onto me for it.

He sets me inside the truck and then leans over to start it. Once heat is flooding inside, he gives me a chaste kiss on my cheek.

"I'll be right back."

Ten minutes later, he tosses the bags in the back and climbs into the truck. He reaches over and takes my hand.

"This one?"

It doesn't hurt like it did when I first fell. Just sore. Maybe bruised. I want his hands on me, so I simply nod.

Gently, he pulls off my glove and tugs my coat sleeve back. "A little swollen." His hands are warm as he rotates my wrist. "Does it hurt when I move it like this?"

"No."

"Good," he rushes out. "I don't think it's broken. You better rest it a few days, though, just in case."

"I have to go home."

"Not until that heals." His tone brooks no argument.

I scowl, feigning anger, but my heart squeezes inside my chest. When he's being sweet and attentive, I don't mind spending time with him. It's when he ignores me and keeps his distance that I nearly die.

Once we're back on the road, I look over at him.

"She misses you," I tell him bitterly.

"Who? Cassandra?" He lets out a heavy sigh. "We were just friends. We're nothing now. She's pregnant and with a guy I went to high school with."

Relief floods through me. I'm glad she can't have him. She doesn't deserve him. He's mine.

"I thought you were going to stab her right there in the store," he says with a chuckle.

"I thought about it."

"You're something else, Eve."

"Just protecting what's mine."

"I'm not...I don't need protecting...never mind."

When we finally make it home, he's once again being distant Atticus. I want to stab *him* now. Once he pulls up beside the house, I unbuckle and scoot over to him. His eyes widen when I straddle his lap to sit and face him.

"Eve," he warns.

"I just wanted to look at you."

"And it's not appropriate."

"Says who?"

"Says the State of Alaska."

I narrow my eyes at him. "They're not here, though."

His lips press into a line. My mouth waters to kiss him. I lean forward and capture his lips with mine. He's stiff at first, but then gives me the tiniest peck back. It makes me detonate. I slide my fingers into his long hair and tug on the golden locks. His mouth parts at the pain, granting me access. I kiss him hard and probing as I grind against his cock that's now hard as stone. His hands find my hips and for a moment I'm afraid he'll pull me off him. Instead, he digs his fingers in, returning my passionate kiss.

I want to devour him.

Mark and claim him.

Keep him.

Moaning against his soft lips, I use his body, seeking friction for the part of me that aches for him. When my nub rubs along his length, I let out a needy whimper.

"Fuck, Eve," he growls. "You really are a temptation."

His words are cold water drenched on me. I freeze and jerk away from him.

"What?" he demands. "Are you okay?"

I shudder when he grips my thighs. "H-He said that to me."

His gaze darkens. "Who?"

"Papa."

I'm yanked to him in a big hug. I claw at his coat, burying my face against his hot neck.

"I'm sorry," he murmurs, stroking his fingers through my hair. "I didn't know."

chapter fifteen

ATTICUS

I'M LOSING IT.

Completely fucking losing it.

When she was sitting in my lap, grinding on my dick, I lost all sense of reality. But the moment I said something that triggered her, we were brought back to our current situation. The one where I'm too old for her and she's just a kid. We since gathered her supplies and brought them inside. Watching her pack away the stuff is gutting at me.

I don't want her to leave.

She's so small and tiny. No match against the harsh wilderness.

But she's fierce and has claws. Her spine is made of steel and her heart is an inferno.

Eve belongs out there.

"What do you want to have for dinner?" I ask, unable to tear my gaze away from her.

She's squatted in the middle of the living room with

her blind dog sprawled out beside her as she unzips hidden places on her backpack.

"Eve…"

Her head snaps my way and she frowns. "Squirrel."

I roll my eyes. "I was thinking pancakes."

Despite her mood, she smiles. Brilliant. Beautiful. Soul consuming. "I love syrup."

And I love you.

"I know. I could teach you how to make pancakes. Over the fire."

Her brows lift. "I could make them at home?"

"Yeah, little fox."

She abandons her task and throws herself into my arms. "Thank you."

Greedily, I wrap my arms around her. "Of course."

Neither of us lets go.

I just hold her until her stomach growls.

"You're shivering," I point out.

Her teeth chatter, but she shakes her head. "I'm not."

"Liar."

I love how her smile seems brighter despite it being dark outside. The flames reflect on her pale face, making her eyes dance with delight. We're both bundled up against the cold, but I'm hot on the inside. Every time she licks syrup off her lip, it drives me insane.

"What if you stayed for a little while?" My words are out of my mouth before I can stop them.

"My hand?"

"No," I utter, scooting closer to her on the log. "What if you stayed because I want you to?"

Her brows crash together. "Why?"

"Why what?"

"Why do you want me to stay?"

"Because the very idea of letting you go out there alone kills me. I don't want to lose you."

She tilts her head up and bats her long lashes at me. So fucking pretty. Snow dusts her cheeks and hair. I run my hand over her cold hair and then I lean forward rather than backing away. My lips press to hers softly. And I don't pull away after that. No, like the stupid fucker I am, I swipe my tongue out, tasting her bottom lip.

Syrup.

She tastes sweet and addictive.

I groan, overcome with the urge to devour her. Her mouth parts, allowing me access. I kiss this sixteen-year-old girl because I fucking love her. And that's so incredibly twisted that I can't wrap my head around it. It's wrong, but nothing about being with her feels anything but right.

She squeals when I grab her hips and hoist her into my lap. Her legs spread and she straddles me. Like before, in my truck, she uses my body to bring pleasure to herself. It's fucking hot as hell.

I tried to be good.

I really did.

But in the cover of night and the heat of the fire licking at us, I feel wild and free. Out here, I'm able to touch her without guilt or repercussion. My hand slides under her coat and she yelps when my icy fingers skim up her bare spine under her shirt. She rubs her fingers through my beard and sucks on my tongue, making my dick jolt in response. I push my hand down the back of her pants, desperate to touch her wherever I can. A moan rattles from her when I grab her ass hard. Her jeans are just tight enough that I can't get to her everywhere I want. I reach under her coat, undoing the button and unzipping her jeans. When they fall slack, I slide my longest finger down her ass crack, brushing against her hole, before seeking out her pussy that's already sticky with want for me.

"Fuck, Eve. You're already so wet." She whimpers when I push my finger inside her tight depths. "This pussy is maddening. I can't ever stop thinking about it."

Her hips rock against me, no longer interested in my dick, but the way I finger her. The angle sucks, so I abandon ship to access her from the front. She whines in protest when I pull my hand out but then moans when I find my way into her panties between us. I rub at her clit, loving the breathy mewls crawling up her throat.

"You like your clit touched, hmmm, babe?"

She nods, kissing me hard as she lets me rub her. I tease her until she's nearly on the edge and then I work my fingers through her wetness back into her cunt. Slurping noises can be heard as I fingerfuck her. When I push a second finger into her, she squirms.

"My cock's bigger than my fingers," I warn.

"I want it."

My dick jumps in my jeans. She might not want it, though. I'd probably destroy her tight little pussy. I squeeze another finger inside her heat, loving the scream that escapes her and echoes through the trees.

"If that hurts, then you can't take my big dick." I nip at her lip.

"I can take it."

I fuck her roughly with three fingers because the angle is awkward, but she likes it based on the way she rotates her hips. My middle finger brushes against her G-spot. Her pussy clenches around me in response. With new determination, I massage that spot until her body is trembling so wildly I think she's having a seizure. Warmth gushes over my fingers as her cunt tries to milk my fingers like it's a dick.

Holy shit, she's perfect.

"Eve," I growl, pulling my hand out of her pants. "What I want is so not okay."

"I want it too. Put your cock in me."

"You're so fucking blunt." I stand with her in my arms. "I'm not doing it out here." With those words, I stalk inside with her, her blind dog on our heels.

I carry her inside the cabin and into the bedroom. The moment I stand her on her feet, we start ripping off clothes. She's the first one naked and I get a hot view of her ass as she prances over to the bed. I remove my boxers and then prowl after her.

I pounce on her, pinning her with my naked body, and seal my mouth to hers in an owning kiss. Mine. She's mine. I know it's not fucking okay. But no one has to know. It can be our secret. I devour every inch of skin I can get my lips on. My mouth marks up her pale neck, making my dick seep with need knowing I'll get to stare at these marks later.

"Atticus," she breathes. "I need you."

I need you too, baby.

Gripping my criminal dick, I rub it through her juices on her cunt. I press the crown into her slowly. Achingly slow. Her tight body stretches—just barely—to accommodate me. Nails dig into my shoulder, making me pause.

"You okay?" I rumble. The restraint it takes not to buck the rest of the way into her is incredible.

She digs her heels into my ass and lifts her hips up, forcing my dick the rest of the way in. Hot. Wet. Tight. I'm overwhelmed by the pleasure of being inside her that I almost can't move. Stalling for a moment so I don't blow my load, I kiss her hard. My palm strokes roughly down her cheek and down her throat. I pin her gently to the bed. Cage my little animal and keep her for myself. Pulling away from our kiss, I watch her feral brown eyes gleam. I give her neck a little squeeze, letting her know she's mine and doesn't get to leave me. She must understand my unspoken words because she smiles.

I buck into her hard, making her scream. I attack her lips with mine. Gentle and soft doesn't work for someone like her. She's wild and I want to be wild with her. We bite and suck and fuck. I'm getting close to nutting when I remember I don't have condoms. I don't want to finish on her stomach, but it's better than knocking her up.

The thought of Eve filled with my kid and unable to leave my side is a maddening thought. I could claim her right now. Keep her forever.

I may be fucking a teenager, but I'm not an asshole.

With a groan as my nuts release my seed, I reluctantly pull out my spurting dick and splatter her pretty red pussy with my cum. Then, I rub the cum with my fingers all over her clit roughly until she screams out my name in pleasure. The moment she's found her release, I fall on top of her, pinning her small body with mine.

Small.

Like a child.

Fuck.

Regret hits me right in the stomach, yet I don't move.

Why?

Because she's running her fingers through my hair and humming "Stairway to Heaven" by Led Zeppelin. Of course I don't fucking move. I'm transfixed by her. Obsessed. Completely out of control. I love her and it's insane. It's against the law. It's wrong.

Yet my dick is already hardening at the thought of having her again.

Hard as stone pressed against her thigh, still wet from her juices. It would be easy to… One small adjustment and my dick is sucked back into her warmth. It feels right being inside her. Like we fucking belong together.

This time, we make love slower. Calmer. More touches. More kisses. I catalogue every whimper and moan. She scratches her fingers along my flesh, marking me as hers. And when I come, I pull out.

Of course I pull out.

Any sane motherfucker would.

But not before feeling that first squeeze of her pussy as my cock jolts with a burst of hot, claiming cum. I take that moment and save it as something I'll remember forever. The moment I made her mine for one second.

Tomorrow I'll get condoms.

Tomorrow.

Tomorrow.

I watch her as she sleeps.

Peaceful and serene. Beautiful.

Her dark hair is messy and half covering her face. Gently, I swipe it away so I can look at her up close, unobstructed.

Last night, I fucked her.

Twice.

And then I washed her in the shower before taking her to bed with me. Now that the line has been crossed, I have no interest in going back. We've done the crime and now I just have to figure out how to keep from doing the time.

I run my fingertip down her spine, dragging the covers down with it, and then along her ass crack. Her cute little ass has put some meat on it and I love it. My dick is hard as stone, but I don't dare try to fuck her again. After the savage fucking last night, she's no doubt sore as hell. I squeeze her ass before seeking out the warmth of her pussy with my finger.

I play with her clit enough to get her to wake up. It's swollen and needy, throbbing with blood. Makes me want to bite her there.

"Morning," I say, my words raspy from sleep. I continue to strum her clit in a teasing way.

"Morning." Her voice is breathy. "Your manhood is hard."

I chuckle. "Cock. Manhood sounds cheesy as fuck."

Her smile lights up my soul. She reaches toward me

and grips my dick. As I play with her, she strokes me with expert knowledge. I wonder if she learned how to do that with her brothers or her father. If they were alive, I'd kill them myself.

Pushing those horrible thoughts away, I focus on bringing her pleasure.

"Atticus," she murmurs. "I want you inside me."

How will I ever tell this girl no about anything?

Answer is, I won't.

"You're dry," I growl. "Too sore."

"Make me wet."

The challenge in her tone is my undoing. I scoot down the bed and mimic her position between her spread legs. She makes a choking sound when I spread her cheeks and lick whatever sensitive flesh I can find. I want my tongue in every crevice of her. I want to own her everywhere. My tongue circles her asshole and teases it for a bit before finding her swollen pussy. I suck on her lips and run my tongue along her slit, seeking out her musky taste. Each passing second, she gets wetter for me. Needier. Desperate to quench my thirst for her. When I'm sure I have her good and wet, I spit on my hand before stroking my dick.

"Ready?" I ask as I crawl up her small body.

"Mmmhmm."

I run the tip of my dick down her ass crack, teasing her asshole and pressing slightly against it. I want inside every one of her holes. I'm fucking crazed for her now and I don't know what to do about it except give in. She cries out when I push in the crown. As much as I want in here too, we need lube for that. Reluctantly, I pull my mushroom head from her tiny asshole and then tease her juicy cunt.

Her fingers fist the blankets when I push all the way into her with one hard thrust.

Heaven.

Being inside her is fucking heaven.

I'm crazy for her and I don't fucking care what a prick that makes me. Pressing my hands down over her wrists, I spike my hips forward, reveling in her moan. Her body is slippery and inviting. An accomplice to my crime. I squeeze her wrists to the point she yelps, which makes my dick thump inside her.

Fuck, I'm losing control.

I want to pin her down and fuck her forever. Fill her up and breed her. Keep her, goddammit.

"You like this, little girl?" I groan, my teeth nipping at her ear.

She nods. "More."

I shove her arms up under the pillows, my grip still tight, as I flex my hips hard. Over and over. Our bodies make a slick slapping sound that fucking sings to me. I nip her ear, her throat, her shoulder. I try to bruise her with my teeth because she's mine and I need to see it whenever I look at her. Each time I bite her, she clenches around my dick. Eve's my wild fucking animal. Of course she loves this shit.

Harder and harder.

I pull out almost all the way and slam back into her, making her scream. The entire bed shakes and the dog whimpers nearby. I don't fucking care. We can break the bed for all I care. I'll buy a new one. Bringing her wrists together, I take the two tiny things in my large hand and rake my fingertips roughly down her body to her hip with my other. Then, I dive my hand beneath her, seeking her clit. I know when I have it because she cries out.

"Good girl," I growl. "I'm going to make you scream because you're mine. My girl. My sweet fucking teenage wild girl with a tight little pussy that was made for my cock."

My dirty talk sets her off because she explodes like a bomb. I pinch at her clit, raggedly thrusting against her until I find my own release. My nuts seize up and I spill. Hot and furious. Fuck. I slip out, my dick still spurting, and press against her tight asshole, just barely feeding the puckered hole the rest of my cum.

Holy shit.

I fall onto the bed, yanking her to me so I can comfort her and stroke her hair. "I'm sorry. I just want to…I don't fucking know. Consume you. Eat you alive. What are you doing to me, baby?"

She lifts her head, her plump pink lips curling into a smile. "Being a good wife."

I freeze.

Wife.

She's still so fucked in the head over that shit.

And because I'm a sick sonofabitch, I roll her over and kiss her to show her just how much I like that answer.

Wife.

Out here, in my cabin, we can fucking pretend.

We're not hurting anybody.

chapter sixteen

EVE

I PACE AROUND THE CABIN, UNSETTLED. ATTICUS IS sitting in his chair reading, but I can't sit still. Blind Bear sits in the corner, gnawing on a bone he found in the woods, happy as can be. I wish I could relax.

"Come here."

The command is one I feel down to my toes that have been curling several times a day thanks to Atticus. He consumes me. Once he was freed from his mental cage, he's been on me like my dog with his bone.

I love it.

I love him.

My feet take me over to his chair. He pulls me into his lap, abandoning his book on the table. Against his warm body, I feel calm again.

"What's wrong?"

"I don't know."

"Is it me? Us?" Guilt tinges his tone and I hate that. We've been fucking as he calls it for weeks now.

"No."

"Then what?"

I nuzzle my nose along his scruffy jaw, inhaling him. My tongue flicks out and I lick his Adam's apple, loving his salty taste on my tongue. He laughs, making it bob.

"You're such a little weirdo."

"I don't know what a weirdo is."

"It's you, Eve. Licking me and marking me. Very cute, though."

I sit up, my eyebrow hiked up. "You're a weirdo because"—I lift my shirt to reveal my breasts that wear purple bruises from his mouth—"you do it too." I let the shirt fall back down and his green eyes glimmer in that predatory way that makes my heart beat faster.

His finger trails along my throat. "I like these marks on you. They're pretty."

I melt a little at his words. He sometimes says soft, sweet things that make my head spin. I'm mesmerized by him.

Toying with a strand of his golden hair, I stare at his handsome face. He keeps his hair down for me, though he puts it in his "man bun" when we go to town. I love it when it's free and I can run my fingers through the silky tresses.

"Something's bothering you," he murmurs, his brows crashing together.

I massage the wrinkle there with my thumb. "No."

He rolls his eyes. "Nice try."

"I just…I want something, but I don't know how to ask for it."

At this, he tenses. "Anything, babe. Tell me what you want and I'll go buy it for you right now."

Atticus is a good husband.

I pick up the book that has words on it I can't understand. "I want to know how to read. Mother tried when I was a child, but I was more interested in playing with Esther's hair or chasing butterflies. I loved to look at my reflection in the water and make silly faces or pick flowers for my mother. All her lessons were for nothing. I didn't care then. I care now."

He pulls the book from my hand and sets it back down before squeezing my thigh. "You want to go to school?"

I cock my head to the side. "I don't know school."

"It's a place where you go with other kids to learn—"

"No." I lean forward and kiss his mouth. "My husband."

He darts his attention away and clears his throat. "Fine. No school. But I can't teach you with George Orwell's *1984*. If you don't know any letters or words, then we need to dial it back to basic. I can pick up some learning books for children." He winces at his words.

"Yes. I want the books. Can we go now?"

He chuckles, the tension leaving his body. "Yeah. You're full of energy. I knew buying you Mountain Dew was a bad idea."

I stick my tongue out at him like I've seen them do on television when they don't like what someone's said. This makes him laugh and then he digs his fingers into my ribs. Loud laughter rips from my throat as I thrash. It's too much. Too intense. Why am I laughing so hard? Tears roll down my cheeks as I giggle. He pulls me to him, stroking my hair.

"I love that sound, baby. So beautiful."

He's loving me just the way I like, and if I didn't already have this in my head, I'd strip down for him so he could touch me everywhere. But this is important to me. Reading. I want to know what the words say on television. I want to know what Joey's T-shirts say or what the words are that sometimes blink on the screen before and after the show.

"Come on," he says, slapping my thigh. "Let's go before I decide to spend the night making you laugh with my nose buried between your legs."

I love the grocery store.

It's my favorite place ever.

So. Many. Things.

There are more jars of peanut butter than I can count!

Atticus cuts me off at five jars, but I toss in another one when he's not looking. My husband is patient as we go up and down each aisle, shopping as he calls it. Shopping is wonderful. A few people shoot us curious stares. I notice several women looking at Atticus as though he's a jar of peanut butter. It makes me want to pull my knife out and tell them to walk away before I make them.

They're all so pretty.

Like Rachel and Phoebe and Monica.

And I'm...

My lips aren't shiny like theirs and my eyelids don't sparkle. I don't wear dresses that show my legs. Judith sent one. I tried it on once, but it felt too open. Now, I wonder if open is a good thing. Is that so your husband can shove it up your hips and put his cock inside you when the need arises?

Maybe I could wear dresses if that's their purpose.

A woman with blond hair walks by, her dress swishing. I realize she doesn't have a husband. She's alone. And keeps sneaking looks at mine.

Does she think…that he would…

No.

Rage, hot and violent surges through me.

"Stop looking at my husband or I'll make you blind like my dog," I hiss at her.

"Eve!" Atticus barks, grabbing my bicep and pulling me back.

"Oh," the woman croaks. "I'm so sorry. I thought she was your daughter."

She rushes off toward the end of the aisle. I relax the moment she turns.

"What the fuck was that?" he demands, turning me to face him.

"She thought she could take my husband!" I yell, jerking from his grip.

He stares at me with wide, horrified eyes. That's what I thought. She had no right!

"Listen," he snarls, stepping close enough that our chests touch. "You can't blab that shit out in public." He strokes back a tendril of my hair, tucking it behind my ear. "You know those traps you make for the rabbits?"

I nod, frowning.

"They make those for men. But made of metal as strong as your knife blade. If they know, they'll tell the police I'm fucking you, and then they'll put me behind those bars. I'll stay there, baby. Do you understand?"

Realization dawns on me. "They'll take you away from

me? Why?" I choke back my tears, hating how the loneliness floods inside my chest cavity.

"Because…" He sighs and drops a quick kiss to my forehead. "Because they won't understand what we have. You and me, baby, it's not right."

"So I'm supposed to pretend you're not my husband when we're around these monsters?" I practically shriek at him, hot tears rolling down my cheeks.

His nostrils flare and he casts a look over his shoulder. "That's exactly what I'm saying."

"But the women will take you from me," I whisper. "If they don't know, they'll think you could be theirs."

He pulls me to him for a hard hug. "No one is taking me from you. As long as we play this right in public. Please. Do this one thing for me, baby. I don't ask for much."

"Yes," I mutter, my voice quivering. "I don't want to, but I will to keep you safe."

"Thank you."

"But if a woman tries to take you, I'll cut her throat."

He laughs as he steps back. "My violent little fox. What would I ever do without you here to protect me?" His green eyes dance with amusement.

Get mauled by hordes of females in the peanut butter aisle apparently.

"Fuckin' hell. If it ain't little Atticus."

We both snap our gazes in the direction of an older man and a younger one. I step close to Atticus for protection. I don't know them and they're both larger than me, unlike the women. I'm not sure I could take two at once.

There's something familiar about them both.

Green eyes. Green eyes. Green eyes.

"Will," Atticus says, his voice tight. "Evan. How the hell are you guys?"

The older one hugs Atticus and then Atticus playfully hits the younger one in the stomach. The younger one stares at me, eyes wide and mouth slightly parted.

"Look away," I warn, my hand going around the hilt of my knife in my pocket.

The younger man snaps his mouth shut and darts a confused look toward the older one. His cheeks blaze red.

"Who's this?" the older one says, no longer playful. He regards me with suspicious eyes.

"Will, meet Eve. Eve, meet my older brother Will. This is his son Evan." Atticus gives me a look that begs for me to keep quiet. "Will is a policeman."

Police.

I remember the term from earlier.

If he knows we're fucking, they'll take my husband away.

"Is she some long lost kid we didn't know about?" Will asks, his eyes assessing me.

"Nah, she's my friend Reed's daughter," Atticus lies. "I'm looking after her for him."

Will jerks his head his brother's way. "Is that so?"

Atticus, always so confident, shifts under his brother's hard stare.

"Can I talk to you for a sec?" Will asks, drawing Atticus away by his elbow.

I'm left with the wandering eyes boy. He stares at the ground, his face bright red. I watch him in case he makes any sudden moves.

"You like peanut butter, huh?" he asks, gesturing to the basket.

I flinch at the movement. "Yes."

He chances a gaze my way. "You go to school around here?"

"No."

"How old are you?"

I bristle at the line of questioning. I remember his friend Rex said they were seventeen. If I tell him that age, he might think I'm a suitable wife for him. I have a husband! I want to scream it, but I bite on my bottom lip. For Atticus.

"Fourteen," I lie. Sounds far enough from his age maybe he'll go bother another woman. Maybe the one we just saw.

"Wow. Fourteen? Really? No way. You're older than that, right?" He smiles in a shy way. "Pretty, though." He glances over at where his father is talking to Atticus. "Dad would kill me if I messed around with a fourteen-year-old. I turn eighteen soon."

My curiosity gets the better of me. "What happens when you turn eighteen?"

"I become legal." His cheeks redden further. "Messing around with some young girl would get me slapped with statutory rape charges. I'm too pretty for prison." He laughs at his words, but they're not funny at all.

"What if I was eighteen too?" I probe.

He swallows and his eyes widen. "Uh, we could, uh…" He trails off. "Like date and stuff. I could take you out. It would be okay."

My mind spins. I should have told Atticus eighteen instead of sixteen. That will fix everything.

"I'm really eighteen," I lie. I force a smile.

"Oh," he squeaks out. "I, uh, okay. Sure. So you lied to me about your age so I wouldn't ask you out?"

I nod. I'm not going anywhere with him.

He laughs. "I understand. You probably have some hot boyfriend back home, huh?"

"Husband," I correct him.

"Wait…what?"

"I have a husband and—"

"Eve," Atticus says sharply, cutting me off. "I was just telling the guys we'd catch up with them another time. You ready?"

We've only gone through a few aisles. No way am I ready to go. He must sense my words before I say them because he gives me a firm shake of his head.

"Fine," I snap, throwing my hands up in the air just like Rachel does it.

Will laughs, Evan looks at his feet, and Atticus glares.

"Typical teenager," Will says under his breath.

"Hey now," Evan grumbles, playfully hitting his father. "I resent that."

They walk off in the other direction and Atticus gives me a warning glare.

"I don't like your brother." I lift my chin, daring him to challenge me.

"That makes two of us."

chapter seventeen

ATTICUS

HOLY SHIT.

That was a close one.

And I don't even know if I avoided it. My brother is a hound dog. Once he gets a sniff of something sketchy, he hunts it down and then dismantles it like a bomb. When he pulled me aside, he drilled me with questions. I lied through my fucking teeth.

Every time I looked at Eve, I thought how much closer to Evan's age she looked than mine. It was glaringly obvious. And, fuck, if she didn't have hickeys all over her neck. Of course Will asked about those too. I lied and said some boy was coming by the house for her.

We need to get the hell out of here.

The cashier takes forever, but eventually we get the truck loaded. It's dark out and snowing again. Before she can climb back into the truck, I grab her hips with my hands and pin her ass to the truck.

"That was bad," I growl, resting my forehead to hers. "My brother…he just doesn't know when to quit."

"I should have stabbed him."

I laugh, kissing her forehead. "Yeah, you should have. Kidding. He's my brother. We can't kill him. I'm just saying he won't let this go. I lied to him about you."

She tilts her head up. "Tell him I'm eighteen." With her wide brown eyes fixed on me and her plump lips pouted out, she makes me crazy with need.

"But you're not eighteen, are you?"

She shakes her head.

"Maybe we should get out of town for a little while." I steal a kiss. "What do you think?"

"Are there prisons there?"

My smile becomes wicked. "Not in the wild. We'll go visit Reed and Devon. Stay for a few weeks."

"The thought of seeing them isn't as frightening as it once was. I think I'm getting used to people now," she says absently. "Maybe Devon will sing to me."

"But she sings so horribly," I joke.

Eve stands on her toes and kisses me in a possessive way. It makes me wonder if she saw one of those women again. The thought has me pulling away from our kiss. Making out with my teenage girlfriend slash wife in the parking lot of the Piggly Wiggly where my cop brother may or may not be loitering still is a bad idea.

"Let's roll."

The drive back home is quiet. Eve is deep in thought. When I finally pull up beside the house, she unbuckles her seat belt and climbs into my lap.

"Yes."

"Yes, you want to visit?"

She nods. "It'll keep you safe."

So protective, my little fox.

"I want to keep you safe too. You wouldn't like it if they took me away. They'd want to put you somewhere that I can guarantee you would hate."

"They could try," she snarls, pulling out her knife.

I take the knife away and fold it back up before sticking it in her pocket. "You can't shank everyone."

"If they try to keep me from my husband, I will."

I close my eyes. I really should have stopped this husband shit. But now we're two weeks into me allowing it to happen. Because behind closed doors, I get off on it. I love the possessive feeling it evokes in me.

In public…

It's embarrassing.

Not because of her. Eve is fucking perfect.

Because of me. I'm a grown ass man. Almost forty, for fuck's sake. People will see me as a predator. They don't understand us.

"Be a good little wife and take my cock out," I murmur, squeezing her thigh. We're home, so our little game is good here.

Her eyes flash with satisfaction that makes my dick hard as stone. She makes quick work of pulling me out. Her small hand wraps around my thickness and strokes me with expert ease.

"Fuck," I hiss. "You're so fucking good at that."

She works me up and down with her dry hand. I want wetness and heat. I want her.

"Take off your clothes." My words are raspy and harsh.

Within seconds, she's ripped away all of her clothes. My tiny, naked *wife* rubs her pussy up and down along my shaft, her needy juices coating me.

"Sit on it, baby. Fuck me."

Her hand grips my wet dick to guide me into her tight body. We both hiss. I buck my hips up, driving the rest of the way in.

"Touch my clit," she tells me in that bossy tone of hers.

At least we've graduated from nub to clit. I obey my sweet woman and rub at the sensitive bundle of nerves with my thumb. With my eyes on hers, I push my middle finger between her fat lips.

"Suck."

Her eyes grow hooded as she face fucks my finger the same way she fucks my cock. Once it's good and wet, I slip it out, letting a string of slobber drip down her chin. I lick up her sweet taste, my tongue tangling with hers, as I locate her ass blindly. My slick finger runs along her crack until I find the bud I'm looking for. I massage the tender muscle until she's whining with need. Slowly, I push inside her asshole with my finger, loving the way both holes clench in response.

"I'm going to put my dick here one day," I tell her. I push as deep as I can go. "All the way in there."

She bobs up and down my cock, her ass clenching each time. When her head tilts back, I attack her pretty throat with my teeth and tongue. I suck her neck, uncaring that I'm leaving more marks. I love the way they look on her.

With my finger in her ass, my cock stuffed in her pussy, and my thumb on her clit, she unravels quickly. Her pussy leaks with her arousal, signifying her upcoming release.

The moment she comes, her entire body jolts and tightens as a scream crawls up her throat. She's hot as fuck when she goes wild for me. Her fingers yank at my hair as she rides her orgasm out.

"Oh fuck," I grunt against her mouth.

Pull out. Pull out. Pull out.

My balls tighten and I bite her neck. She claws at my shoulders, still trembling. Cum shoots into her needy body, spurt after heavy spurt. I fill up my wife and it feels fucking amazing. No guilt washes over me because claiming her this way takes precedence over everything.

"I might get you pregnant," I tell her, my words hot against her flesh.

"Good husband."

Fuck if that doesn't make me want to do it again the moment my dick hardens back up, consequences be damned.

Domestic bliss looks good on Eve.

With each passing day, I realize I'll never be able to let her go. Planning a visit to see Reed and Devon is a good idea. We need to get away. Maybe not be so strained all the time hiding our true feelings. Reed of all fucking people won't judge. He has every right to considering I judged the hell out of him over the fact he fucked his daughter.

"Smelly dog, smelly dog, what are they feeding you?" Eve sings from the dresser, sounding very much like Phoebe from *Friends*, as she folds clothes in a basket.

Blind Bear rolls over on his back and lets out another doggie fart. Enough bacon for that big boy. His bowels can't handle it.

"Gross. Send him to the woods."

She finishes putting her clean panties in the top drawer and tosses the laundry basket in the corner. "How about I send *you* to the woods instead?"

Her challenge gets my dick hard.

"You're awfully sassy lately." I stand from the bed and prowl over to her. "Maybe I ought to spank you."

"With a switch?" she winces, her dark eyes growing stormy.

"Not like whoever the fuck beat you into submission before," I growl. "I'm talking a good ol' hand to the ass kind of spanking. Knowing you, your little pussy would get so wet over it. You're a very naughty girl, Eve."

Her smile grows wicked. "Can I spank you back?"

"Fuck. You're a little sadist, you know that?"

She hooks her thumbs into her yoga pants when something shatters. I shove her behind me and rush for my Glock. The dog tears out of the bedroom toward the sound.

"Stay back," I bark at her as I stalk down the hallway and into the living room.

Cold wind blows in through the kitchen window. A rock sits on the floor and the basket of fruit that was on the table is gone.

What the fuck?

Bears?

I stuff my feet into my boots and grab my coat before walking outside. Blind Bear runs out into the snow sniffing. What I see stops me in my tracks.

Shoe prints in the snow on the porch.

Large. Male if I had to guess. Human.

I squint against the darkness but make out nothing.

"Who's there?" I call out.

Silence.

No cars. No bikes. No anything.

Just a trail of footprints going into the woods.

"BB," I call out and then whistle. "Get back in the house."

After a few minutes of nothing, Blind Bear goes back inside and I follow him. Eve wears a nervous expression I don't see from her too often.

"Bear?"

"Nah," I grit out. "Human."

She eyes the window letting in cold air. "He wanted fruit?"

I hope that's all he fucking wanted.

"Probably just hungry," I assure her. "A drifter. He'll be gone before morning."

"What if he comes back?"

I grip her jaw and press a kiss to her supple mouth. "I'll shoot first and ask questions later."

We may be playing pretend about this husband and wife shit, but my heart thinks it's real and that's all that matters.

If anyone touches my wife, it'll be the last thing they do.

chapter eighteen

EVE

ATTICUS BORROWED A COVERED TRAILER FROM HIS dad because in his rush to get me back to town for medical help, he left his at Reed's. It's been a couple of days since the man stole our fruit and I can't help but look over my shoulder every time we bring another box to pack inside the trailer.

"Everything okay?" Atticus asks as he exits the trailer.

"Yes."

"Liar."

I shrug. If I learned anything from Atticus, it's sometimes we have to lie. Like now. I lie because if I tell him my concerns, he'll scour the woods again for hours looking for the man. And when he does that, I feel isolated and alone. I don't like being in his cabin without him. I'd rather keep him by my side.

"Want to go to Muskies for dinner?" His hands grip my hips and he stares at me as if I'm the most lovely thing he's ever seen.

"I might stab Rex. Better not. Oatmeal it is."

He snorts. "You've been watching too much *Friends*. You're becoming quite the comedian."

"We could go into the bedroom and I could pretend to be Rachel and—"

His lips fuse to mine, silencing my words. I smile into his kiss. It's cold outside, but in his arms, I'm warm. Our kiss grows heated quickly. He takes to nipping my lips and then my jaw and then his favorite place…my throat. I groan, loving the way he feels there, and roll my head to give him better access.

"This." He sucks hard. "Is." Another claiming suck. "Mine."

I giggle when he tickles my side and it isn't until Blind Bear barks that we realize a car is driving down the path to his cabin. I'm shoved behind him as he reaches for his Glock at his belt. He always carries it around now.

"Oh fuck."

"What is it? The man?" My fear bleeds into my words.

"No. Worse."

What could be worse?

The car stops and a woman screeches. "You have a phone, son. Use it."

He groans. "My mother."

My heart swells. It makes me miss my own mother tremendously. The blond woman is small like me but has Atticus's face minus the facial hair.

"Hey, Ma," he says, stepping forward to hug her.

She accepts his hug and then moves him aside. "Let me see the girl."

Atticus shoots me a reassuring look. "Ma, meet Eve. Eve, this is my ma, Susan."

The woman starts for me and I nearly trip over my own boots trying to escape.

"A bear got you?" she asks.

I nod and make a clawing motion across my chest.

Sadness gleams in her green eyes that match Atticus's. When she reaches for me, I stumble again in my effort to get away.

"She's skittish around strangers," Atticus says. "Why don't we go inside and have some coffee?"

His mother studies me intently. "I think I'd like that."

I crave to take Atticus's hand, but I know now's not the time. She's his mother, but how do I know she won't turn on him and take him to prison?

As soon as we make it inside, his mother sheds her coat and starts tidying up. I shoot him a questioning look, but he simply shrugs as if this is normal. He steps into the kitchen to start the coffee and I linger by the door with my dog.

"What in the heavens happened to your window?" she gasps, hands on her hips. "Bears?"

"Man," I say harshly as though the word is bitter on my tongue.

His mother blinks at me and then darts her gaze to Atticus.

"Rock through the window. The guy stole our fruit."

"I see," she replies and then turns her scrutinizing glare on me. "Where did you come from, honey?"

I open my mouth, but Atticus answers for me.

"Reed. A friend of mine. It's his daughter."

His mother's lips purse into a line. "Same spiel you gave your brother."

"It's not a spiel," Atticus mutters.

"How old are you?" she asks.

"Sixteen," he answers as I say, "Eighteen."

He winces and I stand taller. I don't know why he's afraid of this little woman. I'm not. I dig my hand in my coat pocket, checking for my knife. Atticus watches my actions and rolls his eyes.

"Hmmm," his mother says. "I'll take that coffee now. Got anything strong to lace it with?"

"No, Ma."

"Tragedy." She sits at the table. "So you got a boyfriend, huh? That's what Will told me. A little too young to be having a boyfriend. Young ladies should be focusing on their future. What college do you plan on attending—"

"Ma," Atticus snaps. "Enough with the interrogations. Jesus. You're worse than Will and he's a damn cop."

"She's a mystery and you're hiding something. I'm your mother. I know these things."

"There's nothing to know," he mutters.

I wince at those words.

"You're not seeing that Rex boy, are you? I swear Evan can keep better friends than him. I heard he has tattoos." She shakes her head.

"I have tattoos," Atticus reminds her.

"Yours are art, my boy. But he's too young. Do you have any tattoos?" This question is aimed my way. She leans closer, her elbows resting on the table. "What's that on your neck? Has this boyfriend been putting his hands on you?"

"Ma! Enough!"

Her brow deepens. "You both should come for dinner."

"We're leaving in the morning to go see her dad." Atticus's tone is final.

"Lovely. Tonight I'm making lasagna. See you at seven."

"What's wrong?"

I blink away my tears and stare out the window. I don't answer him because I don't think I can speak without crying.

"Baby," he says, reaching across the cab of his truck for my hand. "What's wrong?"

I jerk my hand from his. "Don't."

"Don't what?" he demands, his voice harsh.

"Don't touch me."

He lets out a growl of frustration. The truck slams to a stop on the side of a dark road. I can feel his penetrating glare on me.

"Baby, look at me."

"No."

"Jesus, woman! Why are you so stubborn?"

I give him a scathing glare. "Fuck you."

He gapes at me in shock. "Did you just curse at me?" His fingers run through his hair. "You watch too much television."

"You say that word a million times a day!" I accuse. "Why can't I say it?"

"Because you're sixteen goddamn years old!"

"I'm not sixteen," I snap back.

"Oh, here we go again. You're eighteen now. I

remember. You keep telling everyone that now like it'll stick. Newsflash, baby, it's not fucking sticking."

"Drive." I face forward, ignoring him.

"You don't get to order me around, Eve."

"Drive!"

"Get over here."

"DRIVE!"

He unbuckles my seat belt, grabs my hips, and hauls me into his lap. I struggle against his hold, but he has no problems settling me with my legs spread. I'm wearing my only dress—hoping his mother would like it—and feeling especially vulnerable.

"Calm the fuck down and tell me why you're upset." His green eyes plead with me.

Now that his anger has dispelled and given way to concern, my own fury evaporates like a mist. My shoulders hunch and I tremble.

"You want me to lie to everyone." Hot tears streak down my cheeks. "I don't want to lie."

"I don't want to lie either," he admits, pressing a kiss to my neck. "But we have to."

"They're your family, though."

"I wish it were that easy. We need to just make it through tonight. Tomorrow we'll go see Reed and Devon."

His words don't help the gaping hole in my chest. Nothing feels right. I feel half full. Incomplete. I start to slide off his lap, but his fingers bite into my thighs. Familiar heat burns in my stomach, chasing away the achiness.

"Everything is going to be okay, Eve. Even if we have to wait two years to tell anyone. We'll survive this. I love you too much not to."

Rather than returning his sentiment, I crash my lips to his. His strong hands grab onto my bottom, squeezing and pulling me against his hard cock between us. Frantically, he works at his belt and then jeans to free his cock. I greedily rub against him. His fingers pull my silky red panties to the side and he taps the tip of his cock against my clit.

"Get on there," he orders.

I fight a smile as I slide down over his length. When we're together like this, I forget I was even mad at him. Once I'm seated, I go back to kissing him as he bounces me on his cock.

"We gotta be quick, or we'll be late to dinner," he murmurs, nipping at my bottom lip. He massages my clit in an expert way that has me seeing stars. Over and over again until I lose all sense of reality.

"Oh!" I cry out, losing myself to the pleasure.

His thrusting becomes harder, faster, out of control. Then, he groans as his heat fills me. With his cock still throbbing inside me, he pulls away to look at me.

"I'm going to be hard as fuck through dinner knowing you're full of my cum." He presses kisses along my jaw to my ear. "*Wife.*"

He gives my thigh a squeeze and flashes me a smile. "Relax. You look like you're about to take off running."

I consider it. Now that we're in his parents' driveway, I wonder how far I can make it. Probably not far in this impractical dress. What was I thinking?

My panties are wet as Atticus's cum slowly trickles out of me. It makes me squirm in my seat, wondering if they'll notice. Then our secret would be out. Would they try and drag him away from me? My palm curls around the hilt of my knife in my pocket. They could try.

The truck door opens and Atticus watches me with narrowed eyes. He takes my hand, helping me out of the big truck. Instead of releasing me, he steals a chaste kiss.

"You're so fucking beautiful, Eve. Trust me, I'd much rather brag to the damn world you're mine. One day I will. For now, we have to take what we can get and that's each other. The rest can wait."

His words cause chaotic fluttering in my belly. "Your cum is leaking out of me."

"Eve," he growls, his nostrils flaring as he caresses my cheek. "You can't say shit like that to me right before we walk in to see my parents."

I touch him through his jeans. Hard as stone. "It's the truth. We're about to have to lie. I just wanted to tell the truth while we still could."

"Later," he murmurs, dragging his palm down the side of my neck, "I'm going to pull those silky panties off with my teeth, wrap them around my dick, and jack off all over your sexy little ass."

I thread my fingers in his hair and kiss him deeply. My heart races in my chest with the need for him to consume me. In the end, he pulls away with a harsh groan as if it physically pains him to do so.

It pains me too.

"Come on," he says, his voice husky, as he takes my hand.

Together we walk toward his parents' large home. I lean

against his shoulder, stealing what little time we have left before he pretends I'm nothing to him again. I'm lost in thought when I feel it.

Awareness.

The hairs rising on the back of my neck.

A cold chill down my spine.

I pull my knife out, halting on the snow-covered path. Atticus abruptly pulls his hand from mine and I wonder if he's readying himself to fight too.

"Hey, Dad," Atticus says toward the dark porch.

A giant man appears from the shadows. I stumble back a step. His hair is white and the length is nearly as long as Atticus's. He's bundled up all in black with a cap on his head. His beard is also white, but trimmed short against his face.

"This is Eve." Atticus's voice is tight and it makes me nervous. Is he afraid of his father like I was of mine? "Eve, this is my dad, Abel." His palm finds my back and he gently guides me toward the man.

As soon as his brown eyes come into focus, I tense up. I know this man. The knife in my grip falls to the ground as I shake, a terrified mewl crawling up my throat.

"Hey," Atticus croons. "It's just my father. He's not going to hurt you."

The look on Abel's face says otherwise. Stern. Almost angry. Disgusted. I cringe, hiding behind Atticus's back. My heart stampedes in my chest as fear makes the world around me darken and spin.

I don't feel so well.

The spinning gets worse.

It stops as black bleeds into my vision, stealing me from this moment.

chapter nineteen

ATTICUS

EVE JUST COLLAPSES.

Scares the fuck out of me too.

Dad's footsteps thunder as he rushes for us. I scoop my little fox in my arms, panic surging through me.

"She okay?" Dad grunts out, his worried eyes meeting mine.

"She passed out." I storm up the steps. "I think she was freaked the fuck out."

He doesn't say a word, simply follows me into the house that smells like Ma's amazing lasagna. I can hear my brothers and sister teasing each other and Mom nagging at them to quit. Ignoring them all, I carry Eve over to the sofa and set her down.

"Eve," I croon. "Wake up."

She's so pale. In the lamplight, wearing her big coat, she seems so small and fragile. So young. Guilt threatens to gnaw at me, but I don't let it. I promised her we could be together as long as we kept it quiet. Her age is something I have no problems forgetting about when my cock's buried deep inside her.

"I'll get Vic," Dad says, stalking off.

I pull her coat off her and then drape it over her bare legs.

Less than a minute later, my brother and EMT, rushes over to us. He has the same golden blond hair as I do, but he has Dad's brown eyes. Vic has also adopted Will's clean-cut look and has his hair clipped short to his head.

"What happened?" he asks, launching right into first responder mode.

"She got scared, I think, and passed out."

He checks her pulse with his fingers and then gives me a nod. "Pulse is steady. I think she'll wake soon—"

Her brown eyes pop open and like a cornered animal, she hisses. I nudge him out of the way to sit next to her on the sofa.

"You're okay," I assure her, taking her hand. "You fainted."

"What in heaven's name—" Mom starts as she enters the living room with Will, Evan, and Judith in tow.

"Peanut butter crackers, Ma," Vic says. "Grab a Sprite too. Could be low blood sugar. When was the last time she ate?"

I don't remember.

My mind is blank because my worry over her has consumed every thought.

Dad gently touches Vic's shoulder. "Give them some air. Everyone is overwhelming them." He gestures for everyone to leave, but he remains.

Eve's narrowed eyes pin him in place. She trembles as though she fears he might hurt her.

the wild

"It's okay, little one," Dad says and then grins at her.

Her head cocks to the side, her gaze fixated on his mouth. "He has teeth."

Dad snorts. "Perceptive, this one."

I squeeze her hand. "He does. How are you feeling?"

Vic returns with a package of crackers and the soda. She loves peanut butter, so she devours all six crackers just as fast as I can hand them to her. When she sips the Sprite, her eyes light up with delight. My girl loves soda.

"Better?" I ask.

She nods and eyes the home with guarded curiosity. I don't let her hand go. Not now. Not when she's frightened out of her mind. With Rex and Evan, she wasn't intimidated. But with both Will and my dad, it's like their size terrifies her. It's strange because I'm about the same size as Will and am nearly as big Dad, yet she's not afraid of me.

Her fingers thread with mine, making my heart rate quicken. I should tug them away, but I can't. She's so broken. They can drag my ass to prison. I'm not letting her hand go.

"Tell me how you know this little one again," Dad says, his voice soft as to not startle her.

I flash her an apologetic look. "My friend Reed's daughter. She was hurt by a bear. I am looking after her until she heals. We're actually headed back there. I think we'll leave tonight instead of tomorrow. Just have to swing by the house after this to grab her dog and my trailer."

"Hmmm," Dad says.

He and Vic share a look I interpret all too well. A look that says, *He's lying.*

409

"Hi, Eve," Judith chirps. "You don't know me, but you're wearing one of my old dresses." She grins at Eve. "Looks totally cute on you."

Eve fidgets, but chances a look in my sister's direction. Judith sits on the arm of the couch, giving the rest of us an eye roll.

"You guys just gonna stare at her all night like a bunch of fuckin' creeps?" Judith softens her words with a sassy smile that used to get her ass grounded in high school.

Dad chuckles. "Watch your mouth, girl." Then, he pats my shoulder. "Mind if we talk for a sec?"

Eve's eyes widen. Before I can calm her, Judith inches her way closer. At least Judith knows the whole story—aside from the part that I actually did what she assumed I'd do and fuck Eve—but I'm guessing she'll figure it out on her own.

"Did you like the flashlight?" Judith asks her. "You know the one." She waggles her eyebrows.

"Batteries," Eve chirps.

Judith laughs and then starts chattering about her usual nonsense. I mouth to Eve I'll be right back. Reluctantly, I release her hand and stand to follow my dad out of the room. Vic hovers nearby in case he's needed. Dad pulls me into his study, a worried look on his face.

"You sleeping with the girl?"

"W-What?"

His lips press together in a firm, disappointed way I remember all too well when I was a boy. "You must think I'm nine kinds of stupid, son."

"Dad," I huff out. "I'm not...whatever you're thinking..."

the wild

"You seemed close out by the truck."

"She was worried. I was reassuring her."

His eyes narrow, the browns flickering with distrust. "And just now? Holding her hand?"

"You're reading too much into shit," I growl. "You take what Will and Mom say and add to it to create this fantastical shit?"

"Tone it down," he snaps. "I'm just making sure."

"Well, I'm sure. I'm not sleeping with her." I pin him with a glare. "Why do you even care anyway?" I grumble, irritation fueling my words. "It's not like you didn't start dating Mom when you were young. Wasn't she still in high school when she got pregnant with Will?"

His features darken. "You misunderstand."

"No," I challenge. "I understand clearly. There's always been a code your kids have had to live up to that you and Ma didn't. Will? Vic? They deal with it. You molded them into perfect pillars of the community."

"Atticus," he warns.

I'm done holding this shit in.

"Me? I tried. I disappointed everyone when I didn't follow Will onto the force. Chose football and couldn't even cut it at that." I grit my teeth. "Your boy's been living off his NFL earnings and hasn't found a job."

"Atticus…"

"Want to know why I can't find one? Because I don't want to be a fucking cop. I want to be out there." I wave my hand toward nothing. "Remember when I wanted to be a park ranger and you told me to get my head out of my ass?"

Apparently now's the time to get all the shit off my chest that's been festering for the last couple of decades.

Dad's eyes gleam with fury, but he remains silent, allowing me my rant.

"And Judith…fuck. I should have watched her better." My voice cracks. "Fuck."

"That wasn't your fault. Accidents happen." His voice is soft and his features have lost their edge.

"She doesn't fit the mold either, Dad. We're both fucked up because we can't make our personalities fit into your and Mom's perfect world."

"Are you done with this rant?" Dad asks, crossing his arms over his chest.

"I guess." I deflate like a balloon.

"I'll ask you again. Are you sleeping with the girl?"

"No, Dad. I'm not." Despite his own love life starting with a teenager, I don't push it. Those were different times back then. Nowadays, you just can't get away with that shit. If I give him the truth, it will not fucking set me free. It'll give me a free ride to the station in the back of my brother's police cruiser.

"Good," he breathes out.

"I'm glad you're pleased."

He scrubs his palm down his face. "Just…just wait here. I want to show you something."

As soon as he leaves the office, I head out looking for Eve. The couch is empty when I make my way to the living room. Panic assaults me.

"Bathroom," Judith says, a knowing grin on her face.

I walk down the hall and rap on the door with my knuckle. "You okay in there?"

Eve opens the door, suspicion in her stare. When she confirms it's me, she throws her arms around me. I wrap an arm around her waist before walking back into the bathroom and closing the door behind me. I lift her by her waist and set her on the edge of the counter before cradling her cheeks in my palms.

"We can leave," I murmur, pressing a kiss to her forehead. "They'll get over it. I'm sorry."

She darts her eyes away. "We can stay."

"But you're scared."

"No."

"Eve, baby, don't lie to me."

Her head tilts up and she regards me with fire in her eyes. "I'm not scared."

"Not right now. Ten minutes ago, you passed the fuck out from fear."

"He has teeth."

I blink at her in confusion. "So do I. So do you. It's a thing."

A knock on the door has me jerking away from her.

"It's me," Judith says. "Everyone's looking for you two. I suggest if you don't want them making their own conclusion, you get out here."

"Be right out," I grunt.

I step back over to Eve and gently grip her throat, my thumb running along her jaw bone. My lips fuse to hers and I kiss her in a protective way that's filled with vows to take care of her.

"We'll eat and bail," I assure her. "Come on, beautiful. Let's get this over with."

413

chapter twenty

EVE

H IS FAMILY IS LOUD.
Kind of like all the friends when they gather in Monica's apartment. It's chaotic and filled with laughter. A longing burrows its way deep in my chest. I'm beginning to think families are supposed to be this way. On television, here, at Reed and Devon's, it's all the same.

My home was the wrong one.

When my mother was around, I remember our days being happy. My brothers weren't cruel then. There was laughter and love. It all changed when my mother got sick. Everyone grew angry and quick-tempered. She died, but it never went back to the way it was.

They replaced her.

Papa took Esther and forced her into my mother's role. I was confused, but I loved Esther. She sometimes was like a mother to me. I tried to accept what happened as something natural.

But then my brothers got involved.

They never touched my mother, not like they touched Esther. She became something for them to stick their cocks into or beat with their fists. Papa allowed it. Simply looked the other way. And then Ezekiel hurt her for good. Was so rough with her she bled out and died.

I became the woman of the house then.

A shudder wracks through me as I force away horrible memories of them. Papa would whip me on occasion and bed me, but it was my brothers whom I hated so much. They prowled around like starving wolves, just waiting for my father to go hunting or fall asleep. Like I was their dinner, they'd drag me away someplace where they could all take turns pawing at me. One by one they'd try to breed me like I was some animal meant for carrying their young.

An ache forms in my chest as I remember the blood.

Tears well and roll down my cheeks.

"Eve."

I'm snapped from my inner thoughts as Atticus regards me with furrowed brows. His family all watches me like I don't belong in their home. With his hand on my lower back, his fingers brushing along my bottom over my dress, he guides me into the room with a giant table. Delicious looking foods sit arranged on top, just waiting for us to devour.

"Do you feel faint again?" he asks, pulling a chair out for me to sit.

"No."

"What're you thinking about then?"

"My family."

His features darken. "You don't have to be afraid of them anymore. They're gone."

He sits next to me and brushes a hair behind my ear. I lean into his touch. When I catch his mother's glare on me, I pull away and look down at my lap. Judith takes the seat next to me. His parents sit at each end while his two brothers and nephew sit across from us.

Will, the policeman, sits directly across from me. His penetrating glare burns into me. He reminds me of Ezekiel with his intensity. That thought makes my heart speed up, thumping violently in my chest.

"Well, I think I can speak for the entire family when I say we're glad to have you here, Eve," Judith says, winking at me.

I like Judith. She's nice and funny. Reminds me of a smaller version of Atticus.

The rest of the family mumbles out some sort of agreement. Then, the dinner gets a little loud as everyone starts scooping food onto their plates and passing dishes. Atticus makes my plate and his. I love that he always looks after me. I've just picked up my fork when Will speaks up.

"Reed, you say?"

He's staring at me, but I think he's talking to Atticus.

"Yes." Atticus's voice is clipped.

"Reed Jamison who you sold your extra land to?"

"Are you fucking kidding me right now?" Atticus growls. "You couldn't let shit just lie?"

"Language," their mother huffs.

"Language," Judith mimics her under her breath. "They totally won't mind their language. Watch."

"When you act shady, I have a civic duty—" Will starts.

"To be fucking nosey?" Atticus snaps. "Seriously, man. Back the fuck off."

"Told you," Judith says with pride in her voice.

"Atticus," Abel warns, making the hairs on my arms stand on end.

"Why invite us over if we were just going to be walking into an ambush? The nasty looks are getting old, Ma," Atticus bites out, giving Susan a pointed look. "And Will, for once in your damn life, stay the fuck out of mine."

Will's nostrils flare. "Who is she really? Because when I researched this Reed guy, he has a wife and daughter with blond hair." He points at me. "Not her."

"She's Eve. Still someone I'm looking after," Atticus growls, clinging to his lie harder than ever.

"How old is she really, man?" Will demands. "Because I'm tired of all the lies. I asked Suma—"

"For fuck's sake!" Atticus slams his fist down on the table. "Stop!"

Will stands, his face turning red with anger. Vic tries to pull him back into his seat while Evan's face burns red with embarrassment. Judith whispers that they're animals and do this sort of thing a lot.

"Suma said you were being inappropriate with the girl," Will hisses.

Their mother gasps. "Oh my God."

"Oh shit," Judith whispers.

"For the tenth goddamn time, I'm not sleeping with her!" Atticus's words are practically screamed at them.

Each syllable rattles my bones and poisons my blood. His lies sound so real.

Thank goodness I know the truth.

He loves me.

"Everyone just calm down," Vic says, finally managing to jerk Will back down into his seat. "Eve, hon, how old are you? We're all family here. You're not going to get into trouble and neither will Atticus. We're just trying to make sense of all this."

I dart my eyes over to Atticus. I'm not sure what answer he wants me to tell them. He pinches the bridge of his nose, defeated. Will pins me with a glare that dares me to lie. I decide to tell them the truth.

"I'm…"

"Nineteen?"

My head snaps over to Atticus's father, who watches me with interest. I squirm under his stare.

"Yes."

"What?" Atticus snarls, turning his anger on me. "Are you fucking kidding me right now?"

I wince at his tone. When he reaches for my hand, I jerk it back. Judith gently touches my shoulder and I don't shake away her hand.

"You told me you were sixteen!" Betrayal shines in Atticus's stare and I hate that I've somehow put it there.

I don't remind him it's because he practically force-fed those words into my mouth. I thought that's what he wanted to hear. Then, I realized eighteen was the number he wanted. It was too late then. They were both lies anyway.

"You must be thrilled," Will deadpans. "Now you can fuck—"

"Enough!" Abel booms. "You two boys need to put a goddamn lid on it."

Both Will and Atticus radiate with fury.

"I've already checked with Atticus," Abel tells Will. "He's not having a sexual relationship with her. And that's good. Really good."

"So this is awkward," Evan mutters.

"I think it's delightfully entertaining," Judith disagrees.

"Eve, darlin', what are your parents' names?" Abel studies me as though he can see right into my brain.

"David and Rebekah."

A beat of silence.

Susan drops her fork and gasps. "Abel…"

"I knew it," Abel mutters. "Holy shit."

Abel reaches past Atticus to hand me something. A photograph. As soon as I see it, I recognize it. My parents had one just like it. It was of them when they were children. The one from the photo they never spoke about…

"David and Rebekah are my brother and sister."

Atticus freezes as Abel's words sink in. I'm too busy staring at Abel with new eyes. He has Mother's smile. The eyes are Papa's. While my parents were gaunt, Abel is filled out and muscular. But all the similarities are there.

"You're confused," Atticus whispers to Abel. "Really fucking confused, Dad."

"I'm going to be sick," Susan chokes out before rushing from the table.

Vic follows after with Evan hot on his heels. Will continues to glower at me. Judith has taken to stroking my hair in a soft, reassuring way that makes tears form. It reminds me of Esther.

"Impossible," Atticus growls.

Abel shakes his head. "I saw your parents when they

419

had you," he tells me. "Almost twenty years ago. Your mother was having trouble and they brought her to the hospital. A friend of mine at the hospital called me." He frowns. "You look just as I remember my sister when she was young. They looked so different, though."

They were unclean.

Wild.

Toothless.

Compared to these people, I can see that they would be very different.

"Stop," Atticus pleads.

"Are you…" Will scrubs his palm over his face. "Are you saying the aunt and uncle we never knew…"

"Were fucking," Judith blurts out. "Call a spade a spade, Will."

"That's…" Will trails off.

"Incest." Atticus's hand shakes.

I reach for it and he yanks it back as though I'm diseased.

"The children were a product of incest," Abel agrees. "But they're still our family. I don't know how you happened upon Eve here, but I'm glad you did." He turns his eyes my way. "Do you have any siblings? They had a little girl in tow with them at the time, but I didn't see any others with them. How are David and Rebekah?"

"Everyone's dead," I choke out, my bottom lip trembling.

Atticus stands so quickly, the chair falls back and hits the tile with a loud bang. "Do you know what they did to her?" His fury is aimed at his father. "Her brothers…her father…"

"Wait," Will growls. "Did what? How old were you?"

"Policeman Bob, now's not the time," Judith warns.

"They fucking raped her repeatedly!" Atticus bellows. "Your fucking brother—my uncle—and his shit for brains sons! They killed her sister!"

I start to cry because all I can think about is Esther's pale face as the blood and life drained from her body.

"No," Abel says, his voice a choked whisper. "That's… why would…I can't…"

"I'm calling this in—" Will starts.

"You call this in and I'll fucking kill you." Atticus points a finger at Will. "Do you understand? You will not drag Eve through a media circus over this."

I tense at the mention of my name.

Will stands too, not backing down from his brother. "Fine. But I think it's high time you stop putting your dick in our cousin."

chapter twenty-one

ATTICUS

THIS ISN'T HAPPENING.

This isn't fucking happening.

"Let's go." I march back into the dining room and snag Eve up by her wrist.

Dad and Will swarm me, but I'm not having any of it. I need to think. I need to get the fuck away from this house. Away from the bomb Dad just dropped on me.

"Man, I don't like the way you're fucking handling her," Will barks out after me. "Calm your ass down."

I turn mid stride, releasing Eve, to shove his chest. "She's not yours to concern yourself with."

"And she's yours?" he challenges.

My gut twists.

Was.

She was mine.

But now?

Fuck.

"Everyone just relax," Dad orders. "Tempers are hot.

That was some heavy information I unloaded on you all. But we can—"

"Do what, Dad?" Undo the fact I've been fucking my cousin?

"Where are you going?" he asks, his tone defeated.

"I'm going back home. I need to think."

"Do it without your dick," Will warns.

"Will, go sit your ass in the dining room," Dad barks out. "Now!"

Eve flinches and cowers behind me. Protectiveness roars up inside me like a beast. It screams: mine, mine, mine.

But that's not true.

She's family.

Blood.

My goddamn cousin.

Shame boils my blood and bile rises in my throat. I'm disgusted. Flashes of what we did in the truck on the way over here make my stomach twist violently.

"We'll talk later," I growl at my father. "Let's go."

I toss Eve her coat and she hurries to put it on. The moment she does, I grab her wrist and haul her out of the house. She stumbles in the snow, but catches herself before falling. When we reach the truck, I let go of her hand and climb inside. It isn't until I have the truck started that I realize I've always helped her get into the vehicle.

My mind and heart war with each other.

Don't be an asshole, man.

Apparently I am an asshole, though, because I don't fucking move. It isn't until the truck door opens and my dad's angry face meets mine that I release the breath I've been holding. He assists his tiny niece into the truck.

"If you can't cool off over this, maybe you should take a breather from each other. I can send Judith—"

"Close the door," I say coolly. "Now."

He slams it shut, making Eve jump. I rake my gaze over her, my stomach churning. She looks too fucking pretty to be my cousin. Your cousin shouldn't have your cum still leaking out of her body.

Eve's panties are probably soaked.

Oh fuck.

What if I got her pregnant?

I've barely driven down the street before the bile rears its ugly head. I pull over and fling the door open in time to puke my fucking guts up.

My cousin.

I fucked my cousin.

This isn't something that goes away after two years like when I thought she was sixteen and we'd have to hide her age.

This is worse.

Not right.

Her gene pool is probably so fucked up and if we were together…

I puke again.

A hand touches my shoulder and I shake it away. It's not her fault. She doesn't deserve my wrath. But I'm too fucking broken right now. Her touching me could make things a helluva lot worse than they already are.

We have to get to Reed's.

He'll say the right things. Make me feel better.

What do I want him to say?

Deep in my bones, I know what I want. And, oddly

enough, Reed would give me that reassurance I crave. But that's not right. At least with him and Devon, they weren't blood related. Their shit was fucked up, but not like this.

Eve and I are cousins.

She's a product of incest. If she stays with me, our children…

Who the fuck knows what our children would turn out like.

Life is cruel as hell. What kind of shit karma is this? Did I really fuck over Cassandra so bad that God was like, you just wait…?

I have to get Eve to Reed's because I need to leave her with them.

It's the best way.

A clean break.

My heart slams inside my ribcage, angry at that thought. It's the only sensible one, though. The only one that fits in this world we live in. The alternative is twisted and wrong.

Eve and I can never be.

No matter how much I love…

I shake away that thought as I spit out the last of the puke and slam my truck door. Love doesn't matter because karma has spoken.

A big bear and a little fox don't belong together.

That's just the honest to God truth of it all.

The truth fucking hurts.

425

The moment I park the truck, Eve launches herself out of the truck. Good. She can pack her shit while I get the trailer hooked up. I busy myself with my task, trying to desperately ignore the shitstorm going on inside my heart.

Silence.

I've given Eve silence, and oddly enough, she hasn't spoken a word either.

I spend the next half hour hooking the trailer up to my truck. I'm circling the trailer when I notice the door isn't latched. Fucking bears. I peek my head inside. It's dark and all the stacked boxes of supplies seem to be intact. I count my blessings—because after this day, I need a win—and shut the trailer. After I latch it closed, I make my way back inside. When I see her, it kills me.

Her hair is wet.

She showered one last time.

That revelation hits me hard in the heart.

Am I really taking her back?

I need time to think.

"Put a hat on so you don't catch cold," I grumble, walking past her to look in my room. All of her stuff is gone. With a heavy sigh, I grab a backpack and throw my clothes and toiletries into it. I'm not sure what'll happen when I get out there, but it'd be dumb to not bring stuff I might need. After brushing my teeth to get rid of the puke taste, I head back to the front room.

She stands in the kitchen, her shoulders slouched and her stance defeated. My body physically thrums with the need to go to her—to pull her into my arms and stroke through her now tangled hair. To kiss away this day and start fresh tomorrow.

Her teary brown eyes lift to meet mine.

I look away.

"Let's go." I grab a few more things and then usher her and Blind Bear out the door.

She has one of the backpacks strapped to the damn dog and he looks proud to be carrying her shit for her. At least someone can be a motherfucking hero for Eve.

I thought I was that someone.

I thought wrong.

We load the truck and within minutes we're leaving our little slice of home. I'd like to say I regret every second with her, but that's a big fucking lie. Those moments with her are going to be ones I'll never forget. I just can't give her more of them. Not now. Not after what I know.

All those books I gave Devon about incest…

I read them all.

I researched the fuck out of incest.

My holier-than-thou self thought I was helping. And had they truly been blood related, I think they should have been worried. In the end, that asshole reveals after the fact he'd adopted her. It was all for naught.

Though, now, I have all this knowledge spinning around in my brain.

Psychological disorders. Genetic mutations. Physical abnormalities.

We could never be happy. We could never continue on like a normal couple because the cloud of worry would always be there. Our future would be threatened because of the same blood that ran through our veins. The last thing I want to do to Eve is bring more heartache into her life. If we had a child…if it were deformed because of our blatant

427

disregard to the facts, I wouldn't be able to live with myself. At least now, we can have a clean break and move forward. She can continue to be the wild thing she is and I'll try to forget the fact I'm madly in love with my cousin.

The drive is long. Hours and hours. She sleeps off and on, but otherwise remains quiet. It isn't until we finally pull up to Reed's cabin I helped build that's surrounded by a fence to keep bears out, that she finally speaks.

"Atticus…" Her voice is small, unsure.

I look over at her. Tiny and frail but with the fiercest brown eyes in the world. Same eyes as my father. Fuck. I scrub my palm over my face in frustration.

"Eve."

"We should get inside. It's late." Her bottom lip trembles and tears well in her pretty eyes.

Regret slams into me like a freight train, but I power forward. "I…I'm not going."

"Yes." Fire blazes in her eyes, stealing little bits of my soul in the process.

"Stubborn girl, I'm not going. I'm leaving you with Reed. I need to…I need to think."

"Think here."

I stare at her, wishing I could reach up and swipe away the tear on her cheek. "I can't." My voice cracks. "It's not wise."

"You're a stupid man, so it's fine."

Her insults don't cut me like she intends.

"It's not fine, Eve. We both know it's not right."

"It is right," she argues.

"Bab—er, Eve, I'm not going to fight with you about this."

She blinks her lashes hard, sending more tears racing down her cheeks. "You promised."

"That was before."

"Nothing's changed!" she screams and then sobs.

"Everything's changed!" My body trembles with rage at our situation. It's unfair as fuck, but it's the reality we have to deal with.

"I love you," she whispers as she unbuckles and crawls my way. "Please."

I close my eyes when her palms find my cheeks. "It's unnatural. Wrong."

Warm lips press to mine. Doesn't feel fucking wrong.

"You're my husband. You can't leave." The pain in her words slices my heart right in two. She can keep the other half of my heart because it'll be fucking broken after this.

I open my eyes and grip her delicate jaw, pulling her slightly away. "I'm not your husband."

"Yes!" she cries out, hitting my chest. "Yes, you are!"

Grinding my teeth, I fight the tears in my own eyes. "I'm your fucking cousin, Eve. Get it through your god-damn head already."

She breaks from my hold and kisses me hard. I hate that she tastes like sweet forbidden fruit that I'm starved for. I hate that she's an addiction I'll die breaking myself of.

I grab her shoulders and push her away. "Stop."

"No."

"Yes," I bark out.

"You're my husband," she whispers again, her bottom lip wobbling.

Sucking in a sharp breath, I shake my head. "Did we

429

have a wedding? Like Chandler and Monica? I'm not your fucking husband just like your goddamn father wasn't either. We're just sick fucks who have a thing for sweet little Eve."

She fucking slaps me. "Liar!"

"It's the truth," I hiss. "You don't have a ring, you didn't have a wedding, but goddammit, we sure do share that same last name, Eve Knox. Fucking hysterical, huh? I thought so too. Life's a fucking cunt and it fucked us. It fucked us bad. Now we're stuck picking up the pieces that are left over. We've gotta figure out how to make our lives work again. Without each other. You have Reed and Devon. They'll take care of you. You're not scared of people anymore. They love you. Let them love you, goddammit."

"Fuck you," she sobs.

"Already did, babe, and it was a mistake."

I launch myself out of the truck so I don't do anything stupid like pull her into my arms and promise her everything will be okay. I can't lie to her like that. Nothing will ever be okay again. The tears on my own cheeks are hot and shaming. I unhook the trailer and unlatch the back so Eve can get to whatever shit she needs. Once I'm ready to go, I walk over to her side of the truck and open the door.

Her tears are gone.

Hate for me shines in her brown, violent eyes.

Hate for me.

The newest monster in Eve Knox's world.

Big, bad bear with a razor-sharp words meant to cut into the little fox and make her bleed.

I'm sorry.

The apology is to both of us. I can't say it aloud. It hurts too much.

"Tell Reed…I'll be back."

She swallows, shaking away my offered hand, and jumps out of the truck. Her backpack looks heavy, but she slings it over her shoulders like it weights nothing. No longer wearing the dress from earlier, she seems more like her normal self. Feral. Angry. Suspicious. Ready to cut throats. Blind Bear follows her out and they both stand beside the trailer as she straps the pack on his back. The dog whines while Eve glowers at me.

I want to go to her.

I want to kiss that frown right off her face.

Which is exactly why I need to get the fuck out of here.

"Stay with Reed. You're safe with him. No bears with him. Understood?"

She flips me off. I almost smile knowing she learned this too from television, but I bite it back.

"Goodbye, Eve."

She turns her back to me, her body shaking with sobs, and I climb into the truck.

Drive away.

Drive away.

My heart aches and bleeds and pleads and bargains and makes excuses.

I put the truck in reverse as though I can somehow rewind through every forbidden second with Eve.

My traitorous eyes find her tiny form as she cuddles her dog in the snow beside the trailer.

I look away.

And then I drive away, leaving my heart with her.

chapter twenty-two

EVE

I'M NUMB.

Completely numb.

Sick, horrified, devastated.

He left. He left me. He left me here. He left me here to die.

Blind Bear whines, nuzzling his big face against mine and licking away my tears. I failed my dog. He's punished to this existence along with me.

No more bacon.

No more macaroni and cheese.

No more *Friends*.

No more Atticus.

I fall into the snow, the ache inside me threatening to rip me in two. It's quiet tonight as the snow silently falls. I should go into the gate and call for Reed or Devon. They would pull me into their warm home, feed me fruit, and promise me I was safe.

I consider it.

I really do.

A warm bed.

Food.

The kids to cuddle and play with.

Creak.

At first, I think it's the sound of the trees as they bear the weight of the snow. But when I hear it again, Blind Bear growls.

I should call out and warn Reed it's me. Just little Eve lying in the snow feeling like she's going to die of a broken heart. Nothing to see here.

Crunch. Crunch. Crunch. Crunch.

The hairs on my arms stand on end. That's not Reed. That's…something else.

Click.

"Easy boy," a gruff voice says from behind the trailer. The glint of a gun can be seen, making my heart stop in my chest.

"BB," I whisper, grabbing onto his fur. "Stay."

A man steps into view. Dirty. Long, stringy hair. Grinning a toothless smile at me.

"What do you want?" I demand, slowly rising to my feet, feeling unfairly weighed down by my pack.

"I came for food, girl," he says, but then grabs his crotch. "I think I'll leave with more."

I'll gut him if he even thinks about touching me.

"The big man left ya, huh? Didn't want young pussy. I ain't discriminatin' over no pussy. I love pussy. 'Specially young pussy."

Blind Bear's growls become louder and I think if I weren't

still clutching onto him, he would've already tried to attack. The man advances and I eye the tree line. I know there are a set of stairs Reed built that will take me down the side of the cliff. It's steep and not ideal to run down, but if I can make it to them, the snow-covered trees canopying over the stairs should provide cover.

"Why don't you come over here to the trailer and take those clothes off so I can look at ya?"

No.

No.

No.

"If you show me your cock, I'll cut it off and feed it to you," I warn, sliding my hand into my coat pocket to grip my knife.

"Feisty bitch. I'll look forward to makin' ya scream—"

His words are lost to me as I take off in a sprint toward the stairs. Blind Bear, attuned to me, runs with me. A gunshot goes off, splintering the bark on a tree nearby. I don't stop or scream or anything.

I focus on my goal.

The stairs.

The stairs.

The stairs.

I remember when Reed built them. I watched from afar. Devon would waddle out with a baby in her arms and another on the way, bringing him snacks and drinks. He'd stop his heavy lifting to press an adoring kiss to her lips and then say something to make her giggle. I'd been mesmerized by them. Their relationship was unlike anything I ever knew.

Aching loneliness settles in my stomach.

I did know it eventually.

With Atticus.

He made me smile like Reed does Devon. He loved me—loved my body—like I never knew was possible. And then the moment he found out who my parents were, he cut me off. As though I were a diseased limb that needed hacking off.

Another bang makes me cry out, but I'm at the stairs. I grab the handrail and try hard not to slip on the steps. Blind Bear fumbles his way down ahead of me. Heavy footsteps thud behind me. I'm quick and know these stairs, though. I race down them, eager to get to the bottom. Once down there, I can make it to Reed and Devon's old cabin. Maybe hide in the crevasse.

Each icy breath I take, I cramp in my stomach. I'm out of shape having been laid up in Atticus's house for so long. I never should have let my guard down. I willingly allowed myself to get weak.

Run.

Run.

Run.

I'm close to the bottom of the steps and when I see the snowy bottom that Blind Bear's already run through, I leap off the bottom step. I take off running toward the old cabin. The rush of the river is loud nearby. I'm not worried about wolves or mountain lions or bears. No, the predator that wants me is close and he's hunting me down with his gun. Nothing is more terrifying than him in this moment.

As I run, I wonder how the man got here. He most certainly came from the trailer. Which means it's likely he rode all the way out here with us. Was he the man who stole our fruit? My heart races faster than my legs can carry me through the heavy snow.

After what feels like hours of running, I realize I'm no longer being chased. I stop and listen for sounds. Wind whistling. River rushing. Wolves howling in the distance. No grunts or gunshots.

I reserve my energy and walk, knowing the way by heart. I could close my eyes and find the little cabin. It makes me understand how Blind Bear uses his other senses to get by.

My toes are numb and I'm exhausted. Thirsty. Starved. I can't stop, though. We need shelter and safety. I didn't realize until I'd been freed of the wild that I didn't like it out here. Atticus teased me with a life I loved—one that didn't require constantly thinking about survival—and I grew addicted to it. Had I never left, I would've never known what was out there. Now I know, though. It's a devastating reality that I'll never watch television again or eat ice cream or take a hot shower. I won't learn to read or go grocery shopping. I won't go to school or go to any more dinners at Muskies. I won't have sex.

The last thought makes me think about Atticus and it hurts too badly. A sob chokes me, but I swallow it down as I continue to trudge through the snow. When I see a structure, I nearly cry out with happiness. We can stop there and rest for the night.

"Here, boy," I croon to my dog. "We'll get warm in there."

I manage to get the gate open and then slide the lever in place. At least Reed took necessary precautions to protect them. I guide my dog into the cabin and then pull down yet another lever that will keep out predators—even those of the human variety.

Blind Bear shakes off the snow and slumps onto his side. I relieve him of his pack first. Then, I set to making a fire in their fireplace. They keep this cabin stocked with items in case Reed is ever kept away hunting or something. As soon as the flames flicker, I pull off my pack and then strip out of my cold, wet clothes. I grab the quilt off the bed and wrap up in it. Blind Bear scoots over to the fireplace, his tail swishing back and forth.

"We're not quite home yet," I tell him. "Tomorrow we'll make our way there." I don't have the heart to tell him it's not as nice as Reed and Devon's cabin. He'll learn that hard truth on his own.

The heat warms the space quickly and I'm thankful. I should eat something from my pack or drink water from one of the bottles I brought. Anything but sit here and feel sorry for myself. I just don't have the energy or the willpower.

My tears have run dry. They burn and sting. The ache in my chest feels as though it'll be a permanent part of me. I'll have to learn to get used to it. To cheer myself up, I think about Phoebe and Joey. Their antics. Ross and Rachel's annoying way of never getting together and staying together. And finally, I think about Chandler and Monica. Those two don't cheer me up at all. Those break my heart even further.

A big yawn has my eyelids drooping and me slumping over. Tomorrow will be a better day. I'll regroup and figure out what to do next. Until then, I'll sleep away the pain.

Two days later...

"That's a good boy," I praise when Blind Bear trots back with a dead squirrel in his mouth.

Before BB, I'd relied on my traps. With him, I just have to tell him to get it and he does. It's nice having a dog to hunt with me. I scratch him behind the ears and then use my knife to hack off the squirrel's tail. It'll give him something to play with until I can cook it for us.

At home.

My home.

We set off from Reed's hunting cabin early this morning. It took a couple of days to recover from the loss of Atticus and then the chase with the man. I needed my energy before trekking to my home.

The sun is burning bright in the sky, blinding me with its reflection on the snow. I'm squinting and stumbling slightly when I see it. A little shack in the forest.

Home.

Warmth doesn't flood me.

Only cold.

For so long, it was just me with them. Scared and lonely without my sister. They twisted up their own wants and made me feel as though I had to do as they said.

Never again.

Atticus, though it hurts to think about him, trained me in a different way. Showed me small things to make me happy. Treated me as though I were something he cherished and loved. For the first time in my life, I wasn't continuously afraid. He gave me a strength I didn't know I needed.

He's gone, but I'm still strong.

It buzzes in my veins.

An ember that's caught flame and become an inferno.

Anger and determination obliterate despair. It's all I have left.

"We're home," I tell BB. "It'll have to do."

He barks as though he understands and trots off. I stuff the dead squirrel in my pocket before walking over to a large tree beside the shack. It's where everyone I loved is buried. Not my father or my brothers. Papa and Ezekiel were killed in Reed's hunting cabin. I'm not sure what he ever did with their bodies. My other three brothers were left in my shack after Reed slaughtered them. One by one, I dragged them down to the river. I wanted them away from me. The river did the job for me.

No, under the tree is my mother and my sister Esther.

And them.

Kneeling at the base of the tree, I push snow away from their spot. When I reach the ground, I find four stones. Beneath each stone are the tiny little things I somehow loved even though it didn't make sense.

They weren't like Devon's children she bore. I'd watched the birth of Rowdy—assisted even—and it was not the same. She screamed and pushed and worked to get that giant baby out of her womb. It kicked and howled and breathed life. Devon went on to birth two more. Children that would grow to cry and laugh and crawl and talk. These were different.

Bloody.

Tiny.

Incomplete.

My body seemed to reject them, painfully so. Thankfully, each time one would come out, I would get myself alone, squat, and pull it out of me. It wasn't like when she gave birth. Not even close.

Mine never made sounds.

They never cried or squawked.

Not once did they ever move.

But I cried for all four of them. Each and every time. I kissed their tiny skulls that resembled a baby squirrel's and named them all.

Love. Mercy. Faith. Goodness.

I sang my mother's favorite hymns as I buried them.

I buried my little beings between my mother and my sister so they'd never be alone. So they'd never be cold or hungry or sad.

For a few moments, I sit in the quiet as I think about them. As I dream about what they could have been had they had a strong father like Atticus. They might have grown to be loud and busy like Rowdy. Always smiling like Ronan. Or a little fussy boy like Ryder. If Atticus were their father rather than Papa or my brothers, they would've had beautiful smiles. Infectious laughs. Generous hearts.

I start to cry, hating that I always cry when I think about him. I hastily swipe at my tears and stand. Blind Bear cocks his head at me, his fluffy tail wagging.

"Let's get a fire lit and get dinner cooked."

He barks.

And tomorrow, we'll start anew.

chapter twenty-three

ATTICUS

Two months later...

I SNORT AT THE TELEVISION, TRYING TO SQUINT MY eyes so Monica will become one person instead of two blurry ones. No matter how many times I blink or rub at my eyes, I still can't make out her form.

And it pisses me right the fuck off.

With a rage-filled roar, I throw my nearly gone bottle of Jack Daniel's at the television. It makes a loud *thwap* sound before going black. I can't tell if I've cracked it or shattered it. Hell, I can't tell anything anymore.

Everything's a blur.

Nothing makes sense.

Now that the television is silent, I'm bombarded with thoughts I try every day to ignore. Thoughts that rape my mind whether I like it or want it. Always there. Fucking me painfully. Against my will. Goddamn abuse.

Her.

My thoughts always go to her.

Little fox.

Cousin.

Behind every angry growl of frustration is heartache and loss. But more importantly, guilt.

What I did was wrong.

I just dropped her off at Reed's. Dumped her into his lap as though she were his problem now. I didn't even fucking stay to tell him my sob story. Just dump and run.

Deep down, I know she'll be fine with them. Reed and Devon have always looked after Eve over the years, bringing her care packages and trying to get close to her. Maybe, this time, she'll even speak more than a couple words to them or try and get to know them better.

Or, in typical Eve fashion, she may just bail.

That's where the guilt really starts to gnaw at me. What if she left? What if she's hurt? What if another bear got her? I lie awake at night, my heart racing in my chest, as I worry about if she has enough to eat or if she's warm or if she's scared.

So many times, I make a decision in my head. Just go to her. I'll get as far as getting the truck packed. And then my head catches up to my heart. It reminds me things can't go back to the way they were. She's family. I can't continue fucking her. It's not right.

Knock. Knock. Knock.

They've all tried to come by—Ma, Will, Vic, Judith. I never answer. I don't pick up the phone. All I do is make frequent runs to the liquor store and try to drown in Jack. I just want the pain inside my chest to lessen.

It. Never. Lessens.

Each day it grows maddeningly worse.

I need her.

Fuck, how I need her.

I hear the jangle of keys and I roll my eyes. So far, no one has tried to come inside, knowing I need the space. This person doesn't care.

"The place smells like a distillery, son."

Dad's gruff voice echoes through my cabin. I don't even bother turning to look at him. I manage out a grunt and that's it.

He closes the door behind him and then I hear him rooting around in the kitchen. The smell of coffee suddenly permeates the air. It reminds me of Eve. She loved coffee. God, she loved everything. Nearly every single thing I'd offer her, she'd be in happy awe over.

Dad turns on the overhead light in the living room and begins picking up the shards of glass. I close my eyes, not interested in looking at him. A few minutes later, he sets a steaming mug beside me on the end table. He drags a chair from the kitchen into the living room and sits it right in front of me. Sipping from his mug, he leans back in the wooden chair and studies me.

"You look like shit," he finally says.

"Yeah, well, you have two heads, so I guess we're even." He snorts. "You're wasted."

"So?" Anger swells up inside me like a tidal wave of lava—hot, bubbly, violent.

"Want to talk about it?"

"Talk about what?" I spit out. "The fact I fucked my cousin?"

Rather than be shocked like I expected, he shrugs. "Sure. Let's talk about it."

I shoot him a nasty glare. "This fucking funny to you?"

His brow deepens. "The fact my son is a damn near alcoholic and suffering severe depression? Real fucking funny. What kind of asshole do you think I am?"

I pinch the bridge of my nose and sigh. "I didn't know. I didn't know she was family. I should have known, right? She has your eyes, Dad."

Dad leans forward to set his mug down beside mine and then pats my knee. I blink a few times and squint, bringing him back into focus. His brown eyes are full of concern.

"It's coincidence of the century, sure, but there's no way you could have known." His words are soft, tentative. "You can't let your life turn to shit over this, Atticus."

Without her, I don't have a life.

For years, I've worried about this girl. Her well-being has been on the back of my mind for a long ass time. Then, when I brought her here, everything changed. She breathed life into my mundane world and gave me something I'd been missing. Love, companionship, friendship. She filled holes in me that, in the past, only certain people could fill. Eve filled me to the brim with her. Every day was just her.

God, I was so fucking happy.

"You know," he says, his voice turning wistful. "When I was a youngster and was seeing your mom, we knew it was wrong of her to be underage and myself older." He pauses to scratch at his beard. "We didn't care. Our love was all that mattered."

the wild

I pick up my coffee and sip it. The burn feels good on my throat. It punishes me for driving her away.

He continues. "We were going to run away. So we could be together. I didn't want to go to prison and your mom didn't want to leave my side. Though we were so careful, people started to connect the dots that we were together." He frowns. "Your mother was only fifteen when we first slept together. I was old enough to do hard time for that shit."

I wince, not truly down for hearing about their sex life. But the taboo element keeps me interested.

"Anyway, we were all packed and ready, your mom pregnant with Will, when her dad pulled us aside. He told me he didn't give a rat's ass that I was older. What he cared about was her happiness. And if I made her happy, then I needed to remain in her life. He said he couldn't live without his happy little girl, so that meant there were just some things he had to accept."

"This is different and you know it," I growl, chugging more of the hot coffee.

"Is it? Because in the eyes of the law, her being underage was every bit as a fucked up situation as you sleeping with your cousin."

"It was...it was more than just sleeping with her," I croak out, hating that my eyes burn with unshed tears. "I loved her. Fuck, I still do. I can't erase her from my mind. I can't pull her claws from my heart. She owns me and I don't know what to do about it."

Dad gives me a soft smile and squeezes my knee. "She makes you happy. Right now, you're a miserable shit."

I snort and flip him off.

"I love you, son, and it's quite clear that you love her. If you want to be with Eve, then you have your answer. Just like my siblings fell in love. They ran off to be together. No one chased them and no one will chase you. But as your father, I can't sit here and watch you drink yourself to death."

"You're giving me permission to fuck my cousin?" I bark out a cold laugh. "Right. Okay."

He crosses his arms over his chest and leans back. "I'm telling you to do whatever makes you happy, boy. All those years of you traipsing through the woods? That made you happy. Not abiding by the town rules and society. You loved to go out there and be your own man. No matter how hard you tried, you didn't fully fit in regular, everyday life. You living in this remote cabin and still spending most of your days out there in the wild is a testament to that."

"I…I…I hurt her."

"I saw the fire in that girl's eyes. Takes a lot to keep her down."

"You don't understand," I choke out. "I abandoned her. She thought…she called me her husband. What kind of husband drops their wife off in the middle of the damn woods? I fucking failed her." Tears leak down my cheeks and I swipe them away hastily. I've never in my adult life cried in front of my dad except when I brought Judith to him after a long, exhausting search.

"I failed your mother plenty of times," he says. "Ask her. When we dated and then after marriage. So many times I just did stupid shit that made her crazy. But guess what? She's my wife. And you know what wives do?"

I stare at him dumbly. I don't fucking know.

"They stick with you through the thick and the thin.

446

Good and bad. Sickness and in health. The whole gig. All of it. Wives are goddamn angels."

"She's not really my wife," I grumble. "Though try convincing her."

"Then I only see one solution here and it isn't to continue drinking yourself into liver failure."

"If I go to her…if I'll willingly be with her…" I scrub my palm down my face. "I'm disobeying the law."

"You were doing that anyway when you thought she was sixteen."

God, I forget how much he and Will are alike and their uncanny ability to put all the puzzle pieces together with just a sliver of information.

"She's my…it's incest, Dad."

"Eve is a product of incest. Try convincing her it's wrong."

I let out a dark laugh. "I can't convince her of shit. She's the most stubborn woman I know."

He smiles. "No one has to know, kiddo. For as little as you come to town, it won't be an issue. I've already talked to the family about it. We all agreed this is Knox family business. No one else's. And at the end of the day, we take care of our own. You and Eve included."

My heart does a painful thud in my chest. "What if I go and she hates me? It's been two months, Dad. What if she's…" Dead. Pain lances through me.

"If she hates you, it'll only be temporary. Trust me. You woo the shit out of her, grovel like a motherfucker, and then you claim your woman."

Each thump of my heart reminds me I'm alive and my wife is out there. I just need to go find her. I need to get her back. For the first time since Dad explained who she was, I feel hope.

"What if she can't get past it?"

"She will."

"What if...Dad, what if she's dead?"

His lips purse together as he scrutinizes me. "You think she is?"

"Honestly...no."

"And why's that?"

"Because she's wild fire with a spine of steel. Deadly and fierce. She's a survivor and she doesn't give up. That girl is stubborn as hell, which serves her well out there."

"And what are you, Atticus?"

I sit up, my blood burning hot with the desire to hunt, claim, and love. "I'm her husband."

"So start acting like it."

chapter twenty-four

EVE

RUNNING.
　　Running.
　　Running.

Despite every protesting muscle in my body, I push forward with one goal in mind. Get away from him. The man I've taken to calling Wretch in my head, stalks us. Blind Bear and I had fallen into a quiet routine. Away from everyone. Introspective. Living each day to survive and nothing more. If I was hunting or scavenging or building something, then I wasn't thinking about him.

Not Wretch.

Atticus.

Rather than weaken me with the usual ache in my chest, I use him in this moment. I think of his protective nature and strong presence. I draw from him, sucking air into my smarting lungs, and then harness the way it always felt to be near him. Safe. Cared for. Loved. It stokes my inner fire and gives me the fuel I need to keep running.

Wretch must have stolen more guns from Atticus's trailer because he shoots at me with a rifle. The bullets whizz through the air, but BB and I are too far ahead of him to reach us. Had he not stopped to set my shack on fire, we'd be dead already. But because he'd been preoccupied with trying to burn down the home with us in it, BB and I were able to bolt.

I passed Reed's hunting cabin ages ago, which means I'll hit the stairs soon. I just hope I can make it up the steps without getting shot.

I have to get to Reed.

He'll know what to do.

It's what Atticus would want me to do.

As much as I want to hate Atticus, I can't. I don't. He's my Atticus. Even if I can't have him. He'll always be mine. My heart starts to ache when I think about his handsome face that I almost miss the stairs. Blind Bear, having already familiarized himself with all the paths in the past two months, doesn't miss it and bounds up ahead of me. I hobble after him, weak and tired.

Whizz. Whizz.

Two bullets hit the stairs near me, making me scream in shock. I continue up the steps, trying desperately to outrun him. Wretch is relentless. If he didn't always catch me off guard, I would show him how it feels to be stalked and terrorized.

I start to get a pain in my stomach from breathing cold air and running. Ignoring the throbbing, I rush up the last few steps. I've just made it to the top landing when fire hits me in the back.

"Ahhh!" I cry out.

Don't stop.

Keep going.

Tears freely leak out of my eyes, but I keep running toward the gate. When it opens from the inside and my dog rushes in, I nearly sob in relief.

"Help! Reed!" I scream.

Reed—giant and fierce with his dark beard and crazed eyes—comes into view, a shotgun in his hand. He aims it right for my head. I duck out of the way and then he fires.

Boom!

Wretch curses behind me, but I don't think he's been hit. Regardless, now he has Reed after him, so he better run.

Boom! Boom! Boom!

Reed continues past me, popping away on his shotgun. I rush into the gate, right into the waiting arms of Devon. Her pregnant belly presses against me. Suddenly, my fear of getting killed is outweighed with the worry she'll get hurt instead.

"Y-You have to get inside," I tell her, my teeth chattering from a mix of fear and cold. I'd run out of the shack half asleep. No shoes. No coat. Nothing.

"Oh my God," she whimpers. "You're freezing cold. Where are your shoes?"

She guides me toward the big cabin, clinging to me so I don't fall. It's then I realize my feet are bruised and bloody from sticks and brush. There may not be snow anymore and we're pushing into spring, but it's still bitter cold, especially at night.

We make it onto the porch and then inside the cabin. It's warm and smells like apple cinnamon—my favorite oatmeal flavor. The fact I know this makes me smile just a little. I learned a lot while with Atticus. Not nearly enough, but a lot.

"We heard gunshots," she says as she helps me sit on their sofa. "When Atticus had left that trailer a couple months ago, we figured you were healed and he dropped you off too. The gunshots made us think maybe you were in trouble. Reed flew out of here and it looks like just in time too." She grabs a blanket and wraps it around me. "Let me put tea on and throw some logs on the fire. Try to warm up."

Buddy—their old dog—limps into the living room and eyes Blind Bear with interest. Blind Bear wags his tail and then flops on the ground, exhausted from our narrow escape. Buddy sniffs him but must deem him safe because he also falls to the ground. Neither dog bothering to throw a stink about the other.

"Will Reed be okay?"

She smiles and it stretches across her face. "Of course he will. It's Reed. He's the predator. Everything else out there exists because he allows it."

I let loose a giggle. The pride she has for Reed reminds me of how I was with Atticus. At my laughter, her eyes widen.

"I don't think I've ever heard you…" She frowns. "You haven't ever spoken much, but laughed? Never."

I haven't laughed much in the last two months.

"I think I learned it watching *Friends*."

"*Friends*, huh?" She snorts. "I want to hear more of this story when I get back."

As she busies herself, I gently pull down the blanket and look over my shoulder. My hoodie is soaked in blood. That monster shot me. Anger surges through me, but I'm too tired to do anything about it.

The door flings open and Reed steps through, a scowl on his face. "Who was that guy?"

"Wretch. Short for Wretched Man." I shrug and then wince. "He stalks me like I'm dinner he needs to hunt. We've been playing this game for two months."

Reed cocks his head, his brows furling. "You're babbling."

"I'm tired and that asshole woke me up by burning down my house. Then, he shot me. The babbling is keeping me from passing out."

He smirks and shakes his head. "What did he do to you?"

"Shot me."

"No, not him. Atticus."

Tears well in my eyes and I break his gaze. He stares at me intensely before walking into another room. He returns with a kit.

"I thought the only word you knew was fruit," he says as he sits on the table in front of the sofa. "Your eyes spoke volumes, though."

"I haven't spoken to anyone in two months besides Blind Bear over there."

He opens the kit and starts rifling through supplies. "Oh? What about Atticus?"

"What about him?" I ask bitterly.

His eyebrow lifts at my sharp words. "He just dropped you off without even saying hello to us? Seems out of character. He usually stays for weeks at a time when he comes to visit."

"He was in a hurry to get away."

"From what?"

"Me."

Reed narrows his eyes. "Hmmm." He leans forward to inspect my shoulder. "Fucker shot you. Take your hoodie off and let me see the damage. Turn around so I can see your back."

I start to tug it up, but pain stops me. "Owwww."

Devon rushes in with a teacup in hand. She sets it on the table beside the supplies and gives me a sympathetic smile. Ryder starts to cry from the other room. She rushes off as I gingerly slide my arm through the arm hole on my injured side. Then, I tug away the hoodie, twisting to reveal my back to Reed. His fingers are cold as he flits them over my skin.

"That bullet needs to come out. Luckily it doesn't look deep." He starts digging around in the kit. "This is going to hurt. Maybe I should grab some whiskey."

"I can take it," I assure him. "Been mauled by a bear, remember? Wretch is nothing."

"Still same fierce Eve," Reed says with a chuckle. "Now she's a smartass too."

"Better to be a smartass than a dumbass." I learned that one from TV.

He laughs loudly and then cold liquid drenches my injured shoulder, making me squeal. "Sorry," he mutters, his voice amused. "Now stay still. I'm going to dig it out."

Devon returns with her dark-haired baby nursing from her breast. She wears a frown of worry. I can't help but stare at her as she cradles the baby. He's big, chunky, alive. My eyes water as I think about my little beings under the tree. So small and weak.

She comes to sit beside me on the sofa. I can't help myself when I reach forward to touch his fuzzy head. Soft like a baby bunny. I want to pull him to me and inhale the scent of his hair.

Devon's eyes are wide as she regards me with curiosity. I howl when Reed's hand clamps into my shoulder to hold me still and starts digging with some sort of tool into the wound. Devon reaches over to hold my hand, sympathy in her gaze. I sob loud enough that I wake their other two children.

"Daddy," Rowdy says, holding Ronan's hand. "Why are you making Eve cry?"

"She's got a bullet in her," Reed explains. "I have to get it out and it hurts."

Rowdy and Ronan walk closer, eyes shining with curiosity. Ronan breaks away from his brother to climb onto the sofa and sit next to me. Rowdy climbs on the back of the sofa and perches there like a bird, watching me with a cocked head.

"Sorry," Devon says. "They're curious."

I nearly black out from pain, but then Reed exclaims that he got it. He drenches me in liquid that stings and then starts to sew the flesh. Trying to ignore the sting, I focus on Ronan. He watches me with wide eyes and touches my hair with his tiny hands. My heart melts.

"Here." Devon leans forward to grab the teacup and then offers it to me.

I sip the hot but weak liquid and let out a sigh. "Do you have coffee?"

Reed laughs again. "Yeah, we have coffee, city girl. You need rest, though. I promise you a cup in the morning."

I frown and sip more of the tea. "He'll come back."

"Atticus?"

Wincing at his words, I shake my head. "Wretch."

"I'll blow his goddamn head off if he tries."

"Good."

"You going to tell us what happened? Why did Atticus drop you off and bail?" Reed's voice is stern and commanding. He wants answers. I just don't know if I can voice them. It hurts too much.

"He had to," I tell him, my voice quivering as I hug my hoodie to me.

"That doesn't sound like Atticus," Devon murmurs. "He's caring and thoughtful. He doesn't abandon his friends."

Friends.

I choke on a sob.

"He, uh, I'm not his friend."

Devon looks past me at Reed and I can feel the silent conversation between them. They're trying to understand. My heart hurts so much. In *Friends*, they told each other things that hurt and it helped. Devon and Reed are my friends, even if I'm not very good at being one back.

"We…" I trail off. "I loved him." Still do.

Devon sucks in a sharp breath. "Oh."

Reed is silent behind me as he bandages me up.

"Then something happened?" Devon encourages.

I think about my favorite show and explain all my heartache and loss in a way they'll understand being real *city folks* and all. "We broke up."

"Eve—" Reed's voice is lethal, but Devon cuts him off.

"Not now," she whispers. "So he left you here with us? Why didn't you come to us?"

"Wretch must have caught a ride in the trailer. As soon as Atticus was gone, Wretch was there. Shooting and chasing. I ran and ran. Been at my shack until tonight. He set it on fire." Tears well in my eyes. I lost everything. My packs. My stores of food. My clothes. Everything I ever owned was in that shack.

Nausea roils in my stomach.

Defeat infects me as I come to the realization that loss is all I'll ever know.

"I, uh, I need to use the bathroom," I squeak out as I stand. The room spins as I turn. Reed grips my arm to keep me from falling.

"What the—" He yanks my hoodie out of my grip.

Devon gasps.

Rowdy giggles and Ronan stands up on the sofa to touch my stomach.

"Baby," Ronan chirps in his cute toddler voice. "Baby like Momma."

With one arm covering my breasts, I use the other hand to palm my slightly protruding stomach. Hot tears rush down my cheeks. *I wish, little Ronan. I wish I could have babies like your momma.* Every morning I think strong thoughts. I think of Atticus in the early hours, hoping to give the energy to my little being. If I think about burying the little one with the others, it makes me cry and cry. I'm so tired of crying. I want to keep it. I want it to grow and live like Devon's children. It's a piece of Atticus I crave to hold and love.

The room spins and strong arms keep me from falling.

Everything goes blissfully black.

I wake the next morning and the cabin is quiet. I'm wearing new clothes that must belong to Devon. I don't remember changing into them. Last night was a blur of pain and sobbing. As the sun peeks in the windows, I begin my every morning ritual. Rubbing my palm over my stomach, I speak to my being.

"Your father is big and strong. Beautiful. Gentle and kind." Tears leak down my temples. "He would love you if he knew. I have no doubts about that." I let out a ragged sigh. "He's not like the others. The hateful ones who hurt me before. Like Wretch."

Still out there.

Still waiting.

"He won't hurt you," I assure my being. "Maybe…I don't know…maybe you can fight really hard. Maybe you don't have to go with the others between my mother and sister. Maybe you can stay with me. Maybe one day we'll see him again. Together."

Hope is deadly.

It infects me. Rushes through my veins and buries itself in the marrow of my bones. When it's done consuming me from the inside out, it heats my flesh and threatens to devour me whole.

"I may be a little fox, but I'm a hunter. One day you'll be a hunter too. One day I'll hunt you down a television so you can know about pizza and *Friends* and cartoons. I will learn to read and then I'll teach you too. I will be the best mom. I won't let anyone hurt you ever."

My heart blazes with conviction.

As long as Wretch is out there—horrible like Ezekiel and my father and my other brothers—he'll always be a threat. I need to eliminate that threat if my little being has any hope of growing into a baby.

He will.

This being is half Atticus.

Strong. Strong. So strong.

I climb out of the bed and start pulling on the boots that were left out for me. I slip out of the extra bedroom and creep down the hallway. It doesn't take long to find one of their packs and toss some supplies in it. Devon's coat hangs by the door. She won't mind if I borrow this. On the way out, I grab Reed's shotgun too.

"Blind Bear, you coming?"

He groans but then rises, his fluffy tail swishing.

"Good boy. Let's go kill us a rat."

chapter twenty-five

ATTICUS

IT'S LATE IN THE AFTERNOON AND THE SUN HAS warmed the spring day to the point I probably won't need my coat today. Smoke billows from Reed and Devon's chimney. It makes me wonder what they're cooking for supper. My stomach growls because when I left this morning, I didn't grab anything to eat. Just filled my truck with supplies and flew out of there in my haste to get to her.

She'll be upset.

I know Eve. She'll give me her angry scowls and pout. But I have plans to woo her. I brought peanut butter and oatmeal and coffee. She'll forgive me. At least, I hope.

I'm just parking the truck when the gate opens.

Eve.

Eve.

Eve.

But it's not her.

It's my friend.

I shut off the truck and hop out. He has his .45 in his grip. For one second—based on the fierce glint in his eyes—I'm afraid he might shoot me.

"Hey, man," I call out, waving.

His eyes narrow and his nostrils flare. "Why are you here?"

I'm caught off guard by his words. "To visit."

"Who?"

Unease trickles down my spine. This feels like a loaded question and considering it's coming from a man holding a loaded gun, I choose my words carefully.

"Everyone." But mostly Eve.

Reed prowls forward and it reminds me of when he's hunting. His proverbial hackles are raised. The thrill of the hunt is coursing through his veins as violence shines in his eyes.

"Eve here?"

Wrong words.

He pounces on me, his hand finding my throat as he throws me against my truck. I'm technically bigger than Reed, but this man is feral and uncontained. He lost that docile element most people living in society have years ago, probably when Eve's family decided to rape his wife. Reed's been a rabid bear ever since, protecting what's his.

But Eve?

She's not his.

She's mine.

"What the fuck," I snarl, glowering at him.

"Yeah, what the fuck is right, you hypocritical bastard."

Anger surges up inside me and I shove him away. My

throat throbs from the hold he had. I'll probably bruise. Fucker.

"Why are you being an asshole?" I demand, rubbing at my neck, eyeing the way his hand holding the gun trembles.

"Me? You're the one who dropped Eve off on my doorstep like she was an unwanted puppy," he accuses, his eyes flashing with fury. "Real asshole move if you ask me."

Guilt swarms up inside me, stinging me everywhere all at once.

"Does she hate me?" I ask, my words a mere, broken whisper.

He lets out a derisive snort. "Hell no. From what I could tell, she loves you."

Hope surges hot and brilliant in my chest. "I want to see her."

"You can't."

"The fuck I can't!"

He approaches again but doesn't touch me. Just gets right in my face. "All those years you gave me shit about Devon. And here you were fucking a sixteen-year-old. That's called being a hypocrite, man."

"She—"

"And she's not just any kid, Knox, she's Eve. Sweet, scared, little Eve. I don't even want to fucking know how you got her to sleep with you. But so help me if you forced or manipulated her—"

"Fuck you!" I roar, shoving him hard. "I may be a hypocrite, but I'm not a goddamn monster. I love her, dammit. I wouldn't hurt her."

He shoves his gun into the back of his jeans—thank

fuck—and crosses his arms over his massive chest. "When the pussy got old, you dropped that shit on my front lawn?"

"Talk about her that way again and so help me, Reed, I will make you regret that shit," I threaten, taking a step toward him.

"You still can't speak to her."

Fucking bastard. "I need to make things right."

"Boo fucking hoo, Atticus."

I'm going to punch this guy if he doesn't stop his shit and let me see my woman.

"She's gone," he says.

"Gone? Did she go to her shack? Where the fuck did she go?"

"I think she went after him."

I stand there, staring at him in confusion. "Her dog?"

"Fuck no," he snaps. "Not her dog. Him. Wretch. The fucker who has a major hard-on for trying to kill her."

Wretch?

What the hell is he talking about?

"Man, you're not making any sense—"

"She told us about the fruit. The guy who broke the window."

My blood grows cold at his words.

"Apparently the toothless bastard hitched a ride in your trailer."

No.

Fuck no.

"Chased her right off my property. She's been avoiding the bastard ever since. That was until last night when he set her shack on fire with her in it."

I drop to my knees, the fear of her dying consuming me to the point I can't breathe. I clutch at my chest, tears burning trails down my cheeks.

"She got away," he says coolly. "But he shot her."

I snap my head up and growl, "He what?"

"Shot. Her." He gazes off toward the trees. "Pulled the bullet out myself. This morning, she was gone. Took some shit of ours, including a shotgun, so I know she has plans to go after him. I've been packing some shit this afternoon. I'll need to go out there and help her."

"No." I scrub my palm over my face. "You need to stay with Devon and the kids. I'll go. I will find her."

He sneers at me. "I can't trust you with her, Knox. You already abandoned her when she needed you most."

"I was confused and stressed the fuck out," I scream at him. "You don't understand any of it."

"I understand you left her because she's pregnant," he says at the same time I say, "She's my cousin."

"Cousin?" he asks, confused.

I blink, trying to process his words. "Pregnant?" I rise to my feet. "My wife is pregnant?"

Reed's anger has morphed into a softer expression. "Your wife? She didn't tell me any of this. You married your cousin? You? Atticus Hypocrite Knox?"

"Fuck off," I bite out. "She's mine. That's all you need to know."

Pregnant.

Pregnant.

My sweet, fierce Eve is pregnant.

What if something is wrong with the baby? She's my fucking cousin!

But the baby is mine. Wrong or not. Ours. Innocent and created from love. I swipe at the tears and rise to my feet. I'll go to her. I'll find her and drag her back home with me if it's the last thing I do.

The thought of her out there all alone, facing off with some bastard who wants to kill her, is almost too much to bear. Feral protectiveness surges through me as I start scrambling to grab my backpack out of the truck. I have a tent for emergencies that I use for hunting, so I locate that and strap it to my bag. I'm just fishing guns out from under the back seat when Reed calls my name.

"What are you doing?"

"I'm going to her."

"Tell me what happened. Before you go."

I shove my Glock into the front of my jeans and then grab my ax to shove into a loop on my backpack. Once I shut the door, I turn toward him and toss him the keys.

"I took her back. Nursed her back to health. Fell in love. Eve always told me I was her husband. I never argued it because I secretly liked that shit. But I was all fucked over her age because I thought she was a kid. And she thought I wanted to hear that she was sixteen because that's the age I pegged her as and kept going on about it. She doesn't understand laws and age, but she's nineteen, man. I found that out over dinner with my family when she casually mentioned her real age. After I'd been obsessing over it for weeks. This was the same dinner my dad decided to tell me she's his niece. My cousin. A real clusterfuck. I didn't think…it was wrong…" I trail off and give him a helpless look. "I failed her. I failed my sweet little Eve. Told her we couldn't be together because it's fucking incest. Brought her here to you because if I kept her, I'd ignore the laws of the land and never let her go."

He studies me for a long moment. "What changed?"

"Nothing. I was miserable without her. The second my dad told me who she was, I was miserable. Because I couldn't have her. There's no life where she doesn't exist inside it that is worth living." I scrub at my face with my palm. "And now she's pregnant. My cousin who happens to be my wife in both our eyes is pregnant. I need to get to her so we can be a family. We should have never separated. Everything's messy and fucked up and horrible without her."

"What are you going to do when you find her?"

"I'm going to keep her."

He smiles at me, the anger from before slipping away. "Devon has supper ready. At least leave with a full stomach. When you find her, bring her back before you haul her back to your cave. The kids will want to say a proper goodbye."

I scan the woods behind him.

The call of the wild sings to me, beckons me.

Pleads for me to prowl into it and find peace there.

Eve is my peace.

She's my wild.

I always knew I belonged out there. I just didn't realize it's because I'd always been searching for her. Even before I knew her. Before she was born. Just a feeling. A sensation. A need. And now that I've been exposed to the wild, I'm a slave to it. To her. My heart is shackled to hers.

I'll never be free.

I don't ever want to be free.

I want to be chained to her wild heart until the end of this life.

the wild

"Knox…"

"Tell Devon to make me something for the road. I'm leaving in five minutes."

He grins. "Go get our girl."

As he trots back inside the gate, I grab a few more supplies from the bed of the truck. By the time I walk over to the gate, he's coming back out, a thermos in hand.

"Bad bear stew. Devon's specialty."

I take the stew and with a wave, I start out on my journey to find her.

Mine.

She's mine and I'll get her back.

I don't care if I have to search every goddamn inch of Alaska.

I will hunt her down and claim her again.

This time forever.

chapter twenty-six

EVE

Four months later...

I SNIFF THE AIR. LINGERING BODY ODOR. A HINT OF fire. Now that we're well into summer, his stench is easier to find. Also, he's getting reckless. After nearly getting his ass shot last month, he wasted the rest of his ammo, unloading into the trees at me. I had to take cover, which gave him enough time to escape, but I've picked back up on his trail. Silently stalking.

Blind Bear is a good dog and knows when to be quiet. When I stop, he stops. Together, we listen for sounds. Sometimes, he hears them better and starts in the direction we need to go. Other times, we rely on my sight. Wretch leaves a trail behind wherever he goes. Fire remains. Bloody bones from his latest game kill. Though there hasn't been much of that lately.

I smile, knowing he doesn't have a way to kill the

animals and he can't come back to check any of his traps. Not with us on his trail. Hunting him.

Kneeling beside a recent fire pit, I hover my hand over it. Slightly warm. He isn't that far ahead of us. The pile of bones discarded in the fire are small. Maybe a rat or a baby bunny or squirrel. Not enough to keep him fed and strong.

I stand, listening for more sounds, but hear nothing.

I feel everything.

A roll and then a shiver of excitement.

The being is more than a being. It's a baby. A strong one. One that kicks and rolls frequently. Pride surges through me. I knew it would be a survivor. With Atticus being its father, how could it not be?

I rub my stomach. "It's okay, wild one. We'll find him. We'll get rid of him and then we'll visit the kids again. I think you'd like them."

The baby rolls again.

I'm smiling down at my stomach when I hear it.

Crunch.

Blind Bear growls. I quietly shush him. No sense in giving up our location if we can help it. He remains at my side, his head cocked as he listens.

Something heavy splashes into the river. Before I can stop him, Blind Bear tears off toward the sound. I'm staring off after him when the hairs on my arm stand up. I swivel around just in time to see Wretch charging for me.

Boom!

Wretch must get clipped because he howls but doesn't stop. He has a giant limb in his hand. I aim for him again, but he nails me in the head with the limb, knocking me down to the ground.

He grabs a handful of my hair, his putrid scent making my stomach clench violently, and pulls me to my knees. I fire off another shot that misses him completely before he manages to wrestle the shotgun out of my hands. Blind Bear races forward. He releases me to aim for my dog.

No!

I kick Wretch in his gut, making him fall backward. The gun booms again, but at least it's pointing up rather than at BB.

"Run, BB!" I cry out. "Run!"

My voice echoes through the trees. Blind Bear must understand because he takes off into the woods. I'm struggling to scramble away from Wretch when he aims the shotgun right at my stomach. Evil glitters in his eyes and he grins his disgusting, toothless smile at me.

"Someone knocked your skinny ass up," he says. "Should've been me."

"Fuck you!" I scream, kicking at him again.

"You will, bitch. You fucking will. Get on your hands and knees unless you want me to pump the rest of the bullets in this gun into your stomach."

Anger pulses through me hot and volatile. *Think, Eve.* What would Atticus do? *Be strong for you, wild one.* Think. If I protest, I have no doubt Wretch will shoot me. Shooting at me has been his favorite activity since I first met him. I need to stall until I can get to my knife.

"Okay," I murmur. "Just don't shoot."

He grunts, glowering at me. "Take off that backpack."

I wrangle myself from the pack and drop it beside me. The knife I have is tucked into one of the side loops. I'll grab it when he's not looking—

My pack goes sailing as he kicks it away.

"On your hands and knees."

I turn and scan the ground for anything to use as a weapon. Within reach is a rock. I don't know if I can pick it up, but if I can, it'll hurt if I hit him with it. Slowly, I inch forward. The barrel of the gun presses into the back of my head as he grabs the top of my jeans. Since my belly is so big, I can't fasten them. He's easily able to wrench them down my thighs.

Stay strong.

Stay strong.

As I hear him fumble with his own clothes, I'm thrust into the past. For some reason I think of Nathaniel. At one time, I liked to play with him when we were little. He was always nice to me.

Until Ezekiel and Papa were killed.

He came back that night different.

Formed into a predator.

Night after night, Nathaniel transformed from my brother into this monster no better than Ezekiel or the others.

A cock rubs against my ass and then he spits. I'm dragged from the horrible things my brother did and brought back to the now.

Protect my wild one.

No longer a being.

My strong baby.

I inch forward, reaching for the rock. The barrel of the shotgun digs against my skull.

"Don't fucking think about it, bitch. Your hole will still be hot and wet, even with your head missing."

He makes a sick thwack sound and I cringe, wondering what he's doing. I start to reach for the rock again, but his weight crushes me to the ground. I'm barely kept upright and from squashing my baby by my elbows. Heat floods over my back and then he falls beside me. All I need is a moment without a shotgun pointed at my head. I scramble forward and grab the heavy rock. I swing around to hit him with it, but he's not chasing me. He's simply staring at me with his eyes wide-open.

And an ax sticking out of his skull.

My hand trembles and I nearly drop the rock. I clutch it tighter as I whip my head to the right. Another stands there. Big, tall, feral.

Like a big bear.

An overgrown beard and crazed, violent eyes.

A happy, blind dog at his side.

"There you are, wife."

I slump, dropping the rock as a full-bodied shuddering sob wracks through me. He kneels in front of me and his large hand gently caresses my big stomach.

"Our baby," he whispers, his green eyes shining with pride and fierce protectiveness.

"Yes."

He smiles and in this moment, I realize it's truly him. Atticus. My husband. The man who came for me. As though I weigh nothing, he hauls me to my feet and then pulls my pants up my thighs.

"Did he…"

"No."

"Good because I was wondering how I would kill a man who was already dead."

I let out a silly laugh. I haven't laughed in months. It feels good. I missed it.

"Your pants won't zip," he says, frowning.

"Your baby is big."

Our eyes meet and his smile is wide. Proud. Happy.

I let out a squeal when he scoops me in his arms. I wrap my arms around his neck and nuzzle my face against his beard. It's longer than I've ever seen it.

"I let you go for two months," he says, his voice pained as he walks. "Then, I hunted you for four more. I can't ever spend another day without you, babe."

Emotion overcomes me and I sob against his neck. I missed him so much. Every single moment of every day, I thought of him. Of us. Of our baby.

"I'm so tired," I admit. "Do you have any fruit?"

"There's my girl. And don't worry. I'm going to take care of you now. You're safe. You're mine. You'll never have to be afraid or hungry or sad again."

Sounds like a dream come true.

We walk for a long time until we're far from Wretch's expired body. We're in a clearing that overlooks the river with a path leading down to the water.

"We can camp here for a few days. Eventually, we'll make our way back to Reed and Devon. You're far from home, little fox."

My heart warms as he sets me to my feet. I watch as he efficiently begins setting up a camp. For months, I've lived under whatever shelter I could come by. It was the most animalistic surviving I'd done in years. No home. No one other than my dog. My pack supplies long since dwindled. Everything I consumed was something I found or hunted.

I knew eventually I'd need to make a home for me and my wild one, but I couldn't rest until Wretch was gone.

And he is gone.

Dead.

Thanks to Atticus.

Speaking of my big bear, I watch with a ravenous stare as he peels off his shirt to start erecting his tent. His artful—tattoos I since learned—back glistens in the sunlight. Blind Bear is happy as can be now that our big guy is reunited with us. His tail wags happily and I swear it looks like he's smiling.

"Fruit?" I remind Atticus, my stomach growling fiercely.

He looks over his shoulder, a feral glint in his eyes. "I have fruit. But I can do one better."

I cock my head to the side. "Don't keep me in suspense," I sass.

He laughs and it echoes off the trees, filling my soul with joy. "God, I missed that mouth."

Abandoning his half built tent, he rummages through his pack. When he pulls out a jar, I cry out, my hand at my chest.

"No."

"Oh, yes, baby."

His eyes, filled with love and tenderness, gleam in the sunlight as he approaches. He unscrews the lid and the heavenly scent of peanut butter fills my nostrils. A whine bubbles up my throat.

"I love you," I whimper.

"I love you too."

He kisses my forehead as I dive two fingers into the

untouched jar. I suck off the delicious, sticky peanut butter from my fingers and groan with delight. He winks at me before going back to the tent. I happily scoop out the peanut butter while I visually devour Atticus's muscular form.

He's beautiful.

And here with me.

Mine.

With practiced ease, he builds us a temporary home. A fire pit. A tent. He tells me he'll be right back and after about thirty minutes, he returns with my pack and his bloody ax. I've since sat down and closed the jar to save it for later.

"You want to wash up in the river? You look like you haven't bathed in months, Eve."

"And you haven't shaved in just as long." I arch a brow at him.

He smirks. "I brought you a present." I watch as he digs around in his pack that's proven to be filled with wonderful things and pulls out two items I've missed desperately.

Fat, heavy tears well in my eyes and roll down my face. I choose this moment to let it all sink in. I'm no longer alone. We can be a family.

Atticus kneels in front of me and then pulls me to him. I remain locked in his embrace for what feels like a glorious eternity. He strokes my hair and mutters promises I feel deep in my bones until my tears dry up. I'm ready to use his gifts. I want to brush my teeth.

"Let's go," I tell him as I take the toothbrush and toothpaste. "I want to clean up and then I just want you to hold me. I'm so tired."

"I know, Eve. I know."

chapter twenty-seven

ATTICUS

I HAVE HER.

I finally have her.

My chest no longer aches but burns instead. I'm filled up with her. Every empty hole inside overflows with sweet Eve. My woman. My wife.

For four months, I searched for her. Miles and miles and miles I covered. Every so often, I'd come across evidence that she'd been close. Her stinky dog's shits were easy to follow. But I was always just too far behind. Or I'd lose their trail and spend hours circling the same areas. Every night spent without her, a small part of me was erased. The human side of myself was giving up so the animal could take over. I needed to find her.

I'd been probably a mile away when I heard the gunshots. Never ran so fast in my entire life. And then, as if he knew I was coming, BB came out of nowhere barking.

When I walked up on them, I cracked.

Saw red.

Blood red.

His blood.

I wanted it. I wanted his blood for even daring to look at my Eve.

With a well-aimed throw, I launched that ax. Watched with glee as it split open his skull. And then, I had my girl back.

All my thoughts dissipate the moment Eve sheds her shirt on the river banks. BB has already jumped into the river and is splashing around happily. My eyes fixate on the scar on her back. Where that motherfucker shot her. I'm seeing red all over again when she turns.

Fuller breasts than I remember. Pink, mottled scars from the bear attack months and months ago. And a swollen belly, filled with my child. As she pushes her jeans down and gets completely nude, an alpha need to claim her possesses me. I quickly rip off my clothes and prowl over to her. My little fox doesn't run. Instead, she remains waiting.

"Mine," I growl, my palms going to her fleshy ass.

She snakes her arms up my chest and loops them at my neck. I lift her before carrying her out into the river. It's chilly, but it feels good. Invigorating. Clean. Like we might wash away our lonely past of being separated and start fresh. I like that idea.

I dunk us and when we reemerge from the water, she laughs. Best sound on Earth. I fuse my lips to hers and taste her now minty-flavored tongue. I'd never seen someone so happy to brush their teeth. We kiss as I walk us deeper. With only our heads sticking out of the water, we kiss at a slower pace. Enjoying each other. Reconnecting.

Goddamn I've missed her.

I might have once been plagued by the fact she's blood to me. It damn near destroyed me. But then, after my talk with Dad, something shifted. I realized I didn't care. She was my Eve and always would be. Nothing would stop me from having her.

It took forever to get back to her, but I would've searched until my last, dying breath if that's what it took to see her pretty smile one last time.

"I like this between us," I mutter against her soft, pillow lips. "This baby we made."

I feel her smile against mine. "Me too."

I'm hard despite the cold water rushing around us. Not even cold ass water will keep me from claiming my woman. My wife. Mine. I reach between us and probe at her pussy with the head of my dick. She whimpers and wiggles until her warmth slides down around me. A hiss of pleasure escapes me. With my hands on her hips, I bounce her nearly weightless body along my aching shaft. Her kisses become needy and starved. I kiss her back with the same intensity—probably more.

"Eve," I croak, nipping at her bottom lip. "I love you."

Her body clenches me hard. "I love you too."

I fuck, fuck, fuck Eve in the river until she's calling my name and I claim her by filling her up. And then I nuzzle my face in her wet hair and just inhale her.

Breathe her in.

Get drunk on her scent.

Thank God for giving her back to me.

the wild

The summer night has cooled, so I pull my naked, pregnant wife closer. The light from our fading fire allows us to see each other just enough in the dark tent. Blind Bear is curled up near the entrance of the tent already snoring.

"I'm sorry," I murmur, stroking my finger through her now dry hair. "I'm sorry for everything. I was an asshole for leaving you."

"Yes."

I chuckle. "You're not supposed to agree."

She giggles and then freezes. My heart stammers in my chest, fearing she heard a bear or something. Her hand encircles my wrist and she pulls my hand to her naked stomach. I splay my palm over the firm flesh.

"Feel. Our wild one is awake."

When something pushes against my hand, I let out a choked sound. "T-That's our baby?"

She nods, her smile wide and her eyes filled with tears. "Every single day I told the baby about you. About how wonderful and strong you are. How it'll grow up to be just like you."

The baby moves again. I rub my thumb along her skin, completely transfixed over the fact I can feel my child. It's surreal. I'm overcome with happiness.

A dark cloud of worry passes over me.

The what-ifs.

All those incest books I read.

I'll die if our child suffers. Fucking die.

"This one is strong just like you," she assures me, somehow sensing my fears. "The others weren't like this one."

Others?

"What?"

Her brows furrow together. "Before…with Papa and my brothers. There were times we also created something. I called them my beings."

She got pregnant.

By her siblings and father.

"Four of them," she says, her bottom lip wobbling. "No bigger than the palm of my hand." A tear races down her cheek. "I named them Love, Mercy, Faith, and Goodness. They were mine even if they never took a breath. So weak and tiny." Her body trembles and I pull her close so I can keep her tight in my arms.

"You miscarried?"

"I don't know that term."

"The babies died while in your womb?"

"Y-Yes. They weren't babies. They never moved or breathed." She starts to cry and I hate that this woman has suffered so much pain in her life.

"Eve, beautiful, they were your babies. It's okay to say it. Just because they never lived doesn't change that fact. You had four babies that you would have done everything in your power to protect had they survived. You're going to be a great mother to our wild one."

She sniffles. "My babies." Another sob. "My babies."

"Yes," I croon. "They were yours. They'll always be yours. And when our little one is born, you'll get to see firsthand what a good mother you could have been to them."

"I want to visit them," she whispers. "They're buried by where the shack was. Can we visit them? My babies?"

I find her lips and press kisses to her supple mouth. "Of course we can."

Her palms cradle my cheeks and she stares at me as though I'm the most precious thing in the world. Love floods through me, hot, possessive, and wonderful.

"Love me always, Atticus."

"Always."

Our mouths meet for a frantic kiss as I roll onto my back, pulling her with me. It takes a few quick adjustments and then I'm deep inside her where I belong. She sits up and stares down at me. I take a moment to admire how fucking beautiful she is. Her dark hair hangs long over her perky breasts that have grown with her pregnancy. I admire her swollen stomach that continues to grow each day with my child—my strong little baby. She licks her pink, puffy lips, making my dick twitch inside her.

I slide my fingers to her cunt and find her needy clit beneath her dark curls. She whimpers at my touch, sliding up and down along my throbbing cock. Her body is incredibly responsive. It only takes a few moments until she's exploding, my name a war cry on her lips. I grunt, my hips bucking up, as I find my own release. The desire to continue to fill her up until we're old and gray consumes me. I drain my love into her because it's all hers. Every last drop.

She slides off me and lies back down. I curl up behind her, my dripping cock nestled against the crack of her ass and my palm possessively stroking her stomach. We're nearly drifted off to sleep when Blind Bear drops one of his lethal bombs. It only takes a second for the tent to fill with his rancid ass stank.

"Smelly dog, smelly dog, what are they feeding you?" Eve sings in her best Phoebe voice.

I chuckle and then try not to gag. "No more beef jerky, dude. I don't care how sorry I feel for you. You kill us with that shit."

BB's tail swishes, knowing that we're talking to him, which only serves to send the smell fanning our way. Eve squeals and pulls the blanket over our heads. I bury my face in her sweet-smelling hair.

This is perfection.

Her. Our stinky ass dog. Our baby.

Perfect.

We should have left right away, but we didn't. We stayed for a month, simply enjoying each other and getting re-acquainted. Eventually, we packed up our tiny camp and headed to her old shack.

Traveling with a pregnant woman has proven to be difficult. Though Eve is strong and resilient, she's only human. And this pregnancy is taking its toll on her. Some days she just wants to sleep. Our stops along the way have been long ones. If I were traveling alone, it would have taken me a couple of weeks, not two months like it has when we decided to finally take our journey.

But we're finally here.

Her old shack is nothing but a rock, crumbling

fireplace. The wood that once held it up is gone. Everything is gone. She doesn't seem upset about the home. Her interest is in the stones near the big tree. Fall is here and leaves cover the forest floor, an array of orange, brown, red, and yellow. She's already brushed away the leaves around the stones and kneels beside them. Her fingers walk along the stones as she smiles.

"My babies," she says. "All four of them."

I squat beside her, brushing my knuckles over her cheek to make sure she doesn't feel too cold. We've traveled long and far today. I'm sure she's exhausted.

"These, wild one, are your sisters," I tell our unborn baby.

She laughs. "Girls? How do you know?"

"I just feel like with those names you gave them, they were girl names." I kiss the top of her head. "You probably have another little girl inside you."

She shakes her head. "I feel like this one is a boy."

"Do you now? How come?"

"A hunch. Sometimes, I dream about him."

"Him." My heart squeezes. I hadn't really had a preference until now. Now, like her, I feel like it's a boy.

"While you set up camp, I'm going to look for the good sticks to make toys. I haven't made any for Devon and Reed's new baby yet," Eve says, standing.

I rise and give her a soft kiss on her cheek. "Be careful and holler if you need me."

She sets off and I start setting up camp. We're close to Reed and Devon's. Another half day of travel and we'll be at Reed's hunting cabin. Then, it's not far of a hike to their cabin on the cliff. Almost home.

I've just gotten the tent up and a fire started when I hear it.

Screams.

Blind Bear is gone and I hope to God he scares off whatever the hell is making her bellow like that. Yanking my Glock from my pants, I run toward her screaming. I find her at the bottom of an incline, curled over in pain, BB at her side.

"Eve!"

"Atticu—ahhh!"

She screams as I charge down the small hill to her.

"What's wrong? Are you hurt?" My hands roam all over her, assessing for damage.

"I had an—ahhh!" She curls up, hot tears leaking from her lids. "A pain and I slipped. I've been having them all day—ahhhh!"

Fuck. Fuck. Fuck.

"Is the baby coming?" I demand, my heart in my throat.

"I think so—ahhh!"

I scoop her body into my arms and rush up the incline with BB on my heels. She continues to scream, barely getting any words out as I carry her to the tent.

"G-Get my pants off, Attic—ahhhh!" She sobs. "I can feel him. He's coming out!"

Frantic, I begin ripping off her boots and jeans. When I see blood on her thighs, I nearly pass out. *Don't fucking do that, asshole.* I swallow down the fear of her dying from childbirth and rip off her panties.

She wrenches her thighs apart and screams.

It's then I see.

the wild

A head trying to come out.

Holy shit.

Holy fucking shit.

"Eve, baby, he's coming. Holy fuck, he's coming!"

She screams again and then his head slides out of her stretched opening, revealing to me the first glimpse of my child. My heart is in my throat, but I can't stop to marvel over this miraculous moment. She needs my help. I need to deliver our son. Another scream pierces the air and more of the baby starts to come out. But then, it slides back into her, just the head sticking out.

"My God, our wild one is gorgeous, baby. You gotta keep pushing so you can see him too."

She lets loose another blood-curdling scream and bears down. Over and over she does this as I coach her to keep pushing. At one point, she looks so purple in the face and fucking exhausted that I think she'll give up.

Eve never gives up.

She's a fighter.

A survivor.

A mother who'll do anything for her baby.

Screams pierce the air and she growls as she pushes our baby out. A boy. Just like she thought. He slides out of her body and into my waiting hands. I pull him against my chest. He's quiet. Too quiet. With probably a little too much force, I swat his bottom.

This time, the screams come from our boy.

Angry wails that fill my soul up and make it fucking sing.

Mine.

Ours.

We're a goddamn family.

Eve sobs, defeated and exhausted. I need to take care of her. She has a cord hanging out of her body and there's blood everywhere. We weren't prepared for this.

"Can you take your shirt off?" I ask as I kiss my son's wet, bloody head.

She manages to pull it off her body, revealing her breasts. I gently lay him against her. Her shaking hands pull him to her and she starts to cry. Once I have him covered with her shirt, I try to figure out what to do next.

"You're going to have to deliver the placenta," I tell her. "Then I'll get you cleaned up."

She grunts and groans, and then the blob comes out. Using my big knife, I hack through the cord, careful not to jostle our baby or hurt him. I work quickly to get her cleaned up so I can warm them up.

"He's so perfect," she whispers, fatigue in her voice.

"I knew he would be." Truth is, I worried every single day that there'd be something wrong with him. But there isn't. He's perfect and normal. Ours.

I cover them up with a blanket and then bring her a water bottle. Holding it up to her cracked lips, I help her drink it down. Once she's satisfied, I screw on the lid and then peek at my son.

A full head of dark hair like Eve.

"He's a big boy," I say, pride in my tone.

"Like his father."

"Are you a big boy like daddy?" I coo, stroking his sticky brown hair.

Eve's eyes are tender and water as she regards me. "Daddy. You're his daddy."

I can't help but grin. It feels fucking amazing to call him my son. "I am. Rest and see if you can get him to eat. I'll get something to bathe him with."

It sucks to have to leave them, but I do so I can warm water over the fire. While it heats, I bury the placenta away from camp so as not to attract any wild animals. Once I've cleaned up in the river, I rush back to my family. I bring the pot inside along with a rag, setting it beside me. In my backpack, I find a soft T-shirt I can swaddle our little one in once he's clean.

"Did he eat?"

Eve nods. "I think so. He latched on. It hurt, so I'm guessing he found what he was after."

"Can I wash him up?" I wet a cloth and then wring it out. It's warm to the touch but not hot.

"Yes."

I carefully take our tiny baby away from her. He easily fits in the crook of my arm. Quickly, I clean him off. His screams are loud as he protests at my actions. Once he's no longer sticky with birth goo, I wrap him up in the shirt. He quickly settles, his eyes drooping. I scoot the pot closer to Eve. With my baby pressed against my chest in one arm, I use my other hand to clean his mother's chest off. She's falling fast asleep too. Before her eyes drift closed, I brush my thumb along her jaw.

"What do we name him?"

Her eyes open for a moment and then she smiles. "Wild." She closes her eyes and falls asleep, leaving me with our wild one named Wild. It's perfect considering where he was born.

"You hear that, little guy. Mommy said your name is Wild. You like that?"

He trembles in his sleep, his bottom lip pouting out. Jesus, he looks just like Eve when he does that. My heart is bursting with joy.

The night my son is born, I don't sleep.

Not because he cries all night or I'm worried.

I don't sleep because I stare at him. Stare and stare and stare, afraid to miss one second of seeing his perfect face.

One month later...

Snow dusts our face as we walk up the slippery steps. I keep one hand on Eve's lower back so she doesn't fall with Wild in her arms. After our son was born and Eve was able to walk, we made the trip to Reed's hunting cabin. It was good to stay in an actual home and gain our bearings. But Eve wanted to leave eventually, so we set out on our path to their house. Now that we're almost there, I'm giddy with excitement. I can't wait to show off our son.

A dog barking greets us at the top of the stairs, followed by a burly man. Reed. He lowers his .45 when he sees that it's us.

"Holy shit," he cries out, rushing down the steps to aid us. "I thought I'd never see you guys again." He stops to admire Wild. "Brought home a baby too."

"This is Wild," Eve says to him.

I grin at Reed. "Wild, that's your crazy uncle Reed."

Reed's grin is wide, revealing his bright white teeth. "Well, get your filthy asses into my house. You both look worn as hell and like you could use some bad bear stew."

Blind Bear barks because that fucker will eat anything.

He and Buddy take off sprinting toward the house. We all follow after them.

"Devon had her baby too," he tells us. "A little girl. Raegan."

"A girl finally," Eve says happily.

"Boy, I told you not to come out here," Reed calls out to Rowdy peeking around the gate.

He rushes ahead to his son. Eve stops me and turns to look up at me. Her brown eyes are fierce and loving. I could drown in her intense gaze. My mouth meets hers and I kiss her gently.

"Honey, we're home."

She smiles. "Not quite."

"You don't want to stay here?"

"I want to visit. But then…" She sighs. "I want our son to be able to watch television and go to Muskies and see your family. I want to have hot showers and learn to read. I just want more for him than I had. Is that okay?"

I cradle her cheek and kiss her nose. "Eve, baby, we'll give him the world. I'll go wherever you want to go, because you're my home. Your happiness is my happiness." I give her a lopsided grin. "But can we both admit the real reason you want to go back to my house is so you can have more peanut butter?"

She laughs. "You caught me."

"I'll always catch you."

chapter twenty-eight

EVE

Six months later...

"GOD, EVE," WILL GROANS, COVERING HIS eyes. "I don't think I'll ever get used to you doing that shit at the dinner table."

I smirk. "My son has to eat. We're eating. I don't see the big deal."

"Yeah, Will," Judith chimes in, kissing Wild's head. "Stop looking at Eve's tits."

"I, uh, I wasn't—"

"Who's looking at my wife's tits?" Atticus growls as he enters his parents' dining room with Abel, Evan, and Vic.

Will scowls, leaning back in his chair directly across from mine at the table. "I'm just saying, she doesn't give any warning before she whips it out."

"Dad," Evan states with a chuckle. "It's just a boob."

Atticus leans down and kisses my head before running

his fingertip along Wild's cheek. Wild pops off my nipple to gaze up at his father, his green eyes gleaming with delight.

"You're distracting him," I chide, trying to get Wild to latch back on.

"And you're distracting Will with your nipple," Judith offers, not helpfully.

"I'm leaving." Will pouts but makes no moves to actually leave.

Susan enters the dining room with her famous lasagna. It effectively distracts everyone from my breasts and Wild goes back to nursing. He tugs on my hair, his green eyes locked with mine.

He's so precious.

I sometimes stare at him for hours.

Atticus teases me, but I catch him staring at him too.

Not long after we came back home, Atticus had his family over. I wore a white dress and Atticus wore a suit. In front of his family, we vowed our love to each other. At the end, we exchanged rings to bind our promises. It felt just like when Monica and Chandler got married. Two friends who were inseparable and in love. Atticus tells me not to believe everything I see on television, but I believe in them.

"So, Eve," Abel says as he scoops some lasagna onto his plate. "Susan tells me you're making great progress."

I beam at him. "I'm reading *The Boxcar Children*."

"Impressive. Good stories?"

"The best. I've been writing too, but I'm not that good at it."

Susan waves off my comment. "Nonsense, hon. Your handwriting is beautiful. I'm impressed you've come this far in such a short time. Truly brilliant."

"She never compliments me like that," Judith grumbles, nudging me with her shoulder.

I can't help but bask in her praise. I didn't think Susan would want to help me, but when she overheard me asking Atticus about it, she offered to teach me. It's a good thing too because her handwriting is legible unlike Atticus's. His is messy. Every day she comes over to help with Wild and give me lessons. Sometimes she takes him for a walk or into town to give us some time alone. I never knew my grandparents, but I'm thankful Wild will know his.

When Wild is done suckling, he starts wiggling and crying. Evan hops out of his chair and rushes over to take him. They're sweet. Wild's eyes light up when he sees Evan and Evan acts like a proud big brother. I happily pass off the chunky baby to his cousin and then add some parmesan cheese to the lasagna Atticus put on my plate.

I'm happy.

Every day I wake up with that realization.

I love my life. How I wake up to a warm house and don't have to start a fire to get it that way. That I can microwave food and eat it within minutes. Coffee. Peanut butter. M&Ms. There are so many foods I just don't know how I lived without. As a result, I've gained weight. You can't see my bones protruding anymore, which Atticus says is a good thing.

"I arrested Joey," Will says around a mouthful of lasagna.

Judith laughs. "Good."

Joey—the guy she'd been seeing last year—had been with other women besides her. It really broke her heart. I couldn't understand how someone would want to break

Judith's heart. She's my best friend besides Atticus. Now she's seeing a guy who works at the post office. Ben. She calls him boring all the time, but she gets a silly smile on her face when she says it. Boring is better than horrible Joey, who can't keep his cock in one woman. Ben looks at Judith like she's the only woman in the world.

"Where's Ben?" Atticus asks, mimicking my thoughts.

"Fishing with his dad. He'll be back tomorrow."

They continue to babble and I find my stare locked on Evan. He smiles at Wild, stroking his fingers through his hair. It makes me hope that Wild will be a big brother one day and look at his siblings like Evan looks at him.

"We're going to take Wild out to Reed and Devon's in a few weeks," Atticus says, earning the attention of everyone.

"W-What? Why?" Susan cries out. "You can't take my baby boy away!"

"Ma," Atticus grumbles. "Only for a visit. We'll be gone a week tops."

Susan frowns. "I still don't think it's safe out there."

"Can I come?" Evan asks. "I've never been and you all talk so fondly of it. I could help with Wild too."

"No," Will snaps. "You have class."

"Dad," Evan grumbles. "I can talk to my professors. I'll get the work done."

"He can come," Atticus says. "We don't mind. I know Reed and Devon's kids will love to see someone new."

Will scowls but finally gives in. "Your grades better not suffer. You have a scholarship to a college I can in no way afford to pay for if you suddenly lose it."

"I promise," Evan says, grinning. "Did you hear that, little buddy? I get to come too."

The rest of dinner goes like the usual Sunday night dinners we have at Atticus's parents. Loud. Chaotic. Fun. We always finish with one of Susan's homemade desserts. Tonight, it's my favorite of hers. Peach cobbler.

After dinner, Susan steals Wild and cuddles him since she won't see him for a whole week. I help Judith with the dishes while Atticus and the guys sit on the porch talking. Once we're finished, I check on Wild, who's sleeping on his grandma's chest and then look for my husband. I pull on my coat and then find him with the others.

They all exchange smirks before heading back inside, leaving the two of us alone.

"Hey, beautiful," he says, grinning.

"Hey, handsome."

"Want to go for a walk?"

The air is crisp and cold, but I look forward to an evening walk with him. I offer my hand and he takes it. We walk behind the house and into the woods. It's quiet and calm. When we're hidden beyond the cover of the trees, he presses me against a big tree and kisses me hard.

"I missed you," he murmurs between kisses.

A giggle bubbles up my chest. "You were outside for five minutes."

"Twenty. And I can still miss you. Sometimes I can have you in my arms and still miss you."

"You're weird."

"You like it."

He trails kisses to my neck and gets me worked up with his mouth. My body floods with heat, the fire to have him burning at uncontrollable levels. I rake my fingers through his hair, undoing his neat man-bun and making it crazy, just the way I like it. He groans, his breath hot against my neck, when I tug at his golden strands.

"Are you really going to do this with your parents' house so close by?" I murmur, amused at his ravenous nature tonight.

"If they thought I was making them another grandbaby, I'm sure they'd approve."

With those words, he starts unbuttoning my jeans. His long fingers slide between my lips and find my clit. Whatever apprehension I may have had, melts away as he brings me pleasure. The air is nippy, but my body is flooded with heat. He pushes my jeans and panties down to my knees and then works his fingers faster. I bite on my lip, trying to hold back a loud moan. He brings me close to orgasm and then slides past my clit to push inside me.

"Asshole," I grumble.

He laughs and nips my neck. "I just needed to feel how wet you were." His finger probes inside me, looking to bring me pleasure there, too. He finds the spot that makes my toes curl, and works it in a lazy, teasing way. He drives me insane.

"Just do it," I beg. "Make me come."

"So bossy."

"Now."

"Really fucking bossy."

"Atticus…"

He laughs but obeys. His finger expertly brings me over the cliff of bliss. When he's done, he pulls out his finger, grabs my hips, and twists me around.

"Hold on to the tree, woman." He works at his belt behind me.

"Who's bossy now?"

"Keep it up with that mouth and I'll have to fill it."

My cheeks burn hot. When we moved back home, he told me about blow jobs. I didn't know this was a thing. But seeing the way the big, powerful man submitted to me the moment my mouth was on his cock, I became a big fan of the activity.

"I think you'd rather fuck me against the tree," I taunt. He loves it when I talk dirty.

"Eve," he growls, pressing his hard cock against the crack of my ass. "You're going to scream for that comment."

I smile as he pushes the head of his cock into my slick opening and then bucks his hips hard. I do scream. He stretches me and fills me in the most maddening way. My nails claw at the bark and I whine, pushing my ass against him. His fingers dig into my hips as he begins a hard, powerful thrusting cadence.

From his position behind me, it almost hurts. I like it, though. When he loses himself to the moment and handles me too roughly. Atticus says I like poking the bear. Mostly, I like when the bear pokes me.

"This," he snarls against my ear as he cups my pussy, "is mine. Always will be." Then his fingers are sliding between the lips, massaging the throbbing clit again.

Too much.

Too much pleasure.

My legs tremble, too weak to hold myself up any longer. He senses it and locks an arm around me, never skipping a beat with his wild thrusting. The fingers at my clit continue their torturous rhythm. When he brings me to climax, stars glitter in front of me and I let loose a throaty scream.

His heat gushes inside me, hot and claiming. It makes me hope again and again we'll have more babies. Like Reed and Devon. I want a big family like Atticus's. I don't want Wild to be the only child. I know how lonely it feels and don't wish that for him.

Atticus pulls out and his hot cum runs down my thighs. He takes care of me and pulls my clothes back up and into place. Once we're both decent, he pulls me against him, kissing my hair.

"I can't get enough of you, Eve. I don't think I ever will."

I smile and close my eyes as I inhale him. Atticus is everything to me. He befriended me when I was younger and looked out for me. Brought me fruit and tried to get me to talk. When I got hurt, I went to them, knowing full well Atticus was there. It was him I needed. He's all I'll ever need.

I was born wild, but caged and abused.

And with him, I was freed. He broke the chains around my heart and took it for his own. Rather than feel trapped or mistreated, I felt loved. He always made me feel that way. Now, more so than ever.

"Always yours," I whisper. "You ready to get our boy and go home?"

"Yes, ma'am. I'm not done loving you. It might take all night."

I hope it takes forever.

One week later...

Eyes.

I feel them on me.

Staring.

I jolt awake and squint against the morning sun streaming in through Reed and Devon's guest room. Atticus is gone—probably off with Reed. I'm apparently being watched by two little Jamison boys.

They're not watching me because they think I'm interesting. They're watching because they're trying to sneak off with my baby.

Wild squeals with delight at seeing them.

Rowdy has been inching Wild down the bed away from me while Ronan keeps watch. I blink away my sleep and give them my mean stare.

"What are you doing?"

"We gonna play with Wild," Ronan says. "Rowdy's big. He watch him." Then, the two-year-old gives me a silly, toothy grin.

"He needs to eat first. I can feed him and then come with you two."

Ronan huffs. "No girls."

I roll my eyes. From what Devon says, they're not a fan of their new little sister Raegan.

"Tough shit," I grumble, sitting up.

"No, you tough shit," Ronan sasses back.

Rowdy giggles. "Ronan! Daddy'll whip your butt!"

"And Eve!" he argues. "Eve said shit!"

"You said shit twice." I arch a brow at him to argue with me.

"So did you," Ronan says, sticking out his tongue.

"Can Evan come instead?" Rowdy asks, giving me a smile that reminds me of Devon's.

As if on cue, a sleepy Evan walks into the room in his boxers. The kid is skinny. It'll do him some good to be out here with us for a while. Between Reed and Atticus, they'll put him to work and put some muscle on him.

"Boys meeting and I'm not allowed." I pout, making Evan chuckle.

He saunters in and scoops up Wild. "Hear that, little buddy? We get to play with the boys."

"He hasn't eaten yet," I grumble. "Or had a diaper change."

Evan makes a face and hands him back. "Fine. But as soon as you take care of all that, we'll be back. Come on, boys, let's go get bacon."

At the word bacon, BB hops up from the corner of the room and chases after them.

"These kids love you, Wild," I tell my son as I change his diaper. "They'll look after you like a big brother should. Every one of them."

Wild's green eyes bore into me. For such a small little thing, he gives such serious, adult like glares. I pull down my shirt and latch him to my breast. He suckles and watches me, his fingers grabbing at my hair. The boy is a hair puller and if you're not careful, he'll rip a whole handful out. I stroke my fingers through his dark hair and admire him. Mornings are my favorites. Just like when he was in the womb, I tell him all the things I want him to know.

"You're strong, Wild. Just like your daddy. Sweet and

kind and loving. You're going to grow up to be a good man."

Wild's chin moves with each gulp of milk.

"And one day, you'll fall in love too. One day you'll have a family of your own. Be good to them. Love them with your whole heart, unapologetically so."

The floorboard creaks, stealing both mine and Wild's attention. In the doorway stands the man I love. Strong. Powerful. Good.

"We were just talking about you," I say with a smile.

"Don't let me interrupt." He smirks. "Go on. Continue on about how goddamn hot I am."

I roll my eyes. "I'll tell you how hot you are later."

Wild pulls off my nipple and tries to roll out of my arms toward the sound of his daddy's voice. Atticus melts and a goofy grin spreads over his face. He walks over to the bed and stretches out beside us. Wild lets loose a happy squeal when his father pulls him to him.

Time stops, freezing this moment for us. My son tugs at Atticus's hair and beard, making him playfully cry out in faux pain. Wild gets a thrill over hurting his daddy and giggles like crazy.

I thought nothing could be better than *Friends* or peanut butter or coffee.

I was wrong.

The End

And now, please read a tease into what the future Wild & Free world has in store…

wild

Thirteen years old

"YOU'RE GOING TO WEAR A HOLE IN THE floor," Momma says from the kitchen.

I stick my tongue out at her even though she can't see but stop my pacing by the front window. Evan laughs from the sofa. Turning his way, I glower at him. He holds my glare with an amused one until I look away.

Rowdy's coming to visit. Dad went to get him yesterday and will arrive this evening. I'm excited to see my favorite cousin. Not my real cousin, but we pretend. We haven't seen them in six months. With Momma being pregnant again, Dad doesn't want her traveling. He's afraid the stress will make her miscarry.

Again.

I'm becoming immune to her losses.

She's lost three and I remember each one clearly. Momma cried and cried for days. The first one, I was really sad. I cuddled up to Momma in bed and tried to make her feel better. The second one, I was just ready for her to stop being sad. And by the third, I was slightly annoyed. Of course, I never told her that.

Now she's pregnant with twins. A boy and a girl the doctor says. It'll be two more we'll bury beneath the tree out back. I don't tell Momma that though. I let her hope even though hope is a waste of energy.

"Come sit down," Evan says. "You're making me tired."

Evan hides behind his jokes and smiles, but he's a miserable man. He got canned at his job for smoking pot in the bathroom. Grandma lost her shit over that. Uncle Will said he couldn't move back in with him. I think it's because Uncle Will is married to some young college girl and he thinks his son will steal her from his old ass.

I snort at that thought.

I wonder how Uncle Will would feel if he knew his son liked guys instead.

Knowing him, he'd lose it. Uncle Will likes things in order and if they're not in order, he makes them that way.

"Yo, earth to Wild."

I flip Evan off. He lives with us now. Dad hates it. I know he hates it, but he'd never turn down family. But it was after a fight with Evan the other day that he said he was going to go pick Rowdy up. Last time he'd been out there, Uncle Reed spoke to him about letting Rowdy come for a visit soon. He craves a taste of the city life he'd said.

"Why are you so antsy anyway?" Evan asks. "It's just Rowdy."

Just Rowdy.

Rowdy was never just anything.

He's funny and crazy and caring. When Ronan's being a little shit, Rowdy puts him in his place. When Ryder is worrying over stupid stuff, Rowdy calms his fears. And when Raegan is being a big-ass whiner, he tickles her and tells her she's the queen of all the queens to make her smile.

I hate that they all use him.

No one is there for Rowdy.

Except me.

On rare occasions, he tells me things. Things that bother him or upset him or anger him. I listen because I like the way his voice sounds. I like the way his mouth moves. I like the way his overgrown blond hair hangs in his blue eyes, and he flicks his head back to get the strands to move.

"If I didn't know any better, I'd say you love your cousin," Evan taunts.

"Fuck you," I snap.

A little too loudly apparently.

Momma comes flying out of the kitchen with a wooden spoon in hand. Her belly may be huge now that she's pregnant and I may be taller than her now, but she's scary sometimes.

"Did you just curse?"

I glower at her. "It was Evan."

Evan snorts. "Yeah, it was me. I'm the bad guy, Eve."

Momma taps me on the head with the spoon before kissing my forehead. "Be a good boy."

As soon as she's gone, I huff.

"You're welcome," Evan says. "Now come sit with me already."

Grumbling, I stomp over to the couch and plop down. Evan playfully punches my thigh. I swat him away.

Sometimes he says stuff that makes me want to stab him in his damn eye.

"You've got an evil face going on right now, Wild." Evan smirks.

I study his eyes. They're dilated. Evan's fucked up on something. Like always. How Momma and Dad don't see is beyond me. If Uncle Will knew his son was such a loser, he'd probably happily haul his ass off to jail.

"Aww," Evan taunts, "I hurt baby Wild's feelers."

He pulls me to him and pins me against him. I rage and snarl, kicking out of his hold. It pisses me off when he likes to prove what a badass he is. If I were in my thirties too, I'd be able to hold down some kid. One day, I'll be bigger, and he'll regret this shit.

I break my arm free and elbow him in the throat. He shoves me to the floor and clutches his neck, fire gleaming in his eyes.

"Don't be an ass," he hisses.

Me?

I'm about to tell him to go to hell when the front door opens. Our new dog, Neb, bounds into the house heading straight for me. When we lost BB to old age a few years ago, none of us could get over the loss. But then, one day last winter, we came across a Chow-Chow missing an ear. He was scrawny and alone. Dad called him No Ear Bear. Momma shortened it to Neb. He's been our boy ever since.

"Hey boy," I greet, smiling as Neb happily licks my face.

Evan has lost his scowl. His eyes are wide and assessing. I follow his gaze to Dad and *him*. Rowdy. He's taller than I remember, standing every bit as tall as Dad. Not as big, but one day he'll get there.

I burst to my feet and rush over to them. He laughs when I nearly knock him over with a hug. Rowdy smells like fire and wilderness. He smells like a life I'm not allowed to live. I'm trapped here with Momma and Dad. I have to go to school and play football. I have to go to bed by nine and do dumb chores.

Rowdy gets to hunt and build cool shit. He doesn't have to go to school or do dumb stuff like I do. His life is amazing. One day I'm going to leave my house and go live with Uncle Reed and Aunt Devon so I can see Rowdy every day. Maybe I can smell like fire and wilderness too.

"Oh, hi," Rowdy says, his voice deep. At almost eighteen, he's practically a man now. "Evan? I haven't seen you since…"

"Since you were five?" Evan's annoying voice says from behind me.

"Son, you want to help me unload the truck?" Dad asks. He poses it like an option. I know I don't have an option.

"Yeah," I grumble as I break from Rowdy's arms.

"Good seeing you, man," Evan says, pulling Rowdy in for a hug.

I've never wanted to punch Evan more than I want to in this moment.

They're both around the same height. Evan hugs him for a moment too long. Just when I think I might have to pry him off Rowdy, Evan releases him. He stands close, his hand resting on Rowdy's shoulder.

Rowdy, sometimes shy, turns red and wears a stupid smile.

I don't like that smile.

"Evan," I growl. "Make yourself useful and go help Dad."

Evan snaps his head my way and glares at me. "It won't be my ass that gets whipped if I don't go out there. Run along, kid."

Fury burns hot in my veins. I want to grab my pocketknife and stab him a thousand times. When Rowdy sees my murderous glare, he swoops in to save the day. That's what Rowdy does. He saves everyone.

"I'll help you," he says. "Tell me about football. How's it going?"

I hate football.

Hate it with every fiber of my being.

But tonight, I love it because it makes Evan scowl and I get Rowdy's attention back on me. I grab his hand, dragging him outside as I babble about my teammates and the last game we had. Dad smiles at us as he carries a couple of his guns. Rowdy and I make it to the back of the truck, and I can't help but hug him again.

He's my best friend.

"I missed you." I look up at his smiling face and push his messy hair back. "Your hair is long. You gonna get Momma to cut it?"

He smirks. "I'm growing it out."

"Like our dads?" I make a sour face. Dad is the only man I know besides Uncle Reed and Grandpa who have long hair. It's weird. Who wants hair like a girl?

"Yeah," he says, grinning. "It's almost long enough for a man-bun." He runs his fingers through his dark blond hair and pulls it back to prove it to me. In the moonlight, with his hair away from his face, I can see the sharp angle of his jaw. I have to fist my hand so I don't do something stupid like run my finger along the bone.

"Girl," I tease.

He flinches and scowls. It takes me half a second to realize I hurt his feelings. Instead of playfully laughing it off like usual, he grabs a box and storms away. I'm left with my mouth hanging open. Dad arrives a moment later.

"You okay, Wild?"

"I think Rowdy is mad at me."

Dad looks over his shoulder and then ruffles my hair. "Give Rowdy some space. He's going through a rough time. Uncle Reed wants me to look after him and show him town life."

"Why is he having a rough time?" I demand.

Dad shrugs. "Don't know. Life in the wilderness wasn't for your mother either. Maybe Rowdy will get a taste of this life and decide to stay."

The thought confuses me.

In every dream I have, I leave here to go be with my best friend. To spend every waking minute with him. We'll hunt and fish and climb trees. We'll stay up late talking. We'll be together.

Him here is not a part of the plan.

I'm supposed to escape to him, not the other way around.

"I'll make it better. I promise, Dad."

Dad shakes his head. "Space, Wild. Give him some space."

509

I gave him space.

And he ignored me.

Three days into his stupid space and I've had enough. At night, after my parents go to bed, he and Evan sneak outside to drink beer and smoke pot. Tonight, I'm going to join in and reclaim my best friend. Evan can go suck a bag of dicks.

Neb whines when I crawl out of bed and throw on some clothes. Our house isn't big like my grandparents or Uncle Reed's, but it's bigger than it used to be. A few years after I was born, when my parents were pregnant again with the first baby that later died, he and my uncles added onto the house. They added another bathroom and two more bedrooms. One for me and one for the baby. The other room remained empty and now stupid Evan lives there.

"Stay here," I tell Neb.

He lays his head down, clearly fine with not having to go outside in the cold. I grab my coat and slip out the front door. Beyond Dad's truck, in the woods, I see the fire. I hear their laughing and jealousy spikes through me.

My best friend.

Stalking them, I listen in on their conversation as I get nearer. Evan is telling some stupid story about his friend Rex and Rowdy is howling with laughter. They're both wasted. I can smell the pot from here. If it wouldn't keep me from seeing Rowdy again, I'd pull my knife out and stab Evan right in his stupid mouth that keeps spewing more annoying things.

I'm about to storm into their camp and yell at Evan when I stop dead in my tracks.

Their laughter has stopped. Evan leans forward, cups Rowdy's jaw, and kisses him. Freaking kisses him. I'm so stunned, all I can do is stare.

Why are they kissing?

I know why Evan is kissing Rowdy, but why is Rowdy kissing him back? All he ever talks about is one day getting a wife. Having a family. I thought maybe that's why he wanted to get out of the wilderness. So he could have sex for the first time. But now he's kissing Evan. Gross, annoying, miserable, fuck-up Evan.

And he doesn't seem to be hating it.

Rowdy makes a guttural groan that sends heat burning through my veins straight to my dick. I'm shocked and nearly let out a squeak of surprise. I stare, transfixed on the scene before me, until Evan starts to unbuckle Rowdy's jeans.

He lets him!

I let out a pained sound before turning on my heel and running as fast as I can.

"Wild!"

Rowdy calls out for me, but I don't stop. I run and run and run. Confusing emotions war inside me. I want to beat up Rowdy. Punish him for making me see that. I also want to hug him to me and make him kiss me instead. Rowdy's not Evan's. He's mine. My best friend. Mine.

By the time I make it to the house, I have hot tears streaking down my face. If only Momma could see. She says I'm emotionless sometimes. Her eyes grow sad when she says it, but I simply shrug.

I feel emotions.

Anger. Rage. Restlessness.

Now, I feel pain.

Hot and explosive inside me.

Bomb after bomb detonating inside me.

I don't understand it.

All I know is hate bubbles to the surface. I harness it and ride it like I'm a surfer in the Pacific. I own that wave of hatred. It roars inside my ears drowning out the sadness.

"Wild!"

I stop to whirl around and look at Rowdy. He staggers slightly and his face is screwed up in some twisted way I've never seen on him before. My chest heaves as I wait for him to tell me it was a mistake. That it was because he was drunk. That it was stupid. That tomorrow we'll play football in the yard and he can tell me stories about his siblings.

Tomorrow will be better.

I just need to hear him say it.

"Wild…" His bottom lip trembles. "Please…"

I glower at him. "Out with it." *Tell me you're sorry. That you're my best friend. Mine.*

He swipes away a tear. "Please don't tell Uncle Atticus."

My breath is sucked right from my chest. "What?"

"I…I don't want Dad to know. I just…give me this. I need this." He looks over his shoulder and then turns back to look at me, a smile on his face that hits me right in the gut. "I need him."

Not me.

Him.

Evan.

"Hey," he murmurs. "It's just…I've been stuck out

there. I'm finally free. There's a whole world out there I want to experience—the great unknown—and I feel like I'm finding that start. Just give me this. Please."

"Your secret is safe with me," I say in a cold tone. "That's what best friends do."

He gives me a smile that doesn't reach his eyes. "Yeah, Wild. Best friends."

Liar.

I see the lie in his eyes.

I'm nothing to him.

The truth is cold and painful and sickening.

Anger coats my heart like thick ice, hardening it to the point I'm numb.

"Your boyfriend's waiting." I shoot Evan a nasty glare and then turn back to storm into the house.

I climb into my bed and bury my face in the pillow. Dread and hate and despair war within me. I don't know what to do about it. Momma says I'm emotionless. Maybe I'm too full of emotion.

Rather than sobbing like I want to, I suck in a breath and let it go slowly.

I won't feel.

I will turn it off.

He thinks I'm nothing.

Then I'll be fucking nothing.

More from this Wild & Free world to come!

playlist

"Wildest Ones" by Zayde Wolf

"Love is Mystical" by Cold War Kids

"Daddy Issues" by The Neighbourhood

"Love on the Brain" by Cold War Kids and Bishop Briggs

"Born to be Wild" by Steppenwolf

"Bad at Love" by Halsey

"Not Afraid Anymore" by Halsey

"Where is My Mind?" by Pixies

"Glycerine" by Bush

"Judith" by A Perfect Circle

"Girls Go Wild" by LP

acknowledgements

Thank you to my husband…you see the day in and day out of EVERYTHING. You're my rock, my cheerleader, and shoulder to lean on. Love you bunches, honey!

I am so thankful for all my wild ones. Without you guys, writing would be a lot less fun. You cheered me on and supported me through *The Wild*, and I know you'll continue to do that with whatever story I take on next because you're all badasses like that. Don't ever change. Be strong and fiery and brave!

Big thanks to Robyn Crawford and Eden Books for giving books like *The Free* a home. In case anyone doesn't know what "home" means, it means a place where you feel safe to be you, feel loved unconditionally, and can thrive without judgment or hate. I'm proud to be a part of the Eden Books community. Eden Books has given me a home when no other place would. And that will never be forgotten.

A huge thank you to my Krazy for K Webster's Books reader group. You all are insanely supportive and I can't thank you enough.

A gigantic thank you to those who always help me out behind the scenes. Elizabeth Clinton, Ella Stewart, Misty Walker, Holly Sparks, Jillian Ruize, Gina Behrends, and Wendy Rinebold—you ladies are my rock!

Thank you so much to Misty Walker for encouraging me through *The Wild* and cheering me on through *The Free*. Your friendship is invaluable. Irreplaceable. Incredible. I love you more than you'll ever know.

A big thank you to my author friends who have given me your friendship and your support. You have no idea how much that means to me.

Thank you to all of my blogger friends both big and small that go above and beyond to always share my stuff. You all rock! #AllBlogsMatter

Emily A. Lawrence, thank you SO much for editing this book. You rock!!

Thank you, Stacey Blake, for making this book gorgeous! You're a star and I love you bunches!

A big thanks to Nicole Blanchard with Indie Sage PR for holding my hand every step of the way during the wildest legs of my journey. Your friendship, support, and steadiness has helped me get through some tough times. I'm so thankful for you!

Lastly but certainly not least of all, thank you to all of the wonderful readers out there who are willing to hear my story and enjoy my characters like I do. It means the world to me!

about the author

K Webster is a *USA Today* Bestselling author. Her titles have claimed many bestseller tags in numerous categories, are translated in multiple languages, and have been adapted into audiobooks. She lives in "Tornado Alley" with her husband, two children, and her baby dog named Blue. When she's not writing, she's reading, drinking copious amounts of coffee, and researching aliens.

.

keep up with K WEBSTER

books by
K WEBSTER

Taboo Treats:

Bad Bad Bad

Coach Long

Ex-Rated Attraction

Mr. Blakely

Easton

Crybaby

Lawn Boys

Malfeasance

Renner's Rules

The Glue

Dane

Enzo

Red Hot Winter

Dr. Dan

KKinky Reads Collection:

Share Me

Choke Me

Daddy Me

Watch Me

Hurt Me

Play Me

Contemporary Romance Standalones:

Wicked Lies Boys Tell

The Day She Cried

Untimely You

Heath

Sundays are for Hangovers

A Merry Christmas with Judy

Zeke's Eden
Schooled by a Senior
Give Me Yesterday
Sunshine and the Stalker
Bidding for Keeps
B-Sides and Rarities
Conheartists
Cocksure Ace
No Tears with Him

Paranormal Romance Standalones:
Apartment 2B
Running Free
Mad Sea
Cold Queen
Delinquent Demons

Hood River Hoodlums Series:
Hood River Rat (Book 1)
Little Hoodlum (Book 2)
Campfire Chaos (Book 3)
Hood River Zero (Book 4)

War & Peace Series:
This is War, Baby (Book 1)
This is Love, Baby (Book 2)
This Isn't Over, Baby (Book 3)
This Isn't You, Baby (Book 4)
This is Me, Baby (Book 5)
This Isn't Fair, Baby (Book 6)
This is the End, Baby (Book 7 – a novella)

Lost Planet Series:
The Forgotten Commander (Book 1)
The Vanished Specialist (Book 2)
The Mad Lieutenant (Book 3)
The Uncertain Scientist (Book 4)
The Lonely Orphan (Book 5)
The Rogue Captain (Book 6)
The Determined Hero (Book 7)

2 Lovers Series:
Text 2 Lovers (Book 1)
Hate 2 Lovers (Book 2)
Thieves 2 Lovers (Book 3)

Pretty Little Dolls Series:
Pretty Stolen Dolls (Book 1)
Pretty Lost Dolls (Book 2)
Pretty New Doll (Book 3)
Pretty Broken Dolls (Book 4)

The V Games Series:
Vlad (Book 1)
Ven (Book 2)
Vas (Book 3)

Four Fathers Books:
Pearson

Four Sons Books:
Camden

Elite Seven Books:
Gluttony
Greed

Royal Bastards MC:
Koyn

Truths and Lies Duet:
Hidden Truths
Stolen Lies

Books Only Sold on K's Website and Eden Books:
The Wild
The Free
Hale
Bad Bad Bad
This is War, Baby
Like Dragonflies

The Breaking the Rules Series:
Broken (Book 1)
Wrong (Book 2)
Scarred (Book 3)
Mistake (Book 4)
Crushed (Book 5 – a novella)

The Vegas Aces Series:
Rock Country (Book 1)
Rock Heart (Book 2)
Rock Bottom (Book 3)

The Becoming Her Series:
Becoming Lady Thomas (Book 1)
Becoming Countess Dumont (Book 2)
Becoming Mrs. Benedict (Book 3)

Alpha & Omega Duet:
Alpha & Omega (Book 1)
Omega & Love (Book 2)

Elizabeth Gray Books:
Blue Hill Blood
Cognati

CPSIA information can be obtained
at www.ICGtesting.com
Printed in the USA
LVHW051200130122
708377LV00015B/808